THE DAY AFTER YESTERDAY

A JOE HANNIBAL MYSTERY

THE DAY AFTER YESTERDAY

WAYNE D. DUNDEE

FIVE STAR

An imprint of Thomson Gale, a part of The Thomson Corporation

THOMSON
GALE

Detroit • New York • San Francisco • New Haven, Conn. • Waterville, Maine • London

THOMSON

GALE

LIBRARY OF CONGRESS CATALOGING-IN-PUBLICATION DATA

Dundee, Wayne D.
     The day after yesterday : a Joe Hannibal mystery / Wayne D. Dundee. — 1st ed.
        p. cm.
     ISBN-13: 978-1-59414-592-6 (alk. paper)
     ISBN-10: 1-59414-592-X (alk. paper)
     1. Private investigators—Fiction. 2. Serial murderers—Fiction. I. Title.
PS3554.U4655D39 2007
813'.54—dc22   2007012042

First Edition. First Printing: September 2007.

Published in 2007 in conjunction with Tekno Books and Ed Gorman.

Printed in the United States of America on permanent paper
10 9 8 7 6 5 4 3 2 1

This is for my big buddy, Lynn F. Myers Jr., who first introduced himself to me at a Bouchercon a number of years back by marching up and making this announcement: "I've been coming to these things for a dozen years looking to meet somebody bigger and uglier than me, and here you finally are!" It was either fight him or befriend him. One of the best choices I ever made was to go with the latter.

"LET'S ROLL. . . ."

The final words overheard from United Airlines Flight 93—spoken by Todd Beamer via an in-flight phone connection—as passengers prepared to retaliate against the hijackers who had overtaken their plane above Pennsylvania on 9/11/01.

AUTHOR'S NOTE

Contemporary west central Nebraska is a fascinating and wonderful place where there exists a spirit and a work ethic and an outlook on life that is too rare in many parts of the country. To "cowboy up" is a common phrase for dealing with things when the going gets rough, and the flip side of that is a thorough, genuine appreciation for—and savoring of—the better times.

Upon moving here in 1998, I immediately fell in love with the area and its people. I have tried to capture both as accurately as my perceptions and abilities will allow. However, where it suited my purposes for the plot of this story I was not above resorting to the ol' "dramatic license" fallback. This is primarily evident in two areas: one, my "commercialization" of No Name Bay; two, my relocation of the Dismal River out of Hooker County in the north to the southern part of Arthur County, where I renamed it Pawnee Creek. Trust me, I know the *real* Dismal, having visited it many times and having canoed a goodly stretch of one memorable day with several of my compadres from Arnold-Ogallala Electronics.

. . . *"If you can't paddle with the big dogs, stay on the bank."*

PROLOGUE

In the course of our lives, death touches us many times.

Until, ultimately, it touches us a final time—that icy shoulder tap that summons us for our own one-way trip with the grim old bastard riding shotgun.

In my life I had been touched by sudden death, slow death, violent death, and the kind of prolonged death that people call "a blessing" when it brings to an end drawn-out pain and suffering. I had been touched by the deaths of relatives, loved ones, friends . . . and enemies. To the latter, there had been times I delivered death.

As a result of these various passings I experienced the whole range of emotional reactions. Disbelief and denial. Regret. Anger. At times, a cold satisfaction. At other times, the curious kind of guilt that comes with being a survivor. And sadness and grief, to be sure.

But never had I felt a greater ache or sense of emptiness than in the hours and days and weeks following the news that two of my oldest, closest friends in the world had been simultaneously and suddenly snatched from the ranks of the living. . . .

CHAPTER ONE

Jacked on black coffee, Vivarin, and Coke Classic, I made the eight-hundred-mile drive from my home base of Rockford, Illinois, to Ogallala, Nebraska, in eleven hours, give or take a handful of clockticks. Even pushing her at times to eighty and ninety miles per, my trusty old Honda Accord required only one fuel stop, somewhere in the middle of Iowa.

By the time I swung off Interstate 80 at Ogallala's single exit, my gut was raw from too much caffeine and too little food, my eyes were hot and grainy, and my brain was a squirming worm's nest of anguish and bittersweet memories replaying like snippets of film on a jerky projector . . . and questions that I knew I would never know all the answers to, at least not in this world.

When a highway sign just past North Platte let me know I was within fifty miles, I'd called ahead on my cell phone to Abby Bridger—Bomber's niece, the halting voice in the night who had first informed me of the fatal accident—and told her I was closing in. She gave me directions to where she would be waiting to meet me.

The trademark arches of the McDonald's I'd been instructed to watch for rose unmistakably from the string of motels and fast-food joints that lined a frontage road running parallel to the westbound lanes of the interstate. I doubled back on the frontage blacktop, passing a Texaco station, a Best Western, a Runza, and a Qwik Mart convenience store before nosing in under the aforementioned arches. It was three o'clock in the afternoon—

make that two o'clock, I corrected myself, remembering another highway sign some thirty miles back that informed me I was crossing into Mountain Time Zone.

The parking lot was uncrowded, whatever the hour. I had no trouble spotting the somewhat battered yellow Toyota pickup with cab doors bearing the legend: NO NAME BAY GENERAL STORE & LODGE. I pulled up alongside it and cut my engine. The Accord seemed to heave a wearily grateful sigh before sputtering into silence.

I got out, slowly straightening my cramped, creaking legs. The young woman who'd been sitting in the Toyota got out also, flipping away a partially smoked cigarette after taking a hurried final drag.

"Joe?" she said. Her eyes searched my face. She came around the end of the pickup, exhaling a plume of smoke. "You made amazing time. It was good of you to come."

I started to raise a hand and then let it drop to my side again, an empty gesture. "This is a hell of a lousy thing," I said. The statement sounded empty, too; noise in search of the right words.

"Yes, it certainly is that." Abby took another step forward and put her arms around me in an abrupt hug. Although unexpected, the embrace was so natural and warm and genuine that an initial feeling of awkwardness on my part quickly passed. I responded, placing my palms just below her shoulder blades and squeezing her softly, briefly to me.

When we parted, Abby gazed up at me very intently. "Look, I know I'm the blood relative here. But I also understand how tight you and Uncle Bomber were. I loved him the way you're supposed to love kin, but what he mostly was to me was this big, likable guy—my mother's brother—who came out to visit and tell great stories every few years, and then go away again. There's family, and there's family. The bond between you and him—and Miss Grimaldi, too—was clearly special and strong.

Losing them both like this . . . I can only guess how deep your grief must be and I want you to know how sorry I am."

Again, I didn't have the words. "For two like them," I said, "there will be a lot of deep grieving."

"And rightfully so, I'm sure."

I cleared my throat. "Speaking of which, how is your mother holding up?"

"As well as can be expected." Abby's brows furrowed slightly and her already somber expression grew a shade more tense. "Her health is so frail . . . well, she can't really afford to sink any lower."

"I recall Bomber was pretty concerned about her when he started talking about coming out. Emphysema, right?"

"And congestive heart failure. She's a tough old broad but the ailments are starting to gang up on her. I'm afraid it's shaping up to be a pretty rough summer for the two Brannigan brawlers . . . that's what they used to call Ma and Uncle Bomber when they were kids growing up in the toughest Irish neighborhood of Milwaukee."

I grinned a little in spite of myself. "I know. I heard some of the stories. Bomber said she had the hardest punch for twenty blocks—next to his, of course."

"Uh-huh, I'm sure that would be *his* spin." Abby's brow smoothed and she grinned a little, too. "Ma's got a different version, though. According to her, there were a couple years where she could out-punch even her little brother—if you can imagine Uncle Bomber ever being *little*. Regardless, *I* ain't going to be the one to argue with her about it. Getting raised by her, I've already been on the receiving end of my share of smacks from that hair-trigger backhand, thank you. Even sick as she is, if a person was to get her riled I figure she's probably still got a good pop or two left in her."

"I bet she does. Where is she at, anyway?"

"Waiting at home. Having to lug around an oxygen tank and all, she doesn't feel up to coming in to town much. She's looking forward to seeing you, though. She told me not to waste any time bringing you back."

"Well, sure. Sure, of course I want to see her, too. But first . . . where are Bomber and Liz, Abby?" *Their bodies,* I thought; thought it, but couldn't bring myself to say it out loud.

"They're at the funeral home. They've already been . . . adequately identified. You don't need to put yourself through that, Joe."

"Yeah, I do," I corrected her. "But it's not for the sake of making identification . . . it's for me, for the sake of starting to accept that they're really gone. Trying to come to grips with it. I can't make myself ready for that until I . . . I see them."

Abby was studying me intently again. I studied her back. She was rather pretty, in a subtle kind of way. You might glance at her the first time or two and see simply a slender, average-looking girl. But beneath the unkempt spill of wheat-colored hair there were brown eyes that had the sparkle of deep pools of root beer and there were laugh lines around those eyes and around a wide mouth whose full lips could undoubtedly do a sexy pout but could also stretch and twist with a wide variety of other expressions, spontaneous and uncalculated. It was definitely an interesting face, I decided. An unpampered face that had lived hard and laughed hard and loved hard, although— and I found myself speculating on this for reasons I neither understood nor had any foundation for—perhaps not wisely.

Abby blinked once, slowly. "I see. You're looking for closure."

Psychology 101, TV Talk Show U. Whatever. "All I know is it's something I have to do."

"All right, then. Follow me, I'll take you to them."

CHAPTER TWO

Leaving the funeral home, I followed Abby again, this time north out of town.

Ogallala, the seat of Keith County, is situated along the north bank of the South Platte River and on the hinge of Nebraska's westward-jutting panhandle. Once a notorious old cowtown—officially deemed The End of the Texas Trail from 1875 to 1885 and unofficially dubbed "The Gomorrah of the Plains" by the hard-bitten cowpokes who made the grueling cattle drives to its awaiting railhead—it shoulders a much tamer reputation these days but is still a hub for cattle, cattle ranching, and some amount of irrigated farming.

A few miles north of town, the North Platte River angles in out of Wyoming. Beyond that, the flatness of the two river valleys quickly gives way to the vast, rolling, treeless region known as the Sandhills. The land here for thousands of square miles consists of a seemingly endless series of huge sand dunes, all anchored in place by stubborn high plains grasses. Preventing this semi-arid expanse from being the irreclaimable desert it was once considered, is a gigantic underground aquifer reaching all the way down from Canada, nurturing the grasses and actually creating marshlands and a scattering of ponds and small lakes in many of the low-lying places. Thus, while ill-suited for much else, it makes an almost perfect setting for raising range beef.

The other industry that Ogallala serves is a thriving tourist trade attracted by Lake McConaughy, the largest body of water in the state, formed back in the 1950s by damming up a segment of the North Platte. Although envisioned primarily for hydroelectric power and irrigation—functions which it indeed does perform—Big Mac's hundred miles of white sand beaches and the swimming, boating, and fishing activities to be enjoyed in and on its blue, blue water quickly began luring throngs of weekenders and vacationers and outdoor enthusiasts in general. Their needs and spending habits while in the area support numerous businesses and pump plenty of welcome dollars into Keith County's overall economy.

I knew most of these things from dissertations given over the years by my buddy Bomber Brannigan. Bomber's mother was originally from Keith County but as a newlywed moved to Milwaukee where her husband could find better-paying work. After Bomber's father was killed in an industrial accident when the boy was thirteen, his widowed mother moved back to Ogallala with her two children. Although he would come to appreciate the area and return for frequent visits later in his life, as a city-bred, street-tough youth, Bomber hated the small town. He couldn't wait to get away from the quasi-rural setting and did just that when he was sixteen, striking out on his own. His sister stuck by their mother and remained in the area even after marrying and starting her own family.

It was this sister—Margaret, Abby's mother—I was being led to see. I'd met her once before, some years back, when I had accompanied Bomber on one of his visits. We'd done plenty of fishing and some antelope hunting, but there'd also been obligatory time with his family; a Sunday dinner and a few evening get-togethers of banter and tale-swapping that turned out to be no hardship at all. Like Bomber, Margaret was large and gregarious, with a phony-gruff demeanor and a wry sense of humor. Her husband was still alive then—Henry was his name, if recollection served—a small, quiet guy who seemed to bask in the glow of his wife and family, smiling mildly, saying little, always looking to the needs of everybody else. A couple of years after our visit he died one night in his sleep . . . quietly, like he had lived.

It occurred to me as I followed her in her yellow pickup that I must have also met Abby during that visit. I was able to remember her then, but very vaguely. She had been married at the time—to a brooding, surly sort who clearly had little interest in lame family get-togethers and therefore whenever he and Abby showed up it was only for short periods. Which helped explain my fuzzy memory of her. Furthermore, in the presence of her self-centered, domineering husband, that fleetingly encountered Abby had seemed meek and mousy and was relegated to a pale shadow always an obedient step behind him, almost nonexistent. I then recalled Bomber mentioning at some point afterward that she finally came to her senses and divorced the jerk; probably explaining my earlier sense that she had suffered somehow at the fickle hand of Romance.

The lake came into sight, ahead and to our left. It spread out impossibly blue and sparkling in a wash of late-afternoon June sunlight. The white sand of the shoreline made the blue of the water stand out even sharper by contrast. There were several boats on the water, most of them larger motor crafts. In the distance I could see a couple tall sails skimming smoothly along and nearer the shore a swarm of jet-skis cut in and out, throwing their distinctive rooster tails.

We drove across the top of Kingsley Dam, the massive earthen barricade erected to back up the North Platte's flow and turn it into what locals generally called simply "the lake."

To the right, on the spill side of the dam, a second, much smaller lake had also taken shape before the river re-formed into its natural channel. This lower body of water was called

Ogallala Lake, or "the little lake." While somewhat ignored, especially by out-of-area visitors, it had its own quiet charm enhanced by large areas of shaded campground, picnic stations, a walk path meandering between colorful flower beds, and a handful of fishing piers jutting out from its grassy shore.

Past the dam we turned west on Highway 26 and followed the irregular curve of the shoreline. We passed several lake-access roads, most of them marked with Game & Parks Commission signs stating that a permit was required for entry. On the opposite side of the highway there was a variety of homes ranging from quite elegant for year-round living to skirted trailers and simple cottages set up as weekend and vacation residences.

After about four miles we reached a lake-access road with a sign that read: NO NAME BAY and below that, in smaller letters, MARINA & SERVICES. Abby turned here and I followed.

We quickly came to the rim of the bay. Straight ahead was a boat ramp, its wide concrete slab extending out into the water. To the right was a tin-roofed tavern called the Lassoed Walleye Saloon. To the left was a tall, rectangular two-story building with a banner across the front proclaiming it to be the No Name Bay General Store & Lodge. The "lodge" consisted of a half dozen one-room cabins arranged in a horseshoe pattern around the back side of the big building. Abby and her mother ran the business and occupied living quarters on the second floor.

Cutting close past a set of gasoline and diesel pumps, Abby pulled her truck up alongside the building and parked. I pulled in next to her and we climbed out of our vehicles. The smell of the lake filled my nostrils, strong and clean and fresh.

"As you can see," Abby announced, "the place hasn't changed a whole heck of a lot from when you were here last."

"You remember that, eh? Me coming out before? That was quite a few years ago."

"Uh-huh. About ten. Back before Daddy died. I maybe couldn't have picked your face out of a crowd after this much time, but sure, of course I remember you. Uncle Bomber's best pal, a for-real private eye. I thought you were pretty exciting."

"You were young and impressionable. I've never been a particularly exciting guy and being a PI in real life isn't much like it's cracked up to be on TV and in books."

Abby arched a brow skeptically. "Oh, I don't know about that. I've read some accounts—especially those exclusive articles written by your reporter girlfriend—about a few of your cases. And I've heard plenty of other stories thanks to Uncle Bomber. You don't exactly come off as a low-key, everyday nine-to-fiver."

"You know how people can exaggerate," I protested. "Ought not make a habit of believing everything you hear."

"Maybe not. But nevertheless, you seemed exciting to me."

Unable to resist an opening to probe a little bit, I said, "Don't imagine your former husband appreciated that very much. I'm not going to have to worry about him being jealous after all this time, am I?"

Abby's expression tightened. "You don't have to worry about him whatsoever. Like you said, he's 'former'—I'm Abby *Bridger* again, and he's history. He doesn't have the right to give a damn about anything where I'm concerned."

"Should I say I'm sorry?"

"Only that the marriage ever took place to begin with."

"Fair enough. End of subject." I turned my head and looked at the exposed wooden stairway running up the side of the building. "Guess we'd better go on up so I can extend my condolences to your mother."

"Yes, I'm sure she's anxious to see you," Abby said. "But you won't find her up there. With her bad heart and breathing trouble and all, the stairs got to be too much for her. We converted some storage space in the back of the store to a little efficiency apartment and she stays down there now. She probably heard us drive in, she'll be waiting."

If the place around her hadn't changed much in the last ten years, the same certainly couldn't be said for Margaret Bridger. She looked so different from what I remembered that when I was ushered into her presence I was shocked at the sight of her. Formerly such a tall, sturdy woman, she seemed to have shrunk into folds of pale, loose, wrinkled flesh and the eyes looking up at me from her diminished face carried only the faintest trace of the vibrancy that had danced there before.

"Joe Hannibal, you ruffian," she said, reaching with both arms to embrace me. "Look at you. Sound as a dollar and still with shoulders like you're trying to smuggle an ox yoke under your shirt."

I hugged her tenderly, cautious of her frailness. When she kissed my cheek one of the oxygen tubes wrapped around the sides of her face, feeding the plastic fixture inserted into her nostrils, scrunched the corner of my mouth. Over her shoulder, next to an overstuffed recliner that I guessed she occupied much of the time, I could see an oxygen machine bubbling and hissing softly as it supplied the purified air to aid her crippled lungs.

I held her at arms' length and said, "Sad times, Margaret. Sad times. I'm sorry we're seeing one another again under such rotten circumstances."

"He didn't suffer, Joe," she assured me. "Neither of them did. At least there's some blessing in that. I can't say for your friend Liz, but a man like Leslie—so big and powerful and in-control his whole life—it wouldn't have done for him to endure something like this, like what I'm going through. Fade out slow and feeble? No, snuff the candle quick and clean, that's the way he would have wanted it."

Margaret was the only person on earth I ever heard call

Bomber by his given name, Leslie. After earning his nickname early in his boxing career (when an opponent said getting hit by him was "like having a bomb dropped on you") Bomber never let anybody call him anything else.

"But he still had plenty of vinegar left. Plenty of life, both of them. It shouldn't have been their time," I insisted.

"God has His reasons, Joe. And He will sort the souls."

I told myself it would be both pointless and rude to challenge her faith. But that wasn't enough to keep the bitterness inside me from boiling out into words. "Whatever gets you through, Margaret. Me, I'm a little pissed off at God right now so I hope you'll understand if I don't feel like turning to Him for much of anything."

Chapter Three

At the insistence of the Bridger women I took an early evening supper with them and then accepted the hospitality of one of their guest cabins in which to try and catch up on some sleep.

The heavy meal of pork chops and mashed potatoes (which I had a strong hunch was planned especially for me) did a pretty good job of blunting the stimulants still left in my system, but restful sleep nevertheless did not come easy.

I kept thinking about the way Liz and Bomber had looked on the embalming tables at the funeral home. Curiously unmarked by the car crash that had taken their lives, they simply appeared cold and waxen and still—*forever* stilled. The finality of their condition . . . of being dead . . . was irrefutable. Looking down on their achingly familiar faces, faces that would never again talk or laugh, eyes that would never again open and look back at me or at anyone else or anything else . . . the weight of it bore down on me like being caught under the wheel of a gristmill.

Swaggering, gregarious, heart-on-his-sleeve, larger-than-life Bomber Brannigan. All six-foot-six, three hundred seventy-five pounds of him. Former prize fighter and then pro wrestler of considerable renown back in the days before the media giants turned the whole thing into pay-per-view extravaganzas of "sports entertainment." A human rock you expected to somehow endure forever.

And Liz Grimaldi. Soft-spoken, raven-haired, doe-eyed, voluptuous Liz. Bomber's Gal Friday for all the years he ran the

Bomb Shelter, the popular State Street bar he'd started up after retiring from the ring wars. A special lady and a mutual special friend. For me, such a special friend that she and I had long ago reached an unspoken agreement to never allow the attraction we felt for one another blossom into anything more because we didn't want to risk ruining a great friendship with what might turn out to be a lousy romance.

Stilled . . . forever.

Gone . . . forever.

If I had been seeking "closure," seeking to get past the denial stage and accept that they were truly dead, then I had accomplished that much. Now all I had to do was find a way to deal with it . . . and move on.

Life in many ways is cyclical. And the cycles generally change with some sort of bittersweet passage; the death of one stage, the birth of another. One door opens, another closes. The great continuum, and all that happy horseshit. I wondered if there was some sort of cosmic irony in the fact that, as a child, my parents were killed in an automobile wreck and now, on the downslope of my life, my two dearest friends—the closest thing to a family left in my world—had just met the same fate. And was I supposed to give a damn about what the next cycle might bring?

There was irony, too, in the fact that Bomber—that clucking old grandmother of the streets and highways, the most careful driver I had ever ridden with—had somehow managed to fatally flip his beloved, meticulously maintained vintage Buick in a single vehicle rollover.

"It's a twisty, sneaky devil of a back road, Joe," Abby had explained. "They haul an easy half dozen wrecks a year out of its bordering fields and gullies. Even people who've driven it all their lives suddenly misjudge a curve one day, and it's all over."

Maybe that's all life is . . . a twisty, sneaky road we keep venturing out onto until one day we hit that curve that spells the end.

When I slept, finally, it was fitful and storm-tossed with dreams. Upon waking, I could only remember one of them: I was driving along an undulating country road, awash in brilliant sunlight, lined by tall, leafy trees. The trees cast splotches of deep shadow on the roadway ahead of me and after I'd gone for a ways I realized that, at staggered intervals, some of the shadows formed the clear image of a skull-like death's head. Every time I passed through one of these my breath was sucked away by a chill from within the shadow as sharp as an arctic blast.

CHAPTER FOUR

The next five days were a gray blur of sad, somber activity preparing the interments of Liz and Bomber.

Because of my close friendship with each of the deceased and due to the scarcity of actual kin (for Bomber there was just Margaret and Abby and Abby's brother, Roy, a rancher up near the South Dakota border; for Liz there was only her shiftless, ne'er-do-well brother, Tony, somewhere in Minnesota) I was involved in most of the details. There were people to be notified, wills to be checked, lawyers consulted, funeral and clergy services scheduled, burial plots selected; the list seemed endless. Scores of phone calls were exchanged. Shock was expressed by all hearing about the accident for the first time. Tears were shed.

Somewhat to my surprise, I found out that a number of years prior Bomber had made arrangements to be buried in Nebraska. He prepaid for the funeral, a headstone, and a plot in a picturesque cemetery near an historical point on the Oregon Trail called Ash Hollow, where his mother and her parents were already laid to rest, and where Margaret's deceased husband was buried and she would one day lay next to him.

Since most of Bomber's friends and acquaintances were back in Illinois and unable to make the trip out, the service was sparsely attended but nonetheless sincere and moving. Most of the people who showed up were Margaret's friends from around the area. Roy Bridger drove down with his family. Mike

Kolchonsky, the oldest of the two brothers who had taken over running the Bomb Shelter a year or so earlier when Bomber decided he was ready for semi-retirement, flew out to represent the Rockford contingent. My steady gal, Jan Mosby, was in Washington, D.C., on assignment for her magazine. By the time I finally managed a call through to her there was no chance for her to get away in time to attend.

While Bomber's funeral was taking place, Liz's body was being transported back to Rockford where there would be a wake and services and then a procession to her final resting place in the cemetery of the small downstate town where she had grown up and where her folks were buried.

I guess I should have found comfort in the fact that my two friends were each returning home in a sense, back to their families, back to the earth and whatever lay beyond. But, selfishly, the thought that kept running through my head the most was how totally, irreversibly gone they were and how much I would miss them.

Mike Kolchonsky and I traveled back to Rockford together. He turned in his rental car at North Platte and we rode from there in my Honda. I let him drive most of the way while I tilted the passenger seat as far back as it would go and allowed the weariness that had built up in me to finally pull me into the deepest sleep I'd experienced in days.

There was an overflow turnout at both Liz's wake and the church service the following morning. Taking nothing away from how well Liz herself was liked and how many lives she touched, I think it's safe to say this was partly in tribute to Bomber, too, since virtually no one had been able to make it to Nebraska. Everybody around town who knew one of them knew the other. Liz had become as much a fixture at the Bomb Shelter as Bomber himself. She was the favored shoulder to cry on when somebody was down on their luck, the voice of reason when tempers flared, and unofficial den mother to the parade of girls who came and went as dancers hired by Bomber for the added entertainment of his nighttime patrons. With a wry, sad smile I recalled how many of those girls over the years had picked up on the vibes between Liz and me and referred to ours as a "Matt Dillon–Miss Kitty" relationship.

Prominent among those paying last respects to Liz was her brother Tony—sober, for once; looking understandably distraught. I made myself be civil to him and even felt briefly sorry for him, but then I couldn't help remembering all the shit he'd put his sister through over the years with his asshole schemes and stunts that repeatedly ended up with him in hot water that Liz had to bail him out of. My charitable feelings didn't last very long. Yeah, he was distraught all right—from now on when he ended up in hot water he was going to have to stew in it because big sister wouldn't be there to save his sorry ass.

Jan was finally able to get away from her assignment long enough to jet in from the capital, and it was only after she showed up that I realized how much I resented her for not making it sooner. I had needed her and she hadn't been there for me; her job was more important. That was perhaps a selfish and somewhat petulant stance on my part, but things hadn't been going all that swell between the two of us recently anyway, and this was just another in a sequence of scenes that seemed to find us bickering more than anything else when we were together. My resentment simmered in me until it erupted into a full scale blowout that evening after returning to my place from the cemetery. The finale had her storming out to find a motel room in the middle of the night and then heading back to D.C. the next day without so much as a good-bye or a final go-to-hell tossed over her shoulder as she went.

I couldn't remember ever feeling more alone and miserable.

CHAPTER FIVE

Nine days later, on a Wednesday, Abby Bridger called again from Nebraska.

When the phone first went off my heart gave a little skip, the way it had been doing lately whenever a phone rang. Ever since Jan stormed out on me. Thinking it might be her, finally returning one of the numerous voice mails I'd left.

As a matter of fact, I hadn't been doing much else besides that . . . pining away, feeling lousy. I guess you could say I was still in a state of mourning. Mourning the loss of my friends, mourning the general upheaval in my life. Before going out to Nebraska I had off-loaded the active cases I was working and since returning had neither sought nor accepted any replacement jobs. My bank account was in the black for a change and without Necessity pushing me I was basking in the luxury of allowing myself to be unmotivated and unfocused. Maybe you could also say I was feeling a little sorry for myself.

"Joe?" Abby said after I picked up and she had identified herself. "You sound. . . . Are you doing okay?"

"I'm hangin' in, kid," I told her.

"From you, I guess no one would expect anything less."

"How are things out there? How's your mother?"

She hesitated just enough to make it noticeable. "Ma's doing as well as can be expected, I'd say. As far as things out here otherwise . . . I'm not so sure."

"What is that supposed to mean? Is something wrong?"

"Some things seem to be coming to light . . . some facts, allegedly . . . about the accident that claimed the lives of Uncle Bomber and Miss Grimaldi. It's causing some nasty, hurtful gossip that's starting to make me pretty damn mad."

"Gossip about Bomber and Liz, you mean?" At the implication, I felt my own surge of defensive anger.

"More specifically about the accident. About what caused it."

"Bomber was driving too fast on a strange road. He misjudged one of those sneaky curves you told me about. What more is there?"

"Word's going around now that he was drunk. That the bodies and the inside of the car reeked with the smell of booze. That they found empty beer cans and a spilled bottle of open whiskey in the wreck."

"That's ridiculous! Bomber was diabetic, he had to be careful as hell with his alcohol intake. When he drank, it was very selective. It wouldn't have been whiskey and beer and it sure as hell wouldn't have been while he was out driving on roads he'd never traveled before. As far as Liz, when she drank it was vodka. Never anything else in all the years I knew her."

"There's more," Abby said. "Supposedly there were signs that Uncle Bomber and Liz were . . . you know, fooling around. While they were going down the road."

"What do you mean 'fooling around'?"

"What they're saying is that his pants were . . . well, unzipped. And her panties were completely off, and her front unbuttoned. Liz was wearing this short-skirted summer dress, see, with—"

"I don't give a damn what Liz was wearing! Are people out that way nuts or something? Have they got prairie dust or buffalo shit clogging their fucking brains? Bomber and Liz were friends—*platonic* friends—for twenty-five years. In all that time there was never any romantic or sexual attraction between them. If there had been they were both certainly free to act on it, but no sparks ever got struck. So all of a sudden they go out to Nebraska and can't restrain themselves from behaving like a couple of hormone-charged teenagers? Bomber was pushing seventy, for Christ's sake! And although she'd probably come out of her grave if she heard me say so, Liz wasn't exactly a spring chicken anymore, either. No matter who they were, what are the odds of two mature, long-time friends suddenly carrying on like that?"

"Well," Abby replied quietly, "when the police officers and paramedics who were on the scene all stick to the same story—at least all the ones I can get to talk about it—it's kind of hard to ignore."

"Hogwash is still hogwash, no matter who shovels it."

"Don't you think I know that, Joe? I had just spent the better part of a week with them. For the first time, I felt like I actually got to know Uncle Bomber a little bit. Liz, too. Like you said, there wasn't the slightest hint of anything sexual going on between them and if there had been they had no reason to hide it. What's more, I helped them pack a picnic basket for their drive in the country that day. You know what they took to drink? A gallon of lemonade and a six-pack of bottled water. Boozing it up and hanky-panky were no more a part of their plans than . . . than . . . I don't know what! The whole thing is preposterous."

"So then what's the point of the rumors?" I wanted to know. "Bomber and Liz are past being affected by them. Is someone out to embarrass you or your mother? Hurt your business?"

"That seems pretty far-fetched. The Bridger name has already been dragged through as bad or worse over the years and still managed to survive. And the business? Who or what is our piddly-ass little store and lodge a threat to?"

I said, "What does that leave then? Is the rumor mill out there so hard up for something juicy that these bozos—these cops and paramedics—decided maybe to make up some shit for entertainment at the expense of a couple out-of-towners' reputations? See how exaggerated things would get?"

"I accused Clint Barnstable of as much. It made him furious."

"Who's Clint Barnstable?" I said.

"He was the first one on the scene. He's a county sheriff's deputy, although he was off duty that particular day. He was out dirt-biking with some buddies and they happened to come upon the accident sight as they were returning home. They called it in on a cell phone, did everything they could for Liz and Uncle Bomber until the paramedics arrived, but . . . well, there really wasn't much they *could* do." Abby took a deep breath, sighed it back out. "I got in Clint's face pretty bad the other night at the bowling alley, in front of a lot of other people. It had to've been embarrassing for him. I'm so frustrated and mixed up, I don't know . . . I probably should have been thanking him instead of hollering at him, accusing him of things I had absolutely no basis for."

"You had the basis of knowing that the things he reported were impossible and unbelievable," I reminded her.

Abby paused a long moment before responding. "Unbelievable, yes. Impossible? What if . . . what if the circumstances Clint and the others reported *were* what they found. But—as you and I both believe—the way they found things wasn't the result of anything actually done by Liz and Uncle Bomber?"

It took me a second to grasp what she was suggesting. "The accident scene was tampered with, you mean?"

"It's the only explanation I can think of that makes sense."

My hand was suddenly sweating around the phone receiver. "But if the scene was doctored up, then that means the accident itself may not have been. . . ." My voice went tight, I let the sentence trail off.

"Look, Joe, you don't know me very well but I assure you I am not given to delusions or paranoia or an overactive imagination. I'm about as basic and down-to-earth as you can get," Abby insisted. "Yet I'm convinced there's something very wrong out here. Ever since those quote-unquote 'facts' about the accident got out and started causing loose talk, ever since I lost my temper with Clint Barnstable and confronted some others. . . . All of a sudden I feel like I'm being watched. My every move. At the store, when I go out. Sometimes even at night, in my own home. . . . God, it's especially creepy at night." She was managing to keep the panic out of her tone, but just barely. "I don't know what's going on, but I know I don't like it worth a damn. Like I said before, it's got me mad . . . and I'd be lying if I didn't admit it's also got me a little scared."

CHAPTER SIX

"I know bullshit when I step in it, and I got a pretty good detector for recognizing the other kind that folks spread around, too," Margaret Bridger announced confidently. "So we're in agreement that it's bullshit what some are saying about my brother and his friend Liz having their accident because they were boozing it up and going down the road finger-diddling each other, or whatever. . . . No argument on that. But to jump from there all the far way to a notion that the accident might not even have been an accident at all and the stuff found at the scene was planted or rigged or some such . . . I dunno. That just seems like a big jump to a mighty shaky conclusion."

I was seated once again at the small kitchen table in Margaret's cramped apartment. Seated across from me, occupying the table's only other chair, was Abby Bridger. Her mother was sitting in her recliner, hooked as before to the oxygen machine. We were each balancing cups of good, strong coffee that Margaret had insisted on preparing and serving before the start of our conversation.

"What other conclusion can there be, Ma?" Abby argued. "It can't be both ways. If we're all in agreement that it's not possible Uncle Bomber and Liz were carrying on in a manner that fits the condition Clint Barnstable and the others say they found them in, then either Clint and all the rest are flat out lying or what they found was *arranged* for whoever came along to discover the wreck."

Being in the presence of the two debating women was like watching a physical embodiment of the point-counterpoint exchanges that had ping-ponged back and forth inside my head all during the drive out here. I hadn't dead-headed straight through this time; I'd stopped long enough at a motel on the outskirts of Dubuque to eat a room-service supper and catch six hours of sleep and a hot shower before rolling on. Still, I didn't let any grass grow under feet after receiving the distraught phone call from Abby.

Her call had jarred me out of my doldrums—my period of mourning or period of feeling sorry for myself, whichever it had been. For the first time in nearly two weeks I felt energized, felt focused, felt like hauling myself forward . . . even if the goal ahead wasn't entirely clear.

The last time I came out to Nebraska I'd been in such a stunned state by the news of my friends' deaths and then had gotten so immersed in the whirl of activity surrounding the funerals and so forth that the possibility of their fatal car crash being anything other than an accident had never entered my thoughts. There had been no hint, no reason to suspect something like that. But now there was. And no matter how faint the tremors causing these suspicions, the one thing I was certain of all during the drive here this time was that I would neither rest nor leave again until I had run some answers to ground.

Margaret turned to me pointedly. "Tell me, Joe: Isn't it extremely difficult in this day and age to fake a fatal accident and not have it detected by police forensics?"

" 'Forensics'? For Heaven's sake, Mother," Abby groaned. "You sound like you're rehearsing an advertising spiel for the next episode of *CSI*."

"The questions still stands," Margaret insisted, keeping me pinned with her gaze.

I made a catch-all gesture with my free hand. "You've got to remember, there are forensic teams and there are forensic teams."

"What is that supposed to mean?" Margaret said.

"Well, it means all that high-powered, high-tech stuff you see on TV is really out there, true. And it is definitely capable of some pretty incredible stuff. But it doesn't necessarily mean that kind of capability is available to every police force in every burg across the country. Even in places where it *is* available it often becomes a matter of time or expense or notoriety as to how extensively it gets put to use. You take a basically rural, low-population, low-crime area like out here, I'd say it's a safe bet any evidence that may be a candidate for serious analysis has to be sent off somewhere. Maybe as far as Omaha. That brings into play time and expense, like I said before, plus other issues like proper handling, chain of custody, contamination risk, and on and on. To get the full benefit of those amazing results forensic science can produce you need proper training and discipline and competency all the way down the line."

"And you don't think there's any of that out here?"

"I don't know enough about your law enforcement out here to say. For whatever reason, though, as far as Liz and Bomber's accident it doesn't sound like they *did* do much in the way of forensic work. At least I never heard mention of any. Not even an autopsy was performed. If there had been, then we'd have a medical examiner's report to refer to for verification of whether or not there was any alcohol in their blood and all this rumor/speculation crap that's coming out now could be put to rest plenty damn quick. You see my point? *Not* having those facts to either confirm or rebut these vicious rumors leaves the door open for the kind of suspicions Abby is having and I've got to admit I'm starting to buy into."

"But it all seems so . . . so unimaginable," Margaret

murmured. "That the accident might actually have been the result of . . . I want to say 'foul play,' but, God, that term is such a cliché it feels awkward and silly to even use it."

"As long as there's rising doubt about what really happened concerning Liz and Uncle Bomber," Abby said, "it would be a hell of a lot sillier *not* to use it."

"I didn't come eight hundred miles to have this little kitchen confab and then just leave things go their own course," I assured the both of them. "I'm here. I'm involved. I mean to stay involved until I've done everything I can to determine once and for all if—and I got no qualms about saying it—foul play was associated to the wreck that took Bomber and Liz."

"But how will you be able to do that?" Margaret wanted to know. "So many days have passed. And now there's all this confusion. And the only two people we know for certain who can say what happened on that road that day . . . well, they're in the ground, Joe."

"There are still people above ground I can talk to. Ask questions. Review exactly what went into the official report. Check the accounts of the first ones on the scene, try to get them to sort out what they saw with their own eyes and know for a fact against what they maybe assumed or heard as hearsay. It's the kind of thing I do and happen to be pretty good at."

Margaret regarded me. "Yes, you are. I know that. And of course we will pay you for your time, for helping to put this thing to rest."

"Margaret, don't insult me."

"No, I mean it. I can afford it. I heard from my brother's lawyer just the other day—I had no idea before his call, but it turns out I was named the beneficiary in a very sizable life-insurance policy Leslie was carrying. I was told I could expect payment very shortly. So why should you have to come clear out here and do the thing you earn your living at and do it for free when I can pay you just as well as the next client."

"She has a point, Joe," Abby said.

"No, she doesn't," I argued. "You people aren't 'clients'—you're the family of the guy who was my best friend. No way I'm taking payment from you. And as far as coming into some money, don't try to tell me that with medical bills and the upkeep required for your business here you don't have other places you can put it to use. This part of the conversation is ended—finito—you got it?"

Margaret cocked one eyebrow sharply and glared at me from underneath. "No wonder you got along so well with my brother—you're just as damnably stubborn as he was!"

"Maybe it would help if you tried to think of it as tenacity instead of stubbornness," I said, attempting a disarming grin. "That gives it a more positive spin."

"Stubborn is stubborn, no matter what you call it."

"Have it your way." I turned to Abby. "Now what about this other business—this sense of being watched, possibly being stalked? Anything more on that?"

She shook her head. "Nothing different. Still just the . . . well, feeling. Saying that, I guess now I should be the one worried about sounding silly. But I can't really call it anything more. I mean, I haven't actually seen anybody or anything."

"How about you? You pick up on any of the same vibes?" I asked Margaret.

"Can't say as I have." Another head shake. "But then I don't do much for anybody to keep an eye on. Go up to tend the front of the store once in a while, otherwise I seldom leave this apartment. Ain't got the wind to go much farther."

Back to Abby. "Have you mentioned this to anyone else?"

"No. No, I haven't."

"Your neighboring business—the tavern across the way? How friendly are you with the people who run it?"

"That would be B.U. Gorcey and his wife Mamie. They're good people, we get along fine. They've been very attentive and helpful all through Ma's illness and then when the accident happened. B.U.'s a rough-edged old ex–rodeo rider and when Uncle Bomber was here they hit it off straight away, spent quite a bit of time visiting, swapping stories."

"What about hired help? While we're here talking, for instance, you must have somebody up front tending the store, right?"

"Uh-huh. We hire high school kids mostly through the summer when it's the busiest. We're payrolling two girls from town this summer. And a young college guy to do mowing and outside cleanup and so forth. One of the girls is up front now, the guy is outside policing the grounds and doing some trimming. And for years we've used a handyman service—a fella and his son from town—to take care of repairs when they're needed."

"I'll be as discreet as possible, but you understand I may want to talk to all or most of them at some point?"

Abby nodded solemnly. "Whatever you think is necessary, Joe. Like you said . . . this is what you do."

Chapter Seven

Although the other five cabins of the No Name Bay "lodge" were occupied and booked solid through the rest of the summer, cabin number six was empty due to the fact it had been only partly finished at the time of Henry Bridger's abrupt death and in the intervening years was never completed.

The work that remained, however, was all on the interior. It had electricity and running water, even if its wiring and rafters were exposed, its floor was bare plywood, and the inner walls lacked sheetrock or plasterboard. But for me, I decided, those could be livable conditions. All it took was a good sweeping out and a few basics in the way of furniture. A sturdy old Army cot, a dresser, and a chair and folding table culled out of storage filled the latter category. A spare microwave oven was a luxury toss-in. Finally some fresh linens, including a couple extra pillowcases to thumbtack over the windows for privacy, and I had a suitable home away from home.

Margaret Bridger was aghast at the thought of me staying in what she called "little more than an oversized yard shed" but I finally managed to convince her that I could make do just fine with it. The alternatives, I pointed out, were either to check into one of the motels in town, which would be ill-suited to the goal of me being around to try and spot whatever presence Abby could "feel" watching her; or stay in the spare room of Abby's upstairs apartment (formerly Margaret's bedroom), which would infringe on one another's privacy, would feel personally awkward, and since we would be two unmarried people staying under the same roof would only accelerate the gossipmongers' tongues that were already wagging too rapidly about the alleged activities of the last visitors who showed up from Illinois.

At first Abby joined with her mother in protesting my habitation of the partially completed cabin but, for reasons I wouldn't fully understand until later, when I brought up the point about how me staying with her might be perceived by the local gossip network she quickly changed her mind.

Evening had settled in by the time we were done preparing the cabin. The sun sliding down over the western horizon cast a shimmering pinkish-orange stain down the length of the lake and a breeze coming off the water carried some welcome coolness from the heat that had built up during the day. Some of the occupants of the other cabins had charcoal grills going in front of their units, sending tendrils of smoke and the aroma of sizzling meats wafting through the air. Some of them were also shooting off firecrackers and skyrockets, a loud and annoying practice that was making me jumpy and a tad irritable.

On a final trip over from the big building, Abby brought me a plate of sandwiches, two cold bottles of Coors, and a large box fan. "Sorry if the sandwiches are a lame excuse for supper but the afternoon sorta got away from me and I didn't take time to plan anything," she explained.

"It's not your responsibility to feed me, anyway," I told her. "But the thought is welcome, all the same."

"I figured the fan would get you through the night in case it stays too warm for your comfort. I've got a couple spare window air conditioners down in the basement, tomorrow I'll have our handymen come out and install one of them in here for you. Believe me, it gets plenty hot in these parts in the summer."

We had taken seats on the front steps of my cabin. Abby was smoking a cigarette and sipping from a tall bottle of Pepsi that she'd brought along for herself. I'd uncapped one of the bottles of beer.

Abby was wearing black jeans and a mint-green shirt tied in front just above the navel, sleeves rolled to three-quarter length. The shirt had gotten smudged during her rummaging through the dusty piles of stuff in the big building's basement, selecting the items for my cabin. Helping me haul them over, she'd worked up a faint perspiration and as a result the scent of whatever perfume she was wearing had taken on a deepened, tantalizing muskiness that I became very aware of sitting close to her there in the lengthening shadows.

"Knowing you're out here tonight," she was saying, "I hope to get the first good night's sleep I've gotten all week."

"In between volleys of cherry bombs, you mean."

"They'll stop after ten. They'd better. It's the law and it gets enforced pretty strictly."

"I thought most places had fireworks outlawed pretty much altogether, except in the hands of professionals."

"Not out here. Not for the two weeks preceding the Fourth of July. This is the wild west, my friend."

"I guess I'm used to the wild east. My neighborhood, you hear pops and bangs in the night you figure it's gunfire and you'd better either duck or reach for your own piece."

"Life in the big, bad city, eh?"

"Something like that." Two cabins down, somebody set off a string of firecrackers that sounded like a machine-gun riff and once again it gave me a start. "And at least my city gunfire doesn't go on and on and on, like this crap."

"Like I said, Fourth of July is coming up in just over a week. Isn't that a worthy cause to celebrate? Freedom, right? Seems to me people ought to be free to make a little noise about if they want to."

I shrugged. "If you say so. I never saw the appeal myself. And if one of those bozos down the line sets off anything after ten-oh-one I may have to walk over and explain exactly how *un*appealing I find it."

Abby laughed. "Just don't cause a ruckus that makes me have to get out of bed and come deal with it, okay? Like I said, I'm looking forward to a good night's sleep."

"Got it. I'll keep in mind that I'm here to help with your problems, not add to 'em."

She took a long drag of her cigarette, letting the exhaled smoke trail off on the evening breeze, then said, "Calling you the way I did, I guess that must have seemed pretty bold. I mean, we really only barely know each other. And yet it doesn't feel that way, at least not to me. Uncle Bomber told a lot of stories about you over the years. And then you were such a rock when you came out before, looking out for Ma and me, helping with the funeral, so steady and strong when I knew all the while you were being torn apart on the inside with your own pain. . . . That's why, when I started trying to stand up to these lies, started to realize they might signal something a lot more sinister than we'd ever dreamed, there was only one person I thought of to turn to for help. It was you."

"I'm glad you did," I said sincerely.

She turned her head and looked at me. "I can't tell you how grateful I am to you for coming here and . . . well, *doing* this."

"You have told me. Several times," I reminded her. "You don't have to say so anymore, okay?"

She blushed a little. "Not even to compensate for allowing you to sleep in this hollow old shack?"

"We've covered that about enough, too. You need to remember I've got my own stake in this. You talked about me finding closure the last time? How can I claim to ever have closure if I leave the door open to even the slightest possibility that some sonofabitch might have had a hand in bringing about the deaths of my friends and I don't do everything I can to make sure that question gets answered?"

"So this whole thing means a lot to all of us. And what you're doing to try and help settle it means a lot, too—to me and Ma both."

"You sure about that? She acts half sore that I'm here, like I'm butting in or something."

"No, that's not it. Not at all. I think she's just scared that we might be right, that maybe there was more to the wreck than a simple accident. She was coming to grips with the loss of her brother one way—finding her own closure—now she may have to step back and find a way to deal with it all over again. And she's so ill, Joe, so weak, . . . that's what's making her seem so angry all the time, she hates that she isn't strong enough to be in the thick of this fight for the truth."

"She's got all the fight she can handle battling her illnesses."

"Uh-huh. And it doesn't help any knowing that . . . well, ultimately it's a fight she can't win."

I pointed at the cigarette Abby had by then smoked down to almost nothing. "Not my way to lecture since Christ knows I burnt my own share of tobacco back in the day—but seeing what the emphysema is doing to your mother, you ever consider that's a habit you'd be a lot better off without?"

Sarcastically, Abby said, "Really? Darn! Nobody ever explained that to me before."

"Fine. And you won't hear it again. Not from me."

"I'd appreciate it," she said rather peevishly. She leaned forward to stab out what was left of the cigarette. Then, mouth taking on a rueful twist, sighing, she looked back over at me and said, "Look. I *do* appreciate it—both the concern, and the restraint from any more lectures. I'm working on it, okay?"

"I hear you. Like I said, I've been there."

Abby stood up, still holding the bottle of Pepsi in one hand, brushing off her bottom with the other. "I'd better go and let you eat before your sandwiches turn dry. I'm going to drop in, check on Ma, then help Cindy close up the store and call it a night."

"You do that. Sleep tight, as they say. I'll be keeping an eye on things."

"What about tomorrow? Where are you going to start your questioning?"

"With the county sheriff, I figure. I start poking around, he's bound to hear plenty quick that I've shown up and what I'm doing. Been my experience it'll go a lot smoother if he hears it right up front directly from me. He may still not like it, but it'll irritate less than catching wind of it the other way."

"Arthur or Keith?" Abby said.

"What do you mean?"

"Are you going to see the Arthur County sheriff or the Keith County sheriff? The accident took place across the Arthur County line, but Deputy Barnstable and the paramedics called to the scene were from Keith County. So both sheriffs ended up being involved."

"I hadn't realized that. Who actually ran the investigation of the wreck?"

"I'm not sure. Arthur County is as big or bigger than Keith, but it only has like five hundred people in it and they're mostly scattered ranchers. Sheriff Walt Mabry covers it by himself, with maybe one part-time deputy. I can't say for certain, but I'm guessing anything that amounts to a very detailed investigation he gets help either from the state police or the closest neighboring county—Keith, in this instance."

"Then it sounds like I'll be paying a visit to both sheriffs. But before that I'm thinking I'd better sit down with you and make sure I'm not missing any more basic details."

"I open the store at five sharp each morning—you know, for

fishermen heading out early and needing some last-minute supplies."

I gave a pained expression. "God, don't look for me anywhere near that hour."

"I'll make time for you and we can go over things whenever you show up," Abby said, grinning. "I'll have coffee on."

"Another thing. As soon as possible I want to have a look at the spot where Bomber's car went off the road."

"If you go to see Sheriff Mabry, you'll drive right by it. If you wait until after one of my counter girls show up, I can ride along, show you exactly. Then I can introduce you to Walt, too. I know him pretty well—he puts his boat in at this ramp whenever he goes out fishing."

"What do you figure I can expect in the way of cooperation from these two sheriffs?"

Abby considered the question a moment, then said, "I believe they're both fair and decent men. I think they'll work with you. Gene Knaack, the Keith County sheriff, is a little sterner and more coplike than Walt, but still reasonable. If there's something not on the up-and-up, they'd both want to see it uncovered as badly as we do."

"Let's hope so."

"You'll find out. . . . G'night."

As Abby turned and walked toward the store, the slanting rays of the dying light caught the sun-streaked highlights in her hair and it made me think of my Jan, whose hair—although worn much shorter than Abby's—always streaked in the same way and lightened several shades during the summer months. Thinking of Jan made me feel a little lonely and sad, not surprisingly. But then, remembering how pleasant it had been sitting there in the lake breeze chatting with Abby and how aware I'd been of her perfume and the nearness of her, I *was* surprised to also feel a curious pang of guilt.

Trying to process exactly what that meant caused me to hesitate in returning Abby's "G'night." By the time I did, she had drifted out of earshot.

CHAPTER EIGHT

"So what it boils down to," Walt Mabry summarized in his lazy, low-key drawl, "is that you've got a handful of details that seem inconsistent with the habits of the two, ah, victims."

"Very inconsistent," Abby responded.

Propping his knobby elbows on the desktop before him, Mabry steepled his long, bony fingers and let his chin come to rest on the tips of his thumbs. He was a tall, lanky man somewhere between fifty and sixty, all flat planes and sharp angles, with a long, weather-seamed face and iron-gray hair. He wore gleaming black cowboy boots, sharply creased black slacks, and a short-sleeved white shirt with a Western string tie fastened by a turquoise clasp. There was the distinct air of ex-military about him and the stark simplicity and tidiness of his small office, located at the back corner of the Arthur County courthouse, did nothing to curb that impression.

Past his shoulder, through the office's east window, I could see the small white frame building that a sign on the edge of the parking area outside proclaimed to be: "The world's smallest courthouse, as listed in Ripley's Believe-It-Or-Not." The sign went on to further inform readers that the courthouse and its tiny jail—an even smaller white frame building adjacent to it— were actually in use until 1962, when the new, modern county-government building was erected. I guess being listed in Ripley's was a pretty big deal for a town the size of Arthur, population 148, county seat and only town in a county that was geographically larger than some eastern states but whose entire census tallied less than 500. What's more, just down the street it had a second attraction that had also been honored with a mention in Ripley's—a church made of baled straw, built in the 1920s out of faith and out of creative necessity due to the region's scarcity of timber.

Under different circumstances, I may or may not have paid these attractions much attention. But the fact that a visit to each had been on the agenda of Bomber and Liz the day of their fateful drive gave them some noteworthiness where I was concerned.

Tapping the tips of his steepled index fingers together, Sheriff Mabry said, "These habits of the late Miss Grimaldi and Mr. Brannigan that you're both so familiar with—their choice of alcoholic beverages, the man's unfailingly cautious driving practices, the relationship between the two of them—that would be their *regular* habits in their *regular* home setting or around family and friends. Is that a fair statement?"

I could see where he was headed and I didn't have the patience to let him waste time going there. "Other than the limits his diabetes put on Bomber," I said, "the habits we're talking about were matters of choice, not behavior they chose for appearance sake or merely to 'fit in' with some specific peer group. These weren't a couple of repressed thirty-somethings having a midlife crisis who came eight hundred miles out to the middle of Nebraska to shed their inhibitions and go wild."

"Why exactly was Miss Grimaldi along?" Mabry asked. "I understand that Mister Brannigan was here to visit his ailing sister and maybe return to his roots a little, but what was the attraction for the lady? I mean, we're hardly a garden spot that brings people flocking from all over the country."

"She was simply accompanying an old friend to keep him company on the long drive out and back, and have a look at a part of the country she'd never seen before. Like a lot of us back home, she'd been hearing Bomber talk about Nebraska for years. She had some vacation time coming, so she took the chance to get away for a while and see some new sights. That's all."

Mabry accepted the explanation with a faint nod. Then, continuing on, he said, "As far as your friend's diabetes, heck, I know two or three fellas ailing from that—they take a notion to celebrate with some birthday cake and ice cream or go on a drinking binge with the boys, they just shoot up a different dose of their insulin. Their blood-sugar problems don't mean they always steer clear of the stuff that's bad for them, not by a far sight."

"Bomber did that too," I conceded. "*Sometimes*. He'd go a little too heavy on the beer once in a while, for example, and when he did that he'd alter his insulin dose. But he was never a whiskey fancier, even before he got diabetes. And afterwards he found he could safely satisfy his taste for hard liquor just fine with Diet Coke and rum—no sugar, no carbs." Trying to press my point harder, I added, "If he ever *did* want to go on a whiskey bender, he ran a bar, for crying out loud! Same for Liz. She worked for him. But she was strictly a vodka drinker—screwdrivers or bloody Marys. I saw people get her to try dozens of different concoctions over the years but it always came back to vodka. And if she'd taken a notion to change, Jesus, I can guarantee it wouldn't have been a switch to boilermakers while driving around on strange roads in a strange part of the country."

Mabry listened patiently to everything I had to say but when it was his turn to reply he couldn't keep one brow from lifting in the universal sign of skepticism. "I appreciate your sorrow and your deep feelings for you friends, Mr. Hannibal. But it's been my experience that nobody is above veering off in an unpredictable way once in a while."

"Too bad there wasn't an autopsy ordered on the bodies," I said, trying not to make the statement sound too accusatory. "I guess that would have answered this drunk-or-not-drunk question once and for all."

"Maybe." His eyes might have narrowed just a fraction but his tone stayed calm and mild. "But we're a poor county in a state fighting a raging deficit, friend. It was my call that this matter was so clear-cut there was no reason to waste the taxpayers' money on that kind of unnecessary expense. Also been my experience that, unless it's absolutely called for, the idea of an autopsy—the deceased being laid open and examined in the way they do—is often very unsettling to the surviving family or families."

"You think what we're going through now isn't unsettling, Walt?" Abby said.

"Of course it is. But this is now. Back then, if I'd suggested—"

"If you'd have said you thought it was a good idea, Ma and I would have gone along with it. You know damn well we would have. Even still, that's only part of it. What about this other idiotic business that's getting spread around? The unzippered trousers and the pulled-down panties and the rest—you think it isn't disturbing for a grieving family to have to listen to that kind of ridiculous crap?"

Mabry unsteepled his fingers and lowered his hands. "Look, Abby, I've known you and your family since you was a gap-toothed little gal in pigtails." The pitch of his voice deepened and his tone grew very sincere. "I don't mean to offend nor do I want to speak ill of the dead. . . . But I was there that day at the accident scene, I saw with my own eyes the emptied beer cans and the spilled whiskey . . . and the, ah, undone clothing, too. What explanation can there be for those things other than they were there as a result of the actions of the two people in the car?"

"I don't know." Abby was glaring at him fiercely. "But no matter what you saw—it wasn't the way you're all choosing to believe."

Mabry gave a kind of weary sigh and leaned back in his chair. He swung his gaze to me. "Did you stop at the accident scene on your way here?"

"Yes. Matter of fact we did."

"Ain't been that long and there's been no rain to speak of. . . . You could tell where the car left the road and where it came to rest after flipping and rolling, right?"

The flattened grass sprinkled with bits of glass and chrome, the gouges torn in the earth well beyond the gleaming strands of new wire spliced in to repair the gaping hole in the fence . . . yeah, the scene was planted pretty damn clearly in my mind's eye.

"I got the picture well enough."

"You know any explanation other than running off the road at a high rate of speed for how the car could've ended up that way?"

"No, I don't," I said. "Not yet."

"Okay, can we agree on that much as a sort of baseline, then? That the car crashed as a result of excessive speed? From there, the way I see, that only leaves about three scenarios to account for the rest of it." The sheriff again held up a handful of fingers and, one by one, thumbed off the count. "One, it was the accident everybody has already accepted, for the reasons everybody but you two have accepted. Two, it was an accident that somebody for motives unknown—maybe as a sick prank, I don't know—saw fit to tamper with before more responsible people got to the scene. Three, it wasn't an accident at all and the way things were found at the scene was some kind of cover-up attempt. . . . You with me on that much?"

Abby and I exchanged glances then swung our eyes back to Mabry, waiting for him to continue. He took that for the affirmation it was meant to be.

"Much as the first one displeases you, can you see where, objectively, on the face of everything, most people would consider it the most logical?"

"Only if you put two other passengers in the car," Abby said stubbornly.

"Doggone it, Abby, work with me a little bit here. I'm trying to take a look at this thing from your angle, can't you cut me a little slack and try taking a look at it from mine?"

Tight-mouthed, Abby made a motion for him to go on.

"As far as the other two possibilities . . . I don't know, I'm trying but I can't help seeing them as anything but far-fetched and farther-fetched. I mean, what would be the sense of pranksters messing with the accident scene, the bodies? Where would be the kick, the payoff? They couldn't hang around to see the reaction of whoever showed up next, and since the victims were from out of state it's unlikely pranksters could've known about their relationship to anybody local. None of the details other than 'appeared to have been alcohol related' showed up in any of the news coverage of the accident, so they didn't get their jollies having the graphic descriptions titillate a slobbering public. I repeat, what would've been the point? And if there *wasn't* alcohol involved and your uncle always drove sensible, how did the accident occur in the first place to even give anybody an opportunity to mess with it?"

Mabry let the rhetorical questions hang in the air for a moment, then went on. "And the notion that the wreck was somehow *caused,* and the rest of it was some kind of ruse or cover-up. . . . Come on, you got to admit that gets pretty far out there. In the first place, how could the car have been made to flip and roll the way it did? God knows that stretch of road can be mean and twisty, but the land is basically flat—you got no incline so that the bodies could have been placed inside, maybe unconscious or already dead and then, say, the vehicle pushed down a hill to build up speed. The gas pedal could have been jammed there on the straightaway and then the car dropped into gear some tricky way, I suppose, but an examination of the pavement approaching the crash site didn't show any fresh strips of rubber like would have been laid by that kind of sudden take-off. And neither was there any sign of skid marks to indicate somebody might have run them off the road or that there was any other vehicle involved at all."

"I don't care. There was *something* else involved—something besides what you're choosing to believe," Abby insisted stubbornly.

The sheriff looked at me. "Okay, say I'm wrong, say there was something fishy or underhanded about that car crash. What would make somebody set up something so elaborate? Were your friends in some kind of trouble? Was somebody out to get one or both of them?"

"No way. Nothing like that."

"How about a recent altercation with somebody out here?" the sheriff asked Abby.

She shook her head. "No. Everybody took an immediate liking to Uncle Bomber. And Liz, too."

"Unless something happened on the day of the accident, after they left No Name Bay," I said, thinking out loud. "How about here in your town, Sheriff? This was one of their destinations that day—your little courthouse and jail, the baled-straw church. Since they were going south when their car went off the road that would suggest they were headed back, meaning they would have already been here if they followed the agenda they'd put together."

"This is the first I'm hearing that they were ever supposed to be in Arthur," Mabry said.

"So you don't know if they were in town or not."

"No. But I can ask around, for what it's worth. If they went inside the old courthouse they would've had to stop at the front desk here—in *this* courthouse, that is—to get the keys. Darlene out there ain't been off that desk for months and she's got a memory like a steel trap. As big as Brannigan was, she'll sure remember if he came by."

"Is there a guestbook in the old courthouse for visitors to sign?"

"Matter of fact there is. We can check that, too. Before you leave."

"The church?"

"No guestbook there," Abby answered. "you can't go inside. You just pull up and look from the outside. There's a sign out front telling a little about the place."

"Anywhere else in town they might have stopped? For a snack, maybe a cup of coffee or something?"

"Only place like that'd be the tavern," Mabry said. "They run a short-order grill behind the bar. Serve up burgers and fries, lunch specials on weekdays. Coffee if you've a mind for some."

I had run out of questions for the time being. Our conversation lapsed into a somewhat awkward pause.

Sensing that we'd about used up our welcome anyway, I rose to my feet, saying, "Sheriff, I really appreciate the time you've spared us this morning. We didn't come here expecting to sell you our ideas in one fell swoop and we in no way meant to infer that your handling of the accident was lacking in any way. From your perspective, I guess I can see where you had every reason to take the crash at face value. From ours . . . well, we've got these personal angles that I hope you understand are driving us to want a little closer look. All we ask is that you keep an open mind and maybe your eyes and ears open, too, in case anything odd pops up that might have a bearing on this. What I'm mainly hoping for, though, is that you won't object if I continue to do a little more poking around in your county. For the sake of . . . well, let's just say trying to satisfy our curiosity."

Abby had stood up also. Her expression suggested she might not have been ready to let up on the sheriff so soon, but she didn't say anything.

Mabry frowned faintly at my closing query. His eyes fell to the desktop where he'd laid the business card I had handed him when I first came in. "Don't recall ever having a PI poke around in my county before," he said thoughtfully. There was nothing in his tone to indicate whether or not he liked the idea. His eyes lifted again to me. "You realize, of course, this Illinois license don't give you no privileges in Nebraska."

I couldn't suppress a wry grin. "To tell you the truth, it don't give me a hell of lot of privileges in Illinois, either," I told him. "But let's be clear. As far as this business out here, I'm not acting as a hired investigator—I'm just a guy trying to make sure the record is straight on the passing of two good people who happened to be very dear friends."

Mabry held my eyes for a long count. I'm not sure what he saw in mine; what I saw in his was the depths of a decent man wanting to do the right thing. When he spoke again, he said, "Well then. I guess I'd be a pretty sorry excuse if I objected to that, wouldn't I?"

CHAPTER NINE

"Okay. It was a Wednesday. They arrived on a Saturday so it would've been their fifth day here. Up until then they mostly just hung around No Name Bay . . . you know, visiting, catching up, doing some fishing and a little boating. A couple afternoons Liz sunbathed on the beach while Uncle Bomber shot pool and shot the breeze with B.U. over at the Walleye. One evening they talked Ma into going into town and we all had a nice dinner at Front Street and then went next door to the Crystal Palace Saloon and watched the Wild West Review that the college kids put on there each night in the summer.

"So, anyway, on that Wednesday Uncle Bomber decided he would take Liz around to see some of the historical sites and other points of interest in the area. He had it planned as one big loop, starting in Ogallala at Boot Hill and the Mansion On The Hill museum. Then he was going to swing east to Keystone and see the combination Catholic/Protestant church there before heading up to Arthur to see the old courthouse and the rest where we just came from. He figured to finish up out at Ash Hollow where they've got one of the best museums around and you can still see wheel ruts in the ground from wagons traveling the Oregon Trail. In between Arthur and there they were going to stop and hike back to the site of the original Brannigan homestead on Pawnee Creek, and have their picnic lunch there."

We were on our way back from Arthur, traveling south on

Highway 61, eleven or twelve miles out of town. I'd asked Abby to recap once more for me the itinerary Bomber and Liz were following on the day of their fatal crash.

"This is Pawnee Creek coming up just ahead, right?" I said now.

"Uh-huh. There, where the bridge is."

"And the crash site is a few miles further."

"Right again."

"So, since we've confirmed Bomber and Liz made the planned stops in Arthur that day, I guess we can safely assume they also stopped for their picnic as planned."

"I suppose they must have." Abby turned her head and eyed me more closely. "Why?"

I shrugged. "No particular reason. I'm just trying to chew everything as fine as I can, hoping to get lucky and find something solid, like a lead maybe, that I can sink my teeth into."

We were approaching the bridge over Pawnee Creek. I began to slow down. "Where exactly is this old Brannigan homestead?" I asked.

"Off to the east there," Abby said, pointing to our left. "On the opposite side of the creek. It's back off the road quite a ways—more than a mile, I'd say. Been years since I hiked back."

"You can't drive to it?"

"In a jeep or something, maybe. Not in this car of yours, and certainly not in Uncle Bomber's big ol' low-slung gas-guzzler."

I rolled across the bridge and pulled to the opposite side of the road. Past the sand and gravel shoulder, the ground turned grassy and inclined away to the east. Back toward the creek it dropped off sharply. The spring-fed stream was narrow but it had been winding its way for hundreds of years and had worn a deep groove into the land. Two strands of barbed-wire fence running parallel with the road reached all the way down to the water, interrupted up on the higher ground by a cattle gate. The grass on the other side of the gate was flattened in a wide circular pattern and discernable tire tracks had chewed through to the dirt in several places.

I said, "For not being able to drive back, it sure looks like somebody has wasted a lot of time pulling in and turning around."

"There's a guy on Lake Ogallala who rents canoes for going out on the little lake and also for excursions on the Pawnee," Abby explained. "This is his drop-off spot for the Pawnee trips. He does a pickup at another bridge about twelve miles east."

I went quiet for a minute, gazing past the drop-off/turnaround area. For as far as I could see there was nothing but rolling, grass-covered, sunwashed sandhills contrasted by the deep, shadowy seam of the twisting, tree-lined creek. To the west a low-flying, single-engine plane droned in the sky. It banked leisurely before reaching the highway and swept back west again. Property was so vast out here that cattlemen and other landowners commonly used planes or helicopters to check their herds and fence lines.

Finally, Abby said, "What are you thinking?"

"Back there . . . the homestead site, whatever lies in between . . . is it possible Bomber and Liz might have encountered something that threatened them in some way? Or could one of them have gotten injured . . . fallen, or been snakebit, maybe? That might explain Bomber driving at such an uncharacteristically high rate of speed when they got back to the car."

"But it wouldn't explain the rest of it—the whiskey, the business with the clothing. Not unless you buy Sheriff Mabry's theory about pranksters."

"He managed to shoot that pretty full of holes himself."

"As far as running into a 'threat' out there . . . well, there's always the chance of getting crossways of a rattler. But even that is pretty rare unless you're totally careless and foolish."

I rubbed my jaw. "Yeah. Just some more chewing. . . . Trying to make sure I don't overlook anything."

"It's just too darn bad they didn't have a cell phone with them. Reception sometimes isn't so hot out here but, still, if something went wrong, they might have had a chance to make a call before . . . well, you know. As a matter of fact, I tried to get them to take my cell that day. But Uncle Bomber wouldn't hear of it."

"Yeah. He hated cell phones with a passion. Always said he wouldn't be caught dead with—" I stopped short, the bitter irony of my friend's oft-stated claim clamping down on the words. I cleared my throat. "Damn his stubborn hide. Maybe he *wouldn't* have been caught dead if he'd taken one that day."

I found myself gazing in the direction of the old homestead again.

Abby said, "You want to go back there. Don't you?"

"To be thorough, yeah, I guess I do."

She made a face. "I don't discount it as a good idea—like you said, to be thorough. But it's not something I counted on us doing and the time it'd take would put me in kind of a pinch. I've got deliveries due today at the store and I told Mary Lou I'd be back in time to sign for them and to do the re-orders. Plus I need to be there when the handymen show up to put that air conditioner in your cabin. We could come back here tomorrow, or maybe even later today. Or you could drop me off and come back on your own if you want. You don't necessarily need me tagging along. Follow the creek, you can't miss the homestead site. Although there really isn't a lot to see—an old stone chimney, some foundations, some rotted wood fencing."

"Is it still Brannigan land?"

"No. Hasn't been for decades. It was nothing but a struggle

for Great-grandfather, the one who claimed it. He barely scraped by all the years he tried to make a go of it. After he was gone, his sons—who saw the place as nothing but a source of hardship and misery—sold it off for next to nothing."

"Who owns it now?"

"Cameron Terrell." She seemed to bite off the name rather tersely. "Look in any direction. Everything you'll see, except for the road and the bridge, belongs to the Terrell Cattle & Land Company."

I considered returning and hiking back to what was left of the old homestead. It was something I still wanted to do; but not today, I decided. "We'd better get you back to the store," I said to Abby. "This can wait for now. I'll go ahead on to Ogallala and try to catch a meeting with Sheriff Knaack like I was planning. Maybe I'll get a chance to talk to Barnstable, too, the off-duty deputy you said was first on the crash scene."

"Unfortunately," Abby said, "me and my temper have probably made that a harder task for you than it would have been otherwise."

"Don't worry about it," I said, dropping the Honda back into gear. "Just chalk it up as getting some groundwork out of the way for me. I usually have to piss people off all by myself."

CHAPTER TEN

Back at No Name Bay I parked in front of the store and went inside with Abby, deciding to stock some supplies for the cabin before heading out to try and make my contacts in Ogallala. From the store's surprisingly diverse selection I bought a large ice chest, two bags of ice, some sliced salami and cheese, a loaf of whole-grain bread, a jar of instant coffee, a quart of orange juice, and a six-pack of Coke.

When I inquired where she kept her beer so I could grab a six-pack of that, too, Abby said, "You'll have to go over to the Walleye for that. B.U. sells package goods as well as over-the-bar. That's the arrangement that keeps us good neighbors—he doesn't sell groceries or rent cabins, I don't sell alcohol."

"Makes sense," I allowed.

After unsuccessfully trying to refuse payment for the stuff I'd picked out, Abby insisted on helping me carry my purchases out to the car. Once we had them loaded she said, "If you're going over to the Walleye I'll keep an eye peeled to be sure you make it out of there safe and sound and in a reasonable amount of time."

I looked at her. "I don't follow you."

She grinned. "B.U.'s got a day bartender there, a zesty little bit of Italian spice named Tina. Tina Mancini. Many's the unwary male—including the most avid fishermen, mind you—who has gone in there to pick up a pack of cold ones for their day's activity and never been seen again until closing time when

63

they wander out sort of glassy-eyed and adrift in a daze. Under the influence, you might say, but not necessarily from too much to drink."

"You make her sound like one of the Sirens from Greek mythology."

"Say again?"

"The Sirens lived on an island in the Aegean Sea. They were impossibly beautiful temptresses who lured unsuspecting sailors to their doom."

"I don't know that Tina has ever led anyone to their doom," Abby said, arching a brow. "But she surely has led a few men astray. I can guarantee you that."

"Thanks for the warning. I'll do my darnedest to stay on course."

I left the Accord parked where it was and walked across the gravelly sand toward the Lassoed Walleye Saloon. The day was warming rapidly. The lake was already alive with activity and down by the boat ramp they were backed up three deep jockeying to put in more crafts. An almost palpable sense of energy and vitality danced off the water, along with a faint, fresh breeze.

I pushed into the dim coolness of the Walleye. It was a large, low-ceilinged barroom. Tables in the middle, a pool table and an old-fashioned shuffleboard machine off to one end, long bar across the back wall. Montgomery Gentry was playing on the jukebox.

No other customers were in sight. In fact, nobody else at all was in sight.

I went to the bar and rested my elbows on it. "Hello?" I called out tentatively.

On the opposite side of the bar, directly across from where I was leaning, a face popped up. So close we almost bumped noses.

"Whoa!" The face's eyes widened as it pulled away a hasty ten inches.

I gave a start, too, rocking back on my heels. But a second later, after I'd had the chance to appraise the whole apparition that had appeared so abruptly before me, I saw it was hardly something a red-blooded male ought to be retreating from. I realized I was face to face with the heralded Tina Mancini, and she looked every bit as tempting as advertised. Late twenties, trim yet abundantly curvy all at the same time, flashing dark eyes, close-cropped cap of brunette hair, wide sensuous mouth that broke readily into a dazzling smile.

"I didn't hear you come in," she said in a rush. "I dropped an earring and was trying to dig it out from between the duck-boards. You'll have to excuse me, I don't make a habit of leaping out at customers like a jack-in-the-box."

"No problem from this side," I told her. "You got the worst of it, finding yourself suddenly confronted by this mug of mine."

Her smile turned into a lopsided grin. "Aw, I've seen worse. By the way your nose looks sort of bent and banged around, though, I guess more than one person has taken a disliking to it."

"Wasn't much of a nose to begin with." I shrugged.

"Self-deprecating. I like that. I get too many cocksure cowboys coming on like they think they're the next Johnny Depp or something."

"The next Johnny Weissmuller might be more my speed."

"Who?"

I shook my head. "Forget it. We've already trashed my nose, let's not get started on my advanced years, too."

"Old is as old does. You're as young as you feel."

"Swell. Then at least I'm still under the century mark."

"You definitely sound like you need something to perk you up. What can I get you?"

"Actually I'm on a beer run. The take-out kind, for later on."

"Case or six-pack?"

"Sixer'll do. Michelob."

She snapped her fingers in a "just missed it" kind of way. "Darn, I'd have guessed wrong. Usually I can take a good look at a guy and guess his beer brand. You I had figured for either MGD or a Coors man."

"If it's any consolation, I've downed my share of each of those at one time or other. Used to be I was one of those 'a beer is a beer' kind of guys. But these days it's Mick, if you got some."

"Sure do. Fix you right up."

She disappeared through the stainless-steel door of a walk-in cooler behind the bar and emerged a half minute later swinging a six-pack of Michelob. Vaporous puffs of cold air swirled around her as she heeled the cooler door closed again. She was dressed in cutoff jeans and a spaghetti-strapped, midriff-baring tank top. The smoothly tanned skin of her upper arms and shoulders had taken on gooseflesh and the jewel stud glinting in her navel now seemed to glint ice-like.

"Brrr. These puppies are nice and cold I can promise you that," she announced, plopping the Mick up on the bar.

I assumed she was talking about the bottles of beer. By the way her nipples were threatening to poke through the fabric of her top, however, it was hard not to notice that certain other puppies had also taken on a chill.

Grow up, you lecherous old horse's ass, I scolded myself. If I didn't watch out I was going to end up the next drooling victim of the Siren of Lake Mac.

"You want a sack for that?"

"No need," I replied. "Part of them are going straight into an ice chest."

She took the bill I handed her and walked down to the cash

register to ring it up. "Headed out on the lake, are you?"

"No. Not that lucky. Got some work to do in town, but I'm staying in one of the cabins across the way and this'll be the reward waiting for me when I get back later on."

She paused with the drawer hanging open and turned her head to scrutinize me anew. "Wait a minute. . . . Are you that pal of Abby's uncle? The private eye guy? The one she said was coming out to help her check into that accident business that's got her so worked up?"

"You know about that, do you?"

"Sure. Of course. Abby and Margaret are friends. We're No Name Bayers—we stick together, we tell each other things and look out for one another."

I nodded. "All right then. Yeah, Abby's late uncle was my best pal and I was also very close to the lady who died with him in that car crash. And yeah, I happen to be a PI. But I'm not exactly here in that capacity. I came because Abby was clearly upset and I wanted to see if I could help."

She hip-bumped the drawer shut and came back with my change. "A for-real private eye. Far out."

"Remember, though, I'm not on the clock."

"Call it what you want, you're still going to look into this thing for Abby, right?"

"Like I said, I mean to help however I can."

She planted her palms on the bar top and fixed me with a very direct stare. "So does that mean you think there's something to this notion she has about the accident being bogus?"

I turned it back on her. "Do you?"

She pushed out her lower lip, considering for a moment. Then: "Let me put it this way. There are a couple things I think I've learned making observations from behind this bar. One, I'm able to take a pretty good read off people. Two, I'm especially good at spotting the different kinds of sexual come-ons and nuances, catching the vibes when there's something brewing between two people, even in cases where they themselves might not have realized it yet. And as far as anything sexual going on between your two friends during the time they were here—I picked up zilch. They were clearly just a couple of old buddies, as comfortable with each other as bare feet and warm sand. So if you ask me, that foolishness about them fiddling with each other going down the road and maybe getting distracted enough to partly cause the accident . . . well, that's all it is—foolishness."

"So if that part of the accident scenario most everybody seems to have accepted is 'bogus,' where does that leave the rest of it?"

"I don't know." She shook her head. "That's more your department. You tell me."

"I guess that's the general idea," I said. "Before I'm done I hope I can do exactly that."

When I was part way to the door, she called after me, "Hey, if you're around later this evening you ought to come back over for some of B.U.'s Friday-night fish fry. Best you're gonna find. Good food and drink, good prices, good folks to mingle with. How can you go wrong?"

"Thanks for the invite," I said over my shoulder. "I'll be sure to keep it in mind."

Returning to my car, I put the six-pack of Mick in the back seat with the rest of the stuff Abby and I had loaded in. As I started to pile into the front I glanced up and saw Abby looking out the store window at me. I paused, holding up my left arm and pointing to my wristwatch, signaling that I had made it out of the clutches of the temptress without undue delay. Abby grinned and shot me a thumbs-up.

I pulled over to my cabin and unloaded everything onto the platform of the postage-stamp-sized front porch. Then, stepping around the ice chest and other packages, I unlocked the front door and pushed it open a calculated twelve inches. Before opening it any further, I stooped to reach in and around to check for the intruder warning device I had put in place before leaving that morning.

It's a simple system I use that beats the old hair across the door latch gimmick and is as effective as much of the higher tech gear they put out these days. What I do is take a standard mailing envelope (stamped and addressed to my landlord in Rockford with a month's rent check inside, if it matters), fold it once, then place it hand's reach back from the edge of the door with the door open about one foot. If anyone makes a covert entrance while I am away, the folded envelope will be caught by the swinging door and pushed to a different location. If the intruder bothers to notice the envelope at all they will likely assume I accidentally dropped it on the way out and think no more of it, leaving it for me to find when I return. On the slim chance they notice it and make some attempt to replace it as it was, the odds against both matching my hand reach and holding the door open the right distance are somewhere in the stratosphere. Bottom line: If I find the envelope moved I know I've had an unexpected and unwelcome visitor.

You go through certain routines just because you do. The times they pay off are often so few and far between that you wonder now and again why you even bother. But then, one time out of a hundred, you get results that remind you why you started the routine to begin with. This was one of those hundredth times. My searching hand found nothing. The envelope wasn't where it was supposed to be. . . . Someone had been in my cabin while I was away.

CHAPTER ELEVEN

My meeting with Sheriff Gene Knaack was much briefer than the one Abby and I had with Walt Mabry.

Knaack was a middle-aged man, sandy crewcut hair, with a large head and a square, lantern-jawed face that made him look more physically formidable than his average height and build might otherwise have presented. He was professionally courteous but nothing more. His answers were terse, his questions blunt.

When all was said and done, Sheriff Knaack expressed neither much interest nor knowledge as far as details concerning the accident that had claimed the lives of Bomber and Liz. Yes, it was Keith County paramedics who responded and yes, one of his off-duty deputies happened to be the first one on the scene. By virtue of those circumstances Knaack had been peripherally involved. But he had a plateful of Keith County matters he *had* to deal with and so therefore saw no need to stick his nose into Arthur County business that Sheriff Mabry was perfectly capable of handling.

Nevertheless, he was up to speed on things well enough to know about Abby's misgivings and her subsequent verbal attack on his deputy at the bowling alley. "I don't by any means approve of Abby's antics," he stated, jutting out his substantial chin, "but she's basically good people who has more than her share of bumps on Life's road so I'm willing to cut her some slack. After all, it's a free country and as long as they don't cross certain boundaries a person is entitled to their beliefs or disbeliefs and the right to seek their own version of the truth. In this particular instance, of course, it's all a bunch of hooey but Abby still has the right to waste her time with it . . . as long as, like I said, she stays within certain boundaries."

"How about if I wasted some of my time along with her?" I asked. "Would you have a problem with that? Would you consider it crossing any of your unacceptable boundaries?"

Knaack jutted his chin out a little further, pondering my proposal. I wasn't surprised that he didn't seem eager to have me poking around on his turf—that's a more or less standard reaction for any cop facing PI involvement. Some resist it a hell of a lot harder than others. But to give the devil his due, in Knaack's case I got the impression that he—like Walt Mabry—wanted to do the right thing, the fair thing; he just didn't want to appear *too* willing.

To help him along, I said, "I fully understand that my investigator's license has no validity in this state. I don't aim to present myself in that capacity. I'm merely a friend—a friend of many years' standing to the two victims, a more recent friend where Abby and her mother are concerned—who wants to help try and put this thing to rest in a way that won't leave any lingering doubts."

The sheriff's chin retreated a couple of inches. Arching a brow, he said, "I wasn't aware that Margaret shared Abby's dissatisfaction with this business."

"She doesn't. Not completely," I allowed. "But I think she's becoming a bit more inclined in that direction."

"Your involvement, I suppose," Knaack said thoughtfully, "would probably help conclude the matter with greater finality. For Abby and Margaret, I mean—for myself and most other people it's already concluded."

"I understand that. And yes, whatever I'm able to determine

I think the Bridger women would be willing to accept."

He mulled on it another minute or so. Then, cocking his head slightly to one side, fixing me with a direct stare, he said, "We have to be crystal clear on the matter of your license being meaningless in this state and county."

"Crystal clear."

"And in the unlikely event you should actually uncover any evidence of criminal misconduct I would naturally expect you to be immediately forthcoming with it."

"Naturally."

"All right, then." He settled back in his chair and eased up a bit on the stare. "As long as you agree to conduct yourself as nothing more than a friend trying to help a friend find closure on a recent tragedy, I guess I have no problem with you proceeding."

Closure. There was that word again. Fuck closure—if foul play had been involved in the crash that killed my two friends, what I wanted was for those responsible to pay. If it came down to it I'd be willing to settle for what some court called justice. But at my core, I knew, what I really wanted was a harsher settlement than that. What I wanted was vengeance . . . preferably delivered by my own two hands. That would be *my* closure.

As I left the sheriff's office an ominous rumble low in my stomach reminded me that, other than a jumbo cup of wake-up coffee and a muffin purchased from a snack rack in Abby's store, I hadn't taken a meal yet today. Foregoing the lure of fast-food joints clustered around the interstate exchange to the south, I stayed in the downtown area and made a few experimental turns until I spotted a rustic sign that said Front Street. Recalling Abby saying that she and her mother had accompanied Liz and Bomber to a place called Front Street one evening for dinner, I, being a trained detective, deduced that this must be an eating establishment.

The motif—like many businesses in the area, harking back to Ogallala's infamous history—was Western Frontier complete with a weathered boardwalk and hitching rails out front. I parked in the crushed-gravel lot, not bothering to tie up my trail-weary Honda, and went inside. Once my feet hit the boardwalk, I may have sauntered a little.

Front Street was a full-service restaurant adjoining a bar called the Crystal Palace Saloon where, in the summer months, area college and high-school kids put on a Dancehall & Wild West Review each night. I'd gone there with Bomber one evening during my visit years back. I remembered the show as being light-hearted and entertaining, a mix of corny skits and musical numbers, performed with a lot of energy and a surprising amount of talent by the young cast.

It being well past the noon hour, there was plenty of seating available in the restaurant. It was Seat Yourself so I chose a small table near the back, Jesse James–style, a vantage point from which I could watch the comings and goings of everyone else in the place.

In keeping with the Old West theme established outside, the interior was more of the same. Every available space—walls, shelves, ceiling beams, etc.—was adorned with everything from Indian blankets to replicated Remington paintings to circa-1800s photographs to saddles and lariats and even a Gene Autry lunch bucket perched high on a ledge. The menu came folded inside cover pages of old-timey newsprint set to brief articles on historical sites and points of interest in the area.

I ordered the day's special: calico bean soup and a meatloaf sandwich. Lemonade to drink. The latter came in a tall glass of crushed ice and was tart and brain-freeze cold, exactly the way I like it.

Sipping my drink, waiting for the food, I took out a pocket

notebook and began jotting a recap of the day so far. When I got to the part about someone having creeped my cabin, I put a big question mark. What, exactly, did it mean? Nothing was taken or rifled through, so it wasn't a simple burglary attempt. Whoever was there had been careful not to leave any trace of their visit, other than disturbing my planted envelope. So what was their purpose?

Although I hadn't mentioned it to Sheriff Knaack—or anyone else yet, for that matter—the most obvious answer was that somebody was concerned about my association to Abby Bridger and her suspicions and was checking to try and find out what and/or how much I might know. If that was the motive, then the fact I'd been on the scene such a short amount of time and was drawing such a quick response would seem to confirm somebody had something to hide. What's more, the suddenness of their re-action could arguably be viewed as an *over*reaction, maybe even a hint of panic.

When it comes from the other side, signs of panic and over-reaction are good. . . . Now all I had to do was figure out what buttons had been pushed to cause this and keep on pushing them in hopes of making the next response even more reckless and telling.

Chapter Twelve

There was no one home at the address I'd been given for Clint Barnstable.

Said address had been somewhat surprisingly provided by none other than Gene Knaack. Near the conclusion of our meeting he'd said, "Since he was the first one on the accident scene, I suppose you'll want to be talking to my deputy, Clint Barnstable?"

When I answered in the affirmative, he went on, "I don't want you bothering him when he's on duty. He works nights so you might have a chance to catch him yet this afternoon before he starts his shift." He wrote the address on a piece of paper, handed it to me. "In case no one's bothered to tell you, Clint is a kind of temperamental sort. He's always a little pissed off at something, which gives him just the right attitude for dealing with the rowdier element that seems to come out at night. These days, since this business with Abby and the way she chewed him out that time at the bowling alley in front of his buddies, he's feeling especially chapped. He feels he went out of his way to do all the right things—stop at the accident scene, call nine one-one, even administer CPR—and all he's gotten from it is blame and suspicion. . . . So what I'm saying is, you might not find him to be Mr. Warm & Friendly, willing to sit down and open up to whatever questions you've got. If that's the case, I expect you to back off, you hear? I won't have you badgering him."

So there it was. A friendly gesture wrapped in a friendly warning. Neither of them amounting to much, as it turned out. At least not for the time being, not until I managed to catch up with Clint Barnstable.

But the good thing about groping around in the early stages of an investigation—when you're casting for any kind of lead you can get and haven't begun to narrow your focus at all—is that when you hit a dead end you have the freedom to simply back up, turn, and try a different direction.

Abby had given me the names of two of the rescue-team members who had responded when Barnstable called 911. They were both volunteers who worked full-time jobs in town. She'd already had discussions with each of them, finding them cooperative but unable to offer anything other than the popular line as far as what they'd seen or heard at the accident site that day. We had nevertheless decided it would be worth a try for me to pay them a visit and see if my line of inquiry might get something more out of them.

The first guy was named Stadhoffer and worked at a small factory where they fabricated magnetic materials. His supervisor, a bearded bear of a man named Dunley, wasn't crazy about me cutting into his employee's work time but he relented enough to allow me a few minutes. As it turned out that was plenty because Stadhoffer didn't have anything more or different to remember for me than he had for Abby.

Same for the second guy, a tire mechanic named Timmons who worked at a farm-and-ranch-supply store where they sold everything from light bulbs to fence posts and feed bunks. But that didn't mean he was able to supply me with any new information, either.

So much for my "professional" interrogation techniques. Both Stadhoffer and Timmons were good men—community-spirited obviously, honest from everything I could sense, and both seemed genuinely regretful that they couldn't offer anything to help ease Abby's distress. But they had to stick by what they saw and unfortunately that only substantiated what she—and I—refused to believe.

Leaving the farm-and-ranch-supply store, I decided to make one more swing by Clint Barnstable's apartment. But there was still no answer when I thumbed the doorbell.

If you get easily disappointed or discouraged, then the detective dodge is not for you. I forged on.

On the way to Barnstable's place the first time I had passed a billboard advertising an auto-towing service that made me think of something else I wanted to check out the first chance I got. Since I now had that chance, I flipped open my cell phone and called Abby at No Name Bay.

She came on the line and after I identified myself, she said, "So how'd the meeting with Sheriff Knaack go?"

"Not too bad," I told her. "About what you predicted. He was cordial but cool, didn't go out of his way to be much more. Like Sheriff Mabry, though, he was agreeable to letting me go ahead and do some poking around in this thing."

"Well that's good. Like I told you, I think they're both decent and honorable men. Whatever dirty is going on, I don't think they're any part of it."

"I think you're probably right," I allowed. I took time to disclose my unsuccessful attempts at catching Barnstable at home and also the fruitless talks I'd had with the two rescue volunteers.

"Not coming easy, is it?" Abby said, maybe a hint of a forlorn tone creeping into her voice.

"You don't get base hits every time you step up to the plate," I told her. "But the trick is to keep your eye on the ball and keep swinging the bat."

"Stay the course. Got it."

Shifting to why I'd actually called, I said, "Listen, I need to ask you about something."

"Sure. What is it?"

"What became of Bomber's car?"

"A wrecker out of Ogallala came and hauled it off. Toby's Towing, it was. South of town."

"What about Bomber's and Liz's personal effects?"

"I have them here. Packed up in a couple boxes. I collected their stuff from the cabins they'd been staying in, then Walt Mabry brought me some of their stuff from the car and a little while after that one of Toby's guys dropped off the rest of what they took out at the salvage yard. I haven't really thought about it since then. I don't even know what all is there."

"What about the beer and whiskey bottles that were allegedly found in such abundance in the wreckage?" I asked. "Are they included in the stuff you've got?"

"What? The empty bottles? I don't think so. I'm pretty sure not. I mean, why would they be?"

"Make a quick check, will you? To be sure."

She told me to hang on a sec, put the phone down and was gone a minute or so. When she picked up again she said, "No. Not bottle one."

"Okay. Call Toby's, tell them I'll be stopping by. If the car is still there, tell them it's okay for me to go through it. I want to collect some of those bottles."

"What on earth for, Joe?"

I grinned. "Maybe there's room in this thing for some of your ma's CSI-type lab magic after all."

"How so?"

"I've got some police contacts back in Illinois. I can send them the bottles, call in a favor or two and get fingerprints run on them. If they come up with any decent lifts then they can be checked through the FBI data bank."

"Okay. Wow. But I'm still not sure I see what that's going to gain us."

"I know that Bomber and Liz both have their fingerprints on record from filing liquor-license applications. If they handled those bottles and drank from them as alleged, their prints should be all over them, right? If they're not, then that gives us some support for our argument that they're weren't drinking and driving that day."

"What about fingerprints identifying whoever *did* handle the bottles?" Abby said, getting excited. "We might be able to tell who actually planted them!"

"For the time being," I said, "I think we're better off counting on the prints we *don't* find."

"Wow," Abby said again. "That's terrific thinking, Joe."

"What?" I replied. "You think I get by on just my chiseled good looks?"

She gave a little laugh.

I said, "Call Toby's, okay? I'll head over there right now."

"Okay. Sure. But . . . ah. . . ." Abby cleared her throat. "This is a little embarrassing, but you just made me remember I still owe Toby's the bill for bringing in Uncle Bomber's car. It's not that I can't afford to pay it, but with the funeral and everything and then—"

"Don't worry about it," I interrupted. "In fact, that's even better. Call Toby's, tell them that's why I'm stopping by. To settle up. And while I'm there I want to have a last look at the wreck."

"All right. I'll pay you back when—"

"I said don't worry about it, didn't I? Just make the call."

"I will."

"One more thing. I hear your neighbor over at the Lassoed Walleye puts on a pretty good Friday-night fish fry, is that right?"

"Oh yeah. B.U. and Mamie do it up right. Ma and I used to

be regulars before her breathing got so bad and she got too weak. She hardly ever feels up to going over anymore. These days I usually order take-out plates and bring them back for us to eat here."

"Well see if you can't light a fire under her for tonight. I want to give it a try and I'd like to have you and her along for company. My treat. How about it?"

"I don't know about the 'your treat' part, but otherwise, yeah. Sounds great. Since the invite is coming from you, I think Ma will probably go for it, too. She thinks you're the cat's pajamas, you know. I think you remind her of Uncle Bomber."

The comment caught me off guard, made me feel a little funny in the chest. "That's a pretty high compliment," I said. "I'll try not to do anything to let her down."

"I don't think you ever could."

I didn't know how to respond to that so I just said, "I'm rolling now, so don't forget—"

"I know, I know—call Toby's. Get off the line so I can, then consider it done. See you later. G'bye."

Toby's Towing was a small business set in a cluttered area just off South Spruce between the railroad tracks and the river. The guy behind the service counter—whether or not he was "Toby" I never ascertained—was expecting me and was friendly and accommodating. He took my credit-card payment for the towing job, steered me out back and pointed me toward where they'd unhooked the wreck, then left me to my own devices.

Walking up to Bomber's Buick—once his pride and joy, now crumpled and caved-in and abandoned—gave me an eerie feeling. The car was yet another victim of that fateful crash. A silent, battered remnant of whatever had happened that day.

I put one hand on it gently, almost affectionately, the way you might pat a faithful old dog. What had formerly been hand-waxed sheen was now rough to the touch, gritty with dirt and imbedded sand. A hot wind was blowing across the salvage yard, carrying the scent of the river and stirring from within the wreckage a faint odor of soaked-in alcohol and the early stages of mildew. I leaned over and looked through a busted-out side window and the bottles were there all right, strewn across the dislodged back seat and the floorboards.

I glanced once into the front seat. Saw the rust-colored stains on the cushions and dashboard. I avoided looking that way again.

One by one I plucked the bottles out, gloving each with a piece of upholstery cloth I tore loose to guard against adding my own prints to the mix. A breeze-borne plastic shopping bag that I intercepted as it skipped across the grass served as my evidence envelope. I dropped in five beer bottles and one whiskey bottle, decided that was sufficient.

Stepping back, I took a final long look at the Buick. I felt sad for her . . . not the deep, aching kind of sadness I felt over the loss of Liz and Bomber, of course; but sad all the same.

"You poor beat-up old gas-guzzler," I sighed. "If only you could talk. . . ."

I found a pack-and-ship place in downtown Ogallala that had UPS Overnite service. When I presented the collection of empty bottles I wanted to send, the plump little lady who waited on me tried not to look at me like I was totally nuts but I could tell it was a strain. After I explained that I was playing a prank on an old friend, she seemed relieved and even managed to smile a bit as if she was in on the joke.

I had the package addressed in care of Mike Kolchonsky at the Bomb Shelter in Rockford. Returning to my car after paying the bill and satisfying myself that the bottles were securely contained and properly labeled for transport, I gave Mike a call to warn him what was coming and how to handle it. Next I called Ed Terry, RPD Lieutenant of Detectives, and leaned on him to run the fingerprint analysis I wanted once Mike brought him the package. I had to listen to Ed's usual grumbling and moaning about how he wasn't running a damn support service for my PI practice but in the end he finally agreed to do what I asked. The persuader was telling him I had some nagging concerns about circumstances surrounding the "accident" that had befallen Liz and Bomber and I was trying to make sure the matter got properly put to rest. "All right then, if it's for Liz and Bomber," he'd growled. "I know it's only been a couple weeks but I already miss the hell out of both of them. . . . Damn it all, anyway."

Yeah. Tell me about missing the hell out of them. . . . Damn it all, anyway.

With the day winding down, I headed back to No Name Bay.

As I was crossing over Kingsley Dam, I thought of something else that I decided there was still time to check out. Abby had mentioned a canoe outfitter who rented canoes on the little lake, Lake Ogallala, and also arranged group excursions down Pawnee Creek. It occurred to me that if he'd had any canoers on the creek the day Bomber and Liz hiked back to the old homestead site there was the chance they might have encountered each other and perhaps the canoeing group (if there *was* one) might have seen or sensed something that could be a clue in helping piece together exactly what happened next.

It was a long shot but, like I said before, in the early stages of an investigation you reach for any kind of lead you can get.

On the far end of the dam I turned off onto the county blacktop that curled back and down to the west edge of the lower lake. I had no idea what the canoe-rental place was called but I didn't expect the choices would be too numerous to sort out. If I had to I could call Abby but as long as there was some kind of sign I figured I ought to be able to spot what I was looking for.

I was right. I hadn't gone far at all before I came in sight of a hand-painted sign on the side of the road opposite the lake that read: CANOES FOR RENT—SCENIC LAKE & RIVER TRIPS. A bright red arrow underneath the lettering pointed the way to a weedy oval lot upon which sat a double-wide mobile home and large pole building. A pickup truck and a faded, ratty old school bus were parked in front of the double-wide. Over near the pole building was a flatbed trailer equipped with a tall, three-tiered, multi-armed rack holding a half dozen canoes resting upside down across the arms of each tier.

A pair of barking, slobbering spotted hounds came trotting out to greet me. With their long, droopy faces and floppy ears they didn't look particularly menacing but you can never tell for sure. Before I had time to fret too much about it, a guy emerged from the pole building and began calling off the dogs, cussing them roundly but affectionately in the process.

"Beaulah! Beauregard! Get your bony hides back here before I piss a couple mud puddles I can shove up your sorry asses just for the pleasure of stompin' 'em dry."

The guy was a stout, middle-aged, cigar-chomping specimen wearing a cowboy hat, flip-flops, baggy Bermuda shorts, and a green T-shirt with orange lettering that said CANOERS DIP THEIR PADDLES DEEPER. The dogs responded to his shouts, running back and hopping around him in tail-wagging circles.

I cut the Accord's engine and got out. The guy continued ambling toward me, the hounds bumping and rubbing affectionately against his legs.

"Don't mind these two fools," the guy said easily. "They won't hurt you unless maybe they get underfoot and cause you to accidentally trip and break your neck."

"I'll keep that in mind," I said, showing him half a grin.

"So. What can I do for you, mister?"

I gestured toward the trailer and rack of canoes. "You run the canoe-rental business here?"

"Uh-huh. Me and the wife."

"Any other rental places like this?"

"Not for canoes. Just us. Got a regular monopoly going. Do me a favor, though, and don't tell the government, okay?" He grinned around his cigar. "I'm Vic Faber, by the way. Pleased to meet you." He extended a rough-pawed right hand and I shook it. The dogs had now begun to trot in a restless circle around the both of us.

"You interested in renting a canoe?" Faber wanted to know.

"Actually, ah, no. What I'm interested in is finding out who *may* have rented from you about two-and-a-half weeks ago."

He frowned. "Come again?"

"I'm interested in a specific date," I explained. "June sixth, a Wednesday. Do you have records showing if you set up any trips on Pawnee Creek that day?"

"I got records, sure. Not to sound unfriendly, but what I'm not so sure about is that they're any business of yours."

"Technically, they're probably not," I admitted. "But on that same date two people were killed in an automobile accident on Highway 61 not too far from Pawnee Creek. Just prior to the accident they went hiking and picnicking along the south bank of the Pawnee. The exact details of their subsequent accident have become somewhat controversial. I thought there might be a slim chance that while they were around the creek they might have been seen by one of your canoeing groups if you had any on the water that day. If so, I was hoping someone in the group—if questioned and made to think about it in the right context—maybe picked up on something that could relate to the eventual accident."

"Relate how?"

I shrugged. "That I won't know until I talk to the person or persons. Are you saying you did have somebody out there that day?"

Faber knuckled up the wide brim of his hat and scratched above his ear. "Don't remember if I did or not, to tell you the truth. Hell, I have trouble enough remembering to zip my drawers half the time." He turned back toward the pole building and made a gesture for me to follow. "Come on, let's go see what I got in the files. If somebody made a reservation or paid by credit card there ought to be something to show for it."

I fell in step beside him. "Something I *do* remember, though, is hearing about that car wreck out there a couple weeks ago," Faber said as we walked. "You say there's some sort of controversy about it now? Way I heard it the man and woman were drinking heavy and going like a bat out of hell. You get too heavy-footed on that stretch of highway you're just asking for trouble. They ain't the first to find that out the hard way."

"So I've been told."

Faber shot me a sidelong glance, his eyes narrowing shrewdly. "What else I heard is that drinking and driving too fast wasn't the only things those two were up to that day. Sounded like they were trying to start a ground-level version of the mile-high club, if you know what I mean. Before they dug 'em out of the wreck the woman was lying with her head in the man's lap and you know what? She must have been blowing him, see, and the impact of the crash caused her to bite part of his dong right off. The paramedic who went to perform CPR on her had to dig the bloody stump out of her mouth before he could—"

I stopped walking. "Before that mouth of yours pukes out any more exaggerated trash," I said, fighting to keep my voice level, "you ought to know that those people were both good friends of mine. Even if they weren't, I hope I'd have the common decency to stop you from trying to 'entertain' me with the gory details of somebody else's tragic end. Is that clear?"

Faber stopped, too. His face had gone white, mouth hanging open so that it nearly lost its grip on the cigar stub. "Jesus, mister," he stammered. "I—I'm sorry . . . I didn't know . . . I didn't mean. . . . What I *do* mean is that I'm sorry. I'm sorry as hell. Okay?"

I was standing glaring at him, feet planted wide, fists clenched. I told myself that he didn't deserve the full brunt of the anger I was feeling at that moment. He'd triggered it; but it had been building in me long before he opened his mouth—an unfocused rage simmering just under the surface, waiting to boil over at nothing and at everything.

I unballed my fists, straightening the fingers and then curling them again slightly to keep them from trembling. "You didn't know," I said hoarsely to Faber. "But now you do."

We started walking again. I followed him on into the pole building. He glanced nervously over his shoulder a time or two, like he was afraid I was going to sucker punch him from behind.

It was good to get out of the grilling sun. The interior of the pole building was spacious and cool. There were canoes in various states of repair propped on sawhorses and against one wall was a partly dismantled motorcycle, its gutted parts strewn across an oil-stained canvas tarp that had been spread on the ground in front of it.

Just inside the door there was an old-fashioned rolltop desk, its flat surface piled high with papers and beat-up magazines, its vertical cubbyholes overspilling with more paperwork. Hanging on the wall next to the desk was what looked to be a blow-up of a standard-sized business card that read: VIC FABER—FISH-ING GUIDE, HUNTING GUIDE, TAXIDERMIST, MO-TORCYCLE & BOAT ENGINE REPAIR.

I jabbed a thumb toward the sign and, trying to lighten the

tense mood I'd created, said, "No mention of the canoe rental gig. That must be a more recent addition to your resume, eh?"

Faber looked a little wary, then gave a shrug. "Hey, you do what you got to, right? President Bush says the country needs more entrepreneurs. So I'm doing my bit."

"And what do you do in your spare time?"

His mouth twisted wryly. "Keep an eye peeled for ways I can make my next million, what else?"

"That's a pretty popular pastime," I said, still trying to lighten things a little. "Lot of eyes peeled in that direction."

Faber began flipping and rummaging through the papers on the desk. If there was any organization to the way they'd been placed I failed to spot it. And the way Faber was rifling through them guaranteed there wasn't going to be any when he was done. Nevertheless he found what he was looking for quickly enough, a leather-bound ledger book that he held up like a prize raffle ticket. "Bingo! Here we go."

He licked a thumb and began flipping through the pages.

"Lemme see. . . . Lemme see. . . . June sixth. . . . There. Oh hell yeah, I shoulda remembered this."

I leaned in closer. "Yeah? You had some memorable renters on the sixth?"

"Oh I had a memorable renter that day all right. Trouble is, I don't think he's going to serve your purpose very well."

"He who?"

"Cameron Terrell."

It seemed I'd heard that name before but I couldn't place where. Before I had a chance to ponder it at any length, Faber nailed it for me. "You ain't from here so that name probably doesn't mean much to you. If you spend much time in these parts, though, you're bound to hear it plenty. You see, Cam Terrell is about the biggest cattleman and land owner in the state. Hell, one of the biggest in the country. He owns most of Arthur

County and sizable chunks of other counties on into parts of South Dakota and Wyoming. And part of what he owns is the land on both sides of Pawnee Creek for the whole stretch that I run my canoe excursions."

"And on the sixth of June you set *him* up on one of your canoe trips?"

"In a manner of speaking, yeah. What he actually did was book the whole day, lock it out so's no other canoers would be out there. He sent one of his flunkies over to make the arrangements, give me more than fair payment. The guy he sent says, 'What's the absolute best day's earning you ever got from the canoes?' I told him and he says, 'Well here's two hundred dollars more than that. Mr. Terrell wants you to block out the whole day for him and any guests he might have.' So that's what I done. The way the fella who paid me explained it, Terrell was entertaining a bunch of his rich buddies from other parts of the country out at his spread for a few days. The sixth was the day they planned on being out Pawnee Creek way, horseback riding, hunting, target shooting, just sort of generally cowboying it up."

"And canoeing was supposed to be part of that?"

"Not necessarily. Just *maybe*. I was supposed to be ready in case some of them took a notion to try it, but mainly Terrell didn't want me to have nobody else on the water because of the shooting and other carrying-on they'd be doing in the general area. He didn't want no risk of an accident, was the way it was told to me."

I said, "Sounds mighty generous and considerate."

Faber grunted. "Those ain't two words you generally hear connected to the name Terrell. But in this case, yeah, I guess that's what you'd have to say." With a fat forefinger he tapped the entry in the ledger book. "I got no squawk in the matter, I sure came out of it okay."

"But I take it neither Terrell nor any of his rich pals came around looking to do any canoeing out of the deal?"

"Not a soul."

"He ever done anything like that before or since?"

"Don't I wish. But the answer's a big fat nope."

I turned away and stood for a moment, running things over in my mind. Gazed absently out the open door at the hot afternoon, squinting at the brightness slanting in from the descending sun.

"Sorry you got dead-ended here, mister," Faber said.

I shook my head. "I'm not dead-ended yet, canoe man. You may not have had anybody out on the water that day, but apparently this Cam Terrell had people in the same general vicinity. So I still got the same pitch I came here with, I just go knocking on a different door with it."

"Expect you won't have to knock on Terrell's door. I'm pretty sure he can afford a doorbell," Faber said drily. "And you'll probably get a little classier greeting than you got from my slobbering hounds, too."

"I don't know," I said. "My money might be on the hounds. I've never seen any indication that wealth guarantees class." I heaved a sigh. "No matter, I've still got to play the chance that one or more of Terrell's bunch might have run into my friends out there that day. Maybe one of them can shed a glimmer of light on the answers I'm looking for."

Faber eyed me squarely for a long moment before saying, "I hope you find those answers, mister. For your sake. You got a lot of pain and anger in you that needs to be eased."

CHAPTER THIRTEEN

As I pulled up in front of my cabin at No Name Bay, my cell phone began chirping. When I answered, the voice that spoke on the other end of the connection came so unexpectedly it hit me like a physical jolt.

"Hello, Joe."

Jan. Unmistakable, even with just two words. Finally responding to the numerous messages I'd left asking her to call, apparently ready to speak to me again after the knock-down-drag-out we'd had the night of Liz's funeral.

"Hey," I said, holding my voice calmer than I actually felt. "You sure you dialed the right number?"

"Depends. Is this the guy I've been making whoopee with for the past several years? Or the brooding, surly jerk who ran me out of his apartment one night last week?"

"I'm the whoopee guy," I answered. "At least that's the one I want to be."

"That's the one I want you to be, too."

I wasn't sure what to say to that.

Jan spoke again. "I'm calling to let you know I'm back in Chicago—home, in Oak Park. I've wrapped up the Washington story. I'll do some polishing on the final draft over the weekend, then turn it in on Monday."

"That's good to hear."

This time the awkward pause was longer.

Once again it was Jan who broke it. "Look, one of us has to

say this," she sighed. "Things haven't been exactly swell between us for some time now. The other night was about the roughest clash we've had, but it wasn't the first. And that's saying nothing about the little bouts of pecking and sparring that's become too common whenever we're together. I think it's time we sat down and had a talk—I mean a *long* talk, a really meaningful one. We need to sort out where we're at in this relationship of ours . . . and where we're going with it."

My first response was, "I suppose you're right." Then, hearing how half-assed that sounded, I amended it. "No, you *are* right. It's past time we faced up to whatever has soured between us and do what we have to, to get things turned around. The way it's been lately hasn't been much good."

"No, it hasn't. I was thinking . . . I've got plenty of comp time coming. After I turn in this story on Monday I'm going to take some of it, take at least a week off. What are the chances you can get away too? We can go somewhere, just the two of us. A little R&R, a little re-connecting. *Do* some of the sorting out we both seem to agree we need to tend to."

It dawned on me then that she had no way of knowing where I was, what I was in the middle of. Since she wasn't returning my phone calls anyway, I hadn't bothered leaving any word when I headed west again to look into the concerns Abby Bridger had raised and I now found myself sharing with steadily increasing conviction.

I puffed my cheeks, blew out a soft breath. "I gotta tell you," I said, "your timing could use some work, babe."

"What is that supposed to mean?"

I gave her a brief rundown; where I was at, what had brought me here, what I was caught up in.

When I'd finished, she said in a noticeably tighter voice, "So what I'm hearing is that you don't think you can pull yourself away."

"Your tone makes it sound like you think I have a choice."

"Well don't you? With all due respect, Joe, Liz and Bomber are already dead. No matter what you turn up out there, it isn't going to change that. Our relationship on the other hand is still alive . . . though maybe just barely. I'm not sure I understand why what you're doing in Nebraska is so crucial it can't be put on hold for a little while so we can concentrate on *us*. Try to get things turned around, as you put it."

That unfocused rage simmering inside me climbed too close to the surface again. It put more bitterness in my voice than I would've liked to have been there when I said, "Kinda like how I wasn't able to understand why you couldn't put your Washington business on hold long enough to make it out here for Bomber's funeral."

"That's a cheap shot, Joe. Pettiness doesn't become you."

"When I say it, it's a cheap shot, but when you say essentially the same thing, it's okay?"

"I don't believe this. We haven't seen or spoken to one another for how many days? And now we can't go five minutes without the sniping and the jabbing starting in." I could envision her shaking her head sadly. "It didn't used to be like this between us, Joe. Not for a lot of years. A lot of good years. What happened?"

Her words quelled the surge of anger in me. In its place I felt the weight of the same sadness I could hear in her voice. "Hell, I don't know, babe," I said. "Maybe we do need to get away together. Go someplace else, permanent. Maybe too much has changed around us . . . or not enough."

"Maybe *we* have changed."

"At the start and end of each day you're still you and I'm still me. That's what we've got to work with."

"And at the start and end of every day from now on Bomber and Liz are going to be just as dead and gone as they are at this moment. You're going to have to find a way to deal with that, too."

"That's a hell of a thing to say!" I snapped. "You getting some kind of charge out of reminding me my two friends are dead? That's twice you've gone out of your way to bring it up. What the hell does it have to do with what we're talking about, anyway?"

"It has everything to do with why you're bound to stay out there and chase after something that may not even exist instead of joining me to try and mend our problems. What makes you good at what you do is your mix of toughness and compassion. In the midst of all the greed and betrayal and ugliness you deal with, you somehow usually manage to find some part of it you can salvage, square away, leave better than it was. Your own problems you put off, turn away from even—other people's you don't hesitate to dig into."

"I get paid to deal with other people's problems."

"Are you getting paid now? Are you on hire out there in Nebraska?"

"This is a whole different matter. Payment was offered, I turned it down. Surely you can understand I feel a personal obligation to this."

"I understand all too well. Better than you do, I think. You're in denial, Joe. I'm sorry, but I'm going to say it again—Bomber and Liz are dead. You can't change that, so instead you're grasping at this obscure conspiracy theory or whatever it is, hoping to find some association to their deaths that you *can* change, can salvage and square away in some fashion. Isn't that what's really driving you?"

"What's driving me is the chance that my friends' 'accident' may not have been strictly an accident at all. If that's the case then some sonofabitch somewhere had a hand in doing them harm. You think I'm going to stay cool and detached over something like that? What's driving *you*, Jan? For nearly two weeks you avoided all contact with me, now you decide you're ready to patch things up and it has to get started right this instant. Why the urgency? You finished the job you were on, can't you cut me the same slack—to finish this thing I'm involved in?"

"Maybe I'm afraid you'll always have some other priority before you're ready to truly concentrate on us."

"That's crap. How many times did I call you after our fight last week? I had everything else pushed aside at that point, I even offered to come to where you were. I knew I had hurt you, and I was in my own kind of pain. It seemed like each other's comfort was what we both could have used right about then. I was wide open, *you* were the one with other priorities."

"I *was* hurt. And angry. Most of all I didn't feel up to going through . . . this. This damn bickering we seem to fall so easily into these days."

I let out a long, ragged breath. "Look . . . Christ, let's not blow this too far out of proportion. Yeah, we're at each other's throats lately more than we used to be. I don't like it any better than you do. But even through this rougher going neither of us has said or done anything irreconcilable. If what we've got is worth anything—and I believe it is—then we'll find a way to heal it back up. You need to believe that, too. It might not happen tomorrow or a week from tomorrow, but if we both hang in there then we'll find the time and the way to make it happen."

There was another pause. Only this time the quiet seemed somehow deeper, more intense.

When Jan spoke there was a faint huskiness in her voice that hadn't been there before. "I hoped to avoid speaking of this over the phone. But I can't hold it back any longer. . . . That's why all the urgency in trying to get you to . . . well, I wanted to at least have the decency to tell you to your face."

I swallowed. The dryness that suddenly filled my mouth trickled down into my throat like sand.

"You see, Joe . . . maybe one of us did do something irreconcilable."

I waited. I was in no hurry to hear what I sensed was coming next.

"I met someone . . . in Washington. It wasn't planned or plotted, wasn't something either of us were looking for. We both actually fought to avoid it, but . . . I—I still love you, Joe. At least a part of me does. And always will, I think. Yet if that's really true, then I can't explain how I let myself. . . . Oh, Joe, I feel so sick and ashamed and confused. . . ."

She went on talking. Rambling, to some extent. She said a lot of things. I didn't hear all the words over the rushing in my ears and the hammering in my chest. But I heard enough of them. More than I wanted to.

Chapter Fourteen

Once again there was evidence that somebody had been in my cabin while I was away. Only this time the visit was anticipated and the evidence of it having taken place was actually welcome—a window air conditioner installed by the handymen Abby had called in. They'd left the unit set on high and the roomful of cool air that wrapped around me when I stepped through the door was a brisk and refreshing change from the heat outside.

After I was through talking to Jan and had snapped shut the cell phone, I'd remained sitting out in the car for some time. I was angry and hurt and a little stunned. Although we'd left it that I would make contact as soon as I got back to Illinois so we could pursue exploring what, if anything, remained between us, I think we both already knew that our relationship of over twelve years had probably skidded too far off course to be brought back on track.

Sitting there in the car, random bits and pieces of the conversation we'd just had kept swimming through my head. "Things haven't been exactly swell between us for some time now" . . . "Your timing could use some work, babe" . . . "Your tone makes it sound as if you think I have a choice" . . . "You're in denial, Joe" . . . "At the start and end of every day from now on Bomber and Liz are going to be just as dead and gone" . . . "What's driving *you*, Jan?" . . . "Maybe one of us did do something irreconcilable" . . . "I—I still love you, Joe. At least a part of me does. And always will, I think" . . . *"Maybe one of us ' do something irreconcilable."*

I knew with an aching certainty that it would be next to impossible for me to get past her unfaithfulness. There was more to what had gone wrong between us than that, of course, and the argument could be made that the other troubles in our relationship was what had built up in Jan to the point of causing her to seek a kind of reaffirmation in the arms of another. On some sort of cerebral level that might be very sound logic and finding a way to apply it would probably be a good first step toward healing the relationship in trouble. All of that might work grand . . . for somebody else.

My first and only marriage had ended due to infidelity—I'd walked in on my wife and my cop partner. There were surely things I could have done different and better in that relationship, too. Little things; the small gestures of affection that women tend to crave more than men, the displays of spontaneity and silliness that Peg so enjoyed, the cuddling for the sake of cuddling when it had nothing to do with leading up to sex, and so on. And the bigger things like staying as focused on my young wife as I was on my job and my record-time ascension to the rank of detective. Given the chance, I like to think I would have worked on those things, improved on them. The way it turned out, though, the only chance Peg gave me was to make the decision on whether or not to go ahead with drawing my service revolver and shooting the two of them where they lay in *our* bed. I'd actually had the gun out and aimed. But because I felt a loyalty to what the badge and the badge that came with it stood for—a greater loyalty, than what my wife felt to our marriage vows or nearly, felt to our partnership—instead I put it away and just turned and walked out.

Hearing that Jan had repeat of that momentarily with another man didn't spark a fury—I didn't consider going

after her and him with a gun—but at the same time the scar tis-
sue from having been there all those years before was still fresh
enough to remind me of what I could and could not withstand
and what the limit of my capacity to forgive was, no matter how
much love might be involved. I make no case for the rightness
or fairness of this conviction—if the circumstances were reversed
or if I was looking objectively at the same situation between two
other people, I might even try to argue that a second chance
ought to be considered. But this was what it was and I was who
I was, and there was no getting past that.

Curiously, I didn't feel any rancor toward Jan. I only felt pain
and a kind of emptiness, thinking about what was ending
between us. It was, I realized, almost like enduring another
death. Losing Liz and Bomber so recently . . . and now the
death of Jan and me as a couple. The summer of death, it had
become.

Ironically, the relationship between Jan and I had been forged
in the midst of death—sudden death and violence—when we
were thrown together during a case I was working on in
southern Wisconsin where Jan at that time had been running a
small local newspaper. More recently we had again faced life-
threatening danger together when a story she was digging into
as a feature writer for the slick magazine *C2C* escalated into
savage violence from which each of us narrowly escaped. Maybe,
I mused, ours was never meant to be the kind of long-lasting
romance that matured into peaceful twilight years, holding hands
each evening by the fire. Instead, maybe it was destined from
the beginning to be a bursting skyrocket with a finite life.

If that was the case, then the skyrocket seemed to be sputtering badly and the sparks it was giving off all but faded and
gone from sight.

Pondering all of this, I had remained seated in the
hot, still car until the side of my numbed neck were beaded

with sweat and the back of my shirt was plastered wetly to my shoulders. When I finally climbed out and entered the manufactured coolness of the cabin it was as bracing as a plunge into cold water. An even colder Michelob, dug from deep in the ice chest, went to work on chilling my insides as well. I cracked the cap, sat down on my one and only chair and drained half the bottle in one tip-up. Being back in the cabin again, savoring the beer along with the comfort provided by the handymen who'd been there, made me think about the non-sanctioned visit that had occurred the last time I'd been away. That returned my mind to the business at hand, why I was here in the first place.

It was for sure that Jan wouldn't be gone from my thoughts for a long time. But I was damned if the wreckage between us was going to stand in the way of my getting to the bottom of how and why Liz and Bomber had ended up dead in a very different kind of wreckage. I sensed that I had a slight momentum building and now wasn't the time to let up.

Checking my watch, I saw it was past five. I remembered that I had invited Abby and her mother to join me a little later for the fish fry at the Lassoed Walleye Saloon. All things considered, I was no longer in much of a mood to be around anyone else that night. But I *had* made the date and I couldn't think of a good excuse for breaking it at the last minute . . . not without calling down a barrage of questions or evoking unwanted sympathy. Furthermore, I'd need to eat something sooner or later. And maybe the good company of Abby and Margaret would be a welcome balm after all.

I flipped open the cell phone and called over to Abby at the store. Waiting for her to pick up, one of those unbidden thoughts of Jan, thoughts I knew would be popping up for months to come, jumped into my head. Like Bomber, I had for a long time resisted the lure of cell phones. Cussed them and jeered them and swore I would never have anything to do with the lousy things. Then Jan had bought me one for Christmas one year, forced it on me as a gift; and in a matter of weeks I was as addicted to the damn gadget as every other cell junkie you see shuffling through life with a palmful of plastic clapped to the sides of their heads. Just like now, I tended to reach for mine as intuitively as an Old West gunslinger slapping leather to draw his trusty hogleg.

Abby came on the line. "No Name Bay General Store, this is Abby."

"The fish still biting over at the Lassoed Walleye tonight?" I said.

She gave a little laugh. "You bet they are. I've got relief coming to take the counter here in about half an hour. Then I'll need a few minutes to freshen up. Ma is looking forward to joining us. We'll be ready whenever you are."

So that locked it. No backing out for sure. "Say about seven, then."

"Done. I'll be waiting with Ma down in her place."

Since the cabins of the No Name Bay "lodge" had only a commode and a small hand-washing sink but no bathtub or shower, the six units shared a concrete bunker-like showering facility (divided into half for women and half for men) located down at the end of the row of cabins nearest the lake. Which meant the opposite end of the row from where my place was.

By the time I had walked down, taken a shower, and walked back again in the still warm evening air, I was sweating anew. Nevertheless, I felt cleaner and fresher than I had. A few minutes back in my meat-locker-cool cabin took care of the sweat and a generous splash of Old Spice was the only remaining touch before I was ready for public consumption and the company of two fine ladies.

There had been an awkward moment at the shower house

when I'd started to undress and belatedly remembered the hideaway piece I habitually carry in my right boot. It's a 9mm Kel-Tec P-11, no bigger than the palm of my hand. Similar in size to the old two-shot .22 Magnum derringer I'd carried in that capacity for years, but more accurate and packing eight additional man-stopping rounds. I'd left it in the trunk of my car during my visits to the county sheriffs earlier in the day but other than occasions such as those it is seldom not on my person. Over the years I have made some serious enemies and in my wake have left those who would do me violent harm. Therefore, since it's not practical to always walk around packing the Colt GI-model .45 auto that I prefer for heavy-duty situations, the P-11 is a compromise I can—no pun intended—live with.

Nevertheless, that didn't make it a compromise that another visitor to the shower facility might feel so comfortable with should he walk in and catch sight of it. Not to mention that my carry license for the little hideaway was no good in Nebraska. All and all, it would have been smarter to leave the piece back in my cabin. But, not being inclined to walk all the way back just to deposit it there, I settled for stuffing it out of sight in my boot with a sock crammed down on top of it for the time I was in the shower.

It is a comment on my misspent life, I suppose, that I tend to feel more naked without a gun than I do without clothes.

CHAPTER FIFTEEN

The Lassoed Walleye Saloon was everything you could ask for from a rowdy honky-tonk on a busy Friday night. Loud country-western music blaring out of the jukebox, a packed-in crowd of good ol' guys and gals, cigarette smoke haze hanging heavy in the air, raucous conversations and laughter, foamy pitchers in abundance—and mounds of beer-battered deep-fried perch, cod, or walleye piled on platters with equally generous helpings of french fries and cole slaw.

Abby, Margaret, and I threaded our way through the crowd and lucked out finding an empty table over against one wall. Everybody seemed to know my two companions, and visa versa. Dozens of greetings were exchanged by the time we took our seats.

Toward the far end of the room, in a floor clearing just this side of where guys were shooting pool and playing shuffleboard, a handful of gals clad mostly in skintight jeans and bandana tops were dancing with foot-stomping energy and abandon. Notable among them was Tina Mancini.

Grinning and raising her voice to be heard above the music and conversations going on around us, Abby said, "I promised you the food would be good but I guess I forgot to warn you that if it was quiet elegance you wanted for your dining experience, this might be the wrong place."

"Take more than a little noise to stand between me and my appetite," I told her. Especially after I'd gotten a good whiff of the rich aromas wafting out of the back kitchen and off the platters of food surrounding us. "And," I added, "it's a welcome change from those damn firecrackers they're setting off outside again tonight."

Abby shook her head. "Boy, you're a real fuss-bucket about those firecrackers, aren't you?"

I just made a face and bit my tongue to keep from grousing any more on the subject.

"Well this is a thankful change for me, too," Margaret said. "A change from having to listen to nothing but the damn hissing and bubbling of my air machine all the time." Tonight, in lieu of the machine, Margaret's nose piece and breathing tube were hooked up to a portable oxygen tank that she carried in a kind of sling suspended from a strap over one shoulder.

"Cuss it all you want, that machine is a godsend," Abby reminded her.

"I know, I know. I'm well aware how reliant I am on the blasted thing. That's what I hate about it the most."

As the two women made this exchange, I was watching another woman making her way toward our table. She was pretty hard not to notice. Early thirties, blond, bright cobalt eyes, diminutive in height but abundant to the extreme when it came to womanly curves. The latter were provocatively displayed by a halter top and matching lowrider pants made of taut, butterscotch-colored leather. The expanse of skin the outfit left uncovered looked impossibly toned and tanned.

"Abby . . . Margaret!" the blond woman said. "It's great to see you here. What a nice surprise."

"Hi, Mamie," Abby responded. "We had to practically chop our way through the crowd, but, yeah, we decided it's been too long."

"It sure has."

"Doesn't look like you've missed our business too desperately, though," Margaret observed. "But, dressed like that, I guess I can understand what keeps bringing at least the male customers back around."

There didn't seem to be any venom in Margaret's statement, merely a slice of the kind of straightforwardness she was known for. Which the blond woman—Mamie—appeared to accept in stride. She put a finger to her lips and winked mischievously. "Shhh, don't let B.U. know it's not strictly his dynamite cooking and barside manner that keeps packing 'em in."

Margaret gave a tolerant smile. "With all due respect to how fetching you look, dear, just so you know *we're* here for the fish fry."

"Maybe you shouldn't be so quick to speak for everybody, Ma," Abby said. But her eyes were on me, twinkling a little, teasing. "After all, we brought a guest. Maybe Joe has something to say on the matter."

I knew I was being needled a little, and put on the spot. So I rode with it. Grinning crookedly, I said, "I have learned to appreciate a wide range of things in life. What brought me here was word of the excellent fish fry. However," and here I let my gaze drift freely over Mamie's golden form, "that doesn't mean I can't take note and duly approve of the establishment's other delicacies."

Mamie threw back her head and whooped with delight. "Wow! You silver-tongued devil."

"You can say that again," Margaret muttered, rolling her eyes.

"Abby," said Mamie, "you have *got* to bring this big hunk around again! And I do mean without waiting so long in between. Before we go any further, though, how about an introduction?" She spoke with what sounded like a Texas or Oklahoma accent. "Who did I just have the pleasure of being verbally patted on the fanny by?"

Still eyeing me, still with a teasing slant to her smile, Abby said, "Mamie, I'd like you to meet Joe Hannibal. Joe, this is Mamie Gorcey. She and her husband B.U. run the Lassoed Walleye."

Mamie thrust out a hand. "Pleased to meet you, Joe Hannibal."

I shook hands with her. Her grip was tiny but firm. "The pleasure's all mine."

"Joe's from Illinois," Abby said, expanding the introduction. "He was close friends with both Uncle Bomber and Liz, the lady who was visiting here with him at the time of the . . . well, you know." Her smile had vanished by now. "Joe is helping me to look a little closer at exactly what took place that day."

"Oh," said Mamie. "You're the private eye fella. Tina said you'd been around earlier."

"Uh-huh. But out here, remember, I'm not a PI," I said, trotting out the disclaimer I was beginning to think I ought to have printed on business cards I could hand out at the start of every conversation. "I'm just a friend of the family."

"Well, any friend of Abby's and Margaret's. . . . And B.U. is for sure going to want to meet you before you get out of here tonight."

"I'm looking forward to meeting him, too."

Mamie's expression turned more serious. "Good for you, Joe, for getting involved in this thing. There's something damn fishy about some of the stuff that's been claimed since that car crash. Most people might never notice, but plenty of us around here were fortunate enough to have gotten to know your friends pretty good during their stay. And those things that are being claimed now about them . . . well, like I said, it's damned fishy. It's wrong and sure-hell doesn't fit the people I got to know. I'm glad to see Abby getting some support trying to focus more attention on whatever funny business is going on."

"He doesn't need a pep talk, Mamie, he's already signed on," Margaret said somewhat testily. "What we *do* need—what we came here for, in case you forgot—is some food and drinks. You think that can be arranged before my oxygen tank runs dry?"

Without missing a beat and still smiling, Mamie said, "Oh, hold your horses, Margaret. If you run out of oxygen we'll get you some battery acid to slurp on. That should suit your grouchy disposition."

"I wondered when you'd get around to admitting to some of the stuff you serve in here," Margaret shot right back.

"Pay no attention to them," Abby advised me. "They go at each other like this for hours on end." Then, lifting her gaze to Mamie, she added, "But since we *do* have a guest tonight I'm pretty sure he'd rather not wait that long for his dinner."

"Okay, I can take a hint," Mamie said. "I know it's going to be walleye plates for you two ladies. How about you, Joe?"

I told her I'd make it unanimous on the walleye. When she asked about drinks, Margaret and I decided we'd split a pitcher of Coors. Abby ordered Pepsi.

Once Mamie had departed, Abby said to her mother, "The way you two carry on. If you were little kids you'd get a scolding. You had Joe and half the people around us thinking you were fighting for real."

"Aw, that just helps keep the place interesting," Margaret said, waving one hand dismissively.

"Speaking of the place being interesting," I said to Abby, "why did you go out of your way earlier today to warn me about the wiles of the bartender Tina but you never bothered to say anything ahead of time about our hostess?"

Abby looked at me with wide-eyed innocence. "Why, Joe . . . Mamie's just a regular ol' down-to-earth married lady. What reason would I have to warn you about her?" She paused half a beat, then added, "Besides, this time I knew Ma and I would be

106

here to hold you back if you couldn't restrain yourself."

"And for a minute there I thought we were going to be put to the test," Margaret said drily. Then, giving me an admonishing look: "You, a grown man old enough to be her father, gawping at her and panting like an over-het hound dog. And mumbling about 'duly' appreciating her 'delicacies,' for God's sake. Do men actually talk like that where you come from?"

"I wasn't panting," I protested.

"And so what if he was?" Abby said. "Mamie knows the effect she has on men. She doesn't mind."

"No, she sure don't. She likes it a little too much, if you ask me."

"I *wasn't* panting," I insisted. "And I don't even know how to 'gawp.' "

"You know, Ma, sometimes I'm not so sure the banter between you and Mamie is always in fun. Leastways not from your side. Sometimes you play your part of an old-fashioned prude a little too convincingly. You need to be careful that your put-downs of her—and Tina as well—don't cut too close to the bone or one of these times your going to cause some really hurt feelings."

"Maybe I'm doing them a favor," said Margaret. "If they're going to run around exposing that much flesh then they'd better develop thick-enough hides to withstand a few comments about it."

"All I'm saying is that B.U. and Mamie are good neighbors. And neither Mamie nor Tina have been anything but kind to you, and you know it. I just don't want you offending them and risking that friendship, that's all."

"Well of course not. That goes without saying. But don't you think they have a little fun at my expense sometimes, too?" Margaret wanted to know. "How about that remark—that little dig—Mamie threw in just a few minutes ago?"

"What remark? What dig?"

"You heard her. How glad she was that somebody like Joe was finally here to 'support' you in your little crusade. You think that wasn't a dig at me? You think she wasn't implying that I haven't been supportive of you in this thing?"

"Mother. You haven't been."

"That doesn't mean I need to be reminded of it by her. And it's not like I've stood in your way or tried to talk you out of it, have I? Besides . . . the two of you, you and now Joe . . . well, the way you've laid things out have set me to thinking . . . thinking maybe a little differently, I guess."

Abby's face lit up. "Really, Ma?"

"I said so, didn't I?" Margaret answered grudgingly. "No need to wet your drawers over it. Wasn't like I was holding you back. And it ain't like having me in your corner—an ailing old woman sucking manufactured oxygen—is going to gain you some sharp edge or something."

"It gains me plenty, Ma. It means a lot, knowing you're starting to see some validity in all these questions I've been raising."

It was time to get this conversation refocused and I saw the opening to do exactly that. "And she isn't the only one," I said. "Somebody on the other end of this thing has reacted to what you're stirring up, too."

Both women turned their heads. "What do you mean?" Abby asked.

My answer had to wait due to the return of Mamie Gorcey with the pitcher of beer and Abby's Pepsi in a tall, ice-filled glass. "Here's your whistle wetters, folks," she announced, placing the fare on the table before us. "Drink up. I'll be back in a short with your food orders."

We thanked her and let her take her leave. I poured glasses of Coors for Margaret and me, pushed hers in her direction.

"Well?" said Abby anxiously. "You've got us hanging here.

Tell us. What other 'reaction' have I stirred up?"

Checking to make sure no other patrons around us seemed to be paying any attention, I told them then about the intrusion into my cabin. How I'd discovered it, what I reasoned was behind it.

When I was finished, Margaret said with a dour expression, "Damn, that makes me mad. This used to be just a nice, quiet place that attracted nice, quiet people. You could leave your door unlocked, day or night. Go clear out of town if you wanted and leave it unlocked without worrying about some lowdown sneak thief—"

"This wasn't a common thief or burglar, Margaret," I corrected her. "Don't you see? My cabin wasn't rummaged by someone looking for loose cash or valuables they could fence into quick money. This was a professional toss looking for specific information—trying to find out how much I knew about this matter Abby has been raising a ruckus over. At least that's my read on it."

"If that's so, then they reacted awfully fast," said Abby.

"They sure did."

"And if you hadn't pulled that little trick of yours, they'd have left no sign for anyone to know they were ever there."

"Uh-huh."

"Which means there could have been previous searches. The store, my apartment . . . hell, almost anywhere if they go in and out as slick and traceless as you say. And without a warning device of some kind or even a suspicion that something like that was going on, I would have never noticed."

"Except for those sensations you had of being watched all the time," I reminded her.

"Wait a minute." Margaret scowled. "Are you saying some so-and-so was probably sneaking around in our place, too?"

"At some point or other, yeah," I answered. "If they were

worried about what I might know, there's not much doubt they'd be interested in finding out what Abby had in the way of evidence to back up the noise she's been making."

"But I don't have anything, really," Abby said. "Not what you could call hard evidence. Just suspicions."

"Which is why nothing was taken. Nothing missing would be one more reason for you to remain unaware your place had been creeped."

"But what about me?" said Margaret. "Other than tonight, I haven't been out of that building for weeks. Except for the funeral. If some bastard was prowling around, especially upstairs in Abby's apartment, I'd've been there to hear them."

I shook my head. "No, Margaret. With your air machine going, almost anybody taking reasonable care could have cat-footed around without you ever picking up on it."

Her eyes narrowed and I could tell she wanted to argue the point. But after considering it a moment, she relented. "Well, damn!" was all she could say.

Mamie returned at that point with our meals balanced on a large oval tray. She transferred the heaping plates to the tabletop in front of us, saying, "Eat hearty. I'll be back to check on you in a little bit. Remember there's plenty more where that came from."

We dug in and everything was as fine as advertised. Tender, flaky fish, tangy slaw, crisp fries. Either I was hungrier than I'd realized, or the food was so good it demanded to be devoured eagerly. Whatever the reason, I sensed I was in danger of making a pig of myself.

Between forkfuls of walleye, Abby said, "What you're telling us is kind of disturbing, Joe, but at the same time it's also . . . well, *exciting*. I mean, if somebody is reacting this way then it must mean they've got something to hide, that me going around questioning things has them worried. Right?"

"Be the way I'd look at it," I agreed.

"So what did Sheriff Knaack say about this break-in?" Margaret asked.

Again I shook my head. "Nothing. I didn't tell him about it because it's too soon. All I've got is my say-so at this point, that I left the envelope the way I did, that I came back to find it disturbed. That's not enough for either of the sheriffs to do anything with. But it still helps us. Like Abby just said, it tells us we definitely are onto something and, whatever it is, we've got somebody on the other end of it doing some squirming and jockeying around to try and shore up their defenses."

"And what about our defenses in case of retaliation?" Margaret said pointedly. "If the people on the other end of this thing, as you put it, actually caused or contributed to the deaths of my brother and Liz, then that means they're dangerous enough to be a threat to all of us sitting here, doesn't it?"

"We'd be foolish not to make that assumption," I answered. "As far as defenses, all I can offer at this point is my presence on the scene and, now that everybody has an understanding of what might be at stake, the advice that we all keep alert and take every reasonable precaution."

"I'm sorry, but that doesn't sound like enough." Margaret's gaze was direct, demanding. "Me, it don't matter so much. I'm fighting to keep every breath I take from being my last, anyway. And you, I figure you can take care of yourself. But where does that leave Abby? If there *is* a retaliation, wouldn't she be the lightning rod to attract the biggest part of the hit?"

"If the other side gets desperate enough, maybe," I responded. "But right now Abby's best defense is the fact that she's the one who's been so vocal and so active in keeping things stirred up. If anything were to suddenly happen to her, it would cause one hell of a lot of attention to get focused in a hurry, don't you think? We're not that big of a threat yet. We still don't have anything solid put together. We need to stay alert and proceed with caution, but I don't think any of us are in serious danger for the time being."

But Margaret wasn't ready to let up. "Abby told me about the bottles you sent out for fingerprint analysis. It may be true what you say about not having enough hard evidence to be a serious threat right at the moment, but you sure seem hell-bent on gathering enough ammunition to become one. What then?"

"Then I'll make adjustments, revisions," I told her, meeting the hard scrutiny in her flinty eyes. "I'll do everything possible and feasible to keep us ahead of the retaliation curve until I feel confident we've built our threat strong enough to strike with it."

"I don't want no more funerals held for the sake of trying to resurrect those who have already gone. Do you understand what I'm saying?"

"I understand that resurrection is not in the cards," I replied. "But that doesn't mean that some kind of justice shouldn't be." *My kind of justice,* fate willing.

Further debate on the subject was interrupted by the arrival of a visitor to our table—Tina Mancini, flushed and breathless from her activities on the dance floor.

"Hey, everybody!" she greeted. "Good to see you all." She swung her attention to me, smiling. "And good to see you decided to take my advice on where to come for a Friday-night good time."

I spread my hands, welcoming the shift to a lighter mood. "You made it sound too good to pass up."

"And was I right, or was I right?"

"Let's say no one can ever accuse you of false advertising."

"Or false modesty," Margaret muttered, casting a sidelong glance over at Tina as she leaned on the table right beside her, the younger woman's unrestrained breasts swinging freely beneath the thin fabric of the bandana top.

Still smiling sweetly, Tina replied, "Oh Margaret, that's what we miss the most about having you come around regular, like the old days. Your viper-tongued dry humor. God forbid you ever utter a compliment, then I'd be worried you really *are* ill."

"Ah, there's the incentive I've needed so badly," Margaret said, the words dripping sarcasm. "Now I'll have the willpower to fight on, just so I can keep you amused and entertained."

I was glad I'd already had a preview to this kind of back-and-forth pecking so that I knew not to take it too seriously.

Her tone shifting subtly, Tina said, "So tell me the truth, you old sourpuss. I haven't made it over to see for a while—how are you doing?"

Margaret made a palm-down waggling motion with one hand. "Good days and bad, kiddo. Good days and bad."

Tina glanced in Abby's direction, as if for confirmation.

Margaret caught the look and, before Abby could reply in any way, she barked at Tina, "Don't worry, you shameless hussy. I'll still be around to rag on your brazen ass for the foreseeable future. I shudder to think what's going to become of you and Mamie when I'm not around to herd you back onto the straight and narrow, though. This whole place will probably get turned into a fancy house or a topless go-go joint or something."

"Yeah," Tina tossed back, "but you're probably ornery enough to stick around until after my boobs fall. Then where's that gonna leave me?"

An answer was belayed by the high-pitched chirping of a cell phone's incoming call signal. We all did the look-around "is it you or is it me?" thing and then it was Abby who brought her unit up from out of her purse and spoke into it.

"Hello? . . . Yes. . . . Which one? . . . Uh-huh. . . . Damn! . . . Okay, I'll be right over."

She thumbed off the call, expression strained.

"What's wrong?" Margaret said.

"That was Mary Lou from the store," Abby said, rising to her feet. "There's trouble over at the cabins. Sounds like a pretty nasty fight has broken out. I'm going to have to go over there."

"Not without me you're not." Margaret pushed back from the table.

"No, Ma, none of that. You just take it easy, you hear? I can handle this and I need to get over there in a hurry."

Margaret scowled at the command but she remained in her chair.

I did no such thing. Standing, I said, "You *will* take some company, though, won't you?"

Abby nodded. "You bet."

We headed for the door. Over her shoulder, Abby called back, "Bring Ma after while, will you, Tina? And tell Mamie we'll be back around to make square on the bill!"

CHAPTER SIXTEEN

The music and general din of the Walleye faded behind Abby and me as we trotted across the parking lot. The night air was cooling rapidly now. Reflected light out on the lake writhed gently on the still water.

We hadn't gone far before, ahead of us, we could hear the sounds of a disturbance replacing the evaporating noise from the Walleye. Even the cacophony of firecrackers had sputtered to a halt.

Moving past the end of the store I saw Mary Lou, Abby's counter girl, looking out the window with a distraught look on her face. We came in sight of the row of cabins. Small knots of people—renters from other units—were bunched to either side of number three, making it easy to zero in on where the trouble was.

I could picture the occupants of number three. I'd caught sight of them a time or two as I came and went during the course of the day. Young couple, middle twenties, not newlyweds but maybe on the first getaway vacation of their union. Cute little brunette, husky blondish guy with the earnest expression and rolling gait of a perpetual jock.

It became quickly apparent that this unlikely pair was at the center of the problem.

Their vehicle, a gleaming new Ford F-150 extended-cab pickup with Kansas plates, was parked directly in front of the cabin. The young guy was outside of the vehicle, pacing back and forth along the driver's side, moving in and out of shadows and the overlapping spills of illumination cast by the open cabins and the tall light over the store's parking lot. The guy was in a rage, hollering as he paced, cursing, stamping his feet, and flinging his arms wildly. The young woman was in the cab of the truck, hollering and cursing right back; with the windows rolled up her words were muffled and rang with a faint metallic tone.

"Goddamn you, Mandy! GodDAMN you!" the guy was yelling. "You get your ass out of that truck, you hear me! Get your slut ass out of my fucking goddamn truck RIGHT NOW!"

"You go to hell, Ronnie!" the girl shouted back. "I'll rot and die in here before I come out there so you can knock me around some more."

Halfway between the store and the cabins, another young man stood on the edge of a bar of shadows watching the proceedings. I recognized him as Matt Something-or-other, the college kid Abby had on summer staff as her groundskeeper.

Abby drew up beside him and stopped. "What's going on?" she asked, a little breathlessly.

Matt made a gesture toward the feuding pair. "The Wiltons there are having a heck of a row. He must have started hitting her in the cabin—she came running out, screeching like a banshee. Locked herself in the truck to get away from him. He's got the keys so she can't go nowhere, but she's holding the doorlock tabs down so he can't get in at her, either. They been cussing and carrying on like that for quite a while now."

Abby leaned over and peered more closely at Matt. "What happened to your eye?" she said.

The kid tried to turn his head away but before he did I caught sight of what Abby was asking about. A fresh, bright red mouse was swelling under his left eye.

"It's nothing," Matt said.

"Baloney, it's nothing! How did it happen?" Abby demanded.

Matt gestured again. "I went over there. He was being awful loud and abusive . . . threatening to rip her heart out, cave in her skull, really gross shit. . . . When I tried to get him to settle him down, he punched me."

"That sonofabitch!" Abby spun away from Matt and went storming in the direction of Ronnie Wilton. I fell in step beside her.

In the meantime, the two lovebirds were still going at it strong.

"So help me, Mandy, when I get my hands on you. . . . Get out of my FUCKING TRUCK, you bitch!"

"If you want me so bad, why don't you bust out a window and come in and get me? No, you wouldn't dream of harming your precious truck, would you, you bastard—but you don't mind beating me black and blue every time you have a few too many beers and decide you've got a burr up your ass, do you?"

"You keep asking for it, I'll bust out a window—I'll bust out your fucking lungs!"

"Big talk from a big man . . . a big wife-beater man. That's all you are, Ronnie, you sorry shit!"

"I'll show you sorry. That's what you're gonna be when I get hold of you—sorry you were ever born, you whore slut cunt!"

"That's enough." Abby's voice was clear and steady as she moved past the rear end of the F-150. "That's enough right now!"

Ronnie wheeled to face her. His mouth was twisted in a menacing sneer. "The best thing for you to do, I'll warn you one time, is to turn back around and go mind your own fucking business."

Abby stood her ground. "You're on my property and your behavior is disturbing my business and the rest of my guests— this *is* my fucking business."

"Not if you know what's good for you, it ain't."

"What's good for everybody is for you to calm down and quiet down. Quit acting like a maniac. You keep it up, you're only going to make more trouble than you can handle."

"I can handle all the trouble anybody can dish out on this cowshit-surrounded mud puddle!"

"No you can't. You're a fool if you think so."

Wilton's eyes flared like wild embers. "I been itching to slap the fuck out of one ball-busting bitch—you don't get out of my face, I'll be more than goddamn happy to make it two!"

I'd listened to enough. I edged in front of Abby. "Since you clearly don't have any—no man who beats women does—what do you know about balls, busted or otherwise?"

Wilton hesitated a second to size me up. His anger wasn't making him totally without caution. But then his sneer only widened. "You're kind of old to be playing knight in shining armor, ain't you, Pops?"

"I'm old enough to know how to settle down an oversized baby having a tantrum," I told him.

"Hey, fuck you, you old bastard. It'd take me all of ten seconds to clean your clock. And then that skank you're trying to impress will still have her turn coming. Is that what you want? Back off right the fuck now, or I guarantee that's what you're going to get, the both of you."

Inside the truck, Mandy rolled her window partway down and wailed, "Ronnie, stop it! You're letting this get way out of hand!"

"Just never you mind, Mandy," Wilton replied without bothering to look at her. "You've still got your turn coming . . . this will just take a minute."

"First it was ten seconds, now you're up to a full minute. How many more time limits you got?" I taunted him. "You haven't scared anybody away yet."

Wilton pointed a finger at me. "You're pissin' me off, old man!"

Abby put a hand on my arm. "Joe, this isn't the way to handle it—More fighting's not the answer."

I shook my head. "Afraid sometimes it's the only answer, Ab. But don't worry, this isn't going to be much of a fight."

I'd made sure I said the last part loud enough for Wilton to hear. He did, and it got the reaction I wanted it to. He shrugged immediately into a half-assed boxer's crouch and brought up his fists. "That does it, you old fucker. You had your chance, now your mouth just overloaded your ass!"

I moved away from Abby, toward Wilton, saying, "I've got a fish dinner waiting next door that I want to get back to before it turns cold. Let's get this over with."

My taunts had escalated Ronnie's already heightened rage to a point past good sense or any further glimmer of the caution he'd shown at first. All he could think right now was that he wanted to get his hands on somebody and start bashing. He was twenty-five years younger than me, hard and limber and in better shape. But I had thirty pounds on him and my added years also carried added experience . . . experience that included several instances of going up against a hell of lot tougher men than him, not doing my training by knocking around women.

I let him throw some preliminary punches, gauging his rhythm and skill level. I'm not exactly light on my feet, but it still wasn't hard for me to block or evade everything he sent. He was that wild, that enraged. And he'd been drinking. He was still powerful, though; his punches had plenty of pop—any one of them would have been telling if they'd landed where he intended.

I got set as he winged his third or fourth attempt at a right cross. I took it on my forearm and shoulder, let it graze stingingly off the top of my head. He tried to follow quickly with a left uppercut, which I anticipated and twisted away from. His fist hitting nothing but air turned him slightly off balance. I uncoiled then, slamming a backhand hard to his mouth. As he stiffened from that, I drilled a jab to his solar plexus, screwing my feet into the sand, whipping all my weight into it. The tried-and-true old paralyzer of a punch was as on target as any I've ever thrown. It put him down. He buckled like a half-folded jackknife and tipped back, his butt hitting the ground as if he'd tried to sit where there was no chair.

The rage that had been simmering just under my skin all day was on full boil now. It wanted to be released real bad. I started after Ronnie, my hands clawlike, ready to drag him to his feet so I could pound him down again. And then again.

From inside the truck, Mandy let out a screech. The door flew open and she came clambering out. "Ronnie! Don't hurt him any more! Get away from him!"

The anguish in her voice stopped me. I took a step back. Tried to bring my breathing under control. I let my hands fall to my sides, fingers still curled, felt them start to tremble.

Mandy went running to the fallen man who only moments earlier had been threatening to do all sorts of punishing things to her. She dropped to her knees beside him. "Ronnie. . . . Baby," she kept repeating anxiously. Wilton sort of tipped against her and she hugged his head. His eyes looked out of focus and he was making soft, bubbly groaning noises. The fight was clearly out of him.

I told myself to relax, calm down; it was over. Part of me was glad, part of me still wanted Ronnie back on his feet so I'd have an excuse to hit him some more.

As my breathing leveled, I became aware of excited murmurs passing through the knot of onlookers.

And then, a moment later, I became aware of something else: Strobing red and blue flashes of color thrown by the light bar atop a county sheriff's cruiser rolling down from the highway in a cloud of dust and spraying gravel.

"Shit!" Abby muttered, a half step behind me.

The cruiser veered off, swinging around the back end of the store, and came crunching to a halt three yards short of the Wiltons. Its billowing dust trail continued on, engulfing all of us standing in the vicinity.

As the dust cleared, a uniformed deputy climbed out of the vehicle. "Everybody stay where you are. Don't move, don't leave," he ordered in a loud voice. He was a little over average height, thick but solidly built, ruddy-faced.

He walked up to the Wiltons and stood looming over them. "What happened to this man?" he asked of no one in particular.

When everyone else hesitated, Abby said, "He got what he had coming."

The deputy gave her a sharp look. "That's not an answer," he snapped.

"That jerk hit my husband," Mandy said shrilly, pointing at me. "He hit him really hard!"

"That's right, I hit him," I admitted. "But only after he gave me no choice."

Mandy was still cradling her husband's head. She seemed not to notice that a trickle of blood had seeped from his nose and the way she was clutching him she was smearing it in a wider stain across his cheek. "If you all would have left him alone he would have quieted down in a little while longer," she said petulantly. But there wasn't a lot of conviction in the words, more like she was trying to persuade herself as much as anyone else.

Abby made it clear she wasn't convinced, saying, "That's highly debatable considering how long he'd already been carrying on and that he was only showing signs of growing more belligerent."

The deputy turned his attention to her. "Start at the beginning and tell me your version, Abby."

She ran it down for him, quick and succinct. The phone call she'd gotten over at the Walleye, what young Matt had told her on the way over here, what she subsequently saw and heard for herself.

"And that's when Mr. Hannibal here struck Mr. Wilton and knocked him down," she finished.

At the mention of my name, the deputy's eyes darted to me, narrowing. "So," he said, measuredly, "you're Hannibal."

I met his gaze but said nothing.

"Been hearing about you," he continued. "Can't say I've particularly liked what I heard."

"Clint, that's uncalled for," Abby said sternly.

I knew for sure then that I was looking at Clint Barnstable, the deputy I'd tried to catch up with earlier in the day. The man who was first to arrive at the scene of the alleged accident that claimed the lives of Liz and Bomber. I'd had a hunch who he was when he addressed Abby by name and now she'd just confirmed it.

Ignoring Abby's admonishment, Barnstable drawled, "But something I dislike even worse than an outsider coming around poking his nose in my business is a lowlife miserable goddamn wife beater." He turned slowly back to the Wiltons, his narrowed eyes lingering on me half-menacingly before finally sliding away. Hovering once more over the young couple, he leaned forward slightly and shouted down at Ronnie, "That the way you was brought up to treat your women down there in Kansas, boy?"

"He didn't mean it," Mandy protested in her shrill, increasingly irritating voice. "He didn't hurt me that bad."

"Shut up, you fool girl," Barnstable snarled at her. "You stick up for him when he treats you that way, maybe you're stupid enough to deserve it."

Mandy shrank away from the harsh words, clinging even more tightly to her husband.

Barnstable pressed on with his intimidation. "But that don't mean I want it going on in my county, you hear? Answer me, the both of you—do you hear?"

Mandy began to sob. Ronnie, peering up at the deputy with eyes that were finally starting to come back into focus a little, managed a weak nod.

"On your feet, boy," Barnstable barked. "I want to make sure you're getting my point real clear."

"Clint!" Abby said, her voice lifting on a warning note.

But again Barnstable ignored her. He leaned over, pushed Mandy out of the way, and dragged Ronnie Wilton to his feet. Wilton's knees were rubbery and it was hard for him to straighten up all the way. He held his arms wrapped around his stomach.

"Pay attention, son," Barnstable told him as he pulled him roughly over closer to the truck. "I'm going to give you what's called an object lesson. Free of charge. You take it to heart, it'll help guide you on the straight and narrow and maybe save you a lot of grief down the road."

I didn't know what Barnstable was going to do, but one thing I *did* know with a bitter certainty: Whatever this "object lesson" turned out to be, it was intended as much for me as it was for Ronnie Wilton. Maybe more so.

At the driver's side door, hanging ajar from Mandy's hurried exit out of the vehicle, Barnstable stopped. "I want this night to be a turning point for you," he announced. "And for that to happen you need what they call a 'trigger mechanism' that will kick in the next time you feel like putting the boots to your old lady. Make you remember you're all cured of that sort of thing. So here it is. . . ."

With a deft, practiced motion Barnstable drew the nightstick from his utility belt, whirled it once in the air, then slashed it viciously across the chrome-framed side mirror that stood cantilevered out from the door. The glass shattered and fell tinkling to the ground, the chrome puckered and bent away under the blow.

"Now," said Barnstable, his lip curling nastily as he jerked Ronnie's face close to his, "since you're obviously one of those gear-head freakos who gets his rocks off more over his big shiny truck than warm, live pussy, I figure I just made the impression I wanted to leave you with. Not only is this little accident to your precious truck something for you to think about the next time you want to swing on your wife, it's also just a taste of what I'll do if you ever cause trouble in my county again, is that clear?"

Wilton mumbled something.

Barnstable shook him. "Louder! I want to hear it plain."

"I said it's clear, damnit!" Wilton blurted.

Barnstable shoved him back toward his wife. "Now get on inside, the both of you, and don't be bothering nobody no more tonight. Don't go bleeding all over Abby's clean cabin, either."

Hugging each other, heads hung low, their steps together awkward and uneven, the Wiltons went meekly into their cabin. Just before the door closed behind them, Barnstable called, "And if I catch you driving this piece of shit around my county with this busted mirror I'll ticket your Kansas ass!"

Standing with his feet planted wide, Barnstable waved the nightstick in a sweeping motion, indicating the onlookers still clumped to either side of him. "All right, break it up the rest of you, too," he said. "Go on back to your own places now. Show's over."

After waiting to make sure he got the response he had ordered, Barnstable turned back to Abby and me. He was clearly

124

gloating. "Well, that ought to keep things quieted down for the rest of the night. What do you want to bet that when you peek out fresh tomorrow you'll see Kansas Boy and his sweetie have already hightailed it for the border?"

"Either that or to the nearest lawyer to file police brutality charges against you," Abby said.

"What police brutality?" Barnstable scoffed. "I never laid a hand on the punk except to help him to his feet. What's more, I gave him a valuable life lesson. He ought to be thanking me. Him and his little wife both."

"Yes. I'm sure they're inside feeling all warm with gratitude even as we speak."

Barnstable slid the nightstick back into its thong on his belt. "Hey, you oughta know by now how I operate, Abby. You didn't want me to handle it the way I handle things, you shouldn't've called in a disturbance."

"I didn't call anything in."

He grinned. "Lucky for you then that somebody did." His eyes slid over to me and once again they narrowed slightly. "What do you think, Hannibal? Was I too rough on the wife beater? They handle things different back where you're from?"

I avoided taking the bait. Shook my head and said, "I've got a set of skinned knuckles that pretty much rules me out of passing judgment. Besides, when in Rome. . . . If that's the MO that works for you, then who am I to question it?"

His grinned widened. "That's right. Who are you to question a damn thing, eh?"

CHAPTER SEVENTEEN

I woke the next morning to the smell of cigarette smoke and the murmur of voices coming from just outside my front door.

I'm hardly what you'd call a "morning person" to begin with and having tossed and turned restlessly through most of the night put me in an even less charitable mood this morning than usual. Which is to say that the prospect of welcoming visitors right off the bat didn't exactly thrill me.

In the end, though, curiosity won out over irritability. After lying there for a few minutes trying without success to identify the voices, I threw back the covers, got up and got dressed, went to see who was there.

I stepped out into another brilliantly sunlit morning. In my mood I would have preferred gray gloominess. *Wasn't it ever overcast or rainy in this part of the country?*

Squinting down, I saw two guys sitting on the steps of my tiny porch. One of them was young Matt, the groundskeeper who'd gotten socked in the eye by Ronnie Wilton last night. He was wearing baggy cargo shorts, flip-flops, and a Nebraska Huskers T-shirt. Next to him sat a gent of considerably more years, a lean, lanky sort clad in cowboy boots, faded jeans, a black T-shirt, and a battered black Stetson hat. His face was deeply seamed by age and weather and looked permanently tanned to a dull copper color.

They both looked up as I emerged from the cabin.

"Well now. Speak of the devil," drawled the guy in the cowboy hat. A wide grin spread across his face and the stub of a cigarette bobbed from one corner of it as he spoke. "Here comes Mr. Joe One-Punch hisself."

I gauged the words for some hint of recrimination but found none. And Matt's neighboring smile seemed to be one of unabashed admiration. I didn't feel like I was any more deserving of one than the other.

I said, "If you're referring to last night, it sounds as if somebody's been exaggerating a little."

"Aw, don't go spoilin' it for me," the cowboy said, rising to his feet. A short, gray-streaked ponytail trailed down in back, from under his hat. "Point is, you saw something needed doin' and you waded in and got 'er done." He reached up, extending his right hand. "My name's B.U. Gorcey and I'm proud to make your acquaintance."

I leaned over and took the hand, finding his grip firm and leathery. We shook. "Been hearing about you, B.U. Glad to finally meet you."

"Sorry I wasn't around to give you a hand last night. Not that you wasn't up to handlin' it okay without me. I was busy over at the Walleye and by the time I heard what was goin' on it was all over with."

I turned and glanced down the row of cabins. Number three had an empty, deserted look. The F-150 pickup was no longer parked in front.

Following my eyes, Matt said, "They took off just like the deputy predicted. Packed up and bailed out just a little bit ago. Never looked our way, never said boo. I don't think we'll be seeing them again."

I swung my gaze back. Gave Matt a little smile. To B.U. I said, "Don't worry about last night. It worked out okay. I had Matt here backing me up. He'd already taken a round from the troublemaker, had him softened up for me."

Matt's cheeks flushed scarlet. "Yeah, fat lot of good I did," he said, his mouth twisting wryly.

"You stepped up, kid, when nobody else did," I reminded him. "That counts for plenty. You got nothing to hang your head about. And if it had kept going to where it looked like the girl was in real danger, I'm betting you would have charged in again. And this time you would have been better prepared to keep from getting sucker-punched."

"Man's right, son," B.U. chimed in. "Ain't how many times you get knocked down that counts, it's how many times you get back up. You showed your sand by marchin' in the first time. You'd've been in there again if you needed to be."

The kid's blush deepened but at the same time his chest swelled noticeably under the praise. "I dunno. . . . That guy dropped me pretty quick. I wouldn't have been too eager to serve him up another piece of me. Except nobody else was do-ing *anything,* so I was beginning to think . . . well, I'm just glad Mr. Hannibal showed up when he did."

"Hey, I thought we got that 'Mister' crap straightened out last night," I said, frowning. "It's just plain 'Joe,' alright?"

"Sure . . . Joe."

"Good luck with that," B.U. grumbled. "I been tryin' to get the stubborn cuss to quit callin' me 'Mister' since the beginnin' of summer. He's too danged polite. It's unsettlin' is what it is. He's ruinin' the whole lazy, good-for-nothin', inconsiderate im-age for all the rest of today's youth!"

Matt gave a fatalistic shrug. "Why can I say? My Pa was career Army. Around him it was strictly Mister and Missus or Miss, and Yessir and Yes ma'am. Got my butt reddened too many times for forgetting. Not a habit I'm finding easy to break."

"Well, I guess there are worse habits," I allowed.

"Reckon so," B.U. said agreeably. "And one of them, I'm afraid, is keeping a body from their work. Which I been doin' for quite a spell now, bendin' the young fella's ear so's I had somebody to pass the time of day with waitin' for you to come out. You was on your way into town to pick up those lawn-mower blades from the sharpener, Matt—you best go take care of your business before I cause you any more delay."

Matt clambered to his feet. "Yes, sir. I'm on it. Good talking with you, though." He started in the direction of the shower buildings. Over his shoulder he tossed, "See you around, Mist—" he stopped short, turned his head to flash a silly grin, then: "See you around, Joe."

"Now there goes a good kid," B.U. said after him.

I nodded. "No argument from what I've seen."

"He's livin' in that pickup camper parked down by the lake-shore there, just east of the boat ramp. Goin' to college up at Chadron. Wanted to spend his summer on the lake but still earn some extra cash. Hirin' on for Abby is workin' out good for the both of them."

"Seems so," I agreed.

B.U. craned his neck to look up at me. "So then. Since I came callin' uninvited, I figured the hospitable thing to do would be to at least bring some offerin's." He gestured down at a tall thermos that stood on the step next to where he'd been sitting. Beside it were two thick-handled mugs and a grease-spotted paper bag. "I got fresh-brewed coffee and some doughnuts still warm from the bakery, delivered at sunup over to Abby's store. You got time to sit a spell and join me for some?"

"I sure do," I answered. "I'd invite you in but I'm afraid I'm not set up very well for company. I only have one chair to sit on."

"No problem. These steps are right comfortable and the mornin' sun ain't too hot yet. We're fine right here."

He dropped what was left of his cigarette onto the ground, mashed it under a bootheel, then proceeded to pour us each a mug of coffee. When he apologized for bringing no trimmings, I told him black was fine. In the bag there were two plain doughnuts and two chocolate-covered ones. I chose one of the latter and took a seat on the edge of the landing. B.U. settled back down where he'd been sitting before.

"You might find that coffee a bit stout," he warned. "When you was raised ranchin' like I was and it was up and to chores each mornin' before the sun, a good stiff jolt of caffeine was not only welcome it was necessary."

"Understandable," I said. "Coffee's good." In truth, it was the strongest, most bitter brew I'd ever tasted. But I didn't want to appear ungrateful nor was I willing to let this crusty old cowpoke think I couldn't handle it. Thank God I had intervening bites of the sweet doughnut to keep my taste buds from being bludgeoned senseless.

"You probably got investigatin' to go do, so I won't keep you long," B.U. said. "I mainly wanted to stop by and meet you, put a face with the name I been hearin' so much about. And, for what it's worth, to tell you I think it's a good thing you're doin', helpin' Abby chase down these notions that are troublin' her. Also want you to know if there's any way I can be of help, you can count on me."

"It's good to know that. Thank you."

"Abby and Margaret are good people. And it wasn't hard to like Miss Liz and that big ol' Bomber, neither. I understand they was both good friends of yours."

I nodded. "The best I had."

"I'm sorry for your loss."

I didn't respond directly to that. Gave it a beat, then said, "These 'notions' of Abby's, as you call them . . . I appreciate you being in her corner and all, but how do you feel about them personally? Do you share her feelings?"

He took his time answering. Sipped some coffee, chewed a

bite of doughnut. "The idea Bomber and Miss Liz was carryin' on the way has been claimed," he said at length, "don't fit no-how. I can't buy it for a minute. Not from what I saw. But to go any further than that . . . murder, cover-up, conspiracy or whatever . . . hell, I don't know. That gets kinda far-fetched for this ol' cowboy's head. The best I can tell you is that I can't make up my mind what to think."

"Let me ask you this, then. How about the police? What can you tell me about them?"

"What do you mean, exactly?"

"I guess, specifically, I'm talking about Deputy Barnstable."

"Uh-huh. Clint. He can be a handful."

"Yesterday I met at some length with both Sheriff Mabry and Sheriff Knaack. I came away reasonably well impressed. Then, last night, I had my first meeting with Clint Barnstable."

B.U. cut me a sideways look. "Not so impressed, I take it?"

"He showed himself to be something of a bully and not above abusing the privilege of his badge. From there, in my book, it's just a matter of degree. A man who'll step across the line a little ways will eventually start crossing over farther."

"Reckon that's true enough. Sad fact of human nature."

"Barnstable and his dirt-biking buddies play a big role in this whole business. They were the first ones on the accident scene and, ultimately, the first ones to spot the signs of drinking and sexual activity. Up until now, because Barnstable was an off-duty sheriff's deputy and he called nine-eleven and tried to administer CPR and the rest, I was inclined to look past him and his friends for the answers I was after. Now I find myself backpedaling on that—wondering if looking *past* them for answers might mean *over*-looking some possible answers."

B.U. let out a low whistle. "Boy, you don't hesitate to jump right to the throat of something, do you?"

"You think I'm off the mark?"

"About Clint Barnstable bein' capable of some underhanded doin's? No, I can't argue that. Clint's a throwback—he keeps the peace, but he don't necessarily do it to the letter of the law. Most everybody is aware of that . . . even the sheriff, I expect. But the flip side, knowin' Clint is out there keepin' a lid on things so they don't get out of hand, is the balancin' factor that's caused folks to look the other way when his tactics have got a mite raw." B.U. paused, took another long swallow of coffee. "Now, havin' said that, I come to the same fork in the road as before. . . . Do I think a lawman who's too quick to bust heads and bend a few legal fineries is capable of bein' in on this . . . this cloudyin' of the facts concernin' your friends' car wreck, makin' it look like something it really wasn't? Whew! That's a reach. I don't want to say no, but I ain't ready to say yes."

I grinned ruefully. "You have a knack for answers that aren't really answers, B.U. You ever think of running for political office?"

"I'm just tryin' to be honest, hoss. You got to remember most folks out this way are pretty basic—hard workin' and honest. I reckon in your line of work you see the worst in people, and I ain't so naïve that I don't know the lowest behavior imaginable can sometimes be found in the last folks you'd expect. It's just that out here, well, we ain't so used to it."

"And I hope you never *have* to get used to it. But that still doesn't mean it isn't all around and sometimes it reaches in and touches even the best of places and lives."

"I guess that's why Abby's lucky to have you involved."

"The way things are going for me these days," I said sourly, "I'm not so sure I'm carrying around much luck for anybody."

"What makes you say that?"

"Never mind." I waved him off. "The way we left it last night, since Barnstable had heard I was wanting to talk to him about his part at the accident scene and all, was that he'd be available at home around ten this morning if I wanted to stop by again. I guess I'll get my chance to try and take some more reads off him then."

B.U. gave a little grunt. "Might make for an interestin' mornin'."

"Yeah, it might. Look, if you don't mind, I'd like to move on and ask you about another name that's come up in this thing."

"Go ahead. I ain't been able to give you much in the way of bona fide solid answers so far. Maybe this'll be my chance."

I plucked the last doughnut out of the paper bag. I wondered if it would completely disintegrate if I dunked it in the half-cup of coffee I had remaining. Not wanting to risk losing it, I opted for the safer route of taking a bite and then following it with a sip of the vile brew. Swallowing, I asked, "What can you tell me about Cameron Terrell, the big cattleman and landowner from up north?"

B.U. slapped his leg and his face nearly split in two with a leering grin. "Whoooee! Hoss, I don't know how you do it, but you sure know how to keep a conversation lively."

"Glad to be of service," I said drily.

"Now. Before I answer your question, you gotta tell me—how in *the hell* did Cam Terrell's name get dragged into this tumble-bug's nest you're pushing around?"

So I told him. About how Liz and Bomber were planning to pay a visit to the old Brannigan homestead site on the day of their wreck and how I'd reasoned that maybe one of Vic Faber's canoeing groups had encountered them while they were both in the same general area. How that had segued to learning that instead it was Cameron Terrell who had had people in the vicinity that day. "And that," I concluded, "leaves me needing to pay a visit to this Terrell to see if him or any of his guests might have run into Liz and Bomber while they were out there. If so,

I'm hoping they can tell me something about how they were acting, what they were doing—anything that might provide a hint about what came next. It's a long shot, but it's as solid as anything else I've got to chase right now."

"You're right, it sounds like along shot," B.U. agreed. "But at least now I see where you're comin' from and how you've got to play it on through. As far as Cam Terrell, I ain't sure I can tell you much more than you already know. He's so rich he practically shits money, and he ain't ashamed of it nohow. Reckon nobody gets to be that rich and powerful without bein' a mite ruthless, but I can't say Terrell is any worse than any other hard-nosed businessman. Up until a few years ago, mostly all you heard about him was how he kept buyin' land and growin', buyin' and growin'. Naturally, that meant steppin' on a few toes and squeezin' out more than one small rancher in the process."

"What changed?"

B.U. dipped his chin and cut me a somber upward look. "Little event the world came to call Nine One-One. Terrell's wife was on the fourth plane that morning, the one the passengers took down over Pennsylvania after the World Trade Center and Pentagon had been hit."

I grimaced. "Bitch of a day for lots of good people."

"Uh-huh. Just a little reminder that all the wealth and fineries in the world don't mean squat when your number rolls out on the dice in that Big Casino upstairs. Anyway, Mrs. Terrell had been visiting a sister in New York. Was on her way to California where Terrell was plannin' to meet up with her and they was gonna to spend some time vacationing together there on the coast." B.U. paused to drain his cup. Lowering it, he continued, "Afterwards, after the dust settled some, Terrell became a real outspoken backer for hard-line anti-terrorist measures. Maybe he was always what they call a Right Winger, but nobody ever knew it before because he kept his politics and most all his personal affairs to hisself. By the time the first year anniversary mark for Nine One-One rolled around, he'd formed his own paramilitary group. Called it the RBR Militia— Remember and Be Ready. Claimed he'd become convinced American . . . what's the word? Means you quit carin' or bein' concerned?"

"Apathetic? Apathy?"

"Yeah, that's it! Apathy. The way Terrell saw it, the war on terrorism was going to drag out with no clear, quick victories and American apathy was gonna to start settin' in and all the defensive measures and commitments the country swore to right after the World Trade Center attacks were gonna start fallin' by the wayside as inconveniences the weak and the pampered would no longer want to be bothered with. Accordin' to his way of thinkin', if we go ahead and let our guard down it's just a matter of time before we get hit again and in the end it's gonna come down to grassroots, tough-minded groups like RBR to be the backbone of American defense and survival."

I didn't say anything right away. Somewhat to my surprise, I realized that I'd gotten to the bottom of my cup of the potent coffee. "I'm not exactly ready to get fitted for some pretend Army uniform and go goose-stepping with the RBR," I said at length, "but I'll admit to finding it hard to disagree with at least a portion of that outlook."

"Yeah, I know what you mean. I sometimes wonder what it would take to make us, as a whole country, pissed off enough to stand up and fight for anything anymore."

"But," I sighed, "that's not something that's on my particular plate right at the moment. I'm not out to win the war on terrorism. I'm out to get to the bottom—the truth—of my friends' deaths. And as it turns out the road there happens to cross Cameron Terrell's path. I'd intended to go calling on him later today, after my meeting with Barnstable. Are you saying he's so insulated by this militia thing that I'm going to have trouble getting to him?"

"Ain't sure, to tell you the truth." B.U. shrugged. "He's got militia barracks and paraphernalia and training grounds and what not scattered all over different parts of his property. But as far as I know he still conducts regular business dealings from his main ranch—the Standin' T—up north of Arthur." He eyed me somewhat quizzically. "I wouldn't think gettin' to him would be that much of a problem, though. Not for you. . . . Don't you know you got a sort of inside track for that?"

"You lost me," I said. "I don't follow what you mean."

"You got Abby, hoss. . . . Cameron Terrell is her ex-father-in-law."

CHAPTER EIGHTEEN

"When we were at Pawnee Creek yesterday," Abby was explaining, "and I told you that Cam Terrell now owned the old Brannigan homestead, it simply didn't occur to me to also mention he used to be my father-in-law. I mean, I wasn't being evasive or anything."

"I never meant to imply you were," I assured her.

We were in her store, seated in the small snack area where customers could linger over a cup of coffee or a cold drink, maybe an ice cream cone or one of the microwavable sandwiches available from the cooler section. A pair of round-top tables and a mismatched collection of chairs had been pulled together for this purpose. At present we had not only the snack area but the whole place to ourselves.

After my front-porch session with B.U. Gorcey wrapped up, I'd gone back inside long enough to finish my morning ablutions, including an extra long workout with the toothbrush in an attempt to rid my mouth of the aftertaste from his wretched coffee. When neither that nor the quart of orange juice chugged from my ice chest did the trick, I had come over to the store seeking some chewing gum to try and finish the job. Conversation with Abby had inevitably gotten around to the subject of Cameron Terrell and what I'd learned of her association to him.

Lighting a cigarette, blowing a cloud of smoke into the slanting rays of morning sun pouring through the window, Abby said now, "I suppose you might as well hear the rest of the tawdry tale, too, as long as we're airing my dirty laundry."

"Your laundry—dirty or otherwise—is none of my business, Ab. I told you how Terrell's name came up and why I asked for your input on approaching him. That's all. I wasn't trying to pry beyond that."

She blew some more smoke, scowling after it as it tumbled and dissipated into the wash of brilliant light. "No . . . I suppose you weren't," she allowed, somewhat grudgingly. "I guess any mention of the Terrell name tends to get a rather testy reaction out of me." She took another, calmer drag on her cigarette. "But I *want* you to hear the rest of it. There are some things about me you don't know, and . . . well, it's time you did."

This morning Abby was wearing an orange boatnecked pullover, faded jeans, and a pair of cheap flip-flops such as seemed to be the quasi-official footwear for many No Name Bay regulars. The wide neck of the pullover did a nice job of showing off the smooth, graceful lines of her throat; and when she moved, the neck opening shifted from side to side, alternately revealing the curve of first one shoulder then the other, each cut by the thin silky strap of a pale pink bra. For some reason I found these demure, unintentional flashes of exposure strangely provocative.

"All right. If that's what you want," I said.

She tapped some ash into an ashtray shaped like a fish. With her other hand she fiddled briefly with her cigarette pack. "When I was married to Travis—that's Cameron's son, an only child—we had a child of our own. Also a son. Dusty. He's nine now." Her expression softened instantly at the mention of the boy. "During the last couple years of the marriage, when Travis's treatment of me had me ground down about as low as a person can feel . . . before I finally found some backbone and started to fight back . . . I resorted to alcohol as a means to try and cope.

I found out things didn't seem so bad if I stayed just sort of mildly blurred—*numbed,* I guess is what it amounted to, like a novocaine shot for the whole body. I never got hammered to the point of being incapacitated or to where I was neglectful of Dusty. At least not neglectful or impaired enough to put him at risk of being harmed. There certainly were times I could have paid *closer* attention, played more games with him, taught him more things . . . instead of attempting to hide in a bottle." One corner of her mouth jerked briefly in a kind of bitter smile. "He was about the only bright spot in my life and I foolishly wasted what could have been a lot of special moments . . . precious memories."

She paused for a long moment. I couldn't tell if she was searching for her next words or if she wanted me to make some comment.

I gave it a shot, saying guardedly, "Most parents I know look back and wish there were things they'd done differently as far as raising their children. You love them so much you want everything to be perfect for them. But in the end, everybody's only human—parents *and* children—and that's a condition prone to following a less-than-perfect course."

"Boy ain't that the truth." Abby smoked some more. "Eventually I reached a point where I saw that my drinking was not only the wrong answer but it was headed further out of control. With the help of a few friends, an understanding minister, and a series of counseling sessions, I got things turned around. In the process I found the strength—the *real* strength, inside myself—to stand up to Travis. I told him we both had to face the fact that our marriage was no good and I wanted a divorce." She ground out what was left of her cigarette, stabbing it hard into the fish ashtray. "That's when the clout of the Terrell name swung into action. By every logical expectation I should have gotten custody of Dusty. Hell, Travis was never interested in him. He didn't want to be bothered with a child, just like he didn't really want to be bothered with a wife. Traveling all over Hell's creation with his band, playing in one honky-tonk dive after another, trying to make a name for himself—*that* was all he ever cared about. I could never figure out why he asked me to marry him in the first place. I think he did it to shut his parents up. And I think the reason they wanted him married was because they hoped it would settle him down, divert his interest from the band and the music and bring his head to a place where he'd start acting and thinking like the man who was one day going to inherit the Terrell empire."

"So what you're getting to is that Travis was granted custody of Dusty."

Abby spread her hands. "You don't see him running around here, do you?" she said tartly. After a moment she dropped her hands and the aggression slid slowly from her face. "I'm sorry. There's that testiness again."

I waited, letting her get it sorted out.

"They brought in a high-priced lawyer who cut me to shreds," she continued when she was ready. "Made me sound like a totally depressed, wretched, drunken excuse for a mother and wife. After he was sure he'd convincingly painted me as being non-deserving of alimony once the divorce was final, he then compared what my meager ability would be to provide and care for a child against what the same child could expect if provided for instead by Travis, with the support of the Terrell name and fortune. By the time he made his ruling, the judge was looking at me like I was an insect he wished he could squash with his gavel. He acted like it actually pained him to announce I would get Dusty every other weekend from Friday to Sunday evening, and on alternating holidays."

"Where does the boy live the rest of the time?"

"At the Terrell main ranch—the Standing T. That's officially

Travis's 'home' address, even though he's away traveling with his band more than ever these days. They have a fulltime live-in nanny, a huge horse of a woman named Freda, who was once an Olympic shot-putter for Germany, if you can believe it. Dusty adores her and she is fantastic with him, thank God. That's the only thing that makes the arrangement bearable for me. For the rest of them it was all about spite, of course—for Travis as well as his parents. It was never that any of them really *wanted* Dusty, they just wanted to hurt and humiliate me for having the audacity to want to rid myself of the Terrell name."

"Sounds like a family with a vicious streak."

"It's all about control and ego. And *I* will always be the one to carry the stigma of a mother who was judged by the court unfit to raise her own child. I don't know if you can even imagine how demoralizing that is. I tell myself I don't give a damn what other people think, but of course a part of me truly does. What's worse, sometimes I . . . I start to feel like I *deserved* that ruling."

"You shouldn't ever go there, Ab. Don't give in to it."

"I know. But, believe me, it's easier said than done. Sometimes when I'm in that low place I even want to reach for a bottle again."

"I won't lecture you," I told her. "Life isn't fair, not by a damn site, and we go through much of it feeling like we lack more answers than we have. But in most cases, when it comes right down to it, even when we don't know the *right* answer we sure as hell recognize the *wrong* one."

She listened to the words stiffly, wouldn't meet my eyes. I couldn't tell what she was thinking.

Forging on, I said, "B.U. told me that Mrs. Terrell was killed on Nine One-One. Did that change anything?"

"Not as far as softening anyone's position toward me, if that's what you mean. Judy—that was Mrs. Terrell—never had

141

anything directly to do with caring for Dusty anyway. Like I said, that fell to Freda the nanny. The only changes I've seen any sign of since her passing is that Travis's drive to accomplish something with his music seems to have intensified. He's actually cut a couple of albums and has gotten some decent recognition from them, and most of the gigs he plays these days are a big improvement over the roadhouse honky-tonk one-nighters of the past. And Cameron . . . well, you already know about the militia thing. I guess I'd have to say, too, that Cam has taken to paying a lot more attention to Dusty. 'Grampa Cam,' Dusty calls him. He talks about him and the things they do together quite a bit—old movies and video games in the evenings, chores around the ranch when Dusty isn't in school, fishing and horseback riding. It makes me jealous and resentful, I admit, but at the same time I'm happy for Dusty's sake—he's getting the kind of fatherly attention from Cameron that he wouldn't get otherwise, not from Travis."

"And Cameron," I pointed out, "is getting a second chance at influencing a son to follow more closely in his footsteps."

Abby finally lifted her eyes and held mine for a few beats. Then her gaze drifted past me and took on a momentary faraway look. Whatever she saw in that distant place caused a knitting of her brows. "Yeah, there are implications there that I probably ought not be too thrilled about."

My thoughts jumped to a brighter image. "Bomber was always great with kids," I said. "Did Dusty ever get the chance to meet his great-uncle?"

"Oh, yeah. They hit it off wonderfully," Abby replied, smiling. "When Dusty talked about Uncle Bomber, he didn't just call him his great-uncle—he called him his *great-big*-uncle!"

"I'm sorry I haven't had a chance to meet the boy," I said sincerely.

Abby rolled her eyes. "He's away for a whole month and it's

killing me. I miss him to death!" She paused, reflecting on something. Then went on, "The only good thing is that he wasn't here when Uncle Bomber and Liz had their fatal crash. That's why you didn't meet him at the funeral. I know he's going to have to grow up to learn how to face death and loss one day, so had he been here I would have brought him. But he still has disturbing dreams about attending Grandmother Judy's funeral, and I also know the next test is coming soon enough. Let's face it, Ma's not going to be around a whole lot longer. For the time being, I'd rather he remembers his *great-big*-uncle they way he was—vital and loud and larger than life. As far as he needs to know, Uncle Bomber just went away again, back to where he came from."

I wished that was a game I could play inside my head, rather than face the hard finality of what really was. I cleared my throat and said, "So where is Dusty, anyway? Gone to some kind of camp or something?"

"Remember when I said Travis is playing better gigs these days? Well all through the month of June he landed a booking for him and his band—they're called Travis and the Travelers, by the way—to play a guest-starring spot on the Country Bears stage at Disney World down in Florida." Curiously, I thought I caught something almost like a ring of pride in Abby's voice. "So anyway," she went on, "part of the package included an opportunity for Dusty and Freda to go along. Stay in a luxury suite at one of the hotels, attend Disney World and all the other attractions the area has to offer, hang out with his dad on the days he's not performing . . . how could I say no? Could I deny a nine-year-old that kind of chance of a lifetime? I lose him for a couple of weekends but we made a deal for me to get make-up time when he returns. I have no idea *what* I'm going to do as a follow-up to Disney World, but I'm sure looking forward to giving it a shot. The little fart will finally be back next week and then I get him all through the Fourth of July!"

Her eyes shone with delight at the prospect, and I felt warmed simply by the overflow of her deep affection for the boy.

CHAPTER NINETEEN

Clint Barnstable answered the door wearing a dingy white T-shirt and a pair of badly wrinkled boxer shorts with bright yellow cartoon bumblebees on them. His hair was standing on end and it was clear he hadn't been out of bed for very long.

He scowled at me and said, "I was afraid it was going to be you."

"You said ten o'clock, didn't you?"

"Yeah. Sounded good when I said it, but the night took some unexpected turns." His scowl deepened. "Come on in. I guess I can't leave you standing there."

His apartment was spare and tidy but smelled of cheap perfume, sweat, and the tang of fresh beer. The kitchen counter was strewn with empty Coors bottles, some standing, some tipped over on their sides. In their midst was a flat cardboard container of the type used for take-out pizza. Draped across the back of the couch was a pair of pantyhose with one wadded-up leg and a cream-colored bra brandishing industrial-sized cups. I didn't have to plumb my deductive reasoning skills very deep to determine what type of "turns" the deputy's night had taken.

Scratching his stomach as he led the way into the kitchen, padding on bare feet, Barnstable said, "I got a pot of coffee ready here, brewed on one of them automatic timers. Want a cup?"

"No thanks. I've had my limit for the day." If it was anything like B.U. Gorcey's brew, I'd had my lifetime's limit.

"Well *I* sure need one." He waved his hand at one of the chair-backed stools lining the counter. "Have a seat."

I hitched up a leg and climbed onto the stool while he pulled a cup down out of a mounted wall cabinet.

"Clee-ahnt?" A female's nasal voice twanged out of the bedroom. It had that knack that is peculiar to some southern dialects for being able to draw even a short, blunt word into multiple syllables. "What'cha doin', honey?"

"Tendin' to some business out here, Maizey-Jane, that's all," Barnstable called back. "Don't worry about it. Just keep your box springs tight. I'll be back in directly."

He turned and gave me a knowing leer that told me he'd remembered damn well I would be showing up this morning and had been looking forward to this opportunity to show off his virile prowess the way he'd demonstrated his macho toughness last night at No Name Bay.

"Clee-ahnt?" came the female voice again. "I gotta pee, honey . . . really, really *bad.*"

"Well, come ahead and go piss then, for Christ's sake. You need a written invitation?"

"But, honey," the voice wailed, "I plumb lost track of where my panties gone. You yanked my clothes off last night and flung 'em from Hell to breakfast, you big horny bear."

Barnstable took a drink of coffee and rolled his eyes. "For the luva God . . . things a guy has to put up with in order to get a piece of ass once in a while," he muttered under his breath. Then, louder, he called to the bedroom: "You don't need to get all the way dressed to go to the freakin' bathroom, Maizey-Jane. Just wrap something around yourself and go take your piss and be done with it!"

The next sounds that came from the bedroom were the protest of bedsprings being bounced on followed by the thump of feet hitting the floor. A moment later a plump, puffy-faced dishwater blonde emerged, her ample curves barely contained by a trailing purple sheet that she clutched precariously to a pair of basketball-sized breasts. Inasmuch as the area between the bedroom and the bathroom was wide open to my vantage point, it was impossible not to look. And the half-sheepish, half-coy smile that spread across Maizey-Jane's lips as she returned my gaze told me that she didn't mind being looked at, not in the least. In fact, she lifted one hand and wiggled her fingers, signaling a friendly "hi" as she said, "Who's your friend, Clint? He's kinda cute."

"Just go on about your business and never mind ours," Barnstable growled. "Matter of fact, while you're in there why don't you go ahead and take a shower . . . a nice, long, *loud* shower, if you get my drift. Stick with it. When I'm done here, I'll come join you."

Maizey-Jane tossed her tangled mane of hair. "What if I use up all the hot water? You wouldn't want me taking a *cold* shower now would you, hon?"

"You just trot to it like I told you. Maybe throw in a douche while you're at it. When I join you, we'll steam up the shower stall no matter how cold the water turns."

Maizey-Jane tossed her hair again. "You *are* a big ol' horny bear, aincha?" She glided on into the bathroom. Before she slid out of sight she allowed the purple sheet to slip with feigned carelessness, revealing first a shot of cavernous cleavage and then, as she turned, about four inches of fanny crack separating two mounds of mottled white flesh. It was a sad little cry for continued attention and what was sadder still was that I found it vaguely titillating. *Jesus, you've got a serious need to get your pipes cleaned out, old man.*

After the bathroom door closed behind Maizey-Jane, Barnstable shook his head. "Women . . . if they didn't have a pussy, there'd be a bounty on 'em. Know what I mean? Almost makes a body wonder if guys like Ronnie-boy from last night ain't got the right idea as far as knocking 'em on their asses every now and then."

I made no comment.

He took his time refilling his coffee cup. Then he pulled out one of the counter stools for himself, climbing onto it in reverse so that he sat facing me over the backrest.

"Let's get this over with, Illinois. You can see I got bigger fish to fry," he said. "I don't figure this should take very long. I already know what you want to ask me about and I already know what my answers are going to be because they'll be the same freakin' things I been saying all along—since the sorry day I rolled up on the scene of that damn car wreck."

Plumbing lines clattered suddenly under the floorboards and we could hear the shower spray kick on behind the bathroom door.

I nodded. "Good to hear you're willing to be so open-minded and cooperative."

Barnstable spread his hands. "Hey, how much more cooperative can I be? I invited you right here to my home, didn't I?"

"Yes, you did," I admitted. "Frankly, I'm a little curious about that. You obviously don't care much for me. That is to say, you don't care much for what I represent—an outsider showing up to poke around on your turf. No offense, but you don't strike me as somebody who tolerates very well things he so clearly doesn't like. Why *are* you being cooperative?"

"Because it's the sensible thing to do, that's why. You're right, I don't like worth a damn that you're here poking into this business Abby Bridger has got stirred up. And you're right, too, that my first instinct was to not only be uncooperative but to be downright antagonistic toward you—in ways that would send your ass packing back to Illinois as soon as possible, with your tail tucked between your legs."

"So what changed your mind?"

"Let's just say I was reminded that this whole problem stems from suspicion and mistrust. On the part of Abby to begin with, but I hear she's got a few others starting to think her way now. Including you, right? So if I'd gone ahead and refused to talk to you and went out of my way to make things generally hard for you instead—the way I first intended to—that would have only added to the questions and suspicion. Like what was I hiding or avoiding, see? Which brings us to the alternative . . . what we're doing here this morning."

"I appreciate the change in outlook," I told him.

"Yeah, yeah. Let's get to it. Trot out your questions. What is it you want to ask me?"

I shifted on the hard, uncomfortable stool. "Okay. The way you found the two victims and the condition of the car's interior are all well documented. As you know, the implications of these findings are the whole basis for the concerns and questions first raised by Abby."

"Uh-huh. The big old guy was diabetic, neither him or the woman ever drank whiskey, they were just a couple of cozy old pals who wouldn't ever think of bumping uglies with each other, and blah blah blah . . . I know all that. I've heard it until I want to puke. But what I also know—*really* know—is what I saw with my own two eyes when I went digging into that wreck to see what kind of careless fools were in it and if there was anything left of them."

I willed myself to let the "fools" remark slide. Consider the source and all that crap, I told myself. Besides I had a hunch that what came out of his mouth was only going to get coarser before we were through. My powers of self-restraint were about to be tested severely.

"The woman's shirt or dress or whatever it was she was wearing was undone in front. She had a helluva rack and her bare jugs were flopped right out there," Barnstable was continuing. "Her panties were down around her ankles, and her exposed bush was on display big-time. As for the guy, his fly was open and his dong was out of the corral. No, it wasn't bit off in the woman's mouth and there weren't lipstick prints on it like rings around a tree trunk, the way they're saying in some of the stories being circulated. But come on . . . why else would it be like that? Was he in the habit of flopping his Johnson free and giving it some fresh air while he drove around the countryside?"

"Hold it right there," I said, the words raspy through the tightness in my throat. "The people we're talking about were two of my closest friends, and you damn well know it. I'll ask you to choose your words with a little more tact. I've heard all the juicy details—heard them, like you said a minute ago, until I want to puke. There's no way what you're describing fits the two people I knew."

Barnstable's eyes narrowed. "You calling me a liar?"

"I'm trying real hard not to, mister." I met his glare, held it with my own. The only sound for a long count was the snarl of the shower spray on the other side of the wall. "I have no basis to state you're a liar," I went on. "But I *do* have a basis for saying I find it impossible to believe my friends were engaged in that kind of activity together. And it's got nothing to do with morality or passing judgment or anything like that—hell, I wouldn't *care* if they were screwing each other's brains out. I just don't believe that they *were*. You understand the difference?"

"Well it's got to be one way or the other. If they weren't going down the road finger-fucking and hand-jobbing one another, then how did they end up in the condition I found them?"

"That's what I'm aiming to find out."

"There's an old saying that goes, 'If it looks like a duck and waddles like a duck and quacks like a duck, then it's probably a duck.' You get my drift? I know how I found things and I can't see but one explanation for how they could have got that way."

"That's a logical conclusion. But let's freeze it right there and take a closer look, maybe from a different angle."

"What do you mean?"

"What if you and your buddies weren't really the first ones on the scene?" It wasn't that I actually put much stock in the prankster-tampering theory, but trotting it out was a way to keep this dialogue going, keep Barnstable thinking and answering on his feet. If he *was* dirty in some way, then the more I got him to run his mouth the better the odds he might let slip some revealing little tidbit. It was a spin on the old cop interrogation technique of making a subject repeat his story over and over again in hopes he'd trip himself up by failing to keep his alleged facts straight. "What if somebody was there before you, and the way you found things was the way they purposely left it? *Staged* it, in other words, for whoever came along next?"

Barnstable wrinkled his nose like he'd caught a bad smell. "What sense does that make? Why in hell would somebody do that?"

"I don't know. Yet. Like I said, I'm just trying a different angle on the thing. Somebody tampering with the evidence before you got there is one of the few explanations that could make us both right."

"Hey, *I* don't need for us both to be right. I know what I know, and that's all there is to it. Plus there were a dozen other guys there that day who saw the same things I did."

"I keep hearing that, but your name is the only one that keeps popping up. Understandable, I suppose, you being the trained cop and all and the one who naturally took charge out there that day. I've talked to a couple of the paramedics who eventually showed up and, like you say, they seem to have seen things pretty much the same as you. But how about some of the

151

other guys riding with you when you first arrived at the scene?"

"Never mind that," Barnstable said firmly. "Bad enough I'm getting yanked through the wringer over this shit. They're a bunch of stand-up guys who all pitched in and tried to do the right thing, just like I did. That's all you need to know. I won't have you prodding and poking at them, too."

I let it ride for the time being. "At any rate, none of you saw anything that might suggest somebody could have been there ahead of you?"

"Anything like what? Mysterious footprints? A conveniently dropped matchbook cover from the Casbah Lounge? The car left the road, tore through a fence, flipped and rolled the hell and gone out into a pasture, for Christ's sake. There was nothing else out there but prairie grass, cow shit, and hoof prints all over the ground. Leastways nothing else that caught anybody's eye. But hell, none of us are exactly Daniel Boone trackers. A gang of A-rab terrorists could have marched through there and I don't know that we'd've been able to tell. . . . Hey. Maybe that's it, you think? One of those fugitive terrorist leaders that the whole world is hunting for is hiding up in the Sandhills and your friends stumbled on him and recognized him and he had to rub them out and make it look like an accident to keep them from exposing him to Interpol or Homeland Security or whatever. How's that for an explanation that allows us both to be right?"

"I don't appreciate the deaths of my friends being made light of."

"*You* don't appreciate?" Barnstable's face reddened. "You think I appreciate the way my name is getting dragged through the mud over this damn deal? One of the little details you might want to remember is that my buddies and I didn't take a lot of time to look for silly-ass clues because we were kinda busy trying to revive your friends and save their lives."

I took a breath, let it out slow. "Yes, I've heard that. I'm grateful for all you did."

"Yeah. You're grateful. Abby Bridger is grateful. That's why all this shit is getting stirred up, all this finger-pointing and second-guessing with me smack in the middle of it. Right?"

"It's nothing personal. All we're after is the truth."

"See? Saying it that way makes it sound like the truth is something different than what I'm telling you." His face flushed an even deeper red. "How can I not take that personal?"

"Calm down," I said. "I meant no offense."

"No, you just thought you could come into my fucking home and call me a liar to my face but you meant no offense." He stood up suddenly, pushing away from the stool. "I think we're done here. Cooperation time is over."

I stood up, too. "I'd just as soon not leave it this way. I don't want you for an enemy."

"You're damned right you don't!" He began crowding me toward the door.

"What if you're wrong?" I said. "Maybe it seems far-fetched, but what if there was something more behind that crash than what seemed so apparent? Do you want to leave that chance just dangling? Don't you want to make sure that *you* know the truth?"

"I already know the truth. The rest of this is just bullshit that I'm sick of listening to."

Halfway across the living room I dug in my heels. "Let me touch on one last thing."

"You can ask. Ain't saying you'll be around for the answer." He'd backed me up a few steps. In his mind's eye he could envision me turning and fleeing the rest of the way; it was what he was used to, and it fueled the bullying instinct in him.

I said, "You and your buddies were out dirt-biking that day, right? On your way home is when you came to the accident

153

scene. Before that, did you happen to be riding anywhere in the vicinity of Pawnee Creek?"

Something changed in Barnstable. His body language shifted, the aggression in his posture suddenly easing off, diminishing. A kind of shrewd glimmer slid into his eyes, replacing the angry fire that had danced there only a moment ago. "What does Pawnee Creek have to do with anything?" he said, almost cautiously.

I told him. About Bomber and Liz planning to stop there and walk back to the old homestead site; about what I'd learned of Cameron Terrell scheduling activities for his visiting guests in the same general area on the same day. My speculation that their paths could have crossed at some point during the course of events and how I wondered if perhaps some observation might have been made that could offer a hint of an explanation for what happened next. "And now," I concluded, "it occurs to me that since you and your group were biking somewhere up that way, too, is there any chance one of you possibly saw something that could tie in?"

"Don't you think we would have said so if there was?"

"Not necessarily. Not if something wasn't being considered in the right context. Same for Terrell's bunch. Sometimes things can appear totally unrelated when in fact they really are, but only if you understand the whole scope of what they're part of."

"Jesus Christ. Riddles now? The more you talk the more you sound like you're off your rocker."

"I make sense to me."

"Okay. If you got *any* sense, then here's something you can take to the bank: The absolute last thing you want to do is go fucking around with Cameron Terrell. You might have Sheriff Knaack buffaloed for the time being—and Old Man Mabry up in Arthur County, too, from what I hear—but you start stepping on Cam Terrell's toes and see how fast they turn on you."

"I guess I didn't realize this Terrell was some kind of untouchable monarch. I thought we were all operating in a free country."

"Who you shitting?" Barnstable sneered. "Ain't nothing in this life or this country that's free. And that's the whole thing—Cam Terrell's got money. Lots of it. And money is power. Your poking around, your snooping for the high and mighty sake of finding 'the truth' don't amount to squat if it means rubbing Terrell the wrong way. Like I said, you step on his toes and you'll see. Things will come back on you so hard you'll think you got trampled under a stampede of Texas longhorns."

"Why would the things I'm trying to find out rub Cameron Terrell the wrong way?"

Barnstable scowled. "I didn't say that. Maybe it will, maybe it won't. How should I know what's gonna go against his grain? All I'm saying is if you do. . . . Hell, you think you don't want *me* for an enemy? You'd better think some more, Illinois. That's all I'm telling you. You'd better think real fucking hard before you push things much farther."

CHAPTER TWENTY

When I got back out to the car, there was a message on my phone. It was from Abby: "Joe, give me a call when you get this, okay?"

I backed out of Clint Barnstable's driveway and started down the street before thumbing the callback on the cell's dial pad.

"No Name Bay General Store, this is Abby."

"Super Sleuth Mobile to Base," I said.

She gave a little laugh. "Joe? You all finished with Clint?"

"More like he decided he was finished with me."

"Not go so hot?"

"So-so. I got a free peep show out of the deal and a lesson on whose toes not to step on in this neck of the woods. Evasive rhetoric and a touch of tap-dancing in between."

"Wait a minute. A free peep show from Clint?"

"God no. You think I'd go out of my way to mention such a thing? He had a guest when I got there . . . *she* gave us the peep show."

"That's better, but I don't think I need to hear any more."

"I tell you, I get a wrong feeling off the guy but I'm not exactly sure why. I can't make up my mind if he's thick-headed and just plain crude, or actually hiding something."

"No one has ever accused Clint of being overly bright. But he's tough and . . . cunning, I guess is the word. He can be dangerous. I think it would be a mistake to underestimate him."

"Okay. That's a mistake I'll try to avoid."

"Listen, the reason I called. . . . First of all, I got in touch with my ex-father-in-law, Cam Terrell. He'll be around the main ranch all afternoon and he agreed to make some time to talk to you if you stop out."

"Good going," I told her. "I know it wasn't easy for you to call him. Thanks."

"It was the least I could do. But listen, before you go out there, there's something else. . . . Remember that collection of Liz's and Uncle Bomber's stuff that I said I had here? From the car and from their cabins? If you recall, we talked about going through those possessions together some time."

"Uh-huh. We still need to do that."

"Well, it's been slow in the store this morning so I went ahead and started some sifting through on my own. I hope you don't mind."

"No, of course not."

"I think I may have found something interesting." A tremor of excitement crept into her voice. "No, make that what was interesting was what I *didn't* find."

"Go on."

"Remember when I said I helped them pack a picnic basket for their lunch that day? Well, I meant that literally. Liz and I put together a real old-fashioned picnic basket. Okay, actually it was some kind of tin or aluminum lunchbox thing painted to *look* like an old-fashioned basket, with a lid that popped on tight instead of a checkered cloth over the top. But anyway, there's no sign of that basket here. Also, Bomber's insulin kit is missing. He had a little ice pack thing for the insulin itself and a small zippered pouch for his needles and test monitor."

"I know it well," I said. "Chances are it was in the basket, don't you think?"

"Perhaps. But there's more. I don't know if Liz was much of a shutterbug back in Illinois, but all the while she was out here she was snapping pictures of everything."

"Uh-huh. She bought one of those new digital cameras especially for the trip."

"Well, there's no sign of that either. I called both Sheriff Mabry and Toby's Towing and asked them to double-check and see if they had any items that they forgot to return. Neither of them did."

"You thinking theft?"

"I'm not sure what to think."

"The camera was new and expensive. It might have tempted somebody to pocket it after the crash. The people were dead, they didn't need it anymore. Somebody with loose morals might be able to justify it to themselves as a minor offense that nobody was likely to take notice of or make too big a fuss over even if they did."

"And the picnic basket?"

"Doesn't make much sense. Wouldn't seem worth either the bother or the risk."

The excitement in Abby's voice grew edgier. "Okay, I *am* thinking something. I bet you are, too, and it's not as simple as somebody with sticky fingers. If Liz and Uncle Bomber encountered something while they were back checking out the homestead site—something that alarmed or threatened them in some way, like you suggested before—then they could have dropped the picnic basket and the camera because they were in a big hurry to get away from there. Maybe those things didn't get returned to me because they weren't part of the car wreck at all. Maybe they're still somewhere back along Pawnee Creek."

I had to be careful not to jump to any conclusions. But more and more things seemed to be indicating the stop at the homestead site as the pivot point for the events of that day, a point from which the fatal car crash and the rest all culminated. "Could be," I said, keeping my voice level, my tone guarded.

"Just could be. . . ."

I wanted some alone time to roll things over in my mind. To sort and ponder, prepare for my meeting with Cameron Terrell. I had a hunch the old rancher would turn out to be wily and somewhat guarded, if for no other reason than because of the militia movement he was spearheading. I meant to be sure and make the most out of however much time he allotted me.

It was getting close to noon and I was hungry. But even a quiet corner of a busy restaurant didn't suit my mood. I opted instead for the drive-through window of the local A&W where I ordered a giant root beer and a Coney dog smothered in mustard. With these purchases riding shotgun, I drove west out of town and then took the bypass up to the south side of the lake. This put me on Route 26 where I turned west again. I remembered this stretch from traveling it in Bomber's funeral procession on the way to and from his burial plot at Ash Hollow. In particular I recalled a scenic overlook we had gone by, a high swell of grass and sand overlooking an unobstructed expanse of the lake.

There was a gravel drive angling up and a turnaround oval at the summit of the overlook. When I got there I was relieved to see I had the place to myself. I piled out of the Accord and took a seat on its flat trunk, sandwich and drink balanced next to me. The sky was clear cobalt straight overhead but away off to the west a bank of storm clouds appeared to be brewing just above the rim of the horizon. A soft, warm breeze was blowing.

Pulling the notebook from my pocket, I scanned through it as I began to eat my lunch. While I chewed the food I also did some chewing on the things I knew, the things I didn't know, and the things I only suspected. I added a few notations as I flipped the pages but unfortunately I had nothing to add in the category of hard facts. Before I got too discouraged by how anemic the list under that heading really was, I put the notebook away.

The Coney dog was passable, but not in a league with the Chicago-style red hots I frequently lunched on back home. A food staple that, from what I'd noted so far, wasn't available in these parts. Bomber, I recalled with a fleeting smile, had been even more of a hot dog freak than me. I wondered how he survived the withdrawal pangs during his prolonged visits out here?

Thinking of my absent friend caused a wave of sadness and melancholy to drift over me and settle like a weight on my shoulders.

This was certainly more than just another "case" to me, yet at the same time the mechanics of delving into it involved all the familiar sorting-out/grinding-down steps that were essentially no different than a hundred other investigations I'd conducted. This time, though, it all seemed so agonizingly slow.

How long had I been doing this? How often had I back-tracked on the moves and patterns and interactions of other people's lives, seeking some answer, some proof, some . . . resolution?

Jan had claimed I was always looking for something I could salvage out of digging into the problems of others. What else had I accomplished with my life's work? Was that the only difference I'd managed to make—bandaging and patching a few incidental bruises left on those weak enough or unsuspecting enough to fall prey to the predators and victimizers who stalk our society?

"You'd better think real fucking hard," Clint Barnstable had warned.

What had I managed to salvage out of my own problems, my own life? Looking back on fifty. A failed marriage and numerous other failed romantic relationships, including, it appeared, the most recent and most sustained one. No offspring, no living kin, no property or possessions of any note . . . and no close friends. Not anymore. Nobody who gave much of a damn if I stayed or went or took my own turn around that twisty, sneaky curve you don't come back from.

Jan had also said I was in denial. Was that what was really behind this probe into the crash that killed Liz and Bomber? Was I simply grasping at . . . something . . . some straw, some wisp of *hope* that I could prove wrongdoing as a means to once again set square a small block of the rubble left in the wake of my friends' passing? Was I truly interested in the justice I kept telling myself I was after? Or was I merely attempting a kind of pathetic self-validation, demonstrating that if I couldn't bring back the dead then I could at least confirm my pain and mourning by shaking the living hell out of what remained?

I didn't have a way to explain this sudden wash of depression and self-doubt, these questions of justification and motivation. I'd never felt anything like it before in the middle of an investigation, not even ones that had gotten bogged down. But then I'd never had so much personal emotion wrapped up in an investigation before.

I set aside the half-eaten Coney dog and washed home the last bite I'd taken with a hit of the root beer. It made a sweet, gummy lump going down my throat. Sharp contrast to the bitterness that otherwise seemed to want to envelope me, squeeze me in its grip.

I gazed out over the lake. Between it and where I sat, the land fell away in rolling hills of grassy sand—some sharp-edged, some softly blunted. In the recesses between the hills, rain- and wind-scoured gullies twisted jaggedly.

Here and there, even on some of the most rugged points, I could see calmly grazing cattle. A reminder of what this rugged, beautiful, untamed land had been before the roads and the man-made lake and the rest. And yet, even for all the incursions of man, the land out here was not truly tamed. You didn't have to spend very much time here to get the sense that everything was *of* the land, that the land ruled—not the other way around, like in a city where the buildings and streets and people and clutter obscured the land, even blocking out huge chunks of the sky, until all the scurrying little pissant humans were allowed to feel that *they* mattered the most.

Contemplating this, I began to feel soothed almost as abruptly as I'd grown gloomy.

The green of the grass, the impossible pure blue of the water rimmed by beaches of snow white sand. . . . Focusing on this, drinking it in, you'd have to be dead of soul not to find it soothing. The pace of everything seemed slower out here. Steady and purposeful to be sure, and fueled by a kind of rawboned energy, but without the hectic frenzy of a city.

I'd been raised in the country on my grandparents' Wisconsin dairy farm after my mother and father were taken in their own fatal car wreck. As a youth I couldn't wait to get away. But now, sitting in this hot breeze under a Nebraska sun, I felt a pang of nostalgia for that abandoned way of life deeper than any I'd ever known before.

I wondered if Bomber had experienced a similar kind of feeling in this setting, this barely tamed land. If that explained why he returned here more frequently in his later years, why he'd selected a cemetery plot here. Even before this last visit he had talked increasingly about coming back and settling for good. I'd scoffed at such talk. But I wouldn't have scoffed now. Now it made more sense.

I was looking for answers to a specific thing, I reminded myself. But if I didn't watch out I might find answers to questions inside me that I hadn't even known existed.

What I knew, what I didn't know, what I suspected. . . . More questions than answers. More conjecture than proof.

But once again it was enough. Enough to drive away the doubts and melancholy and second-guessing; enough to convince me that what I was involved in had worth, that it needed to be continued.

That *I* needed to continue . . . to keep on doing what I do.

Chapter Twenty-One

I was driving north on Highway 61, several miles past the lake, not quite to the Arthur County line, when an incoming call set my cell phone to chirping. My guess was that it would be Abby. She had waffled back and forth a half dozen times on whether or not to accompany me to the Standing T Ranch, finally deciding that going there with no chance of seeing her son would only be a downer for her and I would have just as good of luck talking to her former father-in-law by myself. I half-smiled as I reached for the phone, suspecting she'd probably changed her mind yet again and was calling to see if I was too far to turn around and come back for her.

The voice that spoke on the other end of the connection after I picked up and said hello was female all right, but it was hardly Abby Bridger.

"Hannibal, you no good cad, I have a heartsick star reporter on my hands and I want you to know I am holding your sorry ass directly responsible for any downturn in either the quality or quantity of her work in the weeks to come."

I had no trouble recognizing the voice. Cybill Deming, Jan's editor at *C2C Magazine,* was a brassy, mature beauty with a razor-sharp mind and an equally cutting vocabulary that could run the gamut from high articulation to gutter-low vulgarities.

"What are you going to do, Cybill," I said, letting the half-smile stay lazily in place even though she couldn't see it, "charge me as an accomplice for misspellings? Sue me for influencing lousy grammatical composition?"

"That statement right there could be my first piece of evidence. I believe it to be pretty lousy grammatical composition in and of itself."

"You can quote me. . . . No, wait a minute, you just did."

"Goddamnit, Hannibal, what the hell's going on with you and Jan?"

"You've apparently been talking to the lady," I said. "You tell me—what spin did she give you?"

"What I could gather, amidst the sobbing and wailing, is that everything that used to be so hunky-dory between you two has gradually been turning to crap, she's gone and made it worse with a foolish indiscretion, and you're so busy tilting at windmills that you won't take time for even a token effort at trying to solve your differences."

"Not a bad summation," I allowed.

"Is that all you've got to say?"

"What do you want me to say, Cybill?" I said, growing irritated. I realized she was only concerned for a friend, trying to do a good thing, but that didn't make getting picked at like I was the scab on the sore any less annoying. "I'm not crazy about the turn things have taken either, and I don't have a magic answer any more than Jan does—but I know enough to be pretty damn certain that the answer wasn't going to be found by hopping into the sack with somebody else!"

"No," Cybill said, "instead your answer is to hop even deeper into the middle of a 'case' that may not even be a case at all."

I'd crossed the Arthur County line and was nearing the spot where Bomber's car had left the road and gone into the series of deadly flips and rolls. It wasn't a good time for her to take a shot at my "case."

"That's Jan talking, not you," I fired back. "You don't know enough about what I'm doing to have the right to comment on it one way or another."

She sighed, then surprised me by relenting a little. "I suppose I don't. . . . Where are you at, anyway?"

"West central Nebraska. On the edge of the panhandle."

"Good Christ, Hannibal, that ought to be enough to settle it right there. In all of recorded history nothing of any real consequence has ever happened in Nebraska."

We talked a while longer but it kept coming back around to the same refrain. . . . Her trying to convince me to be more compassionate and forgiving, me trying to explain that I didn't think I had it in me.

Finally, in exasperation, she said, "Look, Joe, do you love Jan or not?"

I thought about it several beats, then answered, "I did love her. A great deal."

"Past tense, Joe?"

Hell, it wasn't an admission I liked making any better than she liked hearing it. But all I could add was, "It's the best I've got to give, Cybill."

CHAPTER TWENTY-TWO

Cameron Terrell was waiting for me on the open flagstone front porch of his sprawling ranch house. He was seated with another man at an umbrella table off toward one end of the flagstones. They were drinking dark amber liquid from tall, ice-filled glasses.

Terrell rose to his feet as I parked my Honda at the edge of a narrow strip of front lawn, cut the engine and got out. The other man remained seated. A very fit-looking sixtyish, Terrell was; tall and trim, dressed in immaculately polished cowboy boots, rust-brown Levis, and a long-sleeved white shirt buttoned at the wrists and fastened at the throat by a string tie held with an ornate silver clasp. His oversized belt buckle was also silver, engraved with the Standing-T-brand emblem of his ranch. He had a Lincolnesque face, long and narrow and quasi-homely, topped by wavy silver hair combed straight back from a classic widow's peak. He came over to the edge of the flagstones as I crossed the strip of lawn.

"Mr. Cameron," I said, reaching to shake his hand, "I appreciate you agreeing to spare me a few minutes of your time."

His grip, not surprisingly, was confident and strong. "Happy to oblige a friend of Abby's. Her marriage to my son ended rather nastily, as you may be aware, but she's still the mother to my grandson and I've never harbored any ill feelings toward her. I hope I can be of some help to your cause."

You might look into his washed-out blue eyes and think you

saw a kind of mellowed weariness there. But if you looked closer you realized that the pale blue actually pulsed with a cold fire, a subdued yet steady flame radiating aggressive energy.

"I expect Abby gave you some background on why I wanted to talk to you?"

"She did brief me, yes."

The military-like use of the word "brief" sounded out of place, in spite of my awareness of the militia operation he spearheaded. Since turning at the roadside cattle gate and passing under the tall arch that bore the Standing-T-brand emblem in welded twists of iron, I had seen no sign of activity other than that associated to a working ranch. Cattle, horses, corrals, pens and loading chutes, outbuildings . . . all orderly arranged over a broad expanse of rolling, treeless Sandhills terrain. One of the buildings situated downslope from the main house was a long, single-storied structure that I took to be a bunkhouse. And I'd caught sight of a half dozen wrangler types going about various chores, all similarly clad in cowboy hats, boots, workshirts and faded jeans.

The only incongruous touch I'd spotted as I came up the long graveled drive from the road was a pattern of carefully manicured hedges that had been planted at the rear of the main house. Their lushness and rich green foliage stood in sharp contrast to the duller green and faded gold of the yucca and stubborn, durable prairie grasses that grew naturally out of the sandy soil of the surrounding land.

As far as the militia thing, it wasn't like I was expecting to see tanks or armored personnel carriers or stacks of ordnance draped in camouflaged tarps. Not that I had any real clear idea what to expect as far as the day-to-day workings of such an outfit. But from what limited knowledge I did have of paramilitary groups, my impression was that most of them tended to be somewhat secretive; and considering Cam Terrell owned vast properties in at least three different states, it seemed unlikely he'd be staging an overt display right here in his backyard.

Jerking a thumb toward the umbrella table, Terrell said, "I've got some good sun tea ready over there, and ice and fresh-sliced lemons. Looks like a storm is moving in to cut short the afternoon so I was sitting a spell and enjoying some while the weather held. Sun tea should always be taken out of doors. Won't you join me while we have our talk?"

"Sounds good," I said.

Overhead, the bright sky was indeed dimming and off to the west the bank of gray-black clouds I'd seen simmering on the horizon earlier was skimming closer at a steady pace. The air had turned still and hot for the time being, but soon a cold wind would build and then the storm wouldn't be far behind.

The table was a heavy pebbled glass top supported by sturdy wrought-iron legs. It was set with a large tray upon which rested several upturned glasses, in addition to the two Terrell and his companion already had in use. Also sharing the tray were the aforementioned lemon slices in a silver bowl along with an insulated bucket of shaved ice. Next to all of this stood the rich amber brew of tea in an old-fashioned gallon pickle jar with a screw-on lid.

Terrell's tablemate remained sitting as we approached. He had American-Indian features, his bronze, high-cheekboned face one of indeterminable age. His build was muscular—the kind of long, ropey muscles that house both raw strength as well as speed and flexibility. His hair was cropped to a military buzzcut and beneath that his dark eyes were flat and emotionless yet somehow conveyed a sense of danger.

I didn't have to study this specimen very long to decide he didn't fit the wrangler category nor any other you were likely to find as part of a standard ranching operation. His Indian ancestry gave it a slightly different spin, but I'd seen his kind too many times before to miss the signs. He was a hired thug, plain and simple. A hundred or so years earlier he might have been called a "hired gun," brought in to give a cattle baron like Terrell an edge over other outfits on the range. One and the same. Naturally I found myself wondering why Cameron Terrell—a wealthy modern-day businessman, and a legitimate one by all reports—needed to have a gunslinger hanging around.

"This is Mr. Thunderbringer. William. An associate of mine," Terrell introduced him. "On many fronts, he has become my trusted right arm."

Thunderbringer still did not stand, and made no move to shake hands. Neither did I. We were reading each other loud and clear.

"Jap car," he said.

"How's that?"

"Car of yours. Fucking Jap piece of shit. Don't you believe in supporting American products and American workers?"

"I believe in supporting myself," I said. "That means I drive what I can afford. If it makes you feel better, though, my goal is to one day buy a big-ass, gas-guzzling Humvee. Then I can support American workers *and* the Arab oil potentates. Still keep my money in circulation on the global market, but the Japs can go fuck themselves. How's that?"

His expression didn't change. His eyes were like two shards of black glass. "And a smart-ass to boot. You're a real piece of work, aren't you?"

"That's enough." Terrell barely raised his voice, but the words cut sharp. "William, neither your presence nor, especially, your attitude will be needed for this discussion. I suggest you go make yourself useful somewhere else."

Thunderbringer didn't move right away. But then, silently, unhurriedly, without looking my way again, he got up and walked into the house.

After he was gone, Terrell gestured me into one of the chairs that circled the table. He made no comment on the exchange that had just taken place. As if it never happened.

We took seats across from one another. I upturned a fresh glass, spooned in ice and a lemon slice. Terrell unscrewed the cap off the jar and poured from it with a practiced flourish, never spilling a drop as he filled my glass and topped off his own. After re-capping the brew and taking a sip from his glass, he sat back in his chair and said, "So. I understand you're a private detective."

"That's right."

"Needless to say we don't get many of your profession out in these parts."

"No, I don't suppose so."

"I further understand that the two victims of the recent auto accident in the southern part of the county—Abby's uncle and his lady companion—were close personal friends of yours."

"Yes, they were."

"My condolences on your loss. I know how hard it can be."

"The loss is tough. But almost as tough, as it turns out, is trying to deal with certain allegations that have cropped up in the aftermath."

"I'm not sure I follow you."

"The crash that killed my friends is being credited to their driving at an excessive rate of speed while consuming alcohol and, putting it more delicately than has generally been the case, sexually fondling each other."

Terrell's face pulled into a mildly distasteful grimace. "Yes, I can see where it would be disturbing to hear such a report. And those are the kind of lurid details, unfortunately, that people are all too eager to spread around. I pride myself on maintaining a strict rule against participating in gossip yet I have to admit that even I have overheard some rather graphic accounts of your friends' reckless behavior."

"*Alleged* behavior," I was quick to counter. "The thing is, see, neither the relationship between the two victims nor their personal habits can be made to fit those actions, not in the wildest imagination of anyone who knew them. It's not an issue of moral judgment or being embarrassed for them or disappointed they might have been acting that way. It's simply a rock-solid, unshakable belief that they *wouldn't*. It's so incomprehensible that something about it has to be . . . well, just flat wrong."

Smiling indulgently, Terrell said, "Your loyalty to your friends' memory is commendable."

"It's more than blind loyalty. As far as I'm concerned, it's a cold certainty."

"But isn't it true that the first responders to the accident—the men whose findings and observations became the basis for these details, these 'allegations' that you find so troubling—were all credible, responsible individuals? How could their collective accounts be so badly mistaken?"

"I don't know. Yet. That's what I'm trying to sort out."

"I would have thought that a trained detective would be more influenced by the facts. Facts that other trained professionals have already gathered and seem perfectly willing to accept."

"I have all the respect in the world for facts. And I mean no *dis*respect to the emergency responders or either of the two county sheriffs who became involved. But none of them knew Bomber and Liz like I did, and that means none of them can share my gut feeling, which I've also learned to respect. I know, too, that facts—or what appear to be facts—can sometimes be manipulated. That leaves me with a hell of a lot more questions than answers, but it's also what leaves me a far cry from being satisfied with what others are ready to accept."

For a minute Terrell looked as if he wanted to continue the

debate. But then something changed his mind and he shifted gears. "You seem to have set a difficult task for yourself," he said. "But if tenacity and conviction can carry the day then you also clearly have the tools for seeing the job through. What is unclear, however, is where I fit into any of this. Why the visit here? How is it you think I can be of help?"

So I explained to him about Liz and Bomber's planned stop at the homestead site near the banks of Pawnee Creek on the day they died. And how I'd learned he had a group of visitors engaged in activities in the same general area on that same day, leaving me to wonder if an observation or chance encounter might have taken place that could provide some insight on the actions or behavior of my friends in those hours before their deaths. "Admittedly it's a long shot," I concluded. "But like I said a minute ago, right now I have a lot more questions than answers so I have to pursue even the slimmest chance for a lead until I hopefully turn up something more solid to grab hold of."

Terrell listened with no expression on his face, neither commenting nor questioning as I spoke. When I finished, he took an unhurried drink of tea then said, "Your information about my being responsible for certain activities staged on the property bordering Pawnee Creek that day is accurate." He paused, studying me closely for a long moment as if trying to decide something about me. Whatever decision he reached, it was enough for him to continue. "I must admit to a bit of a fabrication, however, as to the exact nature of those activities. If your detective skills are anywhere near on a par with your determination then I assume you must have learned by now that, in addition to my ranching and other business interests, over recent years I have formed a small, dedicated paramilitary organization."

"RBR," I said. "Remember and Be Ready."

He nodded. "Precisely. And while my dedication to this cause is no secret and certainly no threat to any right-thinking American, I nevertheless realize that the average citizen may be made somewhat uncomfortable by the whole concept." Smiling thinly, he added, "My wealth and my business successes are probably the only things that keep me from being treated like some sort of crackpot."

"Money definitely buys more than just the things they sell in stores," I said.

He seemed to ponder the remark, gazing off at the approaching storm. "Yes," he said distractedly, his eyes narrowing as if he were trying to see through the billowing dark clouds, somewhere beyond them. "But, believe me, there is so, so much that it *can't* buy, as well."

I wasn't sure how to reply to the curious comment. So I said nothing. Took a drink of my tea, waited.

"At any rate," Terrell said, turning back to me, "on the day in question, you see, it wasn't actually a group of dilettante businessmen I had engaged in activities along Pawnee Creek. It was a deployment of RBR militiamen on training maneuvers. Some of it involved live ammunition. You can understand why I didn't want a party of Vic Faber's canoers floating through in the middle of things. It was simpler to tell Faber the story about a group of out-of-town sportsmen than to raise unnecessary alarms in the community about what was truly taking place."

"Reasonable enough, I guess. But that doesn't change the questions I came here with. No matter the makeup of the group that was out there that day, I'm still interested in whether or not any of them might have had some kind of contact with my friends."

"No, they didn't." The answer came too quick, too positive. No shred of doubt, no allowance for a challenge.

I pushed one at him anyway. "You're absolutely sure?"

"I wouldn't have said so if I wasn't," he responded rather

stiffly. "In the first place, I am quite familiar with the homestead site you mentioned—the maneuvers my men were performing were taking place well east of there. If your friends went from the highway to the homestead, that wouldn't have taken them far enough to have come within proximity of our exercises. In the second place, I was personally present during much of the day, in an observatory role. So I can say firsthand what did or did not occur. In the third and final place, should anything— anything—unexpected or out of the ordinary have happened, even after I took my leave, my men would not have hesitated reporting it. I have complete confidence in that."

By the time he'd finished speaking his eyes were boring into me with a cold, brittle stare that dared me to raise any more questions as far as the accuracy of his statements. And at the very same time, listening to him, I felt my hackles raise with the intuitive certainty that there was definitely something *wrong* about this man—about his phony hospitality, about his thug companion, about the story he was trying to feed me. It was the same feeling I'd gotten from talking to Clint Barnstable. *"The absolute last thing you want to do is go fucking around with Cameron Terrell,"* I remembered him telling me.

I swirled some ice in my glass and clenched my teeth to keep from saying something I might regret. Willed myself to calm down, take it easy; not push a confrontation until I was on surer footing.

After a minute, I blew out a soft pop of the breath I'd been holding. "Well then. I guess that makes another dead end. Another possible lead I can scratch off."

Terrell's mouth slanted in a faintly condescending smile. "Even discovering where the answer cannot be found still amounts to progress of a sort," he said.

"By that criteria, I'm making progress hand over fist then. But it's progress that's getting me nowhere. I feel more like the hunter shooting ducks on average."

"How's that?"

"Hunter draws down on a duck one day, his first shot is six inches to the left. He takes aim again, this time shoots six inches to the right. On average he scored a direct hit. But that doesn't stop the bird from flying away safe and unharmed."

Terrell chuckled heartily. "I like that. I'll have to remember it."

I tipped my glass high, chugged what was left in it. Pushed back my chair and stood up. The wind was starting to roll in now, a sudden, almost chilling rush of coolness. Dust clouds billowed across the yard, carrying grains of sand that stung the sides of our faces. Tumbleweeds began dancing down over the low, grassy hills.

"Here it comes!" Terrell announced almost cheerfully. He stood also, his carefully combed head of hair trailing out like bony silver fingers reaching away from his face. He walked with me as I started toward my car.

Behind us, Thunderbringer emerged from the house. He planted his feet wide, hands on hips, and tipped his face skyward to frown up at the churning clouds. As if daring them to rain on him.

At the edge of the flagstones I paused and turned to Terrell. "Thanks again for sparing me a few minutes of your time," I said. "If I may, I have one final question."

"What is it?"

Down by the outbuildings wranglers were scrambling to shut doors and shutter windows and otherwise batten down loose items. In the corral a beautiful black mare was pacing back and forth along the fence, whinnying and snorting anxiously.

"Obviously not today," I said, gesturing to indicate the rapidly descending storm, "but first chance I get, if it's okay with you, I'd like to do some poking around that old homestead site where my friends visited. Another long shot, but who knows, one of these times I'm bound to—"

"Mr. Hannibal," Terrell interrupted, "I have gone out of my way to be courteous and candid and have given you my personal assurance that your friends encountered nothing on my property that day to facilitate their demise. Now you insult me by refusing to find that assurance sufficient."

"That was not my intent. I meant no offense."

"Nevertheless, the answer is no. I do not want anyone else traipsing around on my property and continuing to try and drag my name into this . . . this *whatever* it is that you and my former daughter-in-law are so hell bent on pursuing. You can't even be one hundred percent sure your friends actually went back to that spot on the day in question."

"If you allow me to check it out, maybe that's one of the things I can determine."

Thunder rolled across the blackening sky.

"Here is my final consideration to you, sir," Terrell said, shaking a forefinger in my face. "When the weather clears tomorrow, I'll have some of my wranglers walk that ground. They know the land and I dare say they're better outdoorsmen than you can profess to be. If your friends left any trace, my men will spot it. Anything of note will be reported to you. And if it's personal effects you're worried about, I guarantee should the missing camera or anything else of value turn up they will be promptly handed over."

Chapter Twenty-Three

The rain hit just as I reached the end of the Standing T's long driveway. Fat, thumping drops at first, then wind-whipped sheets slashing across in front of me once I'd turned onto the blacktop road. The intensity had abated somewhat by the time I passed through the town of Arthur, but a steady downpour continued as I crossed Pawnee Creek and got closer to the lake.

As I drove I replayed in my mind the conversation I'd just had with Cameron Terrell and also my earlier one with Clint Barnstable, comparing the two, trying to put my finger more specifically on what it was about each that had set off my intuitive alarm bells. Was there a commonality? A connection? Why had Barnstable warned me so strongly about going up against Terrell? Why did Terrell have a thug like Thunderbringer hanging around? Was any of it relatable to what had happened to Bomber and Liz, or did it all have to do with entirely different agendas?

More questions. Always more questions. And no damn answers.

As I rolled down on No Name Bay my attention was quickly refocused by the two cars pulled up alongside Abby's store. One was a Keith County cruiser, the other an unmarked sedan with state police license plates. Underneath the overhang of the front porch, an anxious-looking Abby stood hemmed in by the four passengers from the vehicles. Sheriff Gene Knaack and a uniformed Clint Barnstable crowded close on her right side, a man and a woman in civilian clothes—state cop detectives, unless I missed my guess—were giving her only slightly more breathing room on her left.

I steered over to my own cabin, but I had an uncomfortable hunch that whatever the collection of cops were here for it was going to end up involving me.

It didn't take long to find out I was right.

As I piled out of the Honda, Abby stepped to the edge of the store's porch and called to me. "Joe? Joe, you need to come over here for a minute."

Clint Barnstable moved up to stand just past her shoulder, glaring at me, as if daring me to try and make a run for it.

I hesitated, thinking about the 9mm hideaway piece concealed illegally in my right boot—illegal because the Illinois carry permit for it didn't mean squat here in Nebraska. The thought of sashaying into the midst of four cops with it on my person was a bit unnerving. But hell, I told myself, it wasn't like they were walking around with radar or built-in metal detectors or something. Besides, I didn't have much choice; it wasn't like I could shuck the gun out of the boot and leave it behind in the car, not with all of them standing right there watching.

I puddle-hopped through the rain and ducked in under the overhang. As I did so, I pushed purposely close to Barnstable and made sure I dripped a generous deposit of fresh rainwater on him. He jumped back a step and a half, brushing the beads of water off his uniform front. His face reddened and his glare got fiercer still.

"Pardon me all to hell," I muttered.

"Joe," Abby said quickly, stepping between us and directing my attention to the others on porch. "You already know Sheriff Knaack and Deputy Barnstable. These," she added, gesturing, "are detectives from the state police."

"I'm Detective Lyle," said the male half of the team, giving a curt nod then jerking a thumb in the direction of the woman, "and this is my partner Detective Sterling. We'd like to ask you some routine questions."

The guy was average height and pot-bellied, nudging fifty, with a potato lump of a nose shot through by fine purplish veins indicating a history of being too friendly with the bottle. He slouched inside his baggy green suit and there were yellowish splotches on his tie that could have been egg stains from that morning's breakfast or mustard from some other meal, long past. In sharp contrast, his partner was trim and smartly dressed, thirtyish, honey-blond hair framing an attractive cheerleader-grown-up face with alert, intelligent eyes. The pleated slacks and torso-hugging salmon pullover she wore under a chocolate blazer revealed that the cheerleader theme was being maintained rather well in the body department, too.

"Sure," I said, responding to Detective Lyle. "What's going on?"

"We understand that last night you were involved in an altercation with one Ronald Wilton."

"The 'Ronnie' who was staying with his wife in cabin three? Yeah, I had a run-in with him."

"How did that come about?"

"He and his wife got into a fight inside the cabin. At some point he either struck or attempted to strike her. She ran out and locked herself in their pickup truck to get away from him. She didn't have the keys to actually drive off so it put them at a kind of stalemate with each other. He was stomping around outside the truck shouting at her, cussing her, being verbally abusive and threatening to do worse if he got his hands on her."

"But you intervened before that could happen?"

"Eventually, yes."

"Why'd you do that? What made you figure it was any of your business?"

"I was having dinner at the tavern next door with Miss Bridger here," I explained. "She got a phone call informing her there was a disturbance over at the cabins. I assume you know that, along with her mother, she owns and runs this store and lodge. That made the disturbance legitimately her business, I think you'll agree. And, like I said, I was with her. It seemed appropriate to come along and see if I could lend a hand."

"And the way you ended up doing that," said Detective Sterling, "was by knocking Wilton to the ground?"

"When it got to the point where he didn't leave me much choice," I said. "After he ignored several requests to settle down. After he continued to be verbally abusive to his wife, as well as to Miss Bridger. And after he physically threatened Miss Bridger."

"And also after he threw the first punch at Mr. Hannibal," Abby interjected. "A half dozen or more, as a matter of fact, before Joe hit back."

"Please, Miss Bridger," Detective Sterling said, politely but firmly. "You've had the chance to give your statement. Let's keep this between us and Mr. Hannibal."

"How many times you hit the guy?" Lyle asked me.

"Twice."

He arched a brow somewhat skeptically. "Twice? We heard only once."

"My recollection is that it was twice. A backhand to sort of set him up after he missed with an uppercut, then a jab to his solar plexus. The solar plexus shot put him down."

"You sound like you know something about hitting people."

I shrugged. "My job, you get in situations that turn a little rough sometimes. I've been at it enough years to have picked up a few things."

"You're a PI, that right?"

"Right."

"You got something that says so?"

"I'm not covered for Nebraska. I'm only licensed in Illinois and Wisconsin."

"I understand. Can you show me something that says that much?"

I took out my billfold, withdrew the laminated wallet-size of my Illinois license and handed it to him. He gave it a quick study, flashed it for his partner to see, then handed it back. As I reached to retrieve it his eyes were watching my hands, giving them a close looking over.

"Can you tell me what this is all about?" I asked.

Lyle ignored my question and came back with one of his own. "Where were you about nine-thirty this morning?"

"On my way into town. Ogallala."

"Can anybody back that up?"

"I visited with Miss Bridger inside her store here for a while just before I left."

"And where did you go in Ogallala?"

I inclined my head in the direction of Clint Barnstable. "I paid a visit to Deputy Barnstable at his home."

"You go there straight away?"

"Uh-huh."

"So you would've got there what time . . . a little before ten?"

"Right at ten. That was the time we'd agreed on for me to stop by."

"And what was the purpose of your visit there?"

"It had nothing to do with Ron Wilton, if that's what you're interested in," I said. "What's this all about, anyway?"

Lyle showed a thin, impatient smile. "I don't know how they do things where you come from, Mr. Hannibal, but the way we like to work it around here is to leave the question-asking to the police, 'kay?"

"Fine. Ask all the questions you want then. Just don't expect me to answer any more until you're ready to either tell me what's going on or charge me with something."

Lyle's tenuous smile started to curl into a sneer but before he could say anything Sheriff Knaack spoke up. "What this is about is the fact that within a few hours of leaving here this morning, Ron Wilton was attacked and severely beaten. It happened in the town of Benkelman, south of here, nearly to the Kansas border. Wilton remains in the hospital there, in a coma, and these detectives are trying to find out who did it and why."

So this interrogation of me and anyone else associated to the trouble last night made sense, then. Checking out the possibility of a lingering grudge. Maybe some payback getting delivered. Even though any payback was more logically owed the other way around.

"How about the wife?" I said.

"She's okay," Knaack answered. "They'd stopped at a little convenience store/gas station so she could use the restroom. She didn't see whoever jumped her husband. It happened that fast, while she was inside. Nobody else saw anything, either—at least nobody who's stepping forward. Way it looks, Wilton was clubbed while he was sitting in his truck waiting, then dragged out and stomped."

"If you two are done with this friendly little tête-à-tête, I'd like to get back to my questioning," Detective Lyle cut in, his tone chilly. "And for the record, Sheriff, I don't appreciate having my interrogation stepped on that way."

"The way I saw it," Knaack replied, "your so-called interrogation was stacking up to little more than badgering. You already had testimony covering this man's whereabouts at the time of Wilton's attack, both from Miss Bridger and my deputy. Given the way they interfaced with one another between the hours of nine and ten, it's clear none of them could possibly fit the time frame you've established for the assault clear down in

Benkelman."

"Yeah, I noticed that . . . how conveniently they've got each other's asses covered for the critical time period."

"Dick!" his partner said quickly, admonishingly.

"Well, it's true, ain't it?" Lyle said stubbornly. "Awfully damn tidy, if you ask me—the three principals who had a run-in with the victim last night just happen to have 'interfaced' with each other this morning in a way that cross-alibis all of them for the period Wilton was getting the shit stomped out of him."

"You calling me a liar?" said Clint Barnstable, taking a step forward. Knaack extended an arm across his chest, holding him back.

But Lyle wasn't ready to back down. "If the shit-kicking boot fits, wear it, that's what I'm saying. We've all heard the stories about your roughshod ways, Barnstable. How you think you're some kind of 'town tamer' from the Old West. Well you might get away with that kind of crap in your own backyard, but that's where you'd damn well better keep it or one of these days it's gonna be your turn to get tamed!"

"Dick, that's enough. I mean it!" said Detective Sterling, stepping in front of him and literally getting in his face.

"Let the old rum pot go," Barnstable taunted. "I'd like to see him try and 'tame' me."

"Goddamnit, that's enough *everybody!*" Sheriff Knaack said in a voice loud enough to shake the shingles on the porch overhang under which we stood. Everybody froze and suddenly the only sound was the steady drizzle of the rain coming down.

After a minute, Knaack spoke again. "Well we sure let this deteriorate into a sad demonstration, didn't we? As police officers, every one of us here ought to be ashamed." His gaze found Abby. "Abby, you have my personal apologies for bringing this to your doorstep." Then it was my turn. "Hannibal . . . don't think anything I just said cuts you extra slack in any way, shape, or form. I may not figure you're good for Ron Wilton's beating, but that don't mean I'm comfortable with whatever else you're up to. Not by a damn sight. You'd better know I'll be keeping an eye on you."

I nodded. "Clear enough."

"All right, then. As for the rest of us . . . we'll take this back to my office. There's obviously some air-clearing to be done. But I think we've entertained the public with enough of our dirty laundry for one day."

CHAPTER TWENTY-FOUR

"Well," I said as we watched the police cars roll away, "that was entertaining."

"Bizarre, is what it was," said Abby. She stood hugging herself, cold from the rain. "For a minute there, I thought Clint and that one detective were going to really go at it."

I shrugged. "Not uncommon for jurisdictional friction to flare between state and county cops. But I'd say those two—Barnstable and Lyle—have some kind of history between them that goes back farther than the little bit of pawing and growling we just saw here."

"Whatever. I guess it's Sheriff Gene's problem to sort out. And as far as the couple from cabin three. . . . Jeez, you think there's any chance what happened to the guy *could* be connected to the trouble here last night?"

"I don't see how. Based on the taste we got of Ronnie's sweet temperament, I'd say it's a pretty safe bet that he gets crossways of people on a regular basis. Considering he likely wasn't in too good a mood when he bailed out of here this morning, could be he simply mouthed off the wrong person and got his clocked cleaned. For that matter, he could even have run into somebody from some past encounter who decided to settle an old score."

"I guess. But settling a score, maybe rapping the jerk on his jaw a couple times would be one thing; stomping him into a coma is a whole different matter."

There really wasn't anything to say to that. However, it was no trouble coming up with a response to the next thing out of Abby's mouth—an invitation to step inside for a cup of coffee. I accepted without hesitation and soon we were seated once again in the store's little snack area, a pair of steaming mugs planted between us.

Naturally it didn't take long for our conversation to turn to the subject of my visit to Cameron Terrell at his ranch. I told Abby how it had gone, up to and including my sense that there was something hinky about the man.

"Hinky?" she said.

"You know . . . bent. Wrong. Something not on the up-and-up."

"Crooked, in other words."

"Maybe." I made a face. "That might be too strong, saying he's actually involved in something illegal. I don't know yet. Right now it's more a sense of him being evasive, maybe hiding or covering up something. Like that. At any rate, not being as forthright and honest as he's pretending to be."

Abby sipped her coffee. "Cameron has certainly never been a warm, outgoing man. He's somber, even moody you might say. Driven and ambitious. And of course not above using his money and power to bully, to get his way. But when I was part of the family I never saw any sign—nor did I ever hear it stated or hinted at in any way before or since—that he might be involved in crooked dealings."

"Like I said, maybe 'crooked' isn't exactly the right way to put it. On the other hand, people change. Could be this is some kind of recent development. And what about his 'trusted right arm'—this Indian, this Thunderbringer he's got hanging around? How long has he been part of the scene? Why does an on-the-level rancher/businessman need a thug like that in his corner?"

"You're right, Thunderbringer is a fairly new inductee into

Cameron's circle. He showed up shortly after Cameron started his militia outfit. I think that's Thunderbringer's main role, helping to develop the RBR."

"Who exactly mans this militia of Terrell's? Friends? Business associates? His own ranch hands?"

"I don't think anyone knows for sure. At least I don't. I mean, they're not some deeply secret society like the Ku Klux Klan or anything, but at the same time neither do they go around putting on public displays or openly parading their identities."

"You don't know anyone who is actually a member?"

"No one I can think of. Outside of Cameron and Thunderbringer, of course. As far as Cameron's ranch hands, I suppose some of them may be members but I don't think it's a prerequisite for working for him. He has employees spread over three states, remember, and some of them have been with him since long before he started the RBR."

"How does he recruit? How did he build up whatever force he has?"

"In the beginning, after Nine One-One, he wrote letters to the editorial pages of newspapers all over the country. I imagine he got many responses—both pro and con—to those. Since the RBR eventually sprang out of all that I suppose some of the respondees who agreed with his views likely became candidates for the initial core group. Beyond that, aren't there magazines like *Soldier of Fortune* where a person can advertise for mercenaries and paramilitary types?"

"Is that where he got Thunderbringer?"

Abby shook her head. "I have no idea."

"Does he pay his RBR soldiers?"

She shook her head again.

"How about your ex-husband, Terrell's son—is he a member?"

"No way! Travis is hardly the military type. He despises that whole movement of his father's and is embarrassed by it."

I rubbed my jaw. "So. Back to the big Indian. Thunderbringer. He's like the chief DI over the outfit, then. Whipping Terrell's recruits into shape. Is that it?"

"That's the impression I get, yes. You have to admit he's a pretty intimidating presence." Abby flashed a wry smile. "I guarantee he intimidates the hell out of my ex, Travis. On the other hand, our son Dusty has taken quite a liking to him. Says he is 'way cool'. Thunderbringer seems to have a fondness or at least a tolerance for the boy, too. He spends time with him, teaching him the kind of things a kid is apt to find pretty exciting . . . how to throw a knife, shoot a bow, some new horse-breaking tricks allegedly handed down from Indian lore, even a few self-defense moves."

For some reason I found it irritating to hear that this lad I'd never even met was doing some bonding with a man I'd taken one look at and categorized as nothing more than a run-of-the-mill thug. "You ought to consider monitoring your son's playmates a little more closely," I advised Abby.

CHAPTER TWENTY-FIVE

By late afternoon the wind and lightning had abated and the rain had slowed to a light, persistent drizzle.

I left Abby's store feeling at loose ends and almost as gloomy as the weather. I was full of frustration and suspicion but empty of facts or evidence or even a clear sense of what direction to take next. While I wanted to give the Bridger women's hospitality a break so as not to take advantage of their willingness to afford me time and attention, there was definitely limited appeal in returning alone to the empty cabin. I had little to look forward to there except further pondering on my recent losses compounded by the ineffectiveness of the investigation to date.

As an alternative, I headed instead for the Lassoed Walleye Saloon, figuring to knock back a beer or three and just lose myself in a quiet corner of the crowd for a while.

I expected I would be joining an accumulation of fishermen and boaters chased off the lake by the storm. Upon entering, however, I was surprised to find I had the place pretty much to myself. B.U. Gorcey was behind the bar, looking bored; his wife Mamie was bustling around, rearranging this and that and wiping tables. As she worked she sang along loud and strong and mostly off key to a string of country-western songs piping out of the jukebox.

I climbed onto a bar stool and ordered a Mick. After serving up a foamy bottle and frosted glass, B.U. rested an elbow on the bar top across from me and we settled into an easy conversation. He didn't come right out and ask but I could tell he was curious to know what had brought the police next door earlier, so I filled him in on what that was all about. From there, we meandered through the usual subjects of idle chitchat: sports, politics, the weather. . . . B.U. informed me that the day's rain was especially welcome not only because the farmers and ranchers needed it, as usual, but also because the lake was becoming increasingly depleted due to this being the region's third year of a stubborn drought.

"We don't have a real wet summer or get a good snowpack melt off the Wyoming mountain ranges next spring," he said, "this time next year No Name Bay out there will start being called No Bay Bay because the water'll be clean gone from it."

Eventually we drifted over to the pool table and started shooting some tavern eight ball. It didn't take long to see that B.U. was a much better player than I was; but he kept it somewhat sporting by going after the more difficult shots left open to him, using the opportunity to sharpen his cutting and banking skills for when he was up against a more serious challenge. As we played, I found an opportunity of my own and asked him some of the same questions I had recently quizzed Abby on regarding the RBR's membership in general and William Thunderbringer in particular. On the latter point he couldn't tell me much; he had heard of the big Indian and somewhere got the impression he came from a military background, but had never met the man in person and couldn't add anything beyond that. As far as who made up the "soldiers" in Terrell's private little army, however, it turned out he knew several men from around the area who belonged to the outfit. The ones he was acquainted with were just regular guys, he said, mostly blue-collar laborers professing to be fed up with the U.S. getting treated like a doormat by foreign countries, especially those populated by "rug heads" and "camel jockeys."

By virtue of B.U. cutting me so much slack, we split the first two games. For the tie-breaker, though, he settled down and put me away with four of my balls still on the table.

By then an evening crowd had started to gather and it was necessary for him to set aside his cue and resume duties behind the bar.

But I'd accomplished more than I came for. In spite of being reminded how rusty my pool game had grown, I still walked away with a lightened mood and had learned a thing or two about the makeup of Terrell's militia to boot.

So I said good-bye to B.U. and Mamie and headed off for my cabin.

It was full dark as I went up the steps to the postage-stamp-sized front porch of my cabin. The rain had softened to more of a heavy mist. Ghostly layers of fog were hanging just above the surface of the lake.

Another benefit of the storm, it occurred to me, was that it had kept the fireworks fun and games to a minimum, making this the quietest evening I'd yet spent here.

On the way past the Honda I had reached in and retrieved my cell phone from the front seat. Inside the cabin, I saw that I had two messages waiting.

I let the messages wait while I built a thick salami-and-cheese sandwich and dug a fresh Mick out of the ice chest. Then I let them wait a while longer, for as long as it took to sit down and eat my supper.

When the sandwich was gone and the beer half drained, I punched Callback on the first of the messages. It was Bob Kolchonsky, at Bomber's old bar, the Bomb Shelter, back in Rockford.

"Hey, Joe," he greeted when he heard my voice. "I was wondering when you were going to get around to giving a shout back. Thought maybe you'd met up with one of those cowgirl barrel racers out there who locked her legs around you and rode you off to join the rodeo or something." In the background on his end I could hear jukebox music blaring and the sound of rowdy conversation and laughter, signaling that the Bomb Shelter was doing another good night's business.

"Don't recall any cowgirls locking their legs around me lately," I said. "And I'm pretty sure I'd remember something like that."

Bob chuckled. "Happens to me in my dreams all the times. Maybe that's why it came to mind."

"That why you called? To see if I was living out one of your fantasies?"

"Naw. I might have had my hopes up a little, but mainly Mike and I thought we needed to give you a heads up on some things. Been practically a parade of people calling or coming by here looking for you."

"Oh? Like who?"

"Well, for starters there was Bomber's lawyer—MacAbee. You know him, right?"

"Uh-huh. He's represented me a time or two also."

"Okay. I don't know if you knew it or not, but he's handling Bomber's will. Were you aware that you're in it—Bomber's will, I mean?"

The question made me wince. No, I hadn't known I was in the will. Never thought about it, never wanted to know. Never wanted things to get to a point where there was call to know *what* the damn thing contained.

"No," I said tightly. "I wasn't aware."

"Well, it's true." Bob paused somewhat awkwardly for a moment. Then: "Hell of a thing, ain't it? Finding out you've benefited in some way from the death of a good pal. Mike and I are sorta in the same boat. When we took over the day-to-day

193

running of the Bomb Shelter, see, we couldn't come up with quite enough to cover the whole up-front buy-in price. So Bomber was letting us settle the balance with smaller payments directly to him as we were able to scratch them together. . . . And now, also as part of his will, we find out he left us the whole works free and clear. Can you beat that?"

"Not surprising for Bomber," I said.

Bob sighed. "Anyway, getting back to you. MacAbee wanted to let you know that Bomber had a life-insurance policy naming you as a beneficiary."

"It was my understanding he left that to his sister."

"That was the big policy. This is a second one, a smaller one. You and Liz were co-beneficiaries, actually, with the clause that if either of you preceded him in death then the other would get the whole amount. Which comes to fifty thousand. Mike and I were called in for the reading of the will, that's where most of this came out."

"I'll be damned," I muttered. Like Bob had said, it was a hell of a thing to benefit from the death of a friend. In this instance, the way it worked out, the deaths of two friends. Yet at the same time I knew, with a twinge of guilt, that I surely could and would make use of the fifty grand.

"Anyway. That's what MacAbee wants to get in touch with you about."

"You indicated he was part of a parade. Who else?"

"Well, uh . . . this afternoon, uh, Jan showed up here. Jan, your ladyfriend?"

"I know who Jan is, Bob."

"Of course you do. So she shows up here and she was . . . well, pretty down. You and her ain't getting along so hot I take it. I mean, I'm not trying to nose in or nothing but that's what she said. I guess you know more about that than I do."

"I'm aware we are having problems, yes."

"It wasn't exactly clear what she wanted. Like I said, she was really blue. Maybe she just wanted to talk to somebody like me and Mike . . . you know, somebody acquainted with the both of you. She, uh, got a little plotched in the process, though. Sitting here talking to us and drinking. She was knocking back screwdrivers pretty heavy. Mike finally took her back to her motel room to sleep it off. Far as I know she's still there. She never really said for us to call you or anything, but it wasn't hard to see that's what she was angling for. Or, hell, maybe I'm wrong. Maybe you don't want to be hearing none of this. But . . . well, I guess I just thought you should know."

"Thanks for that, Bob," I told him earnestly. "To tell you the truth I'm kind of at a loss for what to do about the turn things have taken between her and me. Right now I've got my hands pretty full with the situation out here. That's one of the things Jan doesn't seem to be able to understand. Thanks again, though, for letting me know she showed up there like that. Sorry you and Mike had to get bothered about the whole mess."

"Hey, don't worry about that, man. I just hope things work out for the best between you two."

For the best. *Whatever that is,* I thought to myself.

Bob sighed again. "You want something to worry about, this next one's probably the one for that."

"With a remark like that, how can I not worry? But go ahead, lay it on me."

"Your cop buddy, Lieutenant Terry—the guy you had Mike take those bottles to? He's been calling here for you and there ain't no mistaking that he is royally pissed."

"Pissed about what?"

"Something to do with those bottles. But don't ask me any more than that. All he'd say was that you sent him a ticking bomb and if you thought he was going to get stuck holding it in his lap without dragging your sorry ass to sit right beside him you had another think coming. Quote, unquote."

"What the hell is that supposed to mean?"

"We were hoping you'd know. Mike's down at the cop shop now, trying to find out more about what's got everybody so stirred up. He figured since he was the middleman for getting those bottles to Terry he's already part of it anyway. But whatever it is, *you* are definitely part of it and the good lieutenant made it real clear he wanted you to waste no time getting in touch with him if I happened to talk to you before he did."

I suddenly had a pretty good hunch who the second message on my phone was going to be from. Although there was also the possibility that instead of Ed Terry, it might be from a "plotched" Jan. Neither one held the promise of being a particularly relaxing way to close out my evening.

Chapter Twenty-Six

"The chief, the commissioner, the head of the local FBI, and the top-ranking Department of Homeland Security official in this part of the state . . . each one taking a turn shoving my balls into the wringer. Does that sound to you," Ed Terry demanded in a strained voice, "like a fun fucking way to spend an afternoon?"

"Jeez, Ed. Be careful or you'll blow a gasket," I told him.

"Goddamnit, Joe! You could have at least given me some warning you were tossing me that kind of hot potato!"

"I didn't know I was," I tried to explain. "I still don't even know for sure what this 'hot potato' is supposed to be. Between the sputtering and cussing, you're not making yourself very clear."

"Oh give it up, man! You going to keep trying to spoon me some more crap about the fingerprints on those bottles only having to do with 'suspicious circumstances' surrounding Liz and Bomber's accident, and pretend you know nothing about this guy Ivgar Volnokov?"

"Who?"

"You heard me. You know damn well who."

"This is some kind of joke, right? That guy you just said— wasn't he one of Boris and Natasha's henchmen on the old *Rocky and Bullwinkle* show?"

"Believe me, this is no joke and I guarantee it's no time for you to be a smart-ass, either."

"Well what do you expect? You throw out some Russian-sounding name like a line you read off an eye chart and I'm supposed to take it serious?"

"You'd damn well better. Before you know it Homeland Security is going to be knocking on your door and I guarantee they will be taking things serious. You think FBI guys lack a sense of humor? Next to what I've seen of the Homeland Security boys, they are downright jovial. Then we'll see how many smart-ass comebacks you can pop off."

I held the phone away from my ear for a moment and dragged my free hand heavily down over my face. Then I pulled the phone back and spoke into it again. "Speaking of humor, Ed . . . do me a favor and humor *me*, will you? It's been a long day, I'm tired and maybe I'm a little slow on the uptake. So back up the trolley and start one more time at the beginning, okay? Tell me how the bottles I sent and the favor I asked you to do with any fingerprints you got off them turned into this harangue about some mad Russian and the FBI and Homeland Security and the rest."

Terry was quiet on the other end for a long minute. Still seething. I could hear air whistling angrily in and out of his nostrils. Then, his voice settling into weary resignation, he said, "Okay. I received the bottles this morning and, because you said it had to do with Liz and Bomber, I got the analysis on them started right away. Leaned on a lab tech who owed me some favors and got them pushed ahead of everything else he had going. As luck would have it, he came up with some nice clean lifts almost immediately off the first bottle he grabbed. Before he broke for lunch he fed those first lifts into the state and federal data banks to see if any matches would show up. When he returned from lunch he had matches all right—and that's when the shit started hitting the fan."

"The match was this Russian guy? What's the name again?"

"Volnokov. Ivgar Volnokov. Pretty soon you won't have any trouble remembering it because you're going to be hearing it plenty in the next few days."

"I don't care how many times I hear it. That name—or any resembling it—means nothing to me."

"Joe, if you're trying to play some kind of cutesy angle with this, it's not going to work. Not this time."

"I'm leveling with you straight down the line, Ed. I sent those bottles strictly for the reasons I told you up front. How this Volnokov connects with what I'm looking into I have no idea. Are you sure your lab tech didn't somehow get the prints mixed up?"

"No chance."

"Of course those bottles didn't get handled *only* out here where they ended up. I mean, you could possibly trace prints off them back to some liquor-store clerk or maybe a truck driver somewhere, hell, all the way back to the brewery, right?"

"Possibly. But that's a stretch. And the position of these particular prints were such that they indicated being left by somebody holding the bottle the way you would to drink out of it. Big odds they were put there by the *last* person to handle the bottle, not somebody way earlier."

"Okay. So who the hell is this Russian supposed to be? What is it about him that's got everybody in such a tizzy?"

Terry hesitated a minute before going ahead and answering me. When he did, the information he imparted was stitched somewhat raggedly together out of fragments he'd picked up during the "ball-wringing" session he'd undergone. "Until they iron things a little smoother, remember, they're still viewing me with a certain amount of suspicion and mistrust, too," he explained. "I'm the one who introduced the prints in through the side door—no announcement, no fanfare. Not until the damn things started tripping built-in alarms all through the data bank. So with typical Feeb paranoia they didn't exactly talk freely about certain details in front of me."

Nevertheless, Ed had gathered this much: As a child of twelve, Volnokov had been part of a "sleeper" family strategically placed by the former Soviet Union in the Atlanta, Georgia, area. Even at that young age he was completely indoctrinated in the anti-American/anti-West sentiment that was the predominant Communist mindset of the times. He spoke without a hint of Slavic accent and was thoroughly schooled in a full range of American history and trivia. Like the rest of his "family" he was trained to fit seamlessly into the setting that had been selected for them. Fit and function there—performing jobs, attending school and church, shopping, getting involved in social and sporting activities, blending invisibly into the community in every "normal" way—until such time as a situation might arise when the skills and training for their true cause needed to be called upon.

"Christ. I've heard of 'sleeper agents,' " I said. "But I thought that was mostly the stuff of spy fiction."

"Apparently not. Not back in the day. They had guys in place—hell, whole families, apparently, like in this instance—for months and years. Just waiting. Living routine lives. Until they needed to go into action. And sometimes the call never came."

"So when the Evil Empire got breeched by the Old Gipper's cavalry charge, there must have been a lot of them left hanging."

"You got it. And that's exactly what happened to Volnokov's group. Gardner was their American family name. One day they woke up and all of a sudden they weren't 'sleepers' anymore. They were just a phony family stranded in a country not of their choosing or birth. The government system they believed in and the cause they were so dedicated to and so well trained to defend . . . in shambles. All their communication links severed. What was worse, from their perspective, back in the home country intelligence officials and clerks looking to cut deals with the West for their own personal gain were defecting with armloads and trunkfuls of files and names and operation details that busted open the former Soviet espionage networks like a raw egg slammed to the pavement."

"So if the 'Gardners' had wanted to stay in place, lay low and just continue on with the covert lives they'd been leading, they couldn't risk it because there was the likelihood they'd eventually be exposed and sought out by authorities."

"Almost certainly."

By that point young Volnokov was nearly eighteen years old. If it was known what happened to the rest of the "Gardner" family, the details weren't discussed in front of Ed Terry. But Ivgar—strapping, ambitious, now burning with resentment for both the West and the mother country that had abandoned and then betrayed him—fled Georgia and dropped off the radar screen. When next heard from, he was in South America doing mercenary-type work for the highest bidder. His bitterness and natural aggression and covert training gave him an edge in marketable skills for that particular line of work.

"And then, somewhere along the way," Terry went on, "reports indicate he ended up rubbing elbows with a well-paying little outfit known as Al-Qaeda. This would have been before Nine-Eleven, but Osama's bunch was already known and recognized as a dangerous threat. From what I gathered, there are some who suspect our boy Volnokov—who by the way has accumulated a whole string of aliases—served as some kind of link between Al-Qaeda and Timothy McVeigh."

"McVeigh? The Oklahoma City bombings? I thought he was strictly a home-grown loony."

Through the phone connection, I somehow sensed Ed giving an elaborate shrug. "Maybe he was, maybe he wasn't. Not the first time I've heard that theory—that there was a connection between McVeigh and Al-Qaeda. But always before it came off right-wing talk radio. Who ever knows for sure with those guys?"

"Still, a rumor like that, even with minimal substantiation, would be enough to up Ivgar's prominence on the watch lists."

"True. But that still didn't keep him from dropping off the radar screen again a year or so back. . . . Until now."

"And now his fingerprints—provided courtesy of his own former government's files, I take it—pop up from a source way out in the middle of Nowhere Nebraska."

"And the tizzy commences."

"Jeez, Ed. It was never my intent to get you dragged into a meat grinder over this, it really wasn't. I had no idea something like this was going to come out of sending those bottles."

"I believe you. . . . Now. I gotta admit, though, that my feelings toward you weren't so charitable back when I was *in* the grinder."

"So the big question it all leads to is, What the hell is Ivgar Volkonov—or whatever he's calling himself these days—up to in these unlikely parts? And, not so incidentally from where I stand, does it have anything to do with what happened to Liz and Bomber?"

"I think it's safe to say you're about to get a lot of help trying to find the answers to those questions. . . . More help, maybe, than you ever really wanted."

CHAPTER TWENTY-SEVEN

After I was finished talking to Ed Terry I snapped shut my cell phone and remained sitting at the little foldout table. Slowly, thoughtfully sipping what was left of the now-flat beer I'd opened earlier.

Holy shit. What had I stumbled onto? And what—possibly—had Liz and Bomber stumbled onto before me?

Was there really a chance that an embittered former Soviet agent somehow had a hand in their accident? If so, why? How? For what motive? Or was the whole fingerprint thing some kind of bizarre coincidence, or perhaps a clumsy lab mistake (despite Ed's insistence that couldn't have happened)?

My mind reeled.

And now Homeland Security was going to be descending on me. What would that turn into? A blessing, or a curse?

I've never been a Sherlock Holmes–type detective. My results seldom come from clues or broken codes or clever deductions. I don't do complex or complicated all that well. My way is to just sort of bull into the middle of a thing, root around, ask questions, annoy this person or that. Occasionally rough somebody up if I have to. And hope for a reaction somewhere along the way that signals a chink in somebody's alibi or a fishy smell to a story I've been fed, the hint of a lead I can focus on and start digging deeper into. . . .

I deliberated several more minutes before making the decision on my next move. I didn't want to overreact but at the same time neither did I want to later regret not utilizing a CYA option that was available to me. An ounce of prevention and all that.

Twice in my checkered past I had gotten involved in situations that ended up also drawing the interest of a certain branch of U.S. Army Intelligence. In both cases I had agreed to go along with suppressing related facts and details that had little or no bearing on the outcome of the matter where I was concerned but, if leaked to the public, would have been a major embarrassment to the military in general and perhaps career-damaging to a handful of individuals who deserved better. As a result of my cooperation, certain reciprocal perks had been promised me should the need ever arise.

Dismissing the cell unit for this particular exercise, I walked outside to the pay-phone bubble on a pole near the gas pumps in front of Abby's store. Everything was quiet this time of night, the store and the row of cabins, except for mine, dark. The fog over the lake thickening silently. The only signs of activity, murky and muted, came from the Lassoed Walleye across the way.

At the phone bubble I dialed a special toll-free number, one I had committed to memory years ago but had never used until tonight.

After three rings a male voice on the other end said, "Yes."

I responded with a single obscure word, also memorized from long ago.

"Is this a secure line?" I was asked.

"Public pay phone. Best I can do."

"One moment please."

For the better part of a minute I listened to a dull hiss with occasional pops and crackles. Then a different voice, also male, came on the line. "State your situation."

I gave him the pertinent details, stripped down, bare bones.

"And what assistance do you seek from us?" he wanted to

know when I was finished.

"If I get jammed up by Homeland Security can you provide me some fallback? A pass, a good word—whatever you want to call it. I'll allow them to feel their oats by holding still for a little bit of jackbooting, if that's all it takes. But if they try to make the party last too long, I'd like a designated driver I can count on to get me the hell home."

He didn't have to think about it for very long. "Rest assured that we will, as they say, have your back, sir. Let me give you a separate phone number. As with the one you just used, there is someone there twenty-four seven to answer." He rattled off the number. Repeated it once. It went into the lockbox part of my brain. I don't claim to have a photographic memory or anything close, but when a thing is important enough you find a way to make it stick. "If it becomes necessary, have the people you are referring to call that number. They should recognize it. Your standing and clearance will be explained to them. Anything else?"

"Yes, there is. I am licensed to carry a weapon in two states. Where I'm at isn't one of them. Considering the way things are shaping up out here, I mean to continue having a weapon at my disposal. What kind of cover can you give me for that?"

Again an answer with little or no hesitation. "You are, of course, advised to practice discretion. However, in the event it is necessary to discharge your weapon or if a legal situation arises from having it on your person then use the same number I just gave you. Appropriate authorization for your actions will be negotiated."

"Okay. One final thing."

"And that is?"

"I have a couple of names I could use some deeper background on. I expect both of them will show up in your data banks. The first name is William Thunderbringer, the second is

Ivgar Volnokov. The former may be an alias, the latter is bound to have aliases associated to it. Anything your system turns up that you are able to share with me will be helpful and most appreciated."

The voice asked me to repeat the names and their spelling. I gave it my best shot. Then I was told: "I will have these inputted. It will take a while to see what comes back. Call this number again any time after twelve hours from now and the results will be ready."

"I guess that's it, then," I said, relieved and somewhat surprised at how smoothly the whole thing had gone. "I'm obliged."

"As are we, Mr. Hannibal. Good night."

And the line went dead.

Back in my cabin I felt exhilarated, energized. It was late but there was no way I was ready for bed, for sleep. Not now. Not even the over-quota of beer I'd consumed through the course of the evening had mellowed me enough to offset the rush kicking through me.

Bring on the bad guys. Bring on your scheming millionaire rancher militants, your bent cops, your accident manipulators . . . hell, throw in a war-painted Indian and a leftover Russian spy for good measure. And don't forget the newest incarnation of federal stormtroopers, the Homeland Security gang. However things played out, whatever did or didn't end up being connected to the deaths of my two friends, I could now count on the United States Fucking Army having my back. I was ready to get it on. Let's rumble, assholes. Let's rock and roll.

As this mental chest-thumping was going on inside my head I was pacing back and forth in the confines of the cabin, trying to gear myself down.

I dug a fresh Mick out of the ice chest, twisted off the cap, tipped it high. I pulled the cold carbonation thirstily down my throat and felt it mushroom into soothing warmth as it spread through my belly.

I wished it was morning. I wanted to get the expected Homeland Security grilling out of the way. In the process I was hoping to eke out a little quid-pro-quo information. In any event, I wanted to get back to my investigation with the renewed vigor I was feeling, with this fresh angle I had to pry from.

Still, no matter how or if Volnokov actually figured into my interests, I remained convinced that the turning point for the events that ultimately resulted in Liz and Bomber's wreck that fateful day was their stop at the old homestead site on Pawnee Creek. Something happened there. Something changed. Something took a carefree day of sightseeing and turned it into a fatal car crash and manufactured evidence planted to mask the truth.

But what truth?

What had Liz and Bomber seen or done on the banks of that remote twist of water? Did the old homestead hold some dark secret, some evidence of a past foul deed that made their visiting there at that particular time a threat to someone in the present? Had they, in fact, observed something to do with the "military maneuvers" being staged that day by the RBR—something that, if reported, would be harmful to Terrell's outfit? Harmful enough to kill over? Or had they perhaps come across Volnokov—either hiding out, or maybe *he* was the one spying on the RBR activities—and their discovery of him made him feel compromised to the point of having to retaliate?

Any and all of those possibilities sounded so wild, so far-fetched. And yet what else did I have other than the acceptance of the fatal crash as the straightforward accident that so many others already believed it to be? But no, damn it. It *wasn't* just a simple, tragic accident. There was too much peripheral chaff flying in the air, too many other oddities crowded in around the edges of the picture.

A picture unfortunately still forming, not yet in focus. . . .

I thought about the pictures in Liz's missing camera. If found, what would they show? Would they hold the key?

If only—

I stopped pacing so abruptly that beer sloshed out of the open bottle I was holding.

Liz's . . . missing . . . camera.

". . . I guarantee should the missing camera or anything else of value turn up they will be promptly handed over," Cameron Terrell had assured me that afternoon with the beginning of the thunderstorm starting to swirl around us.

But *how had he known* there was a missing camera? I replayed every word of our preceding conversation through my mind. I was positive I hadn't brought it up.

It was earlier that morning when Abby first realized the camera was missing . . . realized it, if my impression was correct, between the time she called Terrell to clear my visit with him and when she told me about it later on, after she'd started going through Liz and Bomber's belongings. If that was the case, if I had the time line straight, then neither could she have mentioned anything about the camera to her former father-in-law, because she wasn't even aware of its absence yet when she talked to him.

Naturally, I had to confirm this. But if I was right, then business had just picked up considerably and I had even more cause for being too jacked to sleep.

CHAPTER TWENTY-EIGHT

"So if you didn't tell him and I didn't tell him," I was saying to Abby, "the way I see it that only leaves about two other ways to explain how Terrell could know about the camera. One, he or his men already found it and have been withholding it for some reason or, two, he overheard you and me talking about it."

Abby frowned. "But how could he have overheard? He was miles away from either of us when we had that conversation."

"Phone bug," B.U. Gorcey said matter-of-factly.

The four of us—me, Abby, B.U. and Mamie—were seated at the bar of the Lassoed Walleye Saloon. We had the place to ourselves. Closing time had come and gone, the last customer had been shooed out the door. The lights were dimmed and deep, silent shadows filled the corners of the big room around us.

I nodded in response to B.U.'s statement. "Yeah, that'd be my first guess. The store's phone is bugged, maybe the whole place. That's why I put everybody through my little bit of subterfuge earlier in order to get Abby over here, hopefully without sending up any signals that we may have tripped to something."

Once I'd clamped onto Terrell's apparently unexplainable knowledge of the missing camera, I wasn't able to let it go. I'd returned to the Walleye shortly before last call and enlisted the aid of B.U. in contacting Abby and getting her to come over. Because I suspected her phone and/or building were compromised I couldn't think of a good way to lure her away at that hour by myself without the risk of alerting whoever might be watching or listening in. And I didn't want to wait to discuss Terrell's remark. I wanted to share it with somebody, toss it around, examine it from different perspectives.

So, for the sake of the electronic eavesdropping I now believed to be in place, I'd gotten B.U. to concoct a ruse about some mutual friend from the past showing up unexpectedly at the Walleye and using that as an excuse to call Abby and insist she join in for a bit of reminiscing. As soon as she showed up I revealed the deception and why I'd set it in motion. Having involved the Gorceys to that extent, I felt like I had little choice but to go ahead and pull them the rest of the way into the loop.

So I gave a quick recap on where things stood, bringing everyone gathered up to speed. The only details I left out were those pertaining to my busted love life and my covert Army contact.

"God, this is all getting so bizarre," Abby said now, giving a faint shake of her head as if to clear it of cobwebs. "Phone bugs and Russian spies and the involvement of Homeland Security and . . . and . . . who knows what else. What's left? What can be next?"

"Whatever it is," B.U. drawled, "you got a safe bet it ain't gonna be boring."

Mamie elbowed him in the ribs. "Be serious. Can't you see how scary all of this must be for Abby? And who can blame her?"

"I'm *not* scared," Abby said testily. But as she tapped a cigarette out of her pack and snapped a flame to it there was a noticeable trembling in her hands. "All right, maybe I'm a little scared," she admitted. "But mostly I'm damned mad. It was bad enough when I found out somebody had probably creeped my place and snooped through my stuff. But now this, the thought of them listening and monitoring everything I've been doing and saying for. . . ."

She turned to me suddenly. "What about your cabin, Joe? That evidence of an intruder the other day—did they bug your place, too?"

"Not that I could spot. I gave it a good going over before I left. I don't pretend to be a whiz at that sort of thing, but I know enough to recognize a damn bug when I see one. My cabin is clean. So the intrusion was just a snoop job like we thought in the first place. Which is what makes me suspect that only your phone—not the whole store—is tapped. Probably a voice-activated transmitter that kicks on whenever you pick up the handset and start talking. Be easier to monitor that way, too—set up a recorder that's triggered the same and just check it periodically rather than trying to man a receiver steady."

Abby blew smoke angrily. "Well I'd like to go over there and pick up that phone right now and give whoever's listening in an earful of what I think about them!"

"Seems to me we pretty much know who's listening in, don't we?" B.U. said. "It's got to be Terrell. . . . Leastways that's where whatever is overheard gets reported."

"But why?" Mamie wanted to know. "What would make Cameron Terrell so interested in what gets said over Abby's phone?"

"It's got something to do with this whole accident business. That has to be it," Abby said. "Everybody knows I'm refusing to let up. But apparently Cam Terrell wants to know more—who I'm talking to about it, what I'm saying, what I might be planning next."

Mamie said, "Okay. But I repeat—why? What connects Terrell to your uncle's car crash?"

"Something that happened at or near the homestead site on Pawnee Creek," I answered. "That's the common ground, that's where their paths crossed, and that's where it all seems to keep going back to. I don't yet know *what* took place there, but whatever it was I'm convinced it somehow led either directly to the crash or at least to the attempt to mask it over."

"So where do we take it from here?" Abby said.

"We keep right on doing what we're doing. Like you said a minute ago, you're not ready to let up. And neither am I. Our poking and persistence has obviously got somebody worried. We keep the pressure on, keep them worried, we increase the odds of getting them to slip up and reveal more and more until we've got enough to nail 'em."

"What about this phone tap? Are we going to share that with the police? Maybe Homeland Security when they show up? Wouldn't that be the kind of thing they're better equipped to handle?"

"First things first. For starters, let's make sure we're not jumping to the wrong conclusion. When you open the store in the morning, I'll come over and check it out. If I find what I suspect I'm going to find, then we can make our decision on what to do with it. Right now I'm thinking that the longer we can keep the other side from knowing what we know, the better chance we've got of finding a way to make it work to our advantage."

"And what about the Russian guy? The ex-spy who left his fingerprints on the bottle?" B.U. asked. "Where does he fit in?"

"I keep thinking that if he truly has ties to Al-Qaeda then it's impossible to believe Cam Terrell would have anything to do with him," Abby insisted. "After Nine One-One, Cam's hatred for terrorism and terrorists has been practically all-consuming. As witnessed by the formation of RBR and all the money and energy he's sunk into it. To think he'd then turn around and have dealings with someone linked specifically to those responsible for the events of that terrible day? No way!"

"Maybe it's as simple as Terrell not knowing about the Russian's ties to Al-Qaeda," Mamie suggested.

"Or maybe ol' Cam knows damn well about those ties and has some wild revenge plan to get the Russian to lead him and his militia straight *to* Al-Qaeda," B.U. offered.

"There are a lot of maybes where Volnokov is concerned. Too damn many," I said. "Maybe the alleged ties to Al-Qaeda are false. Maybe there isn't a connection between him and Terrell at all. Maybe his fingerprints on the bottle I turned in are a lab mix-up or maybe they got there as a result of incidental contact ten states away and only showed up now as the result of freaky coincidence."

Abby eyed me closely. "Do you really believe any of that?"

"Not a bit."

"Maybe," B.U. tried again, "the Russian's the one Liz and Bomber encountered that day on Pawnee Creek. And what ended up happening to them was the result of a retaliation by him that had nothing to do with Cameron Terrell."

"Except that doesn't explain how Terrell knows and is lying about the missing camera. Or why he has a bug on my phone," Abby was quick to point out. "No. Russian or no Russian— Cameron is somehow in the thick of this. That much is for certain."

B.U. made a sour face. "Maybe so. But it seems to me there ain't very damn much about all this that *is* for certain."

I barked a quick, bitter laugh. "Welcome to the detective game, boys and girls. Where questions and speculation are plentiful, but answers and certainty are as scarce as fairy dust."

Chapter Twenty-Nine

Three a.m. found me alone back at my cabin, lying in the dark, still wide awake. Things were churning over and over through my mind like a shovelful of gravel inside a cement mixer. Sleep was a million miles away.

Since we'd left it that I would check out Abby's store shortly after she opened up at five, I was anxious to get that over with. Exactly what my next move would be from there . . . well, that was a big part of what was churning over in my mind. Before I could plan too far, I had to wait and see for sure what I found and then what resulted from the anticipated visit by Homeland Security. Would they grill me and then dismiss me as inconsequential to the bigger game they were playing? Would they try to jam me up, try to neutralize me and take over the whole investigation? Would they be willing to share any further information about Volnokov that might help rule his possible connection to Cameron Terrell either in or out? Would I have to play my Army Intelligence trump card and, if I did, would it truly be enough to gain me the leverage to continue with my own agenda?

The flip side to those kinds of questions, to fretting about DHS involvement and interference, was to consider cooperating with them fully as Abby had suggested. Welcome their help with the case, if they were willing to give it. After all, apart from stories making the rounds that painted them alternately as bumbling incompetents or power-mad stormtroopers, we were *sup-*

posed to be on the same side. They were representatives of my government, part of what I paid taxes for, the new elite force keeping our home soil safe and. . . .Yeah, right. Who was I kidding with that train of thought? They'd be about as thrilled to join forces with a small potatoes PI as I would be to drop into their draft and let them take the lead in trying to get to the bottom of what really happened to Liz and Bomber. Perhaps I shouldn't be so quick to view them as the enemy, but that didn't mean I could quite picture them as comrades in arms ready to go marching shoulder-to-shoulder toward a joint victory.

And then there were the thoughts of Jan I was wrestling with. Deep inside me, I had already come to the realization that there was no putting the pieces of our relationship back together. It was ended. Over. I still believed that the rough period we'd been going through in the prior months could have been worked out and certainly would have been worth the effort. But her unfaithfulness to me was the one thing I knew I would never be able to get past. I wished it were otherwise. But in that same deep-down place, I knew better; knew better than to even pretend there was a chance.

I thought of Jan alone in a motel room in Rockford, feeling sad and troubled. And me alone in a single-room cabin off in Nebraska, also feeling sad and troubled. It was a damned shame. But it changed nothing. I knew what I had to do to fix at least part of the way I felt. Neither Jan's sorrow nor her lamentations to our well-intentioned mutual friends were going to stand in the way. And neither was the arrival of Homeland Security, if it turned out that's what they had in mind.

When everything was said and done, all I wanted was for everybody to stay the hell out of my way so I could finish what I'd started and what I felt I was closing in on.

Finally admitting defeat as far as getting any sleep, I sat up on the cot and swung my feet to the floor. Abby would be opening the store in less than two hours; I might as well be ready to show up as soon as she did and get my bug hunt over and done with.

I turned on the bathroom light and enough illumination leaked out to make the rest of the cabin navigable. I nuked a cup of water in the microwave, then stirred in some instant crystals and called it coffee. It was bitter as hell but still several notches above the vile brew B.U. Gorcey served up.

Sitting back down on the edge of the cot, I pondered things a bit more as I sipped at the scalding brew. Even though I had some pretty good hunches on where this case was headed, there were still loose ends dangling and dubious allegiances to be sorted out and therefore plenty of room for more surprises to pop up before it was through. I reminded myself how much I hated surprises.

After I finished the coffee, I pulled on my pants and boots. Digging clean pairs of underwear and socks out of my duffel bag, I wrapped them in a towel along with my shaving kit and headed down toward the shower building.

The night air was cool, but not unpleasantly so, on my bare chest and shoulders. It hadn't rained for some time but the sky remained overcast and off to the northwest I could see lightning flickering on the fringe of a new storm front getting ready to roll in. Fog still hung low over the lake, blurry tendrils of it reaching down here and there to touch the water.

Emerging from the shower building twenty minutes later, I was scrubbed clean and scraped smooth and feeling reasonably refreshed. As I approached my cabin I was thinking that because my clean clothes supply was running low I'd have to remember to ask Abby about where I could find the nearest laundromat.

As if bidden by the thought, a cigarette ember flared suddenly amidst the shadows pooled in front of the cabin door and then I was able to make out the form of Abby, sitting there on the steps waiting for me. I made an effort to keep my stride even, not letting her see she had given me something of a start.

"You have a sudden, middle-of-the-night urge to jump up and go take a shower?"

"Something like that," I replied.

"I saw your light on, then saw you head down with your towel and stuff. I couldn't sleep either. Figured we might as well keep each other company. Hope you don't mind."

"Of course not."

She tipped her face upward and exhaled a plume of smoke that trailed out in the night air. "Looks like it's getting ready to storm some more."

"Uh-huh. Pretty soon, by the feel of it. We probably ought to step inside before it decides to cut loose."

She flipped away her cigarette and followed me in. She had showered recently, too; I could smell soap and shampoo scents still clinging to her and the trailing ends of her freshly brushed hair were still damp.

I turned on more lights inside the cabin. Waving Abby toward the chair at the folding table, I said, "I've got Coke in the ice chest or I can make coffee, if you don't mind instant."

"I'll take the coffee. I drink instant sometimes anyway, if I'm by myself and want a cup later in the day when it would be a waste to brew a whole pot. One way or the other, getting a caffeine boost started early this morning sounds like a good idea because we're both likely to need it before the day is through."

"We get desperate we can ask B.U. to send over an emergency ration of his brew. I don't know if you've ever had the pleasure, but he makes coffee strong enough to give a caffeine boost to a mummy." Feeling self-conscious about standing there half-dressed, I snagged the T-shirt I'd left hanging over the bathroom doorknob and pulled it on. "Come to think of it, that may be why I'm having trouble sleeping now—I started my day with a couple jolts out of B.U.'s thermos."

"There's an old joke about cowboy coffee that goes: If you throw a horseshoe into the pot and the horseshoe sinks, then the coffee isn't strong enough."

"Only trouble is, somebody apparently forgot to tell B.U. it was a joke. I think he took it literally. And, now that you mention it, I'm not so sure I didn't swallow part of the horseshoe, too."

We could hear the wind picking up outside and a fresh wave of raindrops starting to fall. Thunder growled low in the sky, sounding far away. I finished making a cup of coffee for Abby and another for me. Placed hers on the table in front of her, carried mine over and took a seat once again on the edge of the cot.

"I still feel bad about having you stay out here in this . . . this shack."

"Hey, it's storming outside and I'm sitting here warm and dry. Got wall to wall floors, electricity, and running water. Where's the big hardship? Besides, it's not like I'm setting up permanent residence or anything."

Abby pursed her lips and blew across the rim of her cup. I noticed she had recently applied a touch of pale lipstick. She noticed me noticing. "I'm looking forward to getting all of this over with . . . except for that part. The part about you leaving when it's done."

I drank some of my coffee, not sure what to say.

Abby smiled wryly. "That sounded awfully brazen, didn't it? First showing up at your door in the wee, small hours and then saying something like that . . . I must seem like quite the hussy."

"You're hardly a hussy, Ab."

"You don't know that. You don't know me at all, really."

"I think I do."

"Or did you just mean I'm not flashy enough or pretty

enough to be a hussy?"

"You're pretty and you damn well know it."

"Am I? I see the way men look at women like Mamie and Tina. I don't see men looking at me that way."

"You're not *asking* to get looked at that way. But you still get noticed and looked at plenty. Believe it."

"How do you look at me, Joe?"

I scowled. "Right now I'm looking at you as somebody who's starting to make me uncomfortable. . . . What do you think you're up to, anyway?"

"Do you like what you see when you look at me?"

"I certainly don't find you hard on the eyes, if that's what you mean."

"I haven't been with a man since Travis and I divorced. In fact Travis is the only man at all that I've ever been with . . . like that."

"Seems like a waste. It also seems like none of my business."

"You could make it your business. You could put an end to the waste . . . in case I'm not making myself clear enough."

"Jesus, Abby."

"Is it because I'm Bomber's niece?"

"What?"

"I *have* seen the way you look at me. And you *do* like what you see. I can tell. But you don't intend to act on it, do you? Why? Because of some kind of sense of honor thing, because you'd feel like you were betraying your best friend in some way?"

"That might be part of it. There are all sorts of reasons I don't hit on every attractive woman I meet. For starters, how far do you think I'd get with this mug of mine?"

"You might be surprised."

"I doubt it."

"I like your mug. I liked it from the beginning. It might not be made for selling toothpaste on a TV commercial or prettyboy cologne in a slick magazine ad, but it's got other qualities. It's strong and solid. It's got character."

"Look, Abby, whatever you're trying to prove—enough, okay? For what it's worth, when it comes time for me to head back to Illinois I won't be leaving here without regrets of my own. And that'll be largely due to you."

"But you'll still go."

"I'll go home. That's what people do."

"And never come back."

"Never is a long time."

"You have a girl back there, don't you? The one who's a reporter?"

"That's sort of up in the air right at the moment," I admitted with a grimace. "Whatever I go back to . . . she may no longer be a part of it."

She studied me intently for a long moment. Then: "You hold a lot inside, don't you?"

"Do I?"

"But maybe not as much as you think. Right now there's a lot of pain showing through."

"Sorry, but that's not exactly a startling display of perception. I've recently lost my two best friends in the world, I just admitted to having a romantic relationship on the rocks, and I'm caught in a case that's swerving in more directions than I can keep up with—yeah, I've got some pain. And some frustration, too. But nothing I can't handle."

"I'm offering to help you handle it. We've both got pain. Would it be so wrong for two people to try and ease each other's pain, even if it's only for a little while?"

I stood up, took a measured step over to the table. Set down my cup, reached for Abby's hands and pulled her to her feet. She came easily and then leaned into me, pressing herself against me. I moved my hands to her shoulders, gripping them gently, holding her intent gaze with one of my own as I said, "Maybe it wouldn't be 'wrong' in the greater scheme of things, but that still doesn't make it a good idea. Not for us, not right now. If the kind of sudden, casual thing you're proposing was truly in your nature, then you *would* have already been with a man since your divorce. I'm flattered and I'm tempted, believe me. But if you end up with regrets where I'm concerned, I don't want one of them to be that I took advantage of a vulnerable moment."

"Like I said," she murmured, gazing up at me, "you're so damned solid."

She was wearing a thin pullover top with no bra underneath. I could feel her hardening nipples, twin points stabbing into me like dull dagger tips. "I may be solid, but I'm not made of stone," I said, easing her back a step and holding her at arms' length. "I think it's time for you to get back home."

She grinned. "Why? Afraid you might change your mind?"

"Maybe that's what *you* ought to be afraid of."

"I'm willing to take the risk. Besides," she protested, "it's raining out."

My turn to grin. "A cold shower'll do you good. . . . Now beat it."

CHAPTER THIRTY

By six o'clock I had completed my bug hunt. Without high-tech sweeping equipment, I had to do it the old-fashioned way: checking every nook, cranny, shelf underlip, light fixture, and table and chair bottom throughout Abby's store. As well as her living quarters above. I found no sign of a listening device in any of those places. As expected, however, I *did* find one in the handset of the store's telephone and, some-what less anticipated, another in the phone in Abby's apartment.

Each time with a radio playing loudly and in close proximity to cover the sounds of my examination, I unscrewed the cap over each phone's mouthpiece and there it was—a small disc transmitter about as big around as a dime.

"Those bastards," Abby muttered in both instances. "Those dirty, snooping bastards."

After replacing the mouthpiece caps and leaving the transmitters in place, we retreated to the store's front porch—just in case my search of the interior had failed to uncover something—to discuss what our next move should be.

The new day was elbowing aside the last of the storm, its rain diminished to barely a drizzle. Overhead, the cloud cover was breaking apart rapidly and patches of bright blue sky were beginning to show through.

"For starters," Abby sighed, "I need to bring Mother up to speed on these latest developments. She was already in bed last night when you called me over to the Walleye and she won't be stirring for a little while yet. I don't really want to get her upset. But she has a right to know what's going on, don't you agree?"

"Absolutely."

"Do you think there's any chance there might be one of those damn bug things in her place?"

"I doubt it. But I can check it out to make sure."

"What about Homeland Security? You still expecting a visit from them?"

"Pretty much guaranteed, according to Ed Terry. Hell, I halfway figured they might come banging on my door in the middle of the night."

Abby flushed slightly. "Instead of just a pathetic, horny divorcée, you mean?"

"That's not what I said and not what I meant."

She turned and looked at me. "I guess I should thank you for what you did . . . or rather what you didn't do. I'm not necessarily convinced it would have had the devastating effect on me that you seemed to fear, but still . . . it was a noble act."

"Noble? Me? Boy, that'd get a horse laugh in a lot of circles."

She continued to regard me. "Not in this circle, mister. . . . Not around here."

A couple of vehicles came rattling down from the highway entrance. A Dodge pickup and a battered old Ford station wagon, both pulling trailers with boats riding high and proud. We watched them roll past the store and swing around at the shoreline, jockeying for position, getting aligned with the boat ramp. The pickup started backing down first and two guys in bright yellow rain jackets piled out of the wagon to lend a hand getting the boat ahead of theirs unloaded. Once outside the car, both guys paused to wave at Abby and she waved back, smiling.

"And so it begins," she said. "By mid-morning, with the weather breaking the way it is, they'll be lined up four and five deep to use that ramp."

"Should be good for business."

"Yep. And that, as they say, is the upside."

Steering our conversation back to what we'd been on before getting sidetracked, I said, "Uh-huh. And let's hope there's an upside to the Homeland Security visit when it comes."

"Are you worried about it?" Abby asked.

I shrugged. "I dunno. Just anxious, I guess. I want to get it over with. I want to see how they'll come at me, what their attitude is. Then I'll know how I've got to play it with them."

"Do you really have a choice? I mean, they not only are the Feds but these days they are—big dogs on the federal agency scene. What else can you do but cooperate?"

"There's cooperation, kiddo, and then there's cooperation," I told her. "They show me and our situation some respect—fine. But if they try shoving me aside or bullying me like some citizen who's never investigated anything more serious than an unbalanced checkbook before . . . well, I'm afraid I might develop a bit of an attitude of my own. I didn't drive all the way to this sock hop to end up listening to the music from outside the gymnasium."

"Sock hop? Gymnasium?"

"Us hard-nosed PI types are supposed to speak in metaphors every chance we get," I explained dryly. "Got to average at least one a day or risk getting your ticket yanked. It's in the fine print of the licensing by-laws."

"Well as the one who invited you to the sock hop I don't want to see you left standing outside the gymnasium either. I'm just not sure that copping an attitude or throwing tough-guy metaphors at the Homeland Security G-men if and when they show up is the best way to ensure that."

We didn't have the chance to debate it much longer. As Abby had predicted, the guys in the station wagon and the pickup were just the start of a steady stream of fishermen and/or boaters whose destination that morning was No Name Bay. More showed up before the first pair were even away from shore. Then they just kept coming, most of them making a stop at the store for a few last-minute supplies, keeping Abby busy seeing to their needs. And, since she seemed to already know many of them, a good deal of friendly banter was also part of the transactions.

B.U. Gorcey wandered over from next door, carrying the same old-fashioned metal thermos bottle he'd shown up with yesterday morning at my cabin. After lingering on the front porch long enough for me to report the results of my bug hunt, we went inside and took seats at one of the snack area tables where we fell easily to shooting the breeze about nothing of any consequence. Between customers, Abby sat with us. She seemed to have no objection to B.U. bringing his own coffee, so I got the impression it was probably a regular practice. I had no objection either, as long as he didn't expect me to share any more of the abominable brew with him. Thankfully, Abby did a good job of keeping my cup topped off from the store's coffee maker, providing no opening for a refill to be offered courtesy of the thermos.

A little after seven, Margaret Bridger emerged from her apartment, lugging her portable oxygen tank. She joined us for a cup of coffee (also pointedly avoiding B.U.'s brew) and some Danish. Then, while B.U. covered the counter, Abby took her mother aside and updated her on all that had recently come to light. Margaret seemed morose and uncharacteristically quiet afterwards, almost as if stunned by what she'd been told. Hell, in a way who could blame her. When she was ready to go back to her place, I accompanied her and performed another search for listening devices, this time turning up nothing at all.

By then it was past eight and something else that hadn't turned up was any sign of Homeland Security. Having never possessed an overabundance of patience, this only amplified the feeling of restless energy inside me.

I thought about calling Ed Terry to see if things had changed in some way. But instead, since the twelve-hour wait period had now elapsed, I decided to first try my Army Intelligence contact.

Outside at the pay-phone bubble I once again dialed the number long ago committed to memory and once again, when prompted, identified myself with the single obscure word.

This morning the voice on the other end of the line was female. But the inflection and clipped speech pattern were identical to the male speakers from last night. "One moment, sir."

The voice that came on next was male again, and it was also something a bit more. "Good morning, Joseph . . . Matthew Elwood here. I trust you remember me?"

I could feel my eyebrows involuntarily lift a notch or two. "Of course I remember you, Colonel. This is a surprise and an honor," I said. "I wouldn't have thought my relatively minor distress call would warrant attention from someone at your level."

A dry chuckle briefly filled my ear. "What you really mean, I suspect, is that you didn't figure an old fossil like me would still be taking up space on the active duty roster."

To an extent, he may have been right. But I wasn't about to admit as much out loud. I waited for him to continue.

"Speaking of active involvement," he went on, "aren't you getting a little long in the tooth yourself to still be in the middle of the same kind of rough-and-tumble scrapes as when we first met back a dozen and more years ago?"

I grinned. "You've been reading my mail, sir. And those long teeth are connected to plenty of stiff joints and aching muscles that remind me regularly just how right you are."

"At least I had the sense to put in for retirement . . . even though the brass seems to keep finding reasons to drag me back."

"I hope I'm not the cause for the latest interruption to that retirement."

"Not exclusively, no. I'd already been pulled in on the periphery of this thing. When your name and the news of your phone call yesterday filtered through, that's when some increased involvement from me was requested."

"I guess even being on just the periphery puts you at an advantage over me, sir. I'm pretty much playing catch-up as far as exactly what 'this thing' is. All I know for sure is that what I started out investigating seems to be taking some sudden and mighty curious turns."

"One of those turns, I gather, bringing you up against the name Ivgar Volnokov."

"I also tossed out an inquiry about a guy called Thunderbringer."

"I have no details on that name at this time. The Russian's, however, is quite a different matter."

"Uh-huh. I got that. His name seems hot-wired to alarm bells in all sorts of interesting places. Up to and including, I'm told, the Department of Homeland Security."

"Indeed."

"Are *you* associated with DHS these days, sir?"

Again the brief, brittle chuckle in my ear. "Don't you know, Joseph, that *everybody* is associated with Homeland Security these days. By virtue, I would hasten to point out, of Homeland Security believing they have the right to associate themselves with the business of anyone and everyone."

I hesitated a moment, then said, "There's probably something to be read between the lines there, sir, but I'm not sure I'm picking up on all of it. Like I told you, I'm playing catch-up here."

Now the hesitation was on Colonel Elwood's end. I sensed he was carefully choosing and weighing his words. Finally, he put them in the form of a simple and direct question. "What is your personal stake in the matter out there?"

"As far as the original investigation, my personal stake is considerable. It involves the deaths of two very close friends. To what extent Volnokov and whatever is attached to him may overlap—I don't know. What can you tell me? *Is* there an overlap?"

"The fact that he turned up in your investigation indicates so, does it not?"

"But I repeat—to what extent?"

"I'm afraid I don't have all the details on that. Only those closer to the situation can elaborate."

"I take it I'll be talking with them soon?"

"At some point that will be inevitable, I suppose. For the time being, however, the goal is for this conversation between you and me to relieve the urgency for a subsequent discussion to be necessary."

I suddenly had a much clearer picture of what I'd sensed going on "between the lines" earlier. I said, "Are you asking me to back off on my investigation, sir?"

"That's stating it rather bluntly." The colonel sighed. "But yes, that is the gist of what I was asked to convey."

"If you thought my question a minute ago was blunt," I said, "you'd better brace yourself for the response to any notion of me quitting."

"I can well imagine."

"If they were friends of yours, tell me you'd do it any different, sir."

"Probably not. But my personal temperament and resulting actions haven't always been advisable models for others to follow."

"Same here. But going back to that 'long in the tooth' business, I'd say it's a little late in the game to be looking for any big changes out of either one of us."

"Unfortunately, being too predictable can be a flaw."

"So can being too quick to conform. I'll take my chances sticking with the way I am—it's gotten me this far."

"Would you reconsider for an issue of national security?"

The question froze me, but only for a moment. "If you're ready to convince me something that major is on the line, of course I'd reconsider," I said. "But the only impression I was getting up till now was that my little investigation is an annoyance bumping against the edges of some mysterious something—nobody's bothered to tell me what, remember—that the Homeland Security gang is interested in keeping all to themselves because of this Volnokov's alleged former ties to Al-Qaeda. And now you're suggesting they want me to go into a holding pattern while they continue to play cat-and-mouse with the Russian until they figure out what he might be able to lead them to."

"Doesn't that sound like quite an important matter to get resolved?"

"Only if it turns out Boris can actually deliver the goods. How many different agencies have been trying to keep tabs on this guy for how long? Shouldn't they already know by now what he's got to spill? Otherwise this is just the latest chapter of an ongoing monkey watch during which my stalled investigation may lose momentum that I might not be able to regain. Plus—with all due respect—our boy has a history of slipping surveillances. Who's to say that can't happen again? Hell, I could even argue that letting me continue my investigation has the potential to work to our side's favor by keeping Volnokov's attention partially distracted by what I might be up to and cause him to leave himself more open to a move by Homeland Security."

"A bit grandiose, don't you think, Joseph?"

"Only if it works. And if it comes to that—who's gonna complain?"

The line was silent for several ticks. Then: "If you insist on continuing with this investigation of yours—ill-advised though that would be, in view of what has been asked of you—it would seem prudent to leave our channels of communication open, just on the off chance you stumble across something significant enough to pass along. However, inasmuch as such rogue action would be totally unsanctioned, my group wouldn't necessarily feel obligated to the courtesies and assistance previously available to you. . . . Is this understood?"

"Understood."

At least I hoped it was. What I was pretty sure I was hearing was an unofficial go-ahead to do my thing, with a veiled indication ("leave the channels of communication open") from the old war horse that he would do his best—no guarantees, though—to still cover my ass.

"I trust that it's obvious there are some very dangerous players on the chessboard out there, Joseph. If the overlap between Volnokov and whatever happened to your friends is only peripheral—maybe more than one team. Stay sharp on your point."

"Ride to the sound of the guns, Colonel."

CHAPTER THIRTY-ONE

"So nobody from Homeland Security is going to be showing up after all?" Abby said, sounding almost disappointed.

"Not today. Not any time soon," I told her. *Unless I do something to piss them off enough to make them change their minds.*

We were seated on the steps of the store's front porch, just the two of us. There was a temporary lull in the parade of customers. Abby was smoking a cigarette. The sky overhead was totally clear now and the sun was beating down bright and hot. From where we sat we could see young Matt, the grounds-keeper, going around with a wheelbarrow picking up twigs and small branches that had blown down in the storm. It seemed a more incongruous setting than ever for the kinds of things we were discussing.

"So where does that leave us. You, I mean—your investigation?"

"Been thinking about that," I said, rubbing my jaw.

"And?"

"I've decided it's about time to take a break from puzzling over what's already happened or what might happen next, and to go ahead and *make* something happen."

"You know a way to do that?"

"Sometimes you reach a point where the best hand you can play is to holler 'Timber!,' kick over the poker table, and start swinging at whoever comes in range."

"Sounds a little reckless to me."

"Can't make an omelet without breaking a few eggs."

"Enough with the metaphors already. I appreciate you wanting to move things along but it seems to me you've already got your neck stuck out—"

"Now who's speaking in metaphors?"

"Never mind that! All I'm saying is that I don't see the need for you to be in a hurry to heap more risk on yourself."

"Everything in life is a risk. The trick is to keep the odds in your favor. If I didn't think I had the odds with me for what I'm considering, then we wouldn't be having this conversation."

"Exactly what is it you're considering?"

I stood up, brushing dust off the seat of my pants. "Come on. I'll show you."

She followed me inside the store. From behind the checkout counter I plucked the phone handset off its cradle and began speaking into it. "You know who this is, Terrell. And I know you're either listening directly to me right now or you'll be hearing this shortly. I'm on to you, you lying, conniving bastard. You're dirty. You've got the blood of my friends on your hands. You leave a stain wherever you walk and all the power and money in three states aren't enough to wipe it clean. But I am—I'm the stain remover who's coming for you and there ain't a fucking thing you can do to stop me. If you think you got the balls to try, you don't have to look any farther than Pawnee Creek." Then I put the phone back down.

Abby was watching me, wide-eyed. "You're crazy!"

I grinned. "Am I?"

"You're not seriously going to Pawnee Creek now?"

"Told the man I was. Wouldn't want me to turn out to be a lying snake like him, would you?"

"But you've given him warning. It's his property, with nothing else around for miles. He could rally his whole damn militia to be waiting for you out there and who would know?"

"You'll know. You know I'm going, know to expect me back. If I don't make it, call in the law."

"What if Cam Terrell calls in the law? He'd have every right—you'll be trespassing. What will you have accomplished if he just sends the sheriff to run you off?"

I shook my head. "He's got too much pride for that. He'll want to handle me himself. But if *you* need to get the sheriff involved, the transmitter in there"—I jabbed a finger to indicate the phone—"ought to be enough to damn well grab his interest. And any reaction by Terrell to the message I just sent will be a measure of proof he's the one behind the bug."

"I still say it's crazy," Abby insisted.

"Actually, the idea is to try and push Terrell into doing something a little crazy. I can't see him disregarding the gauntlet I just threw down. He's had too much power for too long, his ego won't let him just stand by and not respond to my challenge."

"That's what I'm afraid of."

"I figure he may try to threaten me or maybe attempt to buy me off. But he won't be prepared to come right out and harm me. Not just yet, anyway. Hell, a lot of what I threw at him was bluff. He'll suspect that, he'll be looking to try and sort out how much was from how much wasn't. And at the same time I'll be angling to trip him into revealing more of what all he's trying to keep covered up. He can't afford to ignore me, but it's unlikely he's feeling desperate enough to do anything too drastic, either. . . . Like I said, at least not yet."

"You'd better hope you're right."

"I'm doing more than hoping. I'm betting my butt on it."

I went back to my cabin and made a few preparations.

First I changed from my boots to a pair of leather-faced sneakers. Straightening up from that, I lifted the 9mm hideaway out of its boot-clip holster and dropped it into the right front pocket of my jeans.

Next I took the GI-model Colt .45 auto I'd snagged from the trunk of my car, checked it for a full clip, then snugged it in place in a flat pancake holster inside the waistband of my jeans at the small of my back. With a pullover shirt worn untucked, it was reasonably unnoticeable. A couple spare clips deposited in my left front pocket and I felt adequately armed and ready. I decided a set of bandoleers strapped criss-cross over my chest would be a bit too showy.

As I drove away, I saw Abby appear at the near end of the store's porch and stand watching me. I gave a little wave but she didn't return it. Her expression looked as somber as a pallbearer's.

CHAPTER THIRTY-TWO

Pawnee Creek was scooting along high and fast, the runoff from last night's storm stoking its current, painting it a muddier brown than I remembered from before.

I turned off the highway at the south end of the bridge and eased my Accord across the bumpy cattle gate that opened to the turnaround area where Vic Faber brought his canoeing customers. I parked on the fringe of the turnaround area, got out and stood for a moment just looking down at the creek, my gaze following it eastward to where it finally disappeared around a bend of the deep seam it had worn into the rugged Sandhills terrain.

The gentle breeze that was blowing and the faint rush of the water seemed to whisper in soft harmony and it should have been an idyllic, soothing moment, standing there listening to it with sunlight pouring down all around. But, for me, the setting had a strangely ominous feel. Continuing to gaze east, I knew that off in that direction a mile or so was the old homestead site that Bomber and Liz had stopped to look at on that fateful day that was their last. I was more convinced than ever that that stop had somehow triggered something—some kind of reaction, some chain of events—that contributed either directly or indirectly to their deaths and then the clumsy attempt to mask the true cause.

A cold shiver passed through me in spite of the warmth of the sunshine.

I shook off the feeling and started hiking eastward along the high bank of the creek. I hit a good stride and it wasn't long before the cold shiver had been replaced by beads of sweat popping out at my temples.

As I walked, remembering that this was rattlesnake country, I carefully scanned the ground ahead of me and to either side. I was also on the lookout for any sign that might be associated to Bomber and Liz having passed this way, even though, as Cameron Terrell had cuttingly pointed out, I was hardly trained for such outdoor tracking. Plus, the recent storm would have obliterated practically all ground signs, even to the keenest eye. Still, despite my main purpose here today being to bait Terrell, if I happened to kick loose a piece of hard evidence I sure as hell wouldn't disregard it.

I wondered if and how Terrell would take the bait. Regardless of my assurances to Abby, I couldn't really be certain he would show up at all. The only thing I felt one hundred percent sure of was that Terrell was the ultimate receiver of the messages being tapped off Abby's phones. So that meant that sooner or later he would be hearing the challenge I'd thrown out. I was hoping for sooner but, hell, for all I knew my words had gone onto a recording tape that no one had gotten around to clearing yet.

I might be in for a lonely afternoon out here in the wide open spaces.

After I'd gone about a quarter mile, the high ground I was traversing broke away in a gigantic, gravel-strewn washout that angled sharply down to a level stretch of bank right at the water's edge. It was easy to see why Abby had advised that the trip back to the homestead site couldn't be made with any conventional vehicle. Which made me wonder how—if he *did* show up—Cam Terrell would be arriving. Would he walk in also? Some sort of conveyance seemed more likely. A jeep? An

ATV? Hell, he was a big rancher—maybe on horseback. For that matter, considering his RBR connections, maybe a personal tank.

I smiled grimly at the possibilities. If I did end up drawing company out here today, it could get real interesting.

I began picking my way down the rugged slope, careful not to step on any rain-loosened rocks and equally careful not to disturb any snakes that might be coiled amidst the rubble. I had to skirt a couple pockets of mud but for the most part the sandy soil had already been wind- and sun-dried in the wake of the recent storm. By the time I got to the bottom I was pouring sweat. The coolness coming off the stream and the shade thrown by an overhang of twisted cottonwood trees felt most welcome. Backhanding sweat from my face, I gave myself a mental kick in the pants for not having the sense to bring along something to drink.

I had to settle for kneeling at the edge of the creek and scooping cupped palmfuls of water to my face and the back of my neck. It felt good but I couldn't help thinking that a follow-up with a cold bottle of Mick sure would have hit the spot.

I stayed in the shade and followed close to the creek's edge until the taller embankments started crowding in again and then it was back up to higher ground, up above the trees and underbrush to where the land seemed only a stark ocean of undulating grass. Before leaving the creek, I managed to annoy a feisty beaver who stood on his hind legs on the opposite bank and chattered angrily at me for showing up in the vicinity of his watery dwelling. And then, climbing up the weedy incline, I disturbed a small flock of wild turkeys who scattered away, also garbling their displeasure with me. At the rate I seemed to be pissing off every living thing I encountered out here, Terrell would have to stand in line if and when he showed up.

Back on the high ground, I proceeded another half mile or so before coming to a broad, flat expanse just above a gentle slope dropping off once again to the creek. And there, in the midst of this naturally graded area, it was: the rubble of an old stone fireplace and chimney, angular ridges of weeds that had once been the walls of a sod hut, some leaning and rotted gray fence posts with a few broken railings hanging off them. . . .

The Brannigan homestead.

I stepped into a squarish depression that I reckoned had once been where the house proper sat, then walked over to the pile of fireplace stones. After checking the base of the pile for any sign of rattlers, I reached out and rested my hand on the stones. They were surprisingly cool to the touch. I stood like that for a minute, feeling a vague sense of all the ghosts associated to this place . . . from determined old Sean Brannigan whose dream was to turn the spot into a home that could be handed down through generations of Brannigans, to his discouraged sons who fled that dream . . . to my buddy Bomber, who had passed here only to pay homage.

In that moment I was gripped by a general sadness for unfulfilled dreams and the fleetingness of life.

Half a second later, the chimney stones six inches above where I was resting my hand blew apart with a sharp crack of sound. My hand and body jerked away reflexively. As I took an uncertain step backward, the report of a heavy rifle rolled across the breeze-blown grasses and reached my ears.

Twice more, in rapid succession, chunks of chimneystone splattered away, each impact followed by the rolling boom of a rifle report.

Jesus Christ, somebody was shooting at me!

I hit the ground in a dive and scrambled to the opposite side of the stone pile, staying low. I reached under my shirt, jerked the .45 free and held it ready. The shots had come from behind me over my right shoulder, from the southwest. Only softly tumbling hills of grass in that direction for as far as I could see. No movement, no wisp of telltale gunsmoke. Nothing.

I hunkered lower in the itchy weeds and willed my breathing to level off, to get under control. *"But he won't be prepared to come right out and harm me,"* I had assured Abby on the subject of what Cam Terrell's intentions would be if he met me out here today. At the moment it appeared as if I might have miscalculated on that. Assuming, that was, it was actually Terrell—or a representative of his—doing the shooting and that they were actually trying to hit me. Even though the shooter was firing from some distance away, judging by the delay before hearing the sound of the shots, I'd been an unsuspecting, wide open target.

Terrell would have sent the best and the best shouldn't have missed under those circumstances.

The shots *might* only be a warning, but I wasn't ready to stake my life on it by revealing myself unnecessarily.

I stayed low and waited. I didn't have to wait long. A fourth shot came sizzling in, hitting the stone pile closer to the ground, directly opposite my head. *Smack!* And then, after half a second, *Boom!*

Without aiming or even looking, I extended my arm and squeezed off four quick rounds in the general direction of the shooter. . . . Just to give the fucker something to think about.

After that it got real still and quiet. Minutes ticked by. The sun beat down, reflecting off the bare stones. Rivulets of sweat squirmed inside my shirt.

I thought about my cell phone lying in the seat of the Accord. I hadn't become enough of a cell junkie to wear it clipped to me at all times like so many do, yet right at the moment I wished I had. I could have used one to call Abby or Knaack or Mabry—hell, all three of them—to report that some lunatic with a high-powered rifle had me pinned down. Given the remoteness of the spot it would take a while for anyone to reach me, but at least I'd have had the solace of knowing somebody was aware of my predicament and was on the way. I considered the irony attaching these thoughts to the discussion Abby and I had had concerning Bomber's stubborn refusal to carry a cell and how it might have served him on the day he and Liz crashed.

If the shooter was indeed out to get me and was dedicated to the task, I was in quite a fix. Yeah, I had the cover of the chimney stones . . . for the time being. But the shooter, armed with a longer-ranged weapon than mine and moving silently and invisibly in the tall prairie grasses a hundred or more yards away, could right now be circling to position himself for another clear shot.

I glanced in the direction of the slope that dropped off to the creek. If I could make it down there, then I could gain the cover of the trees and underbrush and the shooter would have to come in and get me. The odds would be greatly equalized.

The whisper of the breeze passing through the tall grasses blurred all noise to a soft, prolonged sigh. If the rifleman was on the move I had no chance in hell of hearing him or spotting him—not until, that was, he decided to make his presence known with another bullet.

I shifted my position slightly, nudging against the column of stones as I did so and noticing a faint give to the pile. I reached up with my free hand and pushed harder and felt the weather-lashed column actually teeter a bit. A desperate idea started to form.

I could only guess which way the rifleman would try circling, but since he'd started out to the south of me it seemed somewhat reasonable he would continue maneuvering from that general direction. If I was wrong, if he was circling to the north, putting himself between me and the creek, then I risked running right into him. No matter, I made up my mind I wasn't going to stay there in one spot like a sitting duck.

I rolled onto my back and then scooched my butt up against the column of chimney stones, feet raised and knees bent to my chest. Taking a quick breath and holding it, I pressed my shoulders to the ground and kicked with both feet. It took a second double-kick before the pile went over, but over it did go. Rattling, tumbling, crashing down, dust cloud billowing just the way I'd hoped.

It was a minor distraction and the dusty haze provided only a fleeting hint of a smokescreen, but it was the best I could do. Before the haze started to dissipate, I was on my feet, running as hard as I could for the slope and the creek below, zig-zagging in the tall, slapping grass. One shot boomed from behind me, then another. I imagined I might have heard a slug *thurp!* past my head but I couldn't be sure above the pounding of my feet and the slappity-whack of the grass against my churning legs.

I reached the lip of the slope where almost immediately I stumbled and lost my footing. I'd intended to *run* down the incline but that wasn't the way it went. Instead I toppled, flopped, rolled, somersaulted a time or three, and generally hurtled toward the bottom like a one-man avalanche. As a result, I came to a halt bruised and scraped and with a good deal of wind knocked out of me . . . but minus any fresh bullet holes and still with a solid grip on my .45 .

I wasted no time dragging my battered self to cover, eventually nestling into the crotch of a gnarled, thick-trunked cottonwood flanked by a rocky outcropping on one side and leafy underbrush on the other.

Now. Now I felt ready—eager even—to play some more with the ambusher and his rifle.

Come on you sonofabitch, I silently invited. *Step right up and get yourself some.*

CHAPTER THIRTY-THREE

I waited a long, excruciating, nerve-wracking hour.

One whole hour without moving, scarcely breathing. My ears attuned to every rustle, every flutter, every burble of the stream, every ebb and flow of the sighing breeze. My eyes darting, alert, intently watching . . . waiting.

Nothing. No sound, no hint of movement that didn't belong.

The fact I was able to hold out for that long was a minor miracle of willpower considering my low threshold for patience. Even at the risk of drawing more gunfire I knew I wasn't going to be able to hang on much longer, though.

The way I saw it, there were three possibilities where the shooter was concerned. One, his shots had been meant only to rattle me, scare me off but never to actually hit me and therefore, having accomplished that, he had slipped away and was long gone. Two, having failed in his attempt to gun me down and allowing me to reach equalizing cover in possession of my own firepower, he had slunk off to wait and try another day. Three, he was still out there somewhere, stalking me, showing his own infinite patience, waiting for me to expose myself again so he could finish the job.

I'd told Abby the trick was to play the odds. So two to one, those were the odds I had facing me now. And even if I could stand to stay put another three or four hours they wouldn't really change. Not unless I was willing to stick it out the rest of the day and into the evening, until Abby got concerned enough by my failure to return and sent someone looking for me. Barring that, it came down to finding out if the shooter either had fled or was better at the waiting game than I was.

I eased slowly from concealment, stretching the kinks out of my legs and back, holding the .45 tight and ready.

"Bang. You're dead."

I was amazed and stunned to hear the words spoken from only a few feet behind me. The voice was calm, low. But it froze me in place like some paralyzing ray out of an old science-fiction movie.

Seconds as long as days ticked by. Then the voice, still calm and low, spoke again. "First put down the gun and kick it away . . . then turn around. Slow. Easy."

I did as instructed. Once I had about-faced I lifted my gaze and found myself staring into the eyes of William Thunder-bringer. He was crouched on the crown of the rock outcropping four feet above and slightly to one side of where I'd lain in cover. An M-16 rifle rested in the crook of his left arm, its snout pointed casually in my direction. It seemed impossible he could have moved in that close without stirring any inkling of awareness on my part. Yet the undeniable evidence was right before my eyes.

He spoke again. "That was an interesting maneuver, what you did back up there with the old chimney and all. You move fast for a big guy."

"You've got some pretty slick moves of your own," I allowed.

He straightened up in a fluid, unhurried motion then stepped off the crown of rock and dropped seven feet to the ground as lightly as a leaf. The rifle muzzle never wavered off the center of my chest more than a fraction of an inch.

"You realize, of course," he said with absolutely no strain in his voice, "that if I actually wanted you dead that's what you'd already be."

I nodded. "I get the picture," I said tightly. He'd gotten the drop on me with humiliating ease. It galled me to admit it, but he was that good. And no matter how much I thought about the 9mm still in my pocket and longed for the chance to make a grab for it, to turn the tables, I knew with a sinking feeling it was damned unlikely he'd present any opening for me to do so.

He was dressed in a brown T-shirt and baggy cargo pants with big pockets on the sides. High-topped hiking boots with thick soles. It was amazing how different he looked from the common thug I'd made him for the first time I saw him.

He lifted a black plastic water bottle from a holder clipped to his belt, thumbed open the cap, squirted a long stream of water into his mouth. His eyes stayed on me. After lowering the bottle and thumbing the cap closed again he gave it an underhand toss in my direction. "A kick-ass old sergeant I used to have drilled this mantra into us every time we headed out for the bush: 'Worry first about your fresh water supply, then your ammo and your enemy,' he'd say. 'You got the chance to survive practically any engagement as long as you don't panic, but without water you got no chance at all.' "

I caught the bottle and took a grateful drink, trying not to show how desperately thirsty I was. After drinking and recapping, I flipped it back. "Was that a sergeant in Terrell's army?" I asked.

Half of Thunderbringer's mouth smiled. "The old firepisser I'm talking about would've considered Terrell's outfit little more than a pack of barely competent Boy Scouts."

"But that's *your* outfit now, right?"

"I've soldiered in lots of outfits, Hannibal."

"So you're a mercenary. You go where the money is."

"Something like that."

"And today the money sent you here to . . . what? Warn me? Scare me off?"

"*Have* you been scared off?"

"Only a fool wouldn't be scared with bullets whipping around him. But being scared and being *scared off* are two different things."

"Uh-huh. Way I figured you'd see it. Tell me, how did you trip to Abby Bridger's phone being bugged and what made you decide it was Terrell?"

"Let's just say when your boss is running off at the mouth he ought to be more careful not to let on about certain things nobody ever got around to telling him."

With minimum consideration, he said, "The camera and picnic basket, right?"

He was good, you had to give him that. "Has Terrell got them?" I wanted to know.

"Not unless he put on a hell of a good act sending some of his wranglers out here first thing this morning to look for them. They came back empty-handed."

I pushed his willingness to talk, saying, "So what was Terrell afraid might be on the camera? What exactly did my friends see out here that day that made it necessary to kill them?"

For the briefest flicker of an instant something showed on Thunderbringer's face besides the flat, emotionless mask he wore there. Then it was gone, unreadable. His eyes bored into me. "That's all it comes down to for you, ain't it?"

"It's the whole thing," I confirmed.

He regarded some more. Then he did something that completely stunned me for the second time in only a handful of minutes. He opened his mouth and spoke a single word . . . the same single, obscure word I had been given to establish my contacts with Army Intelligence.

"Who the hell *are* you?" I hissed through clenched teeth.

"The short answer is that I'm somebody on the same side as you."

"That doesn't wash."

"Think about it."

I did. After a minute I saw it. "You're working a double setup. You're mercing for Terrell on the outside, spooking for the G undercover."

"Close enough."

"Yeah, well, excuse me all to hell for not seeing it sooner. Guy takes a half dozen shots at me, I pretty much rule him out as being on my side."

"You're lucky I convinced Terrell to let me be the one to come here and take a crack at scaring you off. You had him mighty excited with that phone message you sent. The other response he was seriously considering was to simply kill your ass."

"That would have been moronic! Everybody knows what I'm working on, the questions I've been raising. Killing me would practically guarantee a flood of attention that would eventually wipe away all of Terrell's lies and cover-ups, no matter how much money and power he's got."

"Even still, your death could be rigged to look like another accident or you could simply disappear. . . . Getting to the bottom of something like that takes time. And a little bit more time is all Terrell really needs. You see, you don't understand the big picture."

"Fuck the big picture! You just said 'rigged to look like another accident'—is that an admission, then, that the death of my two friends was intentional?"

"You need to calm down, mister," Thunderbringer said warningly. "I've already broken about forty different clearance levels revealing as much to you as I have. But I never sweat a few wild cards in the deck, so what the hell. In your place, I'd damn well want to settle the score for my friends, too. There's a limit to how far I can let my empathy take me, though, because I *do* understand the big picture and I happen to give a fuck about it. Justice for what happened to your friends will come . . . but it has to wait its turn. There are other things going down that need to be allowed to run their course first."

I shook my head. "Colonel Elwood already tried that wait-your-turn routine with me once today. If I was ever going to hold still for anybody, it'd be him. He should have known better than to send you to make another pitch."

"The colonel didn't send me. This is a joint operation so I'm familiar with Elwood, but he's not part of my direct upchain. Never mind who is, or which outfit. All that matters is that I was given your code word as a means to link with you in case something made it absolutely necessary. I was supposed to use it only as a last resort. But I've never been big on following orders to the letter. I'm an end-results man, they'll have to get used to it. So it was strictly my decision to break cover with you here today. Like I said, I got some empathy for where you're coming from and I figured, a guy like you, the only way to play it is to lay it out straight."

"Volnokov," I said. "He's at the center of this big picture you keep talking about, right?"

"He's part of it, yeah."

"He have anything to do with what happened to my friends?"

"Man, you have got a one-track fucking mind, you know that?"

"Did he?" I insisted.

"He was there that day," was all he would say.

"And you?"

He met my eyes and held them steady. "I was there, too. There was nothing I could do to change what happened. It came too fast. All I would've accomplished by trying would have been to blow my cover, get myself killed, and screw the overall mission. And nothing would have changed for your friends."

"See?" I said, making a frustrated gesture. "That's why I can't go along with this wait-your-turn bullshit! Everybody else sees what happened to my friends as a minor speck in the background of your big goddamn picture. Well I don't. I see *them* at the front and center of things, not your stinking Russian. And I can also see what's apt to come next. If and when you get ready to bring charges against Volnokov and whoever or whatever else has gotten tangled around him, guess what? Minor specks have a way of getting lost in the shuffle or bargained away to nothingness."

"If the people responsible for what happened to your friends go down—and they *will*—they'll go down hard. The charges against them will be numerous, their punishment will be severe. I'm a realist and, like I said, an end-results man . . . the bad guys fry, what difference does a specific charge or two one way or the other really make?"

"For me and for the sake of my friends' memories, it makes all the difference in the world. I want the sonsabitches responsible for killing my friends to pay *directly* for that act."

"Nobody can make that guarantee."

"Give me the chance to put my hands on 'em . . . I can."

CHAPTER THIRTY-FOUR

I returned to No Name Bay feeling battered, weary, frustrated, angry, and confused.

I didn't know what I was going to do next. One thing I did know was that I was going to have to face Abby. But what did I tell her? How much should I reveal? Those questions had plagued me throughout the drive back.

She was watching, of course, when I pulled up and parked in front of my cabin. She was off the store porch and hurrying over before I was all the way out of the car.

It took her no time to spot the bruises and scuffs from my tumble down the slope. "What happened to you, Joe?" she wanted to know. "My God, Cam didn't send some of his men to rough you up, did he?"

I grinned at her use of the rather outdated term. "No, that wasn't it. More like I roughed up myself," I said.

"Don't kid with me, Joe. Tell me what happened."

Her rich brown eyes gazed up at me intently. Concerned, imploring. Looking down into them I suddenly knew that the only thing I could do was level with her completely, tell her everything. Together, we'd decide where to take it from here.

"Come on inside," I said. "We need to talk."

I started up the cabin steps. Abby started up behind me, but then paused to gaze down past the other cabins toward the lake.

"What's the matter?" I asked.

"I dunno. Nothing, maybe. . . . It's just that young Matt, my groundskeeper, hasn't been around all afternoon. And his pickup camper is gone from where he keeps it parked. He hardly ever goes anywhere in it because of the price of fuel and the fact it's such a gas hog. Plus he ought not be gone at all—there's work to be done. That's not like him. The whole thing is curious."

"Guys his age aren't above being a little irresponsible at times."

"Maybe. He never seemed like that."

"Could be some vacationing babe in a thong bikini batted her eyes at him and. . . ."

" 'Batted her eyes'?"

"I'm just saying."

She motioned me on into the cabin. "Never mind. We don't have time to worry about it right now. He'll probably show up after a while with a perfectly good explanation."

Inside the cabin I pulled the last bottle of Mick and a Coke from the ice chest—both barely cool, bobbing in a melted puddle because I had forgotten to add fresh ice (or anything else) before leaving earlier. As I talked I drank the Mick anyway and Abby, listening, sipped at the Coke.

I laid it out in sequence, starting with my Army Intelligence contact but without going into detail on its history. How I'd gotten in touch with them last evening and then again this morning. How Colonel Elwood had asked me to stall my investigation, hinting at issues of national security, suggesting that a greater good would be served by allowing some unspecified scenario involving Terrell and Volnokov to play out first. And then having that request echoed during my encounter with Thunderbringer once he'd revealed his undercover operative role (a capacity I verified via a call to Colonel Elwood as soon as I got back to my cell phone—verification given only on a "confirm or deny" basis, no embellishments).

"Jesus," Abby muttered when I was done. "This is all mushrooming into something so incredible and so . . . I don't know, huge. Government agencies and national security and ex–Russian spies with possible links to Al-Qaeda . . . this is Nowhere Nebraska, for God's sake! All you and I started out after was the truth about a car crash on an obscure highway and now. . . ."

"Isn't that still what we're after . . . what *we* are after?" I said. "So the next question becomes: Do we allow it to get mixed in with these other agendas or do we try to hold our own course and continue after our own conclusions?"

"Do we really have a choice? You keep talking like we can fight the government, not cooperate with them. You apparently have some kind of rough working relationship with this Colonel Elwood and his group but, even still, if you get to be too much of a hindrance he's already told you he can't guarantee backing you up. The flip side—since you like to talk about odds—if we *do* cooperate with these government guys, doesn't that improve our odds of getting to the bottom of everything?"

"Maybe, maybe not." I explained to her my concerns about direct blame and punishment for what happened to Liz and Bomber possibly getting lost in the shuffle of the bigger picture. "The bad guys may still go down, but will the whole truth come out? Do you think the government is going to be eager to reveal that two innocent citizens were allowed to be killed on the periphery of this big joint-agency operation? If it plays out like that, can we really consider that Bomber and Liz have gotten the justice they deserve?"

Abby studied me closely. "That makes a lot of difference to you, doesn't it?"

"Like I told Thunderbringer—all the difference in the world. Doesn't it to you?"

Her eyes fell. "I don't know anymore, Joe. Right at the moment I'm just feeling exhausted and . . . well, overwhelmed I guess. Hell, maybe a little bit frightened. In the beginning I was fighting for the truth all alone. Getting scoffed at, ridiculed. Then it was so wonderful when you came out and agreed to help. But now all this other stuff has gotten thrown in, you've been shot at and banged up. . . ." Her gaze lifted again. "None of it is ever going to bring Liz and Uncle Bomber back. We both know that, right? If the bad guys end up getting punished anyway, is it worth continuing to fight all these obstacles just so we can say we told everybody so? Is that really what we'd be staying in it for?"

I felt myself wilt a little, as if the exhaustion she spoke of suddenly transferred to me and amplified my own weariness. I dragged a palm down over my face, heaved a sigh. Then I swore. "Shit, I don't know either. Maybe you've got a point."

"I'd say that right now we're probably both too tired to think straight. Plus, those scrapes and bruises all over you need taken care of. We should be worrying about tending to those before we worry about anything else."

I tugged at my face some more, squeezing my temples between a thumb and fingertips. Letting the hand fall, I said, "The cuts have waited this long, they can wait a while longer. Right now all I want to do is gobble a handful of aspirins and stretch out on this cot for a little bit. Then I'll walk down and take a hot shower and you can patch up whatever wounds don't wash off."

"All right," Abby said somewhat reluctantly. "I'll go dust off my first-aid kit and be watching for when you head back from the showers."

I dug a bottle of aspirins from amongst the possibles in my duffel bag and knocked back some of the contents with a glass of tap water. Turning once more to Abby, I said, "What about you? You've been going as long as I have. How are you holding up?"

"I got a little rest this afternoon when my counter girl showed up. And I haven't been tumbling around dodging bullets out in the Sandhills either. I'll be fine."

"So will I. Just give me a half hour, forty-five minutes tops. Then we'll talk some more."

"Take as much time as you need. I'll be around."

I sat on the edge of the cot, reached behind me and pulled the .45 from the pancake holster in my waistband. I placed it on the floor beside the cot, aware that Abby was watching and that her eyes had widened somewhat. Then I lay back and rested one arm across my own grainy eyes. I heard Abby get up and head for the door. I was asleep before I heard it latch behind her.

I woke with a start. It was dark outside and somebody was shooting at my cabin! I jackknifed to a sitting position, my hand darting to the small of my back before I remembered that I'd unholstered the .45 that had been riding there.

I rolled onto one elbow and reached down, groping on the floor for the gun. As I did so, some more of the sleep fuzziness cleared from my brain and eyes and I became aware of Abby standing part way across the room. She was leaning over the table, her face turned my way, looking at me in bewilderment.

"Joe?" she said. "Are you okay? Did you have a nightmare?"

Outside, a fresh volley of bangs and pops riddled the night air. Firecrackers. . . . Damn fools setting off firecrackers! That was the noise I had mistaken for gunshots.

I swung my feet to the floor and sat on the edge of the cot. "What time is it?" I wanted to know.

"Not quite ten. Don't worry, your hated cherry bombers will be knocking off soon. The noise wasn't bothering you before this, you must have been getting ready to wake up anyway."

Abby had changed clothes since I saw her last. Now she was wearing faded cutoff jeans, obligatory flip-flops on her feet, and a spaghetti-strapped pullover top colored a shade of peach that seemed to vaguely match the lipstick she had on. No bra under the pullover, if I was any judge (and I reckoned myself something of an expert observer in that category, even when still a bit sleep-groggy).

"Shouldn't you be at your store?" I asked.

"I close early on Sundays. I decided to fix you a nice surprise for when you finished your little power nap."

The room was bathed in a soft, flickering glow from two glass-encased candles sitting on the table. The table was also set with plates of food, I couldn't tell exactly what, and a second folding chair had been brought from somewhere.

"Looks like you've been busy."

"Just a few simple touches."

"God, I guess I practically died."

"You were sawing logs pretty heavy, that's for sure. But I was nearly ready to roust you anyway. I figured you were bound to be starving, right?"

"As a matter of fact. . . . Uh, what happened to my gun, Abby?"

"It looked so ugly and kinda scary laying there. So I put it out of sight in your duffel bag."

"You shouldn't mess with a fella's gun, Ab," I scolded mildly. "You especially shouldn't mess with one if it admittedly makes you nervous."

"If lecture time is through, your supper is over here waiting for you," she replied coolly, her tone making it clear she didn't care much for the chastisement, no matter how mild. "You want the gun back so you can wear it while you eat?"

I let the matter drop. I'm smart enough to back off after

bumbling down an ill-advised path.

I got up and went over to the table. Took a seat at the plate that had been prepared for me. The plate was loaded with a thick sandwich, sliced pickles and green olives on the side, and a mound of potato salad.

"The sandwich is deli-sliced roast beef, Swiss cheese, and horseradish mustard on whole wheat. Hope you like it," Abby said. "The potato salad is homemade so, whether you like it or not, you'd darn well better pretend to, after all the boiling and peeling and dicing I went through to put it together."

It didn't take but a couple bites to discover that *pretending* to like the fare was far from necessary. Everything was excellent. Of course the fact that I hadn't eaten anything all day and was ravenous didn't hurt either; but it was flat delicious, no two ways about it.

"I re-stocked your ice chest, too. Would you like a Michelob to go with that?"

"You are a goddess and an angel." I started to make a crack about marrying me on the spot but, after the events of last night, I thought better of it and held my tongue.

When Abby handed me a cold, dripping Mick I tipped it up and sucked it half-dry in one mighty swig.

Abby had a plate in front of her, too, containing half a sandwich and a much smaller scoop of potato salad. Beside it there was an opened bottle of Pepsi from which she sipped between bites of her food. "While you were zonked out, I was also busy doing more than just being domestic," she informed me.

I arched a brow. "Oh?"

"I thought a lot about what you said and decided you're absolutely right—The people responsible for bringing harm to Liz and Uncle Bomber not only have to be punished, but they need to be held accountable for *everything* they did. Not have part of it dealt to one side in some meaningless, barely mentioned way."

I grinned. "Attagirl. I didn't think you really meant what you said before."

"Furthermore," she went on, "I might've figured out how we can help make sure they get held accountable, even if you and I end up being bulldozed out of the way by the government."

"Fun throwing those metaphors around, ain't it?"

"I'm serious. Do you want to hear my idea or not?"

I made a gesture for her to go ahead.

"Okay. According to your new pal Thunderbringer nobody has found Liz's camera yet, right? So that means it remains out there somewhere, best guess still being somewhere along Pawnee Creek. If we could find it and if, in fact, it does have some pictures on it that show whatever it was Liz and Uncle Bomber saw and we're figuring caused a retaliation against them, *that* would be hard evidence, correct? Something we could seal and have time-dated and notarized, say, and then leave with a lawyer or something." Abby's eyes shone with excitement. "That way, if the government gets hard-line enough to try pushing us into the background and squelching the little Liz/Uncle Bomber sidebar to their 'big picture' operation, we could have the lawyer release the photos to the media and stir up enough inquiries and demands to *force* them to own up to it. . . . What do you think?"

I was leaning forward a bit in my chair, leaning into her excitement. What she was suggesting seemed like quite a reach. Still, just maybe. . . . "There are a lot of 'ifs' in there," I said cautiously. "Namely, *if* the camera is out there and *if* we could find it and *if* it contained anything meaningful after we did. Terrell's men went over that ground as recently as this morning. Our chances of having better luck finding anything, especially after the storm and all—"

"But that's where the rest of my idea comes in. You see, I'm wondering if the *ground* isn't the wrong place to be looking."

I shook my head. "I'm not following you."

"Okay, try following this: You're Liz and Uncle Bomber and you've just seen and taken pictures of something you realize it's dangerous for you to have observed, and you're trying to get away from there. Maybe you know or at least suspect you've been spotted and somebody might be giving pursuit. You're hurrying back to your car, you've got the camera in the big metal picnic basket. In case you don't make it, you decide you want to leave behind some evidence, some clue that might give somebody later on a lead as to what happened, what went wrong. You don't drop the camera accidentally in your flight or toss it off into a clump of weeds—you've got people chasing you, you know they'll be coming across the same ground. But you've got the picnic basket and though it may not be totally watertight it *will* float after a fashion. . . . And what's right there handy beside you?"

"Pawnee Creek," I said, leaning in a little more.

"Bingo. Moses in the bullrushes. . . . Message in a bottle. . . . It may be a long shot, but even long shots have a way of paying off sometimes. Especially if you're desperate and don't have a whole lot of other options."

I was nodding. "Okay. Not a totally illogical sequence. So if the picnic basket went into the creek, where did it end up?"

"Lots of possibilities there. Pawnee Creek is twisty and full of rocks and snags, the basket could have been carried for a ways by the current and then gotten hung up in any one of scores of different places."

"But that was weeks ago. Vic Faber surely has had plenty of canoers go down the river since then. Wouldn't one of them have spotted something like a colorful picnic basket?"

"If they did, nobody turned it in. I checked with Faber. Of

course that could mean somebody just kept it. In any case, though, catching sight of the basket in the first place might be kinda tricky and then, in the second place, getting to it might be trickier still. It might be snagged in a way that doesn't leave it very visible. And even if somebody saw it, it could be jammed in a section of fast water where it's not easy to stop or maneuver over to. A gaudy picnic basket probably containing a few crumbs of leftover food . . . not big incentive for anybody to go to a lot of trouble for."

"Except us. We'd have incentive."

"Uh-huh. That's why, when I was talking to Faber, I went ahead and reserved one of his canoes for us first thing in the morning."

"Whoa." My hand, holding the last bite of sandwich, froze halfway to my mouth. "I admire your initiative, kiddo, but. . . ."

"But what?"

I made a face. "A *canoe,* that's what. Do I look like Hiawatha or Huck Finn or some damn body? I tried canoeing once when I was a kid and all I remember is being underwater and having the stupid thing upside down over my head like some kind of giant wet hat practically the whole afternoon. You put me in a canoe on Pawnee Creek and the only thing you'll spend your time digging out of the snags and jams is me after I keep falling out."

"All it amounts to is finding your balance," Abby assured me. "I can give you some pointers and make sure we stay afloat. I go canoeing every summer, on Pawnee Creek and sometimes on the Dismal and Niobrara rivers up north. That's how my son Dusty and I spend a lot of the weekends we're together. When she was healthier, even Ma liked to canoe."

"Swell. Take one of them then, you'll have a more experienced first mate. You be the Navy, I'll stay on dry land and be the Infantry."

"Aw, come on. A hard-nosed, bullet-spitting private eye like you can't be a weenie about a little boat ride. I told you I'll keep us afloat, and even if we do dump a couple of times the Pawnee is what—four or five whole feet deep? The worst that'll happen is we get our socks wet."

I thought about a case that had once sent me tubing down a stretch of the Mississippi River under cover of darkness. At first light some very bad and unfortunately also some very good people had died . . . none through any fault of the river.

I sighed. "It'd all be for the sake of playing one hell of a long shot."

"What else have we got? Anything better? Any more promising lead to follow? In addition to possibly giving us some leverage with the government, the pictures—granted, *if* we find any—might also give us more to go on as far as proving who's responsible for what happened to Liz and Uncle Bomber. Right now all we've got are some strong candidates, but no real proof and no clear sense of exactly who played what role in either the crash or the cover-up."

I popped the last bite of sandwich into my mouth and chewed it fiercely. "What the hell," I finally said. "Just do me a favor . . . if I end up drowning in a couple lousy feet of muddy creek water, have the decency to haul my carcass up onto the bank and pump a couple slugs in me or something, will you? Make it look like I checked out the way a hard-nosed, bullet-spitting private eye is *supposed* to check out."

CHAPTER THIRTY-FIVE

After we were done eating and the table was cleared, Abby insisted that tending to my cuts and abrasions would not be put off any longer. She plopped her first-aid kit on the table, ordered me to peel off my shirt and stay sitting right there. Then she went into the bathroom and came back out with a washcloth and bar of soap and a bowl of warm, sudsy water.

"Jesus, look at you," she murmured as she squatted beside me and began to dab and clean. "You go belly-flopping down a freaking cliff and get all beat to hell like this yet you're worried about taking a dunk in the water."

"Bullets flying in your general direction sorta take away the luxury of having the chance to fret about a situation. At the time, going down that slope seemed like a lot better—Ouch! Hey, there's already enough skin missing there, thanks, no need to scrub away any more."

"We put this off too long as it is, so it's even more important now to get these good and clean to make sure they don't become infected. So hush up and hold still, you big baby."

"Having already established I'm a canoeing weenie, what say we lay off impugning my manhood any further for a while."

Outside, it had grown quiet, the damnable firecrackers finally ceasing.

It grew quiet inside the cabin, too, as Abby concentrated on nursing my nicks and scrapes. She carefully cleaned, applied antiseptic, selected the right-sized bandage or fold of gauze where she felt a protective covering was needed.

Somewhere in this quietness, something else started to change also. The banter and easy rapport that flowed so naturally between Abby and me gave way to . . . an awareness. A heightened sense of each other, of being close, of being alone together in a softly lit room.

I could smell her hair and her perfume, and I could smell her overall woman-scent, too. I could feel the cool, gentle touch of her hands, and I could feel the heat coming off her body. And although her eyes were downcast, focused on the work she was doing, I could envision with full clarity the depth and rich color of them, and the intensity and vitality that danced like a thousand tiny sparks in those twin pools.

This heightened awareness started slow but encroached steadily, like the shadow cast by a cloud skidding high across the sky. I could feel it, I could sense Abby feeling it as well.

None of it was exactly new, of course. It had been building from the first. We'd both tried to ignore it, leave it unspoken . . . until last night. Last night I'd still fought it. Fought it hard. Now, tonight, I didn't feel like I had much fight left. Moreover, it no longer felt like something I *wanted* to fight.

"Somewhere in here," I said, a touch of huskiness abruptly present in my voice, "I guess I'd better remember my manners and say thank you for all this—the meal, replenishing my ice chest, seeing to my wounds. You're good people, Abby."

She lifted those wonderful brown eyes and looked up at me. "In case you haven't figured it out by now, Joe Hannibal, I didn't come back here tonight with intentions of being completely 'good.' "

I swallowed. "Jeez, Ab, I. . . ."

"Don't 'Jeez' me, damn it. You feel it, I feel it. It's *there*. I think we're fools if we don't let it happen and see where it takes us. I won't beg you . . . but I don't intend to give up, either.

Not for as long as you're around."

She set aside the washcloth and bandages and stood up. Stood directly in front of me, hands on hips, her breathing quickened. Her bellybutton, visible between the top of her shorts and the hem of her pullover top, was at eye level with where I sat.

Now I was the one who lifted my gaze to look up at her. In a voice that came out huskier still, I said, "You don't ever have to beg, Abby."

She fell into my arms with such force that the chair I was in actually teetered momentarily.

Then it righted itself and we became entangled in an urgent, grinding embrace. Our lips met. Hungry, demanding.

I stood up after a couple of minutes, scooping her in my arms. I turned toward the cot. Lay her down upon it, knelt beside her. She kept her fingers laced behind my neck and kept pulling my face to her lips, murmuring my name between the kisses and low moans of pleasure.

I tugged away her clothing. My mouth found her breasts, small and soft and capped with hard, rust-colored nipples. I worked my way down her body, down the length of her rapidly rising and falling stomach, my tongue probing her navel, then lower. . . .

Our first coupling was fast and hard and intense. It concluded on the floor *beside* the cot, amidst a sweaty tangle of blankets that we had pulled down with us.

Afterwards, after we'd caught our breath and rested and cooled down some, Abby said, "Well. I can't speak from a whole lot of experience, but I'd say that rated as a pretty fair practice run, wouldn't you?"

"Hard to disagree with a lovely lady who happens to be lying naked in your arms," I said. "But use of the word 'practice' tends to imply that numerous repeats of the activity at hand will be forthcoming."

"Uhmm. Yes . . . *numerous.*" Her index finger was idly tracing patterns through my chest hair.

"I see. There are, of course, many proponents of practice. Practice makes perfect, and so on and so forth. But there are also those who hold that the gods dole out only a finite number of quality performances for mere mortals to execute. Therefore an over-abundance of 'practicing' might actually prove to be a wasteful depletion of the quality peaks available to a given individual. Meaning that fewer practices might be a more prudent thing."

"Uhmm," she said again. "Interesting theory. I've never heard it before but I promise to give it some deep consideration. In the meantime, however, I think I'll continue to subscribe to the 'practice makes perfect' school of thought."

"Ahem," I said. "Let me put it another way: You see all the snarly gray threads in those chest hairs you're playing with there?" Actually, even as I was saying this her hand was beginning to travel south, in search of busywork elsewhere.

But I nevertheless continued trying to make my point. "Okay, the way it works is that those gray threads signify the body they occupy has reached a lifetime achievement level of practice and should only be called upon to participate in the rarer, big-event quality performances."

"Oh. I think I get it. No more two-fers left in the tired old engine, is that what you're saying?"

"A bit crude. But it sounds like you've got the gist."

By then Abby's hand had begun to occupy itself in new territory. "Oh *I* understand all right," she said. "And *you* may understand . . . but, oops, what have we here?" She beamed a teasing smile. "Unless I'm badly mistaken, it seems I've come across some evidence—some hard evidence, you might call it— that suggests a certain part of you might actually be, ah, *up* for a few more practice sessions after all."

I was hardly in a position to argue the point. Relenting, I said, "Ah, yes. It appears the gods have given you healing hands."

She rolled on top of me, face close over mine, sun-streaked hair spilling down. Within the canopy of spilling hair, her face was lost in shadow. But I could see that the teasing little smile was gone, and the intensity of her eyes shone out. "We can heal each other, Joe. Because we're good for each other. That's what I've been trying to tell you."

I wrapped one hand in that cascading hair and pulled her face the rest of the way down to mine. "I believe you," I said as our lips met. "I believe you."

Then I thrust up into her and she gasped sharply, biting my tongue until we both tasted the blood.

Chapter Thirty-Six

"Well, you got about perfect conditions. A fine clear morning, and nobody else on the water. . . . Have a great trip!"

With these parting words, Vic Faber gave our canoe a shove off the bank and sent Abby and me out into the current of Pawnee Creek. Abby was in the back, I near the front (I didn't know if nautical terms like "bow" and "stern" applied to a canoe or not). She had emphasized that she would do the steering and most of the paddling and would let me know when and on which side I was to pitch in if my rudimentary paddling skills were also needed. I told myself I might eventually build up some guilt over this slacker's assignment, but for the time being I was content to just sit tight and concentrate on keeping my balance.

"See you at Morningglory Bridge in about four and a half hours," Faber called after us.

Four and a half hours, I groaned inside my head, tensing as the canoe gave a little wobble. *Jesus Waterlogged Christ, how did I let myself get talked into this?*

I continued to think we were playing a very long shot with this whole picnic-basket search. But I owed it to Abby to give her idea a try and, besides, as she had pointed out we didn't really have a better option to pursue right at the moment.

Once we were under way, though, I was surprised to find it didn't take long for me to start to relax a little. This was due mainly to Abby's prompt demonstration of competence when it came to handling our canoe. She propelled us along with strong, smooth strokes, guiding us cleanly through the first snakelike twist of the stream and then almost immediately around the snarl of a fallen tree extending out into the water.

"See?" she said. "Balance and easy, controlled motion. That's all there is to it."

"Swell," I muttered. "If I ever get around to unclenching my ass cheeks I'll make sure I do it in an easy, controlled motion."

I heard her give a little laugh behind me and then we were quiet for a while, just gliding along, listening to the sounds of the moving water and the breeze sighing through the leaves of the trees and the high grasses up on the banks.

I wished I had a better view of Abby. She had her hair tied in a loose ponytail this morning and was wearing cutoffs, canvas shoes, and a lemon-yellow halter top. The straps of the top didn't match a previous set of tan lines running over her shoulders and for whatever reason I found this contrast of tanned/untanned skin very stimulating. But then I happened to be finding a lot of things about Abby pretty stimulating this morning. As I had through much of the previous night.

She'd left my cabin some time in the murky pre-dawn with a final lingering kiss and a softly murmured, "Tonight was wonderful, Joe. Thank you."

Thank you? I had been a little stunned and then touched by the words. No woman had ever thanked me before for making love to her. Nor had I ever thanked a woman, for that matter. At least not out loud. Mentally, of course, I had been eternally grateful each and every time. It just never occurred to me to say thanks.

Thank YOU, lovely Abby.

This pleasant reverie was interrupted by the gun poking suddenly into my hip bone, jerking my thoughts back to the harsher side of what Abby and I were involved with. I'd opted to carry only the 9mm hideaway this morning, in my pocket again, this time zip-locked inside a plastic sandwich baggie as a precaution against the dunk in the water I still saw as a very real possibility. As opposed to bygone times, modern-day firearms and ammunition can generally be counted on to function even after a thorough soaking. Nevertheless, if I ended up having to bring the piece into play for any reason, I wanted to be as sure as possible it would fire the first time and every time that I needed it to.

I shifted my butt slightly on the seat, easing the jab of the gun and causing only a minimal wobble to the canoe.

"Doing okay up there?" Abby asked.

"I'm good," I said over my shoulder.

I hadn't advertised that I was packing. Abby didn't seem entirely at ease around guns. I didn't want to make her nervous about me having it and I didn't want to alarm her about why I might think it was necessary. Actually, I figured the chances of needing a weapon out here today were pretty slim, which was why I hadn't included the .45. But at the same time I couldn't help remembering that I also figured my chances of getting shot at the last time I was out this way were pretty slim, too. And this time if the unexpected broke loose there would be more than just my own safety to consider. So the little nine was once again playing the role of an inconspicuous compromise—exactly what it was made for.

"We'll be coming to the stretch of creek by the old homestead pretty soon," Abby said. "Think you'll recognize the spot?"

"I expect so. I had plenty of time to look it over good while I *thought* I was waiting in ambush." My pride smarted once more at mention of the spot and yesterday's incident, recalling how Thunderbringer had totally out-stealthed and then disarmed me there with embarrassing ease.

"If my premise is valid at all," Abby went on, "if Liz *did* toss the picnic basket in the water while her and Uncle Bomber were making their way back to their car, then it could be anywhere along in here. It most likely got carried for a ways by the current, but we'd better keep a sharp lookout, just in case."

Places where the floating basket could have gotten hung up were plentiful. Vic Faber advertised that a navigable channel was kept clear on Pawnee Creek, but otherwise the waterway was left as "natural" as possible. This meant that rocks, deadfall branches, sections of whole trees, breakaway portions of the bordering high cliffs—all these were to be encountered and encountered frequently on the twisty, snake-wriggle course of the narrow creek. And each held the potential of presenting a snag sufficient enough to capture and hold what we looking for.

Hunched near the front of the canoe with the paddle across my thighs, I dutifully and intently scanned each of these places, hoping I was wrong about the remote chance for this search to actually succeed. Behind me, Abby worked her paddle with deft precision, maneuvering us around the various obstacles, only occasionally calling for me to paddle a few strokes on one side or the other in order to help negotiate a particularly sharp turn or the sudden appearance of something to be avoided. My jerky, inexperienced movements when called upon to swing into action allowed a few deadfall scrapes and caused us to wobble precariously a time or two, but for the most part our progress was smooth and steady.

We passed the old Brannigan homestead site, our first mile marker. Abby estimated we were traveling about two and a half miles an hour.

As time and distance went by, we saw no sign of the picnic basket. Other than the natural kind, the creek and vicinity were clean of any debris. Vic Faber's canoeing groups were either very litter-conscious or the current served to be a serviceable housekeeper, sweeping all evidence away.

Not too far past the former Brannigan place, the creek ran relatively straight for a quarter mile or so and was crowded on either side by particularly high, sharp cliffs. Some large chunks of the cliff face on the north side had recently broken away, leaving raw gashes in the grass and underbrush and spilling a jumble of rocks and gravel across part of the Pawnee.

The narrowed channel turned frothy and fast as it squeezed past this jumble.

"Looks like the recent storm finally washed away part of the Tunnel," Abby commented.

"The Tunnel?"

"That's what folks call this section, because of the way the cliffs crowd in. Some of it was bound to crumble sooner or later. Look on the bright side, though—we got an extra stretch of whitewater to shoot through!"

"Oh, yeah. Whoopee," I muttered.

Actually, the newly created rapids weren't all that fast or rough and were relatively short-lived. We scooted through in good shape and, grudgingly, I had to admit to myself that I even got a little kick out of it. Although I maintained my doubts about finding the picnic basket or the camera, the way things were shaping up at least it didn't look like the canoe trip was going to be the total disaster I had envisioned.

An hour passed. Then an hour and a half. No sign of the picnic basket. No sign of much of anything except the water, the trees and underbrush down low, occasional rocky cliffs, and the tall grasses waving up on the blunted tops of the high banks. Here and there we saw scatterings of a cattle herd and down on the low, flat stretches we saw minefields of leftover cowpies marking where they had been. We spotted three elk moving along a high ridge. And from some leafy foliage on the south bank we caught sight of a cautious raccoon peeking out at us like a highwayman laying in wait wearing his robber's mask.

But no picnic basket.

Shortly past the two-hour mark, Abby swung us to shore at a point where the bank was flat and sandy and free of cow droppings. The sun was high overhead in a clear blue sky, already hot and getting hotter.

"We're making good time, we can afford to take a break," Abby announced, hopping lightly to shore.

I made it to shore, too, but in an awkward clamber, managing to plop one foot in the water before the task was accomplished. I didn't care, I was grateful for the break. Even though Abby was doing most of the work, I was sweating freely and could feel the muscle strain from sitting so tensed-up most of the time. Everything is relative, I told myself. Put me in my element, I bet I could freak her out cutting wildly through rush-hour traffic or dazzle her with such urban skills as dodging pickpockets, muggers, and scam artists. On the right turf, I was Daniel-fucking-Boone and "Canoe" was nothing but a cheap cologne worn by guys on the make.

Abby carried to shore a watertight plastic bag that she had brought along. On the sandy bank, she opened it up and produced a fluffy blanket, a fat thermos, and a foil-wrapped paper plate of sandwiches. I helped her spread out the blanket.

"The sandwiches are just cheese—Co-Jack and jalapeno," she said. "But it's good rye bread, and there's lemonade to drink. We're burning up calories and electrolytes, it's always a good idea to stop and replenish the body a little."

"You're practically a pro at this," I told her.

"Like I said, I've done it quite a bit. How about you? Is it turning out as dreadful as you thought it would?"

"No," I admitted. "No, it's not. But I never thought it would be dreadful. . . . No time with you could be all bad."

She gave a little smile and tipped her face down but couldn't hide the bright pink blush that infused her cheeks. "You'd better eat your sandwich before it starts to dry out. We can't tarry here too long or we'll leave Mr. Faber waiting."

She unscrewed the cap off the thermos and poured lemonade into it, which we shared. It was cold and tangy and delicious.

After taking a long drink, I made a gesture to indicate our surroundings, saying, "Since Faber dropped us off we haven't seen a house or building, not a telephone pole or electric line, no sign of a road or even a jeep trail. Don't any *people* live out here at all?"

"Not for miles and miles. Cattle range, that's all it is. So remote you can't even get a cell signal down here in the creek cut. That's why I didn't even bother bringing mine along. The only living things out here are the cattle and the wildlife. Except at roundup time when the cowboys ride out to bring the herds in for market or branding. They do it on horseback mostly, same as it was done a hundred and fifty years ago. The only modern touches are the planes or 'copters they sometimes use to locate the herds. Maybe a jeep or a couple of pickup trucks when they get them in closer to the ranch. Oh, and these days they heat the branding irons up with a propane fire instead of hot coals."

"Progress."

"Same difference to the cows getting their asses burned, I suppose."

I gestured again. "And this is all still Terrell land?"

"All this and plenty more. Like I said, for miles and miles and miles."

We stayed quiet while we finished eating. Then, after pouring the last of the lemonade and lighting a cigarette, Abby rather abruptly said, "Would you be shocked if I went topless for a while?"

The question caught me so off guard I was at a loss for what to say. Before I could spit anything out, Abby decided to expound. "It's something I've always wanted to try. You know, like those la-de-da babes on those beaches in France and other places. All lean and tan and golden all over."

I spread my hands and, finally finding my voice, said, "This ain't exactly the French Riviera, but what the heck."

"Mamie and Tina have got a couple places back on the lake where they sometimes shuck their tops and sunbathe. They're always teasing me to join them, but I keep chickening out. It's just too darn busy around that lake, I don't care how remote the spots they pick. If somebody I knew from the store or the cabins happened to see me that way I'd be embarrassed to death. Besides, stripping down with those two—my saggy little titties next to their super boobs—that would be embarrassing enough right there."

"Now damnit, don't start that again. Don't run yourself down that way."

"But out here," Abby went on, "I mean, this is the ideal setting for a shy gal like me, right? Except always before, like I explained, I had Ma or my son Dusty with me. You can see where those were hardly the right circumstances."

"But *I* am okay circumstances, eh?"

"If you don't mind."

"Am I an idiot? Am I going to stop you from flashing your breasts? You want to shuck the top, be my guest. I'll even lend a hand. My only advice would be to take care you don't sunburn any, er, *sensitive* areas."

Abby pulled a tube of sunscreen from the plastic bag and held it up, grinning. "Am *I* an idiot? And speaking of getting sunburned, we'd better get some of this on that nose of yours and your bare arms. Jesus, don't they have sunshine back in Illinois? You look like you've been living in a cellar and now, after being out here a little bit yesterday and only a couple hours today, you're getting red as a beet."

"What can I say? I'm the sensitive type all over. Inside and out."

"Yeah right. Lean closer here and hold still."

She stabbed out the cigarette after taking a final drag and then began dabbing goop on my nose, across my forehead, and finally my arms. When she was done she handed me the tube and wiped her hands on a corner of the blanket. "Now do me," she said, hitching around so that she was facing partially away from me. As I squeezed some of the goop into my palm she reached behind her back with both hands, unclasped the halter top and did that little shruggy thing that women do, causing the top to fall free and slide down her arms.

Her skin was very warm under my hand as I began applying the sunscreen. She gave a faint shudder from the contrasting coolness of the goop. I could see one of her freshly bared breasts. It did have some faint sag to it but it still looked plenty appealing to me. The nipple was once again—or still?—erect and hard. I remembered how it had felt and tasted under my tongue last night.

"I don't think this stuff is going to do much good," I said, even though I continued to rub in the lotion.

"Why not?"

"Because if you keep having me do this I got a feeling that in pretty quick order it's going to turn into something else and all this lotion is going to get sweated and smeared right off again."

Abby turned her head and smiled coyly. "Awfully sure of yourself, aren't you?"

"Sure of what I *want*."

"What happened to the guy who just last night was lecturing about selectively spreading out his 'performances,' not overtaxing the limited supply?"

"Your healing hands, remember? Plus all this damn fresh air—it must have miraculous recuperative powers."

Her smile was blatantly teasing now. She'd known damn well what she was doing when she started in with the whole sunscreen bit. "What about Mr. Faber? We can't leave him waiting too long."

I could feel myself grinning, too. "The hell we can't."

She leaned back into me and we kissed. When our lips parted, she reached and took the tube of sunscreen from my hand, snapping the cap back closed. "You're right, Faber can wait. . . . But let's not waste the sunscreen, we're going to need it again in a little while."

The rest of the trip was uneventful. Meaning that, on the upside, we experienced no canoe upheavals or shark attacks or any other nautical disasters, in spite of all my initial misgivings. The downside, of course, was that neither did we spot any sign of what we'd come looking for.

The fate of Liz's camera—whether sunk to the bottom of the creek inside the picnic tin, or confiscated by an anonymous someone who never came forward, or perhaps lying undiscovered in the weedy prairie grass out on the periphery of the crash site—was destined to remain a mystery.

During our final hour on the water, both of us grew quiet and somewhat melancholy. I suppose part of this was due to disappointment, the realization starting to sink in that we *weren't* going to find the picnic basket or the camera. But another part, for me, was also due to having the time to reflect on this thing between Abby and I that seemed to be building an almost reckless momentum.

I reminded myself I still had issues concerning Jan that needed to be resolved. Even though I felt there was little or no chance for a fix in the break between us, you don't spend over a decade with somebody then all at once walk away without trying to settle it in some manner, at least attempt an amicable parting. This line of thought forced me to face the distasteful question: Was my interlude with Abby nothing more than a revenge fuck? Had I allowed it to happen for the sake of cheap personal satisfaction ("see, I can get a piece on the side, too, if I want one")? Or to have as ammunition I could throw in Jan's face in case of an ugly confrontation?

And if there was substance to any of this, what did it say about my *real* feelings for Abby? True, there had been no promises, no commitments . . . and no stated expectations. Yet I knew damn well that somebody as basic and grounded as Abby wouldn't enter lightly into a "fling" without some expectations or at least hope in her heart. So, knowing this, what did it imply that I had gone ahead and coupled with her? Was I callous enough that I would still—as I had warned her—simply take my leave when the case was finished? Or were my feelings for Abby genuine enough that, on some level, I too had hopes and expectations for something more?

Such thoughts were disconcerting, to say the least. I didn't care much for the questions they raised nor for many of the answers that might fit.

By the time the pickup point came into view, I was grateful both for the excursion to be over (even though it had gone nothing like I'd feared) and for the shift in activity that would focus my idle thoughts in other directions. Had I known what direction that would turn out to be, however, I wouldn't have been nearly so eager.

The pickup spot was a flat, grassy bank on the north side of the Pawnee, just past Morningglory Bridge. As we passed under the bridge, we could see Vic Faber's truck and canoe trailer parked there. Faber stood near his rig, hands in pockets, watching for our approach as expected. But what wasn't expected were the other vehicles parked to either side of his truck and the other people gathered around him, also apparently waiting for us.

"Looks like we've got a welcoming committee for some reason," I commented.

"Yes. That's curious," Abby said from behind me. "Sheriff Mabry's one of them. And that woman beside him looks familiar, but. . . . Do you suppose Cam Terrell found some basis for siccing the law on us?"

"Could be. But I don't see what—"

Abby cut me short. "Wait a minute! Is that Travis, my ex, standing there? Why isn't he in Florida?" Her voice raised in a tone of alarm. "And where is Dusty?"

Abby stroked our canoe hurriedly to shore. Faber walked over and caught the front, steadying it. Abby was out before the craft came to a complete stop, stepping in the water seemingly without notice, brushing past Faber and me and making a beeline straight for the distraught-looking young man I presumed to be her ex-husband. "What's going on?" she demanded of him. "Where's Dusty?"

Sheriff Mabry moved to intercept her, saying, "Take it easy, girl. There's no reason to panic and every reason to believe at this point the boy is okay."

"Oh, my God, Abby. They've taken him," wailed the distraught-looking man, holding up his hands in a warding-off gesture. "Our son has been kidnapped!"

CHAPTER THIRTY-SEVEN

In the hours that followed I stayed as close to Abby's side as I could, but for a while my role in the proceedings was relegated to little more than that of an observer. If some of the law officials who became involved had had their way I expect I would have been elbowed out of the picture farther still. Even in her distress, however, Abby was insistent that I be given a certain amount of latitude.

From Morningglory Bridge—once Abby had regained some composure after getting walloped with the news about her son—we were driven to the Standing T Ranch. The woman on the bank with Faber and the others turned out to be Detective Beatrice Sterling of the state police, one of the investigators who'd shown up at No Name Bay a couple days back looking into the beating of Ronald Wilton. I rode to the ranch with her. Abby rode with her ex-husband in the back seat of Sheriff Mabry's car. Watching them roll off together caused a curious twinge to pass through me that it took a minute to recognize as jealousy. I swore at myself for reacting like an adolescent jackass when a hell of a lot more serious issue was at hand.

Between the terse recap given by Mabry and a handful of anguished outbursts from Travis Terrell, it was revealed that the kidnapping had gone down quick and brutal. I tried to get some more details out of Detective Sterling during the ride to the Standing T, but she stayed determinedly tight-lipped.

Upon arrival at the ranch, what I knew was this: The snatch

had happened between six and eight p.m., Florida time, the previous evening. Dusty had been taken from his father's hotel suite near Disney World. Terrell was away at the time, performing with his band. The abductors had gained entry apparently without force and once inside shot and killed Freda, the nanny, who was present with the boy. There was no sign she had put up a struggle. A computer print-out note, secured in place by the woman's coagulating blood, had been left on her body. The note was addressed to Terrell, telling him that if he wanted to see his son alive again he should return immediately "home to where the money is" and await further instructions.

I can't think of many situations where the cops would permit somebody to leave the state right after a murdered woman has been found in his hotel room, but apparently compassion over the abducted child combined with the wealth and influence of the Terrell name was enough for the Florida authorities to make an exception. In the wee hours of the morning Travis Terrell had been allowed to arrange for a private jet and by daybreak he was back in Nebraska, back "home", as directed, to receive further ransom demands.

It was here, then—the Standing T Ranch—that a command post was being set up to orchestrate the efforts of the various forces gathering to deal with the kidnapper/killers and work for the safe return of the boy. I could see as we arrived that it was still what you might call a work in progress, playing out for the time being like a scene of quasi-controlled chaos.

The FBI, naturally, was at the forefront of operations. The agent-in-charge was a blocky, red-haired man named Bastien from the state headquarters in Lincoln. He was backed by a pair of regional bureau guys and a Florida liaison who'd flown up with Terrell. In addition to Sheriff Mabry and Detective Sterling, local law enforcement was further represented by the presence of Keith County's Gene Knaack. There was a team of technicians on hand, too, hooking up extra phone lines and stringing wires to computers and other electronics gear.

All of this was centered in Cameron Terrell's den, a sprawling room with a massive stone fireplace at one end and masculine furnishings of leather and dark-stained wood. The man himself was there when we were ushered in, sitting on a couch next to Sheriff Knaack. The old rancher looked as though he'd aged twenty years since I saw him two days ago. When he spotted the entrance of his son and former daughter-in-law, the elderly Terrell rose and went to them. He embraced Abby and then, rather stiffly, as if an afterthought, also Travis. The three of them remained in a close knot for several minutes, weeping, consoling one another, their lamentations now and then rising to a level that leaked out to the rest of us.

Mabry introduced me to the FBI men. Each responded with a curt nod and then a cold shoulder. I also got a snappy nod and a chilly look from Knaack. I figured maybe he was practicing to be an FBI guy.

After that was when I noticed two additional men in the room. Both were tall, lean, narrow-faced, and gray-suited. They stood together against a wall off to one side, unmoving except for their eyes. Mabry didn't offer to introduce me to them and they seemed to have no objection to the oversight.

Finally, also hanging on the periphery of the activity humming through the middle of the room, there was Thunderbringer. Mabry didn't offer to introduce me to him either. But when the big Indian and I locked gazes he gave an acknowledging tip of his chin. It occurred to me that this made his about the warmest greeting I had received.

Mabry eventually saw fit to wander off and leave me on my own. I took the opportunity to pay a visit to the generously supplied wet bar that had caught my eye. Glancing around to make sure no one looked poised to object, I filled a tall glass with shaved ice, splashed in some vodka, topped it off from a chilled bottle of grapefruit juice.

The leather padding around the front edge of the bar seemed like an inviting place to lean so that's what I did. Leaned there, sipping my drink, assuming my own place on the fringe of things, quietly watching events continue to unfold.

Mostly I kept my eye on Abby. She appeared to be holding up pretty well, all things considered. But I knew the strain on her must be almost unbearable.

When we'd arrived at the ranch, before coming inside, Detective Sterling had produced a light jacket which she wordlessly handed to Abby to put on over her halter top and cutoffs. It had been a considerate gesture. Watching Abby now, thrust into the midst of so many men, at least half of them complete strangers, I could see that she was still self-conscious about her scant attire. She stood with her hands jammed deep into the pockets of the buttoned-to-the-throat jacket, her posture unnaturally slouched so that the garment reached down as far as possible on her bare legs.

It tore me up to see her so uncomfortable and sad-faced, so far removed from the happy, uninhibited woman who had lain naked and loving in my arms such a short time ago. Even under the weight of her mother's doomed health and the cloud hovering over the deaths of Bomber and Liz, I had sensed in Abby a woman on the verge of breaking out, ready to come into her own, ready to free herself of repressions that had been dragging on her for years. Certainly since her ego-crushing marriage and divorce, maybe longer.

And now this. Kicked square in the teeth by the latest cruel twist of fate and, what was worse, kicked right back into the arms (practically) of those largely responsible for grinding her down.

I wanted to go jerk her away from the Terrells and take her

into my own arms, comfort her. But I knew that part of the reason I wanted to do this was as much for me as it was for her. So I held back. I also knew that they—Abby and the Terrells—had a bond that, especially under the circumstances, I had to respect. That bond being the boy, Dusty. Travis Terrell might be a punk and Cam Terrell might be a liar and a manipulator and worse, but for the time being what trumped everything was that they were blood. To them, Dusty was a son and grandson. And he was in the hands of a ruthless killer. . . .

I watched as agent-in-charge Bastien marched up and rather brusquely interrupted the family huddle. He began conducting what quickly took on the appearance of quite an intense discussion. After a couple of minutes, he started to focus primarily on Abby, the way he was leaning into her suggesting he was peppering her with a pretty heavy bombardment of questions. Abby, already looking wrung-out and frail, seemed to wither even more under this barrage. She shook her head frequently and kept making I-don't-know gestures with her hands, looking at times bewildered and even a little desperate.

I finally had enough and went over there.

"Excuse me," I said, my voice sounding louder than I'd intended.

Bastien's face snapped around. "We're in the middle of something here, mister," he said unpleasantly.

"I can see that." I fought to keep my tone from being equally unpleasant. "I can also see that this young lady is right on the ragged edge. Look at her, she's practically ready to collapse. Don't you think it would be a good idea to at least allow her to sit down, maybe get her a glass of water or something?"

Travis Terrell apparently felt his opinion was required. "I really doubt Agent Bastien needs your advice on how—"

"Never mind," Cameron Terrell cut him off. "Hannibal makes a valid point."

Bastien scowled. His eyes went from the elder Terrell to Abby and then to me. Grudgingly, he said, "Yeah, maybe he does at that." His expression softening, he swung his gaze back to Abby. "Forgive my lack of courtesy, ma'am. Sometimes I get caught up in things and come on a little too strong. We've all got a high-stress situation on our hands here, certainly you as much as anyone. I should have given that more consideration."

"It's all right. Really," Abby said, managing a weak smile. "I understand you have to ask your questions . . . and if it's for the sake of getting Dusty back, then. . . ."

"We can take a break from the questions," Bastien assured her. "We can come back to them in a little bit. For right now, why don't you go ahead and have that seat like your friend suggested."

Abby's smile tipped a little lopsidedly. "What I really could use," she said, her gaze flicking in my direction, "is a breath of fresh air and a cigarette."

Bastien spread his hands. "Fine. We can resume our talk when you come back in."

I moved up beside Abby. Placing my hand at the small of her back I guided her toward a set of patio doors that I judged would open to a backyard. Travis Terrell scowled after us. I couldn't tell if he was pouting because Bastien had given in to me or if he simply disapproved of his ex-wife's smoking habit. For damn sure he didn't approve of the company she was keeping.

Abby and I emerged not to a backyard per se, but rather to the maze of lush, carefully manicured hedges I had spotted the first time I drove out to the Standing T. Dusk was settling in and the tall, sharp-edged rows of bushes cast bizarre and sometimes eerie patterns of intersecting deep shadows. The evening was still and quiet once we re-closed the doors behind us and shut off the buzz of activity from inside the house.

Abby got a cigarette going and exhaled a long plume of smoke. Then she said, "I feel like my life somehow got crammed into a big cardboard box and then the box got booted down a long flight of stairs. Now I'm in the middle of all the broken jumble and right at the moment I can't even tell which end is up."

I said. "There are lots of people—people who care about you very deeply—ready to help you put things back in order."

"But don't you see? Things *can't* be put back in order, not unless my son is returned! It's been hell enough these past years having Dusty gone from me for weeks at a time. But this . . . if they . . . if he should be taken from me completely . . . I don't think I could stand it."

"Don't go there. Think positive. We'll find a way to get him back."

She gazed up at me with pleading eyes. " 'We,' Joe? You'll stick this out with me?"

"Of course I will. I don't know what I can add that the FBI and every cop between here and Florida won't already be contributing, but I'll sure as hell stick."

"You've become awfully important to me in a short amount of time. You know that, don't you? And all I do is keep asking more of you."

"Let me worry about that."

"And now the thing that's most important to you—finding the truth about what happened to Liz and Uncle Bomber—is suddenly getting pushed farther away."

"Liz and Bomber are in no hurry. They're beyond that," I said, my voice a little thick. "There's no time limit on finding the truth about them. But the minutes are ticking for a little nine-year-old boy out there somewhere, alone and scared and in danger. It's a no-brainer that he is where our priorities need to be focused now."

CHAPTER THIRTY-EIGHT

Because she wanted to remain at the Standing T in case of contact from the kidnappers, Abby asked me to be the one to leave for a while and go check on her mother.

When Travis Terrell had shown up at No Name Bay earlier in the day, looking to break the news of what had taken place, it was Margaret who'd intercepted him and informed him Abby was out canoeing on Pawnee Creek. Inasmuch as he stood before her in the company of Sheriff Mabry and Detective Sterling it was obvious something serious was wrong, so there'd been little choice but to go ahead and reveal to his former mother-in-law that her grandson had been abducted. As anyone who knew Margaret Bridger might expect, she had outwardly taken this like a rock, a mere glistening of tears showing in her eyes. Her main comments were words of concern for her daughter, insisting that someone be waiting for her at the canoe pickup point and that she be told of the terrible turn of events as gently as possible. At first she had further insisted she would go along and see to the task herself, but it became quickly apparent that she was too weak and overcome to turn that intent into a reality. B.U. and Mamie Gorcey had been called over to sit with her, promising to remain for as long as necessary.

Abby got these details from Sheriff Mabry and Travis Terrell during the ride from Pawnee Creek. She had called her mother from the car and spoken briefly to both her and Mamie Gorcey, but now she wanted me to do an in-person follow-up.

Detective Sterling once again chauffeured me, returning me to where Abby and I had left my Honda at Vic Faber's canoe-rental place. I drove alone to No Name Bay from there.

It was full dark by the time I arrived. I parked at the back of the store. There was a light showing in the window of Margaret's apartment, indicating someone was still up. This wasn't surprising, even though the hour was past her normal bedtime. These were hardly normal circumstances.

My soft knock at the door was answered by Tina Mancini, who greeted me with a finger placed to her lips, signaling for me to be quiet, before motioning me on in. I followed her into the small, neat apartment. Margaret was in her recliner, extended back nearly horizontal, asleep. A light blanket had been spread over her. Her breathing was even, the oxygen machine beside her bubbling in faithful concert.

Tina gestured for me to take a seat at the little kitchenette table. One of the table's two chairs was already partially pulled out and a pile of magazines was fanned on the tabletop before it, indicating where Tina had been sitting and how she had been occupying her time. I pulled out the opposite chair and sat.

"Can I get you anything?" Tina asked, soft-voiced. "There's iced tea in the fridge. And beer. Coors."

I shook my head. "I'm good."

She sat down across from me.

I glanced over at Margaret. "Looks like she's resting pretty comfortably."

"Not too bad. Every once in a while she tosses and turns a bit. Bad dreams, I suppose. We called her family doctor and got him to phone in a prescription for some sedatives. B.U. went to town and picked it up. This was all unbeknownst to Margaret—she would hear of no such thing, of course, but the rest of us figured something to settle her down was probably the best thing. So once we got the pills we had to sneak a couple into

285

her iced tea. They went right to work."

"Good," I said. "She doesn't need any more grief on top of everything else she's already fighting."

"Her son Roy—Abby's brother—offered to drive down. Him and his wife. But they're short-handed on their ranch and it's awfully hard for them to get away. Margaret told them to stay put for the time being, there really isn't much they can do right now, anyway. Mamie is going to sit the night with her. She'll be back in a little while, after her and B.U. close up the Walleye."

"That's good of her. Good of you, too, to be here now."

"Are you kidding? It's the least we can do." Her pretty brows furrowed with sincerity and concern. "How's Abby holding up?"

"Well as can be expected, I guess. She wanted me to come check on her mother and also pick up a few personal items to take back to her."

"Uh-huh. She called just a little bit ago, gave me a heads up that you'd be by and went over some of the things she wanted me to be sure and send with you."

"That's a relief. She must have figured I'd be bound to forget some important dainty or other, and she'd probably be right. Your help would be most appreciated."

Tina grinned. "Tell you what. If you want to sit here and keep an eye on Margaret in case she wakes up and is confused or anything, I'll go put together some essentials for Abby."

"Deal."

She slipped quietly away.

I sat there in the small, dimly lit room. Sat listening to the sound of Margaret Bridger breathing and the sounds of the oxygen machine chugging along with her.

I fidgeted. I considered changing my mind about having one of the beers out of the refrigerator. I poked at the stack of magazines on the table but they were all gossipy movie-star/

pop-star weeklies that had zero appeal to me.

I studied Margaret in her peaceful, drugged repose.

The sister of one of my oldest, closest friends. But he was gone now. And she was undeniably fading. One day soon I would be thinking of her in the past tense, too. Like so many other things in my life. A life that was beginning to feel like it was getting too full of the memories of yesterdays, and too void of much promise for tomorrow.

"You've become awfully important to me in a short amount of time. You know that, don't you?" Those were the words Abby had said to me only a short time ago. I wondered why I didn't find the implications in them more disconcerting than I did. Was it because there was a potential for part of my tomorrows to be found in those words?

Had I known how important I was becoming to Abby? Had I knowingly allowed it? If so, did that mean I was also allowing her to become important to me? Would finding the truth about what happened to Liz and Bomber be only part of what I was on the brink of finding out here?

I thought of the lyrics contained in one of Kris Kristofferson's sad, lonesome classic songs about yesterday being dead and gone and tomorrow out of sight . . . *help me make it through the night.*

Liz and Bomber were dead and gone. My relationship with Jan might not be officially declared dead, but in my heart I knew that it surely was. What did that leave of yesterday that remained genuinely important to me any longer? A handful of friends . . . just acquaintances, really, the ones who were left. Others already dead and gone . . . some regrettably, some for the better. Memories. Ghosts. An adopted city that had never truly been all that warm and embracing. . . .

Was Abby meant to be my guide through the transitory night? A hand reaching out to pull me into a tomorrow she was ready to help make richer and brighter?

But what brightness would any of her tomorrows hold if we weren't able to safely retrieve her son from—

My meandering thoughts were drawn back to the moment at hand by the return of Tina Mancini.

She paused partly through the doorway, eyeing me in a curious way.

"What?" I said.

"You," she responded hesitantly. "When I came in you looked so . . . I don't know. Thoughtful? Sad?"

"Not exactly a happy situation we're in the middle of here," I pointed out.

"I know, but. . . . Never mind." She forced a let's-change-the-subject smile, and held up the small blue suitcase she was carrying in one hand. "I picked out some things for Abby. I'm not sure how long she's intending to stay out at the ranch, but this should see her through for a while."

"She wants to be there in case the kidnappers call and there's a chance to talk to Dusty," I explained.

"I understand. Still, it's got to be added stress for her . . . being out there with her ex and all." She tipped her head to one side and eyed me again. "Are you going to stay there, too?"

I hadn't really thought about it before, but the answer came out quick enough. "I'll be around."

A corner of her mouth lifted slightly. "I figured so. . . . That will be good for Abby."

I wasn't sure why but, before leaving, I felt the need to go over and give the sleeping Margaret Bridger a kiss on the forehead. I could feel Tina watching me. When I straightened up and turned back to her I avoided meeting her gaze directly. Took the suitcase she held out to me, thanked her, then departed back into the night.

★ ★ ★ ★ ★

My cell phone was ringing when I got back to the car.

There was a slight pause after I answered, then an unmistakable voice said in my ear, "This is Thunderbringer."

I waited.

"The kidnappers made contact. Two phone calls."

"Two?"

"One to the Terrells . . . one to me."

"The kidnappers called *you?* Separate from the call to the family?"

"It gets a little complex."

"Talk slow, I'll try to follow along."

"You and me, I'm thinking we're going to hit a point pretty quick when we'll be coming from the same place on this thing . . . A different place than some of the others."

I waited again.

"On your way back to the ranch, just before the second curve as you come into the town of Arthur you'll see the county fairgrounds on your right. The entrance gate will be open. If you want to hear the rest of what I've got to say, I'll be waiting by the rodeo arena grandstand. You might want to consider that before this is done I figure the boy's life may end up depending on us."

Chapter Thirty-Nine

A moon the size of a football field hung low in the cloudless, star-peppered sky, tinting everything silver-blue and casting shadows as thick as pools of tar.

The entrance gate to the Arthur County fairgrounds was standing wide open, as I'd been told it would be. I rolled slowly onto the property, my headlight beams sweeping over weathered livestock sheds, a couple of empty pavilions, a row of window-less booths. Farther down, the whitewashed pipe fence sur-rounding the rodeo arena shone like skeletal remains in the moonlight. Overlooking the arena, the unpainted wooden grandstand loomed tall and gray and imposing, throwing a cross-hatch pattern of shadows down off its back side. Within these shadows a bright red GMC Yukon sports ute was parked. Next to it, sitting casually on an upended phone-cable spool, William Thunderbringer waited for me.

I pulled up and braked nose to nose with the Yukon. Cut my engine and lights, piled out. The scent of fresh mown hay hung heavy in the still air, undercut faintly by the smell of cattle and manure.

"See you took me up on my invitation," Thunderbringer said.

"Hard not to. You tossed down some pretty intriguing remarks." From between the fingers of one hand I was dangling two beaded bottles of Michelob that I'd snatched out of the ice chest in my cabin. I held them up. "Last time you furnished the drinks. Figured tonight ought to be my turn. Use one of these?"

A lazy grin came and then faded. "Time was, you could get shot in these parts for offering firewater to an Indian." He held out a big paw of a hand. "Luckily times have changed. But I'd best do my part to help you get rid of the evidence just in case there's somebody still around who ain't got the word yet."

I handed him one of the Micks and we each cracked open our bottle and took a long pull.

"Good stuff," Thunderbringer announced. "Obliged."

"Okay. Now let's get down to it. The boy," I said. "What's this talk of you and me coming from the same place and being the ones his life may end up depending on?"

Thunderbringer took another pull of his beer. Lowering the bottle, he gazed off into the night and began talking.

"The first thing you need to understand is that, basically, there have been two kidnappings. And, to start with, it was all planned and ordered by none other than Cameron Terrell himself."

"The old bastard ordered the snatch of his own grandson?"

"It would have been a setup, see. To everybody on the outside—including the kid, and even Terrell's own son—it would have played like a straight snatch for ransom. The cops and FBI would have been brought in, the money would have been gathered . . . just like is going on now. It was planned to drag out until after July Fourth, and then the kid would be given the opening to miraculously escape or something. Those final details hadn't exactly been worked out yet."

"What was the setup part?"

"While all this was going on, behind the scenes Abby Bridger would have been contacted and informed that the *real* ransom was for her—and you—to back off your investigation and turn the focus away from Terrell. Your agreement to do this and to keep totally mum about it would have been the trigger to allow little Dusty's release/escape."

I shook my head in amazement. "We had Terrell *that* fucking worried?" It was crazy. We were crowding in on the guy, sure, but we were a long damn way from having anything concrete enough to make any kind of serious charge against him.

"Like I told you the other day, your challenge about the phone bug really shook him up. It was while I was away trying to 'scare' you out on Pawnee Creek, in fact, that the old man went ahead and set this kidnap action in motion. It was something he'd been hatching as possible last-resort leverage to use against you and Abby ever since you came on the scene. While I was away that day, there were others on hand who convinced him it was time to insert the lever, that you were raising too many questions too close to July Fourth and it was the only way to make sure you caused no last-minute interruptions."

"Interruptions to what? You keep mentioning July Fourth—why is that date so important to any of this?"

"Because the way Cameron Terrell has been planning to celebrate this coming Fourth of July is at the core of every single thing involved here. RBR—Remember and Be Ready. It's Terrell's intent to force the world to *Remember*, and then show them how to *Be Ready* in order to prevent it from happening again."

"How about sparing me the riddles and giving me a straight answer?" I said irritably. "You're talking but you're not telling me anything."

Thunderbringer drained his Michelob. Then, twisting at the waist, he turned and threw the empty bottle hard against one of the grandstand's uprights. It shattered. Turning back, Thunderbringer tipped his face skyward and howled, "Eeeyowkiiiyiiyii!" Relaxing his shoulders, he shot me a sidelong glance and a satisfied grin, saying, "Little something for my Cherokee ancestors."

It was a curious, tension-breaking moment. I felt my irritability slide away.

"Okay," said Thunderbringer. "We'll come back to the RBR in a minute. But first let me finish telling you about the kidnapping. For starters, how about those who talked Terrell into going ahead with it and then proceeded to be the ones who carried it off? I think you'll be interested in hearing who they were."

"I figure one of them was Volnokov."

"Hell. That was no challenge at all for a trained detective like you, was it? We'll have to see if we can't make the bonus round a little tougher. So, then, who do you figure accompanied Volnokov down to Florida for the snatch?"

I just looked at him. "If I wasn't in the mood for riddles, what makes you think I'm up for guessing games?"

Thunderbringer sighed. "You're going to be a mighty boring partner if you don't pry that tree stump out of your ass, you know that?"

I waited.

He sighed again and then said, "Okay. Try this on for size: Volnokov's fellow snatch artist was none other than everybody's favorite commando cop, Clint Barnstable."

Now *that* I did not see coming.

"I'll be damned," I muttered. Getting past the surprise of it, I began assessing some ramifications of the pairing. "Which explains why they had to kill the nanny. She recognized Barnstable and if left alive would have been able to identify him." And then an even more chilling assessment. "And that means if the boy also recognizes Barnstable. . . ."

"Don't deduce too far ahead there, Mr. Detective," Thunderbringer cautioned. "Remember I said that basically there were two kidnappings? The first one—the way it was ordered by Terrell—didn't allow for anybody getting hurt. Not the nanny and sure as hell not the kid. I don't know all the details because I wasn't there, but Barnstable was supposed to wear a mask or something to keep from being recognized."

"So the mask must have slipped."

"No, I don't think so. I think the nanny getting blown away was intentional and part of the plan—just not Terrell's plan. I think that was where the *second* kidnapping kicked in and started its swerve on the first one."

"You're saying Volnokov and Barnstable took the old man's *staged* kidnapping and turned it into their own version? That now they've got his grandson and they're trying to use him to cut a for-real ransom payoff?"

"Close, but not quite. You see, in addition to the two phone calls from the kidnappers there was another important call that came through to the ranch after you left this evening. It seems the authorities down in Florida recently discovered the body of Clint Barnstable in a swampy ditch not too far from the small airfield he and Volnokov flew down to when they went to grab the boy. He'd been shot twice in the head, execution-style."

"Volnokov getting greedy? Wanting the whole pie?"

Thunderbringer shook his head. "Not so much that, I don't think, as ol' Clint just never being part of the swerve to begin with. I can't see him ever double-crossing the old man. He was fiercely loyal to Terrell and even more so to his cause."

"What cause? The RBR again? You're saying Clint was a member of Terrell's militia?"

"One of the first. One of the most dedicated."

"Well ain't you just full of surprising little tidbits."

"Call me the Indian Al Jolson. I got a million of 'em. Like, for instance, have you figured out yet who Volnokov is?"

"What do you mean *who* he is? He's the Soviet sleeper guy who—"

"Who's been right under your nose practically since you got here. He was the one who planted the bugs in Abby's store and apartment and kept them monitored. Reported back to Terrell everything he heard—and saw. What he didn't pick up with his electronic ears, he got from keeping his eyes open by day and creeping your places by night or when no one was around."

"Who the hell are you talking about?" I wanted to know. "You saying there's somebody at No Name Bay who—"

Thunderbringer interrupted me again. "I'm saying there *was* somebody at No Name Bay. He's gone now, remember, off taking care of a little matter in Florida. Can't you think of any recent absentees from the regular gang out there?"

"More goddamn guessing games," I growled. "If you've got a name to spit out then go ahead and spit it."

Thunderbringer grinned. I was beginning to think he got a kick out of annoying me. Then he laid it on me. "That Matt Hollis, Abby's young groundskeeper . . . he sure seemed like a swell, likable kid to have around, didn't he?"

He couldn't have shocked me more if he'd told me he was wearing a garter belt and nylon hose under his blue jeans.

"Well I *will* be damned," I said.

CHAPTER FORTY

"I know what you're thinking. The smarmy little puke you knew as Hollis looked barely out of his teens but Volnokov has to be, like, pushing forty, right? Yet they're one and the same person, believe me. Must be good Russky genes or something."

Thunderbringer damn well knew he had my attention so he just kept rolling. "It was strictly freak good luck for Terrell, having a key man in place right there at No Name Bay when Abby started stirring things up over that car crash. From the beginning the old man insisted that anybody we used from the outside would be brought in and salted around the area in inconspicuous positions while the operation was being put together. In Volnokov's case, it paid off in ways he never could have foreseen."

"The operation," I said. "That'd be this July Fourth thing you're leading up to?"

"Uh-huh. Operation Stoneface. The thing Cameron Terrell has become obsessed with."

"And Volnokov was brought in especially for it?"

"He has some talents and, more importantly, some connections Terrell saw as crucial."

"Among those connections, from what I've heard, are alleged ties to Al-Qaeda. That's near the top of things I don't get—at least not yet. If Terrell started this whole RBR Militia thing as a kind of knee-jerk reaction to the Nine One-One terrorist attacks that claimed his wife among thousands of other victims, why would he have anything to do with a man who was in thick with the very organization responsible for those attacks?"

Thunderbringer's eyes glinted in the semi-darkness. "Remember I told you how I was an end-results kind of guy? Well so is Cameron Terrell."

"Maybe so. But whatever end result he was going for just got knocked to hell, didn't it, by his pet terrorist turning out not to be quite housebroken? The second call from the kidnappers—the one to you—that would have been Volnokov, right? Saying he was trading in his Operation Stoneface role to go for a personal score, a ransom pay-off for the grandson Terrell had so obligingly placed right in his hands."

The big Indian spread his hands. "What can I say? Little fucker picked up some bad habits from spending too much time down in Central and South America, I guess. Down there, kidnapping is practically a trade taught in vocational schools."

"In other words, he knows the ropes."

"Betcher ass. Don't let yourself be fooled by the baby face and the polite aw-shucks routine he played on you around No Name Bay. Volnokov or Hollis or whatever you want to call him is one mean, nasty bastard. . . . As a case in point, remember that rowdy neighbor you had down there at the lake the other night? The guy you tangled with and then Clint Barnstable ran out of Dodge?"

"Yeah. The guy who liked to rough up his wife. Wilton, his name was. What about him?"

"He ran into a little trouble on his way home the next day, didn't he?"

"Got the snot beat out of him. Somebody lead-piped him then put the boots to him after he was on the ground. The state cops even came around and. . . ." I let my voice trail off as I began to see where he was leading me. "Before I had my altercation with him and before Barnstable showed up, I remember now that he took a swing at Hollis/Volnokov. Rapped him a pretty good one on the jaw. The kid didn't fight back."

"Didn't fight back *then*," Thunderbringer corrected. "He couldn't, because he was putting on his meek aw-shucks act. But the next morning he made a point to catch up with the guy and get even. Put him in the hospital in a coma, right? Bragged, when he was telling it to some of us later on, about how loud the guy's jaw bone and ribs popped when he was breaking them."

All I could do was shake my head, both chafing and marveling at the totally convincing deception by the innocuous-seeming "kid" I had barely taken notice of these past days.

"So how much ransom is he asking?" I said.

"Five million."

I gave a low whistle. "Terrell have that kind of dough?"

"He's good for it. It's the same amount he told them to ask for when he was setting up the bogus kidnapping."

"I take it you've had the chance to inform Terrell of the swerve, right? That the snatch of his grandson has turned into the real deal?"

Thunderbringer nodded. "I was able to get him off alone shortly after Volnokov contacted me. It really knocked him for a loop, let me tell you."

"Does anybody else know?"

"Not yet. Me, the old man . . . and now you. But that doesn't mean there might not be others with a few suspicions."

I finished my beer, fired the empty bottle over into some weeds. Then eyed him squarely. "Why so quick to bring me into the loop?"

Thunderbringer held my eyes for a long moment before turning his face and looking off into the night. "Why so quick is easy—because Volnokov is insisting we move quick. The old man has gone into Mad Scramble mode, starting to pull the money together. As far as why I'm telling you these things. . . ." He swung his face back and locked eyes with me again. "Mainly because I got a feeling about you, and I hope to hell I'm not wrong. You see, the whole thing now turns into saving the kid. The whole thing, that is, for me, for Terrell—and, I'm betting, for you."

"Kinda overlooking the parents, aren't you?" I said, bridling somewhat on Abby's behalf.

"I meant people who can actually *do* anything about the situation. The flip side of the coin from us are those who can impact on the situation but likely have got different priorities."

"The Feds, you mean."

"Who else?"

"Why would they have priorities ahead of the boy's safety?"

"Come on, don't pull up lame on me. Think about it a minute. Any kidnap situation, what are the odds the actual kidnapee ain't gonna make it out alive, no matter what else happens? Especially how they work it down South America–way. Sometimes you can improve the odds if you're willing to cold-blood blow away the 'nappers at the ransom exchange. But those fucks on the flip side of our coin have wanted to get their mitts on Volnokov for too long . . . you think they're going to be in a hurry to pop a cap on him now for the sake of some nine-year-old who, statistically, is already off the board?"

"They already *had* Volnokov, didn't they? You were reporting to the G, didn't you ID him to them?"

"Of course I did."

"Then why didn't they make their move on him before this?"

"Greed, my friend. Yeah, for weeks now they've had Volnokov where they could have nabbed him any time they wanted. But moving on him too soon would have also meant throwing their net at Operation Stoneface before everything was in range, before the biggest bang for the buck could be gotten. That's what they were holding out for."

"Operation Stoneface again. Cam Terrell's pet project. You indicated Volnokov was a key player in that—How much of a monkey wrench *does* his kidnapping double cross throw in the overall operation?"

"Maybe a big enough one to short-circuit the whole damn show. I wouldn't have thought anything less than a nuke to the head would have stopped that iron-willed old dog Terrell from going ahead with his mission. Especially at this stage of the game. But if you could have seen the look on his face when I told him he'd set up his grandson to be abducted for real. . . ."

"The Fourth of July is only a few days away. At this stage of the game, as you put it, there must be a lot of things already in place."

"You ain't wrong."

I started to exhale a breath then held some of it in my mouth, puffing out my cheeks. After a moment I let it the rest of the way out and said, "I think we've danced around it long enough. Why don't you go ahead and tell me what Operation Stoneface is."

Thunderbringer didn't say anything right away. When he spoke, he asked, "You brought only the two beers, huh?"

"Yeah, that was all."

"Shame."

"Firewater to an Injun, remember? Like you said a little bit ago. Let's say I had enough foresight not to want to take too big a chance."

It was hard to tell in the shadows, but I thought I saw him grin a little. Then he lifted his face skyward once more and for a minute I thought he was going to do that Indian yip thing again. He didn't, though. He just started talking with his face tilted up that way.

"Operation Stoneface, in a nutshell, is a plan to blow up the

Mount Rushmore national monument on the Fourth of July and leave a trail of false leads that will bring about the conclusion it was the work of Al-Qaeda terrorists. Even though the human life toll wouldn't be as great as the Nine One-One hit, Terrell is counting on the American public reacting with the same kind of shock and outrage. Only this time—before the anger subsides and the apathy starts to set back in and the left wing ass-punches start moaning for more understanding and peaceful compromises—he will be poised to rally all 'true patriots,' holding up RBR as a shining example, and lead the demand for a sustained, full-out push to wipe Al-Qaeda and all such groups off the map."

"That's a pretty ambitious nutshell," I said when he paused.

"The old boy don't think small, you got to give him that. He has a passion. He's still mourning the loss of his wife and he's appalled and infuriated not only by the fact that those responsible haven't yet been hunted down but also by the lefties in this country who seem more concerned about things like the civil rights of Abu Ghraib and Club Gitmo prisoners than they do about what the camel-fucking lowlifes did to get themselves in prison to begin with. Personally, he's looking for revenge . . . or justice, if you want to call it that. As a country, he wants us to quit getting pissed on and start being pissed off."

"And you bought into all of this?" I said, sensing that some of what I'd just listened to had included more than a little personal bias.

"I've soldiered in a lot of different places for a lot of different causes," Thunderbringer replied. "Once I'd finished my initial hitch for Uncle Sam, the rest of it became just a way to do what I was good at and to make money. After Nine One-One, though, I stepped back and wondered if maybe I shouldn't be doing what I was doing for a better purpose. One that mattered to me, one I at least half-assed believed in. I was actually considering re-upping for Uncle when Cam Terrell got hold of me and invited me to whip into shape this militia thing he was putting together. I saw it as the best of both worlds. I could be on the side of the angels and the pay was a hell of a lot better."

"Was Operation Stoneface part of the picture from the beginning?"

"I'm sure some version of it must have been percolating in Terrell's head pretty much from the get-go. But I didn't start hearing about it until after I'd been around for a few months."

"Blowing up Americans for the sake of America's best interests. You didn't think that sounded a little extreme?"

The big Indian shrugged fatalistically. "Collateral damage is a part of any war. The faces on Mount Rushmore were the main target, making it a symbolic thing, Al-Qaeda shitting on one of our most treasured pieces of Americana. Yeah, there were bound to be some injuries and loss of life. But a justifiable amount, if you look at it a certain way. How many more American lives are going to be lost to ongoing terrorist activities if we don't toughen up and get rid of these rugheaded fucks?"

"And Volnokov, because of his past ties with them, was brought aboard to authenticate the planted leads that would point to Al-Qaeda once the operation had gone down," I said, starting to add together some of the pieces for myself.

"Like I said before, he has talents that can be applied to a lot of things. But you're right, his Al-Qaeda links were what first got Terrell interested in him."

"Only when he popped back up on the Federales' radar you can bet they took an interest, too. Which I'm guessing is what eventually brought them knocking on your door, right? Leaning on you to take on the double-agent role, still functioning as part of RBR but siphoning off info to the G."

Again the fatalistic shrug. "I didn't like doing that to the old man, but they had me in a box. I figured I was still on the side of the angels, though, and setting up Volnokov to dump on Al-Qaeda was a viable option for bringing heat down on them. I decided it was something I could live with. Besides, truth to tell, I was never *completely* comfortable with hitting our own people on our own soil anyway . . . no matter how hard I tried to sell myself on my own ends-justify-the-means mantra."

I took a deep breath, let it out slow.

"Jesus Christ," I said. "And I was afraid Nebraska was going to be dull and boring."

Thunderbringer grunted. "I know what you mean, man. Hell, maybe it was—before riff-raff like us started showing up."

We shared a sardonic smile over that and then neither of us said anything for a while.

Somewhere off to the south, a coyote wailed long and lonesome.

First a howling Indian . . . now a howling coyote. To say nothing about a howling-mad individual plotting a phony yet lethal terrorist attack against his own country, I thought to myself. *What the hell had I gotten myself into this time?*

Finally, Thunderbringer spoke. "Well, I've laid a hell of a lot of stuff on you and in the process finished trashing any security boundaries I missed stomping on the last time we talked. Either you get the picture by now, or you're never going to. Me, every angle I try it from it keeps playing that if anybody else does the exchange for the kid they're liable to be more interested in netting Volnokov than bringing Dusty out alive. I don't intend to stand by and allow it to be handled that way. I could use some backup, but I got this big lack of faith in my esteemed colleagues up at the 'command post.' And there ain't enough time for me to contact any of the guys I know and trust from jobs I've worked in the past. So that leaves me with you, Blue Eyes. . . . How about it?"

Chapter Forty-One

It was that gray, half-light time of morning that some people call false dawn. The sharp edges of the hedge maze behind the Standing T's main house were blurred by damp, thick air that hadn't quite formed into a fog.

Cameron Terrell and I were walking together, slowly making our way through the maze. William Thunderbringer strolled a dozen feet behind us, presenting a buffer to interruption by anyone from inside the house.

"William informs me," Terrell was saying, "that he has told you everything."

"To the best of my knowledge he has, yes."

The old man looked like hell. He obviously hadn't slept. His clothes and hair were rumpled, his eyes red-rimmed.

He heaved an exhausted sigh. "I can only imagine how uncharitable your feelings toward me must be."

"No, I doubt that you can," I corrected him.

There was the faintest hesitancy in his next step but we continued on. "Yet you are still willing to assist in this thing that must be done."

"For the boy. For his mother. What happens to you, whatever trauma you go through . . . I could care less."

"Yes, of course. In your shoes I would feel no different." A corner of his mouth twitched with the hint of a bitter smile. "How ironic that I find myself prepared to rest all of my hopes on two men, one of whom has already betrayed me with his duplicity and another who has cause to hate me. And yet, despite his undercover work for the government ultimately meaning my imprisonment and the collapse of something that has been almost the entire focus of my life these past years, I trust William Thunderbringer's instincts and training above any other to handle the dastardly turn that now threatens my grandson. And if he vouches for you, that's good enough for me."

"Up until now my sole interest in any of this has only been how it related to finding out the truth of what happened to my friends. Thunderbringer finally told me. Now I want to hear it from you."

We had come to a lacquered wooden bench placed at one of the turns in the maze. Terrell went over and sat down on it. I stopped walking and stood at one end of the bench. Behind us, Thunderbringer stopped walking, too, maintaining his distance.

For a long moment Terrell sat running one hand idly over the smooth, treated wood of the bench, gazing out across the tops of the hedges. Then he said, "Does it strike you, Mr. Hannibal, how silly and incongruous this English hedge maze is here in the middle of treeless, barren western Nebraska?"

"Hadn't really thought about it."

"Well it is. It's downright ridiculous if you stop to consider." He sighed again. A great, weighted-down melancholy sigh for the ages. "But it became a consuming desire of my late wife to have the blasted thing. I don't know where she got the idea, but once she had it in her head there was no getting it out."

He continued to run his hand over the bench, almost caressing it now. "I pretended there was no way in hell I would ever agree to such nonsense. The way I always did . . . before giving in to the girlish whims she sometimes had." His hand stopped caressing and balled into a bony fist, resting on the seat beside him. "So in the fall of Two Thousand-One, while she was away shopping and visiting with her sister in New York, I had a crew of landscapers come in and put up this silly damn thing. It was to have been a surprise for her when she returned home.

"As you are aware, however, she never made it home. The events of September Eleven robbed her of her life and of the wonderful surprise I had planned for her. Robbed me of the one true love of my life . . . robbed so many people of so many things." He turned his face and looked up at me. I half expected to see tears in his eyes but instead there was only a cold fury there. "I was angry and in pain beyond words, Mr. Hannibal. I have remained so ever since. On the night of my wife's funeral I brought a can of kerosene and a bottle torch out here, fully intending to turn this pampered pile of brush to nothing but scorched earth. But I didn't. Something made me change my mind. Standing right at this very spot—I was going to douse this bench and make it the ignition point, you see—I decided that instead of viewing this maze as a painful reminder of what I'd lost I would look at it instead as a beautiful reminder of all the beautiful memories my wife and I had shared together. And rather than scorching *my own* earth I would do everything in my power to ensure the scorching of not only the earth but the very souls of the murderous bastards who so deeply wounded me and our country."

Terrell leaned forward and, resting his elbows on the tops of his knees, dragged both hands slowly down over his face. "Now. . . . Now I wonder if I had gone ahead and set that fire, would I have succeeded in burning up some of the rage inside me? Would I have appeased myself enough at that early point to have prevented all the hate and anger from continuing to build and eventually bringing us to . . . to this? To where we are all at now. This terrible place where the life of my precious grandson has fallen under threat. So help me God, I would have burned every acre and every possession I own to have avoided this!"

In that moment I almost felt sorry for him. Almost. We each have the right to deal with grief and the pain of loss in our own way. In my book, retribution against those who have inflicted suffering upon you is both understandable and acceptable. But it can never be acceptable for the sweep of retaliation to purposefully include the innocent and undeserving. Looking down at Cameron Terrell, I knew that not only was he perfectly willing to make such inclusions but in fact was already responsible for having done so.

With his face still in his hands, Terrell began talking again. "On the day your friends showed up at the old homestead sight, I and some of my men were in the field doing practice runs on a stretch of the embankment along Pawnee Creek serving to be a rough simulation for the Mount Rushmore cliffs. I'm sure William has given you the details on the missiles we acquired and how we planned to use them from commandeered helicopters. It was important that, before the day of the strike, we actually do some test firings from the air."

Based on what Thunderbringer told me, I knew that Terrell's RBR had illegally purchased twelve British Blowpipe man-portable missile launch systems. The heart of Operation Stoneface called for them to be released from four helicopters scheduled to be stolen on the day of the strike from a sky-tour business located in close proximity to Mount Rushmore. Two missiles per 'copter, each fired at one of the targeted stone faces. Once the missiles were thrown, the whirlybirds would scatter ground-close ahead of anticipated response out of nearby Ellsworth Air Force Base and drop into pre-determined clearings amidst densely forested areas plentiful to the area. Pickup teams would be waiting to whisk away the 'copter crews and follow carefully selected evasive routes to secure their successful withdrawal.

In truth, it sounded like a stripped-down, brutally simple

plan that just might have worked. But that didn't mean I was ready to pick up a set of pom-poms and start cheering it on.

"Your friends were drawn beyond the homestead site by the sounds of the helicopter and the practice missiles hitting the high, sharp cliffs we had chosen," Terrell continued. As he talked, in my mind's eye I saw the section along Pawnee Creek that Abby had called "the Tunnel", where great raw gashes of the cliff face had recently been torn away, and I knew exactly the spot he was talking about. "They couldn't have fully comprehended what it was they were seeing, of course, but it must have been apparent quickly enough that they'd stumbled onto something that was unwise and possibly dangerous for them to observe. They fled, but not before the 'copter crew spotted them. As it happened, all of the ground team—including me—were on the opposite side of the creek. So pursuit was hindered."

He pulled his face out of his hands and turned it to look up at me. "You must believe that no one set out to harm your friends. Those were not my orders. In all honesty, I suppose I have to admit that such a decision may have eventually become necessary. I . . . I don't know. But for the time being all I wanted was to stop them, bring them back and talk to them. Try to explain somehow. At that point, addressing what they had seen would have been awkward and inconvenient, to be sure, but nothing that posed an immediate threat. Once Operation Stoneface took place and hit international news, however, I had to consider that they surely would have been able to add two and two together and then could have come forward and made things very troublesome for all of us."

"I guess we all know how that little spot of trouble got resolved, don't we?" I said in a tight voice.

Terrell looked away again. "Clint Barnstable and Ivgar Volnokov—who you knew as Matt Hollis, and the bastard it now appears is the mastermind behind this kidnapping double cross—were part of the ground crew. They had brought their dirt bikes along. When your friends made it back to their car and got out on the road, Clint and Volnokov and some of the others gave chase. The helicopter made a couple of passes at the car, too, trying to get them to slow down. But your friend only drove faster . . . faster, as it turned out, than he was able to control. They reached a curve he couldn't negotiate at the speed he was going and . . . well, they didn't make it."

"And the rest of it?" I demanded, a harsh bite in my tone. "The beer and whiskey bottles? The sex-play gimmicks?"

Terrell hung his head. "That was an on-the-spot decision by Clint. He was excited, a little panicky maybe—he was afraid someone might question that the relatively simple curve alone shouldn't have been enough to cause such a wreck. When he checked the IDs of the people in the car and saw they were from out of state, he decided to rig up the scene, give investigators some clearer evidence for the cause of what happened. Prior to that, unknown by me I assure you, the boys had been taking a few nips out in the field. They had some beer and whiskey in the saddlebags of their bikes . . . I don't suppose I need go into further detail on how they put them to use and the other stagings they set up." He paused, then added with a kind of dull bitterness, "Irony again. . . . The very measures Clint thought he was taking to *avoid* arousing suspicion were exactly the ones that caused you and Abby to *be* so persistently suspicious."

So there it was. All the answers I had been seeking for what seemed like such a long time and yet really no time at all.

I was looking at the man responsible for the deaths of Liz and Bomber. He hadn't pointed a gun at them or held a knife to them or given a direct order to end their lives. He hadn't actually threatened them in any way. But he had caused them to die all the same. And, if left to his own devices, to his own warped plan for revenge or justice or whatever purpose he believed he was serving, he was willing to cause the deaths of hundreds more who were just as innocent and undeserving.

My fantasies of clutching the killer of my friends between my own two hands flashed white-hot through my mind. He was an old man, right there in front of me. It would have been easy. Not even Thunderbringer could have moved fast enough to stop me.

Maybe I actually started to raise my hands toward him, the fingers curling menacingly. Maybe I only imagined it. I'm not sure. I know that for a moment I tasted the acidic tang of rage boiling in the back of my mouth and felt the quickened thud of my heart. But then it all faded, lost its intensity, and I realized it wasn't to be.

Not that way. Not this time.

"You said you wanted to hear it from me," Terrell said, his head still hung low. "Now you have. Now what?"

I was ready with the answer. "I want a signed written confession. Exactly like you just told it to me. When Thunderbringer and I leave to make the exchange for Dusty, I'll have Abby Bridger hand the paper over to Sheriff Walt Mabry. I will leave it up to him to see that charges are brought and you're made to answer for the murder of my friends. For the rest of it, as far as I'm concerned the government can sort out their own shit with you."

The rest of the house started waking up after daybreak.

Walt Mabry and Gene Knaack had left and gone to their respective homes sometime during the night. Detective Sterling went to a motel in Ogallala. The government team that had gathered remained on premises, sacking out on couches and recliners. Abby scored one of the guestrooms, which she retired to shortly after I brought her back the suitcase of personal essentials. After she turned in, I opted to go out and fold down the seatbacks in my Honda and sleep there, enjoying my own measure of privacy from the crowd inside the house, until Thunderbringer rousted me for the meeting with Cameron Terrell.

One of the cooks from the bunkhouse showed up at the main house and laid out a huge breakfast spread of scrambled eggs, bacon, sausage links, hash browns, hot cakes, a small mountain of toast, and gallons of hot coffee standing ready in two tall silver urns. Not surprisingly, Abby and the Terrell men only picked at their food. The rest of us ate like field hands. Shop talk was kept to a minimum—largely due, I suspected, to my presence.

After the meal, Abby and I took cups of the excellent coffee and sat together at the umbrella table out on the flagstone front porch.

Abby had washed and brushed her hair to a bright sheen and had applied a touch of pinkish lipstick. She was wearing a white boatneck pullover and faded jeans. To me, she looked as fetching as always. But there was no denying the strain that showed in her eyes and tugged downward on the corners of her mouth.

"It's going to be a long day," she said, gazing off at nothing in particular with a faraway look on her face. "The kidnappers are supposed to make contact again this evening. Cameron thinks he has a chance of having the money raised by then."

Indeed the old man was at the moment inside the house burning up phone lines to various bankers and accountants.

Abby lit a cigarette. "I told you they let me talk to Dusty last night, didn't I? His voice sounded so tiny and frightened, Joe. . . . He's so confused by what's going on."

"This is hard on everybody," I told her. "Kids have a way of being amazingly tough and resilient, though."

"All they gave me time for was to tell him that I loved him

and to be brave, that we would be coming for him soon."

"In his place, I think those would be pretty comforting words to hear."

Her eyes found mine. "But how true were they?" she said in a hush, ragged voice. "I'm neither stupid nor naïve, Joe. I follow the news, I pay attention to the world around us and the depressing nastiness that goes on there. Even if the money is turned over and all instructions followed to the letter, how often do things like this end in tragedy anyway? What are the odds of a high-dollar kidnap victim ending up dead, regardless?"

"I don't know the odds," I said honestly. "I won't lie and say it doesn't happen that way a good share of the time. We both know that it does. But there are still plenty of times it works out the other way, too. Bastien seems like he knows what he's doing. He's got a full crew working the case hard. And Old Man Terrell is willing and able to come up with the money. That's got to be a plus. You need to try and stay positive."

It bothered me that I couldn't tell her the other agenda that was going on behind the scenes. Not that she necessarily would have found it more soothing, I just didn't like lying to her; even by omission. But with the cops and the FBI hovering tight over the situation and the suspicion that still more G-men of one stripe or other were lurking in the wings, if Thunderbringer and I had any chance of pulling off what we aimed to, it was essential that we kept the involvement and/or awareness of anyone else to an absolute minimum.

Abby wasn't smoking her cigarette. She was just holding it, her thumb tapping nervously against the filter-tipped end. "But they killed Freda, just blew her away for no apparent reason. They're obviously ruthless. And did you hear about Clint Barnstable also being found shot to death down there? Do you think it's possible he was somehow part of the kidnapping and the others turned against him for some reason? Even Sheriff Knaack admits that the timing and proximity of where he was killed seems like too much of a coincidence for there not to be a connection. Clint called in sick that day, he wasn't even supposed to be out of town. The last time I saw Sheriff Gene, he was so upset he looked practically sick himself over the whole thing."

"Nothing harder on a good cop than having to face up to the reality of a dirty one."

"They tell me there's a news media pack gathering out at the front gate and more in town, wanting to know more about the two bloody Florida killings with ties to this area. Thank God they haven't caught wind of the kidnapping yet. On top of everything else, I don't think I could bear popping flashbulbs and rude questions and microphones stuck in my face."

"I expect the FBI will do a thorough job of keeping a lid on that . . . at least until after it's over."

My choice of words carried an unintentionally ominous-sounding implication that added a pinch of anguish to Abby's already strained expression. I was debating whether or not to say something more and risk making it worse or just let it ride when Travis Terrell came out of the house and helped make up my mind by walking over and interrupting Abby and me.

Addressing Abby, he said, "Bastien wants us to meet with him in the den in about five minutes. He wants to update us on the latest developments and then discuss options for handling the ransom payoff." His eyes shifted to me. "The meeting is for Bastien's team and immediate family members only."

No ambiguity there.

"I'll be in in a minute, then," said Abby.

Terrell lingered, trying to hold eye contact with me as if challenging me to take exception at being left out of the meeting. I just looked back at him. Pretty soon he averted his eyes, turned and disappeared once more into the house.

It occurred to me that this had amounted to the closest thing resembling a direct exchange between the two of us since he'd shown up at Morningglory Bridge the previous day. When it came to me, he obviously had some kind of bug up his ass. Which was fine—I didn't like him either. In fact, when this was over, I entertained thoughts of maybe giving myself a little treat and popping ol' Trav-boy right on the beak first chance I got.

"Never mind him," Abby said. "He's just as big a jerk as he ever was."

"Relief to know this isn't supposed to be the new, improved version."

Her thumb tapped the filter tip of her cigarette. "When you left to go get my things last night, do you know what he had the nerve to ask me? He wanted to know what 'the deal' was between you and me."

"What did you tell him?"

"I told him it was none of his damn business."

That was an answer and yet a non-answer. *What WAS the deal between her and me?*

"Joe, do you think everybody can tell?" Abby wanted to know. Her expression was very earnest. "I mean, do we give off some kind of vibe or something . . . you know, that we've been together?"

I shrugged. "I don't know. Whether we do or not, it's like you said—nobody else's damn business."

Her expression changed. Her brows knitted with uncertainty. "It's just that . . . I lay in bed last night thinking about a lot of things. I caught myself wishing you were there with me, to take me in your strong arms and hold me and comfort me. It made me feel better. . . . But I've got to admit that part of the time I also caught myself feeling kind of guilty. I couldn't help thinking that in those very moments my son was being kidnapped and terrorized by vicious killers, I was . . . you and me were. . . ."

Before she could say any more or I could respond, the Florida

FBI agent stuck his head out of the house and called to Abby, "Mrs. Terrell, could you join us inside for a few minutes please?"

Abby's face snapped around. "My name is Bridger. Abby Bridger. I am the *ex* Mrs. Terrell, if you don't mind!"

The agent's face colored. "Of course, ma'am. I knew that. My apologies for misspeaking. It won't happen again." Abby stood up, dropping what was left of her cigarette onto the flagstones and grinding it out under a twist of her foot. Then she went into the house.

CHAPTER FORTY-TWO

After Abby left, I didn't remain at the umbrella table.

I got up and walked down toward the corral and horse barns. The sleek black mare that had been alone in the corral the other day when the storm was getting ready to hit was there again this morning. She was a real beauty. All muscle and grace and power, strutting proudly back and forth like she knew exactly how special she was.

I leaned against one of the fence rails and just watched her admiringly for several minutes. I wondered idly if Dusty Terrell had ever ridden this animal. Although I'd never laid eyes on the kid I could somehow picture him in the saddle, horse and boy in fluid motion together, the way it is with a good rider on a spirited mount, galloping reckless and carefree in the wind. God, I ended up thinking, if only that picture in my mind could replace the reality of what the little guy must actually be enduring at this moment instead. . . .

I caught a whiff of aftershave lotion first, then sensed the physical presence of someone moving up behind me. Turning, I found myself eyeball-to-eyeball with the two anonymous gray men who throughout yesterday had done nothing but hover silently on the periphery of the FBI team's activity. From the first I had made them for government spooks of some kind, I just wasn't sure which branch. I got the feeling I was about to find out.

Both were angular in build, pinch-faced, with suspicious eyes and receding hairlines. Both wore white dress shirts and almost identical suits of drab gray. The more daring of the pair wore a maroon power tie, the other a tie of Navy blue.

"Word with you," Maroon Tie said.

"Uh-huh," Navy Tie confirmed.

I looked from one to the other. "Mornin'," I said affably.

"You ought to know," Navy Tie sneered. "You got started on it early enough."

I felt my affability start to slip. "Whatever that's supposed to mean."

Maroon Tie said, "You met with Cameron Terrell in the hedge maze before daylight. We want to know what that was about."

I paused a long beat, considering my response carefully. Then I said, "It shouldn't be a surprise that we talked about the kidnapping of Terrell's grandson. The shock of it, the trauma it must be putting the boy through. The old man is pretty shook up over the whole thing, not much else on his mind."

"Why would he seek out you in particular for such a discussion?"

I shrugged. "I doubt he discusses much of anything else no matter who he's talking with. Like I said, it's weighing pretty heavy on the guy's mind. He's upset, distraught."

"What? You run some kind of grief counseling service as a sideline to your PI racket?" Navy Tie, again with the sneer. "Or is it that you're just an especially good listener?"

"Naw, actually I'm a little too impatient to be a good listener," I corrected him. "For example, right now I can't help thinking that I've listened to about enough crap out of you."

Navy's face turned purple. So purple, in fact, it became a close match to his partner's tie. "Who the hell do you think you're talking to, mister?!"

"I have no idea. You skipped the common courtesy of

introductions and jumped right to making demands, remember?"

"You wanted to know something, you could have asked," said Maroon Tie, almost petulantly.

But Navy was too pissed to back off. "You might be some kind of hotshot PI back where you come from, but that ticket doesn't buy you shit out in these parts, buddy-boy. And if you think your connection to that antiquated old MI outfit earns you any special privileges, you've got another think coming there, too. None of that cuts a damn bit of ice with us."

"And you don't cut no ice with me. So we're even. Let's call it a day," I said.

I started to push away from the corral fence but Maroon Tie, still hoping to salvage a discussion, said hurriedly, "Wait a minute. Everybody needs to calm down here."

"Tell that to your partner."

"I said everybody."

But before we could test our ability to cool it and start over, a car came rolling up the long driveway and veered off in our direction before braking to a stop. The driver's door opened and State Police Detective Beatrice Sterling got out. The clouds of yellowish dust billowing in the wake of her vehicle maintained their momentum and came tumbling along over all of us as she began walking in our direction.

"Shit," muttered Maroon Tie under his breath.

"Good morning, gentlemen," Sterling said as she drew closer. Her blond hair gleamed in the sunlight stabbing through the dust haze.

"You could say that," Maroon Tie replied. "Then again, you could say there's not much good about it."

"No, I suppose not. Not today, not around here. . . . Any new developments?"

"Bastien's holding an update meeting inside right now, as a

matter of fact. Maybe you ought to go on in and find out what he's got to say."

"Maybe I should," Sterling agreed. "But why aren't you in there, Blake?"

"Because we're out here," Blake, aka Maroon Tie, answered rather testily.

"Me, I was pointedly not invited to the festivities within," I offered on a lighter note.

"Careful you don't get a complex," muttered Navy Tie.

Sterling eyed me. "I thought you had an in with the family, Hannibal?"

"Seems to be a lot of that impression going around," I said, holding her eyes for a moment and then cutting my gaze over to Blake and Navy Tie. "Nevertheless, here I stand on the outside looking in."

Blake heaved a resigned sigh. "Okay, why don't the two of you go ahead and enjoy some more of that view, then. Us, we've got to be moving along." He motioned to his partner with a jerk of the head. "Come on, Culver."

Culver moved obediently after him but couldn't resist shooting one more withering glare in my direction before he went. "We'll be seeing *you* around, Hannibal."

"You betcha," I said, beaming a shark's smile.

We watched the two of them trudge off in the direction of the house. When they were out of earshot, Sterling said, "Well. Am I ever the party pooper, it seems."

"Some parties deserve being pooped on," I told her.

"Uhmm. Looked like the two of them had you sorta cornered."

"You could say that."

"Do you know who they are?"

"We got off to a rocky start as far as formal introductions. We were just getting around to that when you showed up."

Her eyes narrowed slightly as they returned to the two departees, now entering the house. "They're a couple of CIA spooks working these days under the umbrella of Homeland Security. . . . You know, what with the various intelligence agencies being all one big happy family now, since Nine One-One."

"Uh-huh. I've heard rumors along those lines," I said. "But then, I've also heard rumors about things like the Easter Bunny and the Tooth Fairy. I figure they all belong in pretty much the same category."

Sterling gave a short laugh. "That's about the size of it. Culver and Blake there, they're every bit as trusting and sharing and flexible to change as a couple of ancient, moss-covered tortoises. And not a hell of a lot brighter, from what I've seen. Yet with all the shit coming down, they're what we get sent. Can you believe it?"

I regarded her more closely. I was surprised and frankly a little suspicious about her suddenly being so open with me. Up until then she had seemed nothing but stern and no-nonsense, and particularly close-mouthed where I was concerned. Part of it was a defense mechanism, I supposed, an attempt to offset her fresh-faced prettiness in order to be taken seriously as a dedicated cop. At any rate, I sensed she had a lot on the ball so I decided to play along with this turn of face in the interest of finding out where it led.

Without turning her head, she said, "Why are you looking at me that way? Trying to decide if a functioning brain could really, truly exist under the blond hair?"

I grinned. "No, I've mostly made up my mind about that. What I'm trying to decide is how much is going on inside that pretty blond head. Who are you really and what are you really up to, Detective Sterling?"

"I'm like Popeye. I yam what I yam," she said, facing me again. "But in addition to my police training I was also selected and trained as a Homeland Security liaison for this region. So when you factor in everything about this case—and I mean everything—you should be able to figure out that what I'm up to goes a little deeper than just the kidnap/murder scenario that is presently playing out on the surface."

"Okay then," I said. "If you're in with Homeland Security you must be familiar with the term 'Operation Stoneface'?"

She arched one brow sharply. "Since learning what I have about you, I supposed it shouldn't surprise me that you know about it, too—But, damnit, *how* do you know?"

"Take it easy. We're on the same side. That's what counts, right?"

"I'm not sure. From where I sit, I see too damn many sides to this thing. Too many different sides, too many different agendas, too many different allegiances. We've got more plots and subplots going on than a freaking daytime soap opera."

"That doesn't make it unmanageable, as long as everybody's got the storyline straight that at the end of the day we're all aiming to safely rescue the kidnapped boy."

"That's the trouble," Sterling said, her expression turning suddenly grim. "Another thing I'm unsure about is if all the players—and yes, I mean all of the ones lined up on 'our side'—see that as a crucial plot element. Some of them, I'm afraid, are approaching this like there's room for a little improv."

I could hear Thunderbringer's words echoing in hers. I said, "Yeah? Well, there's improv and there's improv."

"What is that supposed to mean?" she demanded.

I flashed a quick grin, trying to take the edge off my careless remark. "Basic law of physics, right? For every action there's an equal and opposite reaction. We're the good guys. Have faith. Whatever the bad guys try, we'll come up with something to counter it."

"Christ. Gag me with a snow shovel. I thought all you loner

PI types were cynical and bitter. What are you, the exception that proves the rule? The Mary Sunshine version?"

"Like you said, kiddo. I yam what I yam. Bleak as it might look, I try to hold out the belief that there's always a chance to make things turn out for the better over the worst. If I didn't think that, I'd've bailed off this freight train a helluva long time ago."

She was looking at me a little softer now, but no less intently. "The freight train being your line of work, or life in general?"

"Take your pick. Either way, it's the ride I'm on."

She smiled. "See, now *that* sounded at least a little bit cynical. That's more like it."

"I'll keep working on it," I promised.

"Speaking of what you're working on, what about the case that brought you out here in the first place? The investigation into your friends' deaths? Sheriff Knaack explained to us the other day how you were looking into that, how you were unsatisfied with the original findings. Is all of that on hold because of Abby's son being kidnapped?"

I nodded. "Seems like something that ought to take priority, wouldn't you say? Although, like I told Abby, I don't really know what I can add to everything else that's already being done."

"Hannibal the innocent and uninvolved bystander?" Sterling twisted her mouth skeptically. "Come on, that suits you even worse than the Mary Sunshine bit. Especially after you just admitted to knowing about Operation Stoneface."

"Are you suggesting," I pressed, "that Operation Stoneface has something to do with my friends' deaths?"

"I'm suggesting nothing of the sort. But I do know that I don't like coincidences. And I especially don't like them where somebody like you is concerned. You showing up here suspicious over a fatal car crash and ending up knowing about a highly secret planned paramilitary strike . . . I'm supposed to buy that as being wholly unrelated?"

"Buy what you want. You don't hear me hawking a sale."

"You could do worse than to confide in me, you know. Never hurts for somebody to have your back. Look around . . . I know. You may be low man on the food chain of Feds and spooks and whatever else we've got running around here, but I'm not too many ladder rungs above you."

I got what she was saying. "Why doesn't somebody have *your* back? Where's that partner of yours? The guy who was with you out at the lake the other day?"

"Dick Lyle is off on leave," she answered a little too stiffly, too formally.

"Booze dry-out, eh?" I guessed.

"I didn't say that," she protested.

"No. I did. He had all the signs of needing it."

"It's not the first time," she admitted. "But, one way or the other, it'll be the last. If this trip doesn't take, the department will boot him for good. That'd be a shame, he's a good cop. Good instincts. He may be rough around the edges, but he taught me a lot, showed me the ropes when others made it clear they didn't want anything to do with a female rookie. I miss having the crude old fart around."

"So what *are* you doing for backup?"

"Nothing permanent has been arranged yet. In the interim, I'm supposed to be working closely with Culver and Blake. You saw how well that's going. I come around, they scatter like I'm carrying bubonic plague. Which doesn't exactly break my heart because, as I indicated before, I think they're a couple of morons."

"Sounds like a swell working relationship."

"Believe it or not, I've survived worse."

"Survival. . . . That's what somebody having your back can

come down to."

"Sometimes."

I considered for a moment. Then: "You also up to speed on the big Indian—Thunderbringer?"

Her eyes narrowed. "Uh-huh," she admitted cautiously. "And you are too?"

I nodded. "He's around, I'm around. . . . What I'm saying is, you don't need to worry about somebody having your back."

"Okay. I'm grateful." Sterling blinked, looking somewhat uncertain, maybe even a bit startled. "But Thunderbringer . . . and you . . . I need to know—"

I cut her off with a shake of my head. "No, you don't. Just remember what we were talking about a little while ago—how the boy's safety must take precedent over everything else. Leave it at that."

CHAPTER FORTY-THREE

That afternoon I drove to the Ash Hollow cemetery and visited Bomber's grave.

One of the Standing T ranch hands advised me of a dirt lane that angled across a back corner of the property, accessing an obscure side road that in turn cut over to Highway 61 north of Arthur. I used this route to exit the premises, thus avoiding the thickening throng of newshounds gathered at the front gate.

On the way to Ash Hollow I swung by No Name Bay and sat for a while with Margaret Bridger and the Gorceys. The overall mood was understandably somber, somewhat tense, but Margaret's trademark resolve shone through unfaltering and she kept things from getting too grim with a flash or two of wry humor. The presence of B.U. and Mamie was a quiet demonstration that their supportive strength was unfaltering also.

Abby had elected not to come with me because once again she couldn't bring herself to leave the ranch for fear of missing a call from the kidnappers that might afford another chance to speak with Dusty. Margaret said that, being a mother herself, she understood perfectly. "Besides," she added grumpily, "ain't like Abby don't call on that blamed cell phone of hers practically every hour to check on me anyway. I can't even catch a decent nap!" But you could tell she was proud of the attention, even as she ached for the torment her daughter was going through.

Why I ended up at the cemetery I wasn't exactly sure.

I thought of the overused, overrated word that everybody kept throwing around so often early on, when the funerals were being planned and so forth. *Closure.* Maybe that's what I was still looking for. The one and only time I'd ever been to Bomber's grave was the day of the service, in the presence of the others who had gathered. Maybe all I wanted was a one-on-one chance to say good-bye to my old buddy.

I'm not a praying man, so I knew that wasn't it.

And yet, standing there that day with the sunlight streaming down over my shoulder onto the patch of recently disturbed ground and leftover flowers (no headstone had been delivered yet) I felt a sense of spirituality for the first time in a long time. If there was a God, I knew that for me He would never be found inside a steepled box with colored windows and rows of fashion-conscious hypocrites chanting empty expressions of good will and mimicking archaic rhetoric. But out here, out in the open, on the grand stage of this rolling weather-scoured land under an endlessly kaleidoscopic sky where only the voice of the wind touched your ears . . . in a setting such as this . . . maybe . . . just maybe. . . .

But that still didn't answer what had brought me here today.

Finally, I figured out what it was.

It turned out to be a simple thing, really. A message I needed to deliver personally to an old friend.

In a low, clear, faintly husky voice I spoke to the flower-strewn rectangular plot of ground. "Don't worry," I said. "I'm going to get your grandnephew back safe . . . I just wanted you to know that."

CHAPTER FORTY-FOUR

I was on my way back to the Terrell ranch, rolling up Highway 61 just south of Arthur, when my cell phone went off.

"Thunderbringer here," a familiar voice said after I picked up.

I felt an anxious ripple run through me. "This mean it's show time?"

What sounded like a grunt of disgust sounded in my ear. "Oh, there's a show going on all right. But it ain't hardly the performance we been looking forward to."

I waited.

"The shit has hit the fan around here," Thunderbringer continued. "I'm calling to tell you to stay clear. If we end up conducting our little piece of business later on tonight—and I think there's a good chance we will—then I'm going to have enough trouble slipping away as it is. They've already got me on their radar, no sense you walking back into the thick of it and adding the complication of trying to get both of us untangled in case we need to move and move fast."

"Untangled from what?" I wanted to know. "What exactly is going on?"

"It seems Bastien and his FBI boys tend to take their jobs serious. In checking out the possible connection between Clint Barnstable's murder down in Florida and the kidnapping there, they got a warrant to search Clint's apartment. First, they found evidence of his membership in the RBR. As you can imagine, that perked up everybody's interest more than a little bit. Next they searched some property Barnstable had out on the north side of the lake, where he put up a pole building to store his boat, duck blind, dirt bike, and other outdoorsy toys. They found all the stuff they expected, but they also found a pickup camper parked inside the building—the one registered to Matt Hollis. In the camper there was evidence of Hollis being involved with Old Man Terrell's militia, too. What's more, they turned up a scrap of paper on which Travis Terrell's Orlando hotel and suite number were written."

"And the cheese gets more binding," I muttered.

"Uh-huh. But the real kicker was the fingerprints they lifted out of the camper. When they fed them into the federal data bank and the match to Ivgar Volnokov came spitting out you could hear alarm bells going off all the way back to the Potomac."

"I bet it wasn't long before something else could be heard, too—the hoofbeats of Blake and Culver, those two CIA-cum-DHS goons, galloping up to take over the lead."

"Boy, you *are* the detective, ain't you? But you're sure not wrong—Blake and Culver swarmed Bastien's team like ants on cookie crumbs. They played their Homeland Security trump card and proclaimed the whole operation out here to now be under their direction. They made no bones about the apprehension of Volnokov becoming the main mission, and spilled the beans on Terrell's Operation Stoneface to everybody in the process."

"Morons," I said, echoing Beatrice Sterling's appraisal of the pair.

"Needless to say," Thunderbringer added, "their little revelation earned Old Man Terrell a pretty high ranking on the shit lists of his own son and your friend Abby."

"Excuse me if I can't work up any sympathy for the old

bastard. But more to the point, where does that leave you? Did you get 'outed' by the dynamic duo as well?"

"Let's just say my role in things was acknowledged. I'm not officially one of the bad guys, but I guarantee you I'm not part of the inner circle either. They're making it pretty plain they don't trust me. Among other things, they're mighty curious about my presence during your little stroll through the hedge maze with Cam Terrell earlier this morning. That's why I said they've got me on their radar. And they're tracking hard to try and get a bead on you even as we speak. You can bet they'd feel a lot better if they had you back on the screen, too. For some reason, they have this lame-ass hunch the two of us might be up to something."

"I'm mortified," I said.

"Hard to believe—a couple of choirboys like us, eh?"

"Speaking of 'us,' I take it Cam Terrell didn't crack under all this added pressure and spill about the little side arrangement we've got going?"

"Not a peep. No matter what else he's done or what you might think of him, all of his focus right now is on getting his grandson back safe. He still figures we're the best bet for that."

"Let's hope like hell his judgment about that is better than it's been about some other things."

"Hey, throw that doubt bullshit out the window, kemosabe," Thunderbringer growled. "We *are* the kid's best bet. You don't believe that, go ahead and thumb a ride back home—I'll light this fucker up by myself."

I growled right back at him. "Loosen your war bonnet, chief. The only ride I'm thumbing is with you when you go to face Volnokov, and about that there damn well *ain't* no doubt."

The connection between us was only soft background static for a long minute. Until Thunderbringer spoke again. "That's better, then."

"You said you expect to be contacted tonight?" I said.

"That's what my gut is telling me. Terrell's got the money pulled together for the public kidnap scenario that everybody else is watching. Once Volnokov hears that, it should be his signal to set up the real deal with me. When he does, his exchange demands will be complicated and they'll come fast, not giving us time to try and get cute from our end. That's why we've got to be as ready as we can be before he sets it in motion."

"Then are you sure I shouldn't be there with you—you know, in the 'ready' position?"

"Not with the G swarming all over here. Like I said, when the time comes we're going to have to move and move fast. What's best is for you to stay out of range and ready so we can quick-connect once I peel away."

"But you said they've got their radar out for me even as we speak. How am I supposed to stay out of range yet accessible both at the same time?"

"As far as they know you don't know they're on the lookout for you. Mostly they're expecting you to show up back here at the ranch. Any additional looking they do is likely to be in other obvious places—No Name Bay, maybe Ogallala. Where you at now?"

"Coming up on Arthur," I told him.

"Perfect. Hide in plain sight."

"What?"

"There's a little bar right there in town. Park around back or on a side street where your car isn't obvious, go in and nurse a few beers. Listen to some hillbilly music on the jukebox. Act like any other guy with an evening to kill. You'll be invisible. Wait for my call. When I blow out of here I've got to come through Arthur anyway—you'll be right there for the hookup."

It sounded just loose enough and simple enough to work.

"But there's just one hitch," I said.

"What's that?"

"Little matter of the signed confession Terrell was supposed to have ready for me."

"You and that damn one-track mind of yours." He gave it some quick thought. "Tell you what. I'll get the confession from the old man, put it in Abby's hand. Tell her what to do with it when the balloon goes up. That's how you were going to handle it anyway, right?"

"Something like that."

"Done and done, then. Okay?"

"Done and done."

"Be ready. Be waiting for my call."

"I'm there."

Chapter Forty-Five

My phone rang again at nine o'clock.

"This is the one," Thunderbringer said on the other end of the connection. "This time it is show time."

"Let's do it, then."

"I don't hear any jukebox music in the background. You not at the bar I suggested?"

"Oh, I'm there all right. The ol' Long Branch. Not big on originality, but quaint as hell."

"Quaint," Thunderbringer echoed.

"It's just me and Homer the bartender and a Colorado Rockies baseball game on TV. Get me the fuck out, I'm begging you. I'm up for Volnokov and the whole Russian army rather than sit through one more inning of this boring-ass game."

"You might want to consider that old saying about being careful what you wish for."

"Not a chance. Where we hooking up?"

"You remember where we met the other night?"

The rodeo arena at the fairgrounds. I said I remembered.

"I'm rolling. Fifteen minutes."

"Gotcha."

Once again the moon hung low and large in a starless sky. I parked in the shadow of the old grandstand, got out and walked around the upended cable spool. Three hours of killing time at the Long Branch—sipping Bud Lite drafts, munching beer nuts, fighting not to snore in the face of Homer's monosyllabic mutterings or the dreadfully slow "action" of the televised game—had left me stiff and sluggish. I needed to shake the feeling, walk some of it off.

The fresh air helped. I breathed it in deep, grateful for the lack of cow manure stink tonight.

I had myself refreshed and mentally stoked by the time I spotted headlight beams swinging onto the grounds. To my surprise, however, it wasn't Thunderbringer's big sports ute that came pulling up but instead an unmarked Ford sedan with state police license plates. I braced myself. And then, even more to my surprise, the Ford's doors popped open and Abby and Detective Beatrice Sterling got out.

Abby came over to me. "Joe," she said somewhat breathlessly.

"Abby, what are you doing here?" I wanted to know.

"Sticking her neck out," Detective Sterling answered. "Which pretty much covers what we're all doing."

"Where's Thunderbringer?" was my next question.

"He shouldn't be too far behind. We're running interference for him."

Before I could ask what that was supposed to mean, Abby said, "I turned Cameron's confession over to Sheriff Walt, like Thunderbringer said you wanted me to. I hope you don't mind that I read it first."

"I'm sorry you had to find out that way," I tried to explain. "Sorry I wasn't able to tell you sooner myself."

She was looking up at me intently, her eyes bright. "What counts is that you did it, Joe. You got to the truth about Liz and Uncle Bomber's car crash."

"*We* did it," I corrected her.

"But there was so much more! My God, can you believe Matt Hollis is that Russian spy we've been talking about? And Cam's insane plan to stage a fake terrorist strike, the extremes he was willing to go to. . . . He actually *arranged* Dusty's kidnapping!"

"One version of it," I allowed.

Another set of headlights came bouncing onto the property. This time it was Thunderbringer's Yukon that rumbled up and crunched to a halt.

The big Indian piled out amidst a tumbling cloud of dust. He spread his arms. "My loyal tribe awaits."

I wasn't in the mood. "Tribe, my ass! What's the idea of dragging these two into this?" I demanded.

"If it wasn't for 'these two,' buster," Sterling said rather tartly, "you might not have any of 'this' going on. Your commando partner here may have remained landlocked back at the ranch."

"She's right," Thunderbringer agreed. "Blake tried to button down the whole ranch at sundown. Nobody out, nobody in. He didn't say it in so many words but it was pretty clear I was the main one he was looking to hold in place. And if it hadn't been for some well-timed distraction he might have been able to make it stick."

"I take it I'm looking at the distraction," I said, my eyes cutting back and forth between Abby and Sterling.

Thunderbringer grinned. "See? Ain't he the detecting-est sonofogun you ever saw?"

"Finish telling it," I growled.

Thunderbringer shrugged. "It was simple enough, really. I got Abby to pitch a fit about wanting to leave and go visit her sick mother. Detective Sterling picked up on what we were trying to do and joined in on Abby's behalf, insisting that she had every right to go. Offering to drive her and escort her if that would help take care of the matter. Blake didn't like having his authority challenged, but the two of them raised enough of a ruckus to not only talk their own way out but to give me the chance I needed to slip away, too. It only seemed right to clue them in on where you and I were hooking up."

"That man Blake—him and his partner, whatever government agency they represent," Abby said, scowling fiercely. "All they kept talking about was capturing Volnokov and 'securing' his Al-Qaeda contacts. It was clear that for them getting Dusty back was merely . . . incidental."

"All too willing to write him off as one more piece of collateral damage." Sterling's face held no particular expression, but her tone had a scornful and bitter edge. "That's a concept that players in the terrorist game—on both sides—seem awfully fucking quick to accept and get comfortable with."

"You should all know," Thunderbringer said, breaking the moment of grim silence that followed Sterling's remark, "in another time and life I was part of that kind of thinking. All I can say is that under certain circumstances it can somehow seem right. Ain't especially proud to speak of it now, but . . . well, like I said, I figured you should know." His eyes found Abby. "But your boy ain't going to end up collateral damage, Abby. Me and Hannibal are going to see to that."

I took Abby's hand in mine, squeezed it reassuringly.

"I don't want either of you to fall to harm, either," Abby said.

"Sure not our plan," said Thunderbringer.

I looked at him. "We've *got* a plan? I'd like to hear it some time."

"Well, the exact details we're gonna need to sort of fill in as we go."

Sterling rolled her eyes. "God, I put my career on the line for this? Hope and Crosby on the Road to Rescue?"

Thunderbringer raised his wristwatch and tapped it. "One thing's for sure—we got to hit it. Volnokov is going to run us through a series of checkpoints to make sure we're not being tailed or tracked. We've got ground to cover and time to make up before he calls again."

Abby pulled her hand from mine and clutched my arm instead, fingers digging in hard. "Finish it, Joe—bring my boy home safe!"

Chapter Forty-Six

"Just across the Colorado line, on the outskirts of the town of Julesburg," Thunderbringer was explaining, "there's one of those interstate rest areas. We got fifteen minutes to make it there. I'm supposed to pull in and circle the parking lot with my left turn signal blinking for identification. Once he sees this and is satisfied we're not being tailed, Volnokov will call again with further instructions."

"But you don't expect him to try the exchange at the rest stop?"

"Highly doubtful. Too public, too big a risk for witnesses, even this late. Besides, Volnokov will be looking to frazzle us some, jerk on our nerves. I expect him to run us around a lot more first, if for no other reason than that."

We were blowing down Interstate 80 at ninety miles an hour, traveling west. We'd just passed the turn-off for Big Springs and were closing on the Nebraska–Colorado border.

"When it comes, the exchange will take place somewhere remote, deserted. With a fair amount of concealment around— old abandoned buildings, something like that—and high ground or some kind of observation point close by. Plus quick access to more than one getaway route." Thunderbringer was speaking in a steady, confident drone. As if reciting some deeply ingrained lesson from long ago. "I figure there'll be no less than three of them working the exchange," he continued. "There'll be Volnokov, naturally, to do the talking and negotiating; one more holding the bonnet, and probably one more positioned out of sight as backup, a sharpshooter or something like that on the high point."

"What do you mean one of them will be 'holding the bonnet'?" I asked.

In the greenish glow of the dashboard lights, Thunderbringer's mouth pulled momentarily into a tight, razor-thin line. He didn't answer for a long moment. Then: "Something Volnokov said when he called before. I asked him how the boy was doing and he answered that he was just fine but couldn't come to the phone right at the moment because he was busy getting fitted with his shiny new bonnet."

I waited, frowning. I still didn't understand.

"It's called a 'Columbian bonnet,' " Thunderbringer went on. "Little something the South American gangs hit on when they found out that kidnapping rich city businessmen or their family members for ransom was a quick, relatively easy way to score big money. The trick, for both sides, is always the exchange. What they came up with—to give themselves the edge and cut down on any last-minute heroics or tricks the money payers might try to pull—was to start bringing their victims to the exchange fitted with a Columbian bonnet. What this consists of is the muzzle of a sawed-off double-barreled shotgun placed against the victim's temple and secured there with wraps of duct tape around the end of the barrels and the victim's head. Then the gun's triggers are wired back and the hombre holding the gun and walking beside the victim thumbs the hammers to full cock and you see what you've got. Anything goes wrong, any trap is sprung or rescue attempted, any reason at all causes the gun holder's thumb to release those hammers . . . things turn real *un*-pretty. No matter what else happens, the victim don't make it."

"Jesus Christ," I croaked. The inside of my mouth had turned as dry as sand.

Thunderbringer shot me a sidelong glance. "In case it wasn't clear before, *that* is the kind of people we're going up against," he said. "Don't be misled by my casual remarks or if I seem all loose and relaxed—I've been doing this kind of shit too long to be rattled by it, that's all. But the fact remains we are going to be crashing the party of some very nasty-ass motherfuckers. You straight on that?"

"Straight," I said. "But one thing—if Volnokov is working with backup, where did he get it from? He killed off Barnstable, his original kidnap partner."

"Only because ol' Clint would never have gone along with double-crossing Terrell, not because Volnokov didn't still need somebody," Thunderbringer pointed out. "As far as where he found replace-ments, it's hard to say for sure. He could have even recruited some out of the ranks of the RBR. He sure as hell wasn't above bragging about his past exploits, and some of the younger Rambo wanna-bes were mighty impressed by his tales. Wouldn't have been hard for him to lure some of them astray. They were all pretty green by his standards, though. I'd be more inclined to guess he found a couple of professionals, maybe somebody he worked with in the past."

"That would take some time and forethought. That mean he was planning a swerve on the old man all along?"

"Not necessarily. Guy like Volnokov don't survive as long as he has without keeping his ass covered. Terrell was paying him handsomely to authenticate the Al-Qaeda tie-in to Operation Stoneface. Handsomely enough to make it worth the risk of coming back and operating here in the States again for a time. But the risk was still there, and Volnokov would have wanted a back door to duck out through in a hurry if something went wrong. I'm guessing he had a couple of hirelings in tow to make sure that back door got held open for him. When you came along and stirred up enough shit to make the success of Operation Stoneface begin to look threatened and Terrell started acting a little too panicky . . . well, that back door was there waiting and so was the chance for ol' Ivgar to drag five million bucks out through it with him."

"Too bad for him," I said, "but he's about to find that doorway a little more crowded than he figured on."

For the next hour and a half, exactly as Thunderbringer had predicted, Volnokov kept us on the run.

From the Julesburg rest area he sent us west on Highway 30 to an old abandoned sugar-beet factory in the town of Ovid. From there south to the aroma-laden vicinity of a huge hog farm down near Holyoke. Then north and west again, re-entering Nebraska's panhandle, picking up I-80 once more and headed for Sydney.

The back roads we traveled were flat and empty. Traffic was almost as light even on the stretches of interstate we covered. With minimal observation from two or three key points along the route it would have been easy to determine that no other vehicle moving out there this night was in any way associated to ours.

As we drew within a mile of Sydney, Thunderbringer's cell phone chirped once more and he received the final set of directions. "Uh-huh. . . . Uh-huh," he kept repeating as he listened. Then at one point he said, "The old Army depot. Yeah, I know it."

When the call was finished, Thunderbringer's expression became set in stern, deep lines. "Okay, that was it," he said. "They're waiting for us somewhere among the igloos of the Sioux Army Depot. That's where we'll do the exchange."

"Igloos? Sioux Army? What are you talking about?" I wanted to know.

He jabbed a thumb, indicating a general direction off to our right. "North of here, due north off the Sydney exit, there's an old World War II ordnance complex. The Sioux Army Depot it was called. Been closed down for years now, but back in the day it was quite a deal. They built it during the second big war, like I said, and it stayed in operation up through part of the 'Nam thing, I think. Covers something like twenty thousand square acres of land, had miles and miles of service roads and railroad tracks when it was in full swing. It's all empty and falling apart now, tracks all torn up, roads broken apart and choked with weeds. Still quite a few structures standing along the front boundaries of the property last I knew—dilapidated old warehouses, a few administration buildings and the like. And the igloos are still standing, too, the only difference being they're still sound as the day they were built. They're where the goods got stored. Everything from small arms weapons to jeeps to ten-thousand-pound bombs. They claim there were even a few ICBMs housed in them at one time or other."

"You keep using the term 'igloos.' Obviously you're not refer-ring to ice-block houses for Eskimos. How about a little transla-tion?"

We had peeled off the interstate and were turning north on Highway 385 now, passing through a sort of strip-mall area that had been built up around the home base for Cabella's, the world-famous outdoor outfitters. The cluster of parasite busi-nesses included everything from a Chinese restaurant to a winery and of course local representation for both McDonald's and Wal-mart. All save a couple of twenty-four-hour gas stations were closed at this hour. Off to our left, about a quarter-mile to the north and west, a blanket of silently twinkling lights marked the slumbering town of Sydney proper.

As we rolled away from this blip of population, Thunder-bringer answered my question. "The Army depot igloos," he said, "are pretty much like the picture that comes to mind. Except these are domed structures of concrete blocks instead of ice and they've been sodded over on the outside so that they look like big humps of grass and weeds. Would've made them invisible to World War Two–era bombers from the air, see. And they're massive. Fifty or sixty yards in diameter, probably twenty-five feet high at the peak of the dome. These days they rent a lot of them out for storage units. Some of the area farmers store grain and equipment in them. But there's still plenty that are just left empty. Hell, you got like eight hundred of these things plopped out in the middle of nothing but prairie grass and leftover buffalo shit. You first come upon it, it's a pretty eerie sight, let me tell you."

"Sounds like it. Sounds like the setting for some kind of nineteen-fifties science-fiction movie."

"Yeah, well that's where we're headed but this ain't no kind of fiction, it's reality about as cold and mean as you're gonna find."

"You don't have to keep reminding me of that," I told him. "I may not be some kind of jungle-trained mercenary like you and Volnokov but I'm not quite a paper-shuffling greenie who's never thrown down in a firefight before, either. Okay?"

"Fair enough. I guess I had that coming." Thunderbringer flashed a grin, his teeth iridescent green in the dashboard glow. "Hell, maybe I'm a little nervous myself."

"Gee, I wonder why," I muttered.

"Now don't jump down my throat if I ask this—but you're carrying heavy enough, right? That .45 you pulled on me at the creek the other day?"

"That, and a close-in 9mm hideaway."

"You might want to consider something longer-ranged for a second piece. I got a selection in the back—Glock, Colt, S&W, and more. And I got a couple vests, too. If we mean to walk away from this thing then I suggest we give ourselves every edge we can."

I didn't argue. He pulled over to the side of the road.

The lights of the town and the exit-ramp businesses were a mile and more behind us now. Out here was nothing but emptiness. No buildings, scarcely any trees; only grassy, rolling hills tumbling away in every direction. The bloated moon surrounded by a skyful of stars bathed everything in pale blue illumination that, except for pools of heightened shadow, gave almost as much clarity as an overcast day.

Thunderbringer opened the back of his rig and dropped the tailgate. Four large, deep suitcases stood in a row in the cargo bay, held fast by a multi-colored bungie cord. He unhooked the cord, pulled out the end suitcase, laid it flat on the tailgate and opened it. Two layers of flat, bubble-wrapped triangular objects were revealed. Separating the layers were two folded Kevlar vests. On the bubble-wrapped objects I could see strips of clear tape with felt-marker writing that read "S&W .38", "Glock 10mm", and so on.

"Christ," I said, "you've practically got your own ordnance depot on wheels right here."

"Some nice pieces to choose from. Two or three different Glocks, any of which would give you a manstopper good for more distance than the hideaway you described."

"Before I decide on a weapons upgrade, exactly what role do you see me playing in this little shindig we're about to kick off?"

Thunderbringer tugged out the two vests and handed one to me. After stripping off his shirt he began fitting the second vest around himself. Thick muscles bulged across his bare shoulders and rolled up and down his arms.

"If I'm right," he said as he fumbled with the vest clasps, "if they've got a three-man setup waiting for us, then I'll be pretty much occupying two of them. That'll be Volnokov and the shotgunner he's got with the boy. What that leaves is the third one for you to try and get a bead on. If he's there, his purpose will be to take me out as soon as Volnokov is either satisfied the exchange has gone in his favor or becomes convinced it's turned hopelessly to shit. Either way, they'll be looking to blow me off the board."

"And my job is not to let them."

"If you please."

I skinned out of my T-shirt and started putting on my own vest. "But no matter which way it goes, how are we going to get the boy out from under that shotgun?"

Thunderbringer tipped his head, indicating the remaining suitcases in the cargo bay. "I've got a little something in there that I'm counting on to give us some negotiating leverage in that department."

"But not money."

His eyes narrowed. "Nobody's going to *pay* these mother-fuckers for doing what they're trying to do . . . leastways not with money."

"Okay. I'm down with that. But if you're successful in getting the shotgun off the boy, then what?"

Thunderbringer's eyes stayed hard. "Then your priority changes. That's where you've got to turn cold-blooded. No hesitation, no second thoughts, no worrying about some kind of fair-play bullshit. The instant—and I mean the *instant*—that shotgun lifts off the boy, you put down the sonofabitch holding it. Empty a whole goddamn clip on him if you have to."

"And what about Volnokov and the sharpshooter who'll have you in his sights?"

"If there actually is a sharpshooter."

"You seemed pretty convinced a minute ago that there would be."

"Okay. If there is, then that's where I'll be hoping this vest buys me something. Once the lead starts flying, I'm not exactly going to be standing there with my thumb up my ass, am I? I figure I can probably take Volnokov out before the sharpshooter even reacts. Then all I have to do is get past a round or two—a miss if I'm lucky, maybe a hit to the vest—before one of us is able to land our sights on that third fucker and he's toast, too."

"You've got it all figured out."

"Piece of cake. . . . Let's go slice us some before the frosting starts to melt."

Fifteen minutes later, as we crested a low hill and started down the back side, Thunderbringer announced, "There they are."

I hitched forward in the Yukon's back seat and gazed past his shoulder. Ahead and to our left, stretching for as far as I could see into the murkiness, stood row after row of huge earthen humps. It was indeed an eerie sight, as if someone had littered the undulating countryside with giant upside-down egg cartons. The crowns of these grassy domes were tinted bluish green by the moonlight, their bases swallowed in velvety shadow.

"Good God, they go on forever," I marveled.

"Like I said, there are hundreds of them. Literally," Thunderbringer replied. "That last side road we passed back there would've led off to the old warehouses and barracks and other buildings, but this right here was the real heart of the operation—the igloo field."

We'd left the highway some ways back, angling north and west through a series of turns on narrow, roughly paved back roads until we reached this spot. Other than a set of railroad tracks and a grain elevator and some accompanying buildings where we'd turned off the highway, we had seen nothing but open country—range grass and a handful of tended fields.

"How are we supposed to find Volnokov in there?" I wanted to know.

"See those ruts leading off periodically through the high grass?" Thunderbringer jerked his chin. "That was an old grid-work of streets running between the igloos. Lanes, I guess you'd call them. They're all broken up and weed-choked now, but can still be followed. My instructions are to turn off on the sixth lane and follow it back. We'll be signaled."

"Okay. By my count, then, this is the fourth lane coming up. . . . So two more and you make your turn."

"Got it."

Thunderbringer slowed his rig and swung onto the sixth set of ruts leading off the edge of the road. In the spill of the Yukon's headlights there was indeed a lane of sorts cutting through the weeds and grass and sagebrush. There were even sporadic patches of pavement showing through. We rolled ahead slow, weeds and sage noisily slapping against the undercarriage of the vehicle, tires bouncing in and out of gaping potholes.

Now there were tall, shaggy igloos rising up on either side of us. I leaned over in my seat and craned my neck to look up at the nearest one. "The top of one of those would make a dandy spot for a sharpshooter to set up," I noted.

"I was thinking the same thing," said Thunderbringer. "But if that's where they put one, he'll have the disadvantage of having to skyline himself when he raises up to shoot down. Time comes, that's what we make work for us."

We had rolled maybe a quarter of a mile through the igloo field when a bright light stabbed out of the shadows ahead on the right. It stayed on for five seconds, then winked out.

"That's them," Thunderbringer said, his voice sounding a little tight. "Get ready."

I slithered over the rear seatback and wedged myself down beside the suitcases in the cargo bay. The idea was for me to stay there, out of sight, until Thunderbringer opened the rear to bring out the suitcases supposedly filled with ransom money. At that point I would slip out and squirm into position under the dropped tailgate, where I would have decent cover and a reasonably good field of vision.

I reached up and checked the dome light over the cargo area, making sure it was switched off. Having my presence suddenly illuminated when Thunderbringer opened the back hatch would hardly be conducive to the success of our plan.

I stayed hunkered down while the Yukon jolted over some rougher terrain, angling toward the signal light. Then it braked to a halt. The door opened, Thunderbringer got out, the door closed again.

Both cab windows were rolled down. I could hear voices, clear in the still night.

"Well, well . . . the big Indian buck delivering the big greenback bucks. That's what I like to see." It was Volnokov talking. I tried to match my memory of Matt Hollis's voice to this one, but it didn't really fit. This smug, superior tone was too different from the polite, condescending one that had been such a carefully calculated part of the Matt charade.

"Means a lot to me, doing something that makes you happy," Thunderbringer responded dryly.

I raised my head cautiously and peered out through a crack between two of the suitcases. Volnokov stood directly in front of one of the igloos. The unit's broad doorway was at his back, its heavy steel door standing ajar. The gloom inside was impenetrable. Thunderbringer stood facing him from a distance of about twelve feet.

"We could stand here all night exchanging pleasantries," Volnokov sneered, "but let's get this over with. You bring the money?"

Thunderbringer jerked a thumb over his shoulder. "In my rig."

"Let's see it."

"You see the money when I see the boy."

Volnokov folded his arms across his chest. A big-handled automatic pistol was shoved in his belt, meant to be seen. "You think you're in a position to be making demands?"

"You see the money when I see the boy," Thunderbringer repeated, his voice steady.

Volnokov kept his arms folded for a long count, scowling. Then, heaving a dramatic sigh, he lowered them and turned to motion at someone inside the igloo. After a moment, two figures reverse-melted out of the blackness inside the dome. I laid eyes on Dusty Terrell for the first time. He was tousle-haired and wide-eyed, the strips of duct tape around his forehead flattening one ear. My gaze followed the wraps of duct tape to the barrels of the shotgun they held fast against the side of the boy's head. And then up the length of the gun to the grim-faced, grizzled-looking Hispanic who gripped the piece with its wired-back triggers and the hammers full-cocked under his thumb.

"William!" the kid blurted when he saw Thunderbringer.

"You okay there, Dusty-boy?" Thunderbringer said. He was trying like hell to keep his voice light, but I could hear the strain in it.

"You can *see* he's okay, can't you?" said Volnokov, his own voice tense. "We ain't got time for no family-reunion chitchat, so both of you shut the fuck up. You got your look at the boy, big chief—now I want a look at my goddamn money."

I watched the Hispanic holding the shotgun grin a greedy, rotten-toothed grin and my whole body ached with wanting to put a bullet between his eyes.

"Hold your horses," Thunderbringer said, turning and walking toward the Yukon. "I got what you're asking for right over here."

He opened the cargo bay and I rolled out, blocked by his big body. Hit the ground on the back side of the vehicle, pivoted on my rump and bellied into the weeds and deep shadows under the dropped tailgate.

Thunderbringer left the suitcase containing the guns where it was. He took out two of the others and set them on the ground. The remaining one he pulled out and carried toward Volnokov.

"Come have a look," Thunderbringer invited. "The score of your lifetime."

Volnokov advanced to meet him.

From where I lay I was scanning the peaks of the surrounding igloos, looking for movement or a shape that didn't belong. I saw nothing.

Thunderbringer set the suitcase down and gestured to Volnokov. "It's all yours now. Be my guest." He backed away.

Volnokov dropped eagerly to one knee before the suitcase. He laid it flat and popped it open, smiling as he gazed down at its contents.

The smile took on a strange kind of slant but stayed frozen in place for several clock ticks. Then it faded suddenly and his eyes lifted, his gaze snapping up to Thunderbringer. "What the fuck is this?!" he demanded in a harsh voice.

"You should recognize it. Ain't like you haven't seen any before," Thunderbringer said calmly. "It's a block of plastic explosive big enough to blow you into dime-sized pieces of hamburger. Oh, and by the way, when you popped the lid on that suitcase you activated a timer set to trigger it, counting down from two minutes."

"*Two* minutes? Two minutes, you stupid fucker?" Cords in Volnokov's neck bulged out. He started to rise. "In two minutes you and the boy will be so—"

"Hold it right there," Thunderbringer interrupted him, raising one hand in which he held what looked like a small black box. "Before your mouth makes a bunch of threats your ass can't back up, you should know that what I've got in my hand

349

here is a remote override on that timer. My thumb's on a little button here, see, sort of like that greasy partner of yours has got his thumb on those shotgun hammers. Anything causes my thumb to relax on this button, the timer zeroes out automatically and that block of plastic blows instantly."

Volnokov stopped moving, which left him crouched in an awkward, half-standing posture.

The Hispanic with the shotgun wasn't grinning anymore. Dusty's eyes were wide and shiny, locked on Thunderbringer.

I could feel my heart hammering so hard against the ground I was afraid it might be audible, like the beating of a tom-tom. All the while I kept scanning the tops of the igloos, looking for some sign of the sharpshooter I had reason to believe was atop one of them.

"You're bluffing," Volnokov hissed.

"Call it, then . . . if you got the balls."

"If you set anything off, you and the boy are both too close! The explosion would get you also."

"Maybe. Maybe not." I couldn't see Thunderbringer's face but I somehow knew that he was grinning. "But there damn sure ain't no doubt it'll get you, is there?"

Everything went completely still.

The only sound was the hammering in my chest. I gripped the .45 in my fist and kept sweeping my eyes over the igloos.

"Clock's ticking, Ivgar," Thunderbringer said. "Tell ol' Greasy there to cut the boy loose and step away. He does that, there's still a way for me to stop that timer. Then we can talk it out from there. Maybe we all walk out alive."

Volnokov's eyes were getting wild. "Fuck you! I'm supposed to trust you? Having that little bastard under the gun is the only guarantee I got."

"The only guarantee out here tonight is that if any harm comes to that boy, you're going to die. Let him go, there might be another way. Think on it. But do it quick . . . like I said, the clock is ticking."

In the murky light I could see beads of sweat popping out across Volnokov's forehead. Finally, with a jerky motion of one hand, he called back over his shoulder. "Vasquez! Cut the boy loose."

Vasquez, the shotgunner, looked uncertain. "But, amigo. . . ."

"Do it, goddamnit! Be quick about it!"

With his free hand, Vasquez pulled a lockblade knife from his pants and snapped open the blade. Slowly, carefully, he began sawing at the wraps of duct tape around the muzzle of the shotgun.

"Hurry the hell up!" Volnokov shouted, his eyes wilder than ever as they bounced back and forth from looking down into the suitcase and then up again at Thunderbringer.

I squirmed backward half a foot in order to keep in the shadows. Brought the .45 up, extending both arms, cupping the butt of the gun and the heel of my right hand in my left palm. Took deliberate aim on the center of Vasquez's forehead.

And then, out of the corner of my eye, I caught a flicker of movement—up high. One igloo east from the one Dusty and Vasquez were standing in front of. A man-shape shifted his position there. Against the star-filled sky I could make out something in his hands, a long object . . . a rifle.

The sharpshooter was up there, drawing a bead on Thunderbringer. I couldn't take him out now, not with the shotgun still at Dusty's head. And as soon as the shotgun dropped I would have to open up on Vasquez. Once I did that, once the shooting started and hell broke loose, there would be nothing to stop the sharpshooter from firing on Thunderbringer.

Shit!

Fuck!

My aim wavered for a fraction of a second, but then steadied again on Vasquez. Saving Dusty was priority one. That's what this whole thing was about. Thunderbringer knew the risk he was exposing himself to. He was willing to accept it, I had to be, too. The best thing I could do for him was concentrate on being fast and accurate in putting down Vasquez and *then* return my attention to the sharpshooter, hopefully before he did too much damage.

The last strand of duct tape parted and the shotgun muzzle swung momentarily away from Dusty's head.

My heart stopped hammering. I clenched my teeth, held my breath, and put three bullets into Vasquez's head as fast as I could squeeze the trigger.

BAM! BAM! BAM!

Vasquez jerked away, his head spraying a rooster tail of gore. The shotgun discharged with a shattering but harmless roar as his body did half a backward somersault before crashing hard against the igloo's steel door and then sliding down, still and lifeless.

"Duck inside, Dusty!" I heard Thunderbringer yell.

I caught a fleeting glimpse of the boy darting for the doorway of the igloo.

By then I was swinging my aim up and over toward the top of the east igloo where I'd spotted the silhouette of the sharpshooter. But he was already firing before I could get a round off.

Hell, at that point everybody was shooting.

Volnokov had drawn the gun from his belt and was firing wildly at Thunderbringer as he tried to back away from the suitcase. Thunderbringer had his own gun out and was returning fire on Volnokov as he backpedaled for the cover of the Yukon. Only difference was, Thunderbringer's shots weren't wild. The Russian's body jerked and spun in reaction to the impacts.

I scrambled out from under the tailgate and emptied the rest of my clip at the sharpshooter up on the igloo. I saw him take at least two hits and topple back, but not before I also saw Thunderbringer stagger and fall.

The .45's slide slammed back. Empty. I shifted the Colt to my left hand, drew the Glock from my waistband. Stood poised and ready, breathing hard, the sound of gunfire reverberating in my ears.

My eyes jumped to the explosive-rigged suitcase . . . *The timer!* . . . *The override!*

Suddenly realizing the way I'd exposed myself, I took an instinctive step backward. Why hadn't—?

And then there was one more shot. Volnokov—on the ground, dying—squeezing off a final wild round . . . directly into the suitcase and the block of plastique it contained.

I was aware of a brilliant flash, followed instantly by a terrible ear-splitting wave of noise and heat that lifted me off my feet and sent me crashing against the side of the Yukon. I obviously must have fallen to the ground after that, but I don't remember it. I only recall having the sensation of floating for a long moment, hearing the echo of the explosion rolling, rolling softly off into the distance, and then . . . nothing.

CHAPTER FORTY-SEVEN

I spent nine days in the Sydney hospital. The tally of the injuries I sustained included a concussion, a blown left eardrum, second-degree burns on the side of my neck and left arm, numerous incidental cuts and contusions, and a busted right hip from being slammed against Thunderbringer's sports ute.

Thunderbringer's vest saved him a bullet through the heart, even though the punch of the round still knocked him off his feet and left one hell of a bruise across his massive chest. And getting knocked down, as it turned out, took him out of the path of most of the blast.

By ducking back inside the thick-walled igloo, Dusty Terrell also escaped harm from the explosion.

Ivgar Volnokov and his two cohorts were pronounced dead at the scene from gunshot wounds and blood loss.

During the course of my hospital stay I received many visitors. Their moods ran the full gamut from highly pissed off to nurturing, loving concern.

Leading the charge for the Pissed Off contingency, no surprise, were CIA/Homeland Security agents Blake and Culver. But I was still pretty heavily medicated through most of their ranting so it was even easier than usual to tune them out.

Bastien and his FBI team also dropped by to express their displeasure with my part in "jeopardizing" the Terrell kidnapping case, although there didn't seem to be a lot of steam in their chastisement. And local law enforcement, as represented by sheriffs Mabry and Knaack, took their turns with a couple of terse but stern lectures on "citizens involving themselves in matters best left to the proper authorities." Once they'd fulfilled that obligation, however, they put considerably more enthusiasm into a bit of verbal back patting for the safe rescue of the boy.

The only other "official" contact I received was a phone call late one night from Colonel Matthew Elwood. In that veiled way of his (never saying anything too directly) I think he may have complimented me on a job well done. "No one can argue that the world isn't better off minus the likes of Ivgar Volnokov," he opined. Before ringing off, he wished me a speedy recovery and suggested once again that I take stock of my advancing age before continuing pursuits that heightened the risk of any more such recuperative hospital stays.

To the disappointment of some, no legal charges of any kind were filed against me or Thunderbringer. After all, in spite of our unsanctioned actions, we still had our ties—however tenuous—to the G. And like the colonel pointed out, nobody could argue that the world wasn't better off with Volnokov removed from it. Plus there was the little matter of getting the boy back safely. Maybe it was all as simple as something Thunderbringer had said at one point: We were on the side of the angels.

The day he completed his own brief hospital stay, Thunderbringer swung by my room. He was in the company of Detective Sterling. It didn't take long for me to decipher, somewhat to my surprise, that she wasn't exactly on the clock.

"When you're tough like me," Thunderbringer boasted, "bullets mostly just bounce off and you don't have to rack up a lot of unnecessary hospital time."

"It wasn't a bullet that put me here, you crazy-ass redskin," I reminded him. "It was that cockamamie pack of explosives you dropped into the middle of everything. What the hell was that all about anyway?"

"It was a ruse. A ploy. It worked, didn't it? It got Dusty cut loose like we wanted."

"If it was a 'ruse,' did it ever occur to you to use a *fake* block of plastique so we didn't almost get ourselves blown to smithereens?"

"Volnokov had been around too much plastic E. It had to be authentic or it might not have fooled him."

"Yeah, well I guess there's no doubt he got convinced it was real. After you were careless enough to get yourself shot, the damn stuff was bound to go off one way or the other anyway—either the timer would have run out or you would have lost your grip on that override gizmo."

"Joe," Thunderbringer said impatiently, "read my lips . . . it was a *ruse*. The timer wasn't actually hooked up to any kind of trigger device. And the override? It was a garage-door opener I swiped from one of Terrell's gas-guzzlers back at the ranch. Hell, I don't think such a thing as a remote override even exists." His face split into a wide grin. "But the threat of one sure puckered up ol' Ivgar's asshole didn't it?"

"You *are* freaking crazy," I told him.

"You're both crazy, or you never would have been out there in the first place," Sterling said.

Thunderbringer jabbed a finger at her, still grinning. "My chauffeur. She doesn't trust me to drive myself with my 'injuries.' She don't know how damn bulletproof I really am."

"My job is to protect and serve the citizenry. It would be shirking my duty to turn you loose on an unsuspecting public," Sterling said. A little grin was playing about her pretty mouth, too; a wry twist of the lips that seemed to say, "What am I getting myself into here?" Yet she seemed perfectly willing to find out.

"Well, then that settles it," Thunderbringer said. "Far be it from me to expect a young lady ever to 'shirk' on my account . . .

at least not on the first date."

They departed arm in arm.

The remaining visitors who came and went were all caring well-wishers.

The Gorceys, Tina Mancini, even Margaret Bridger with all of her own ailments insisted on making the trip. . . .

And of course Abby. She was at my bedside frequently and for lengthy periods of time. On a few occasions she brought her son Dusty, and he and I started to get to know each other. Travis Terrell sent wishes for my quick and complete recovery and expressed his gratitude for my role in getting his son back. I grudgingly had to admit that showed some class, especially considering the other role I had played—the one that had helped to bring about the battery of charges against his father. The Terrell patriarch was currently behind bars awaiting what likely would become an endless series of trials and appeals that would drain the bottom right out of the Terrell estate and drag on until the old man's natural death, maybe beyond.

While the details of the Dusty Terrell kidnapping was downplayed almost to a nonevent, the rest of it—the foiling of Cameron Terrell's Operation Stoneface, prominently featuring the role of Ivgar Volnokov and his links to both Al-Qaeda and the former Soviet Union—all made national and international news. My name got mentioned here and there, but not to any significant degree. My hospital confinement served as a buffer zone that saved me from direct media probing. I never saw or heard Thunderbringer's name pop up at all. I couldn't decide if that meant he had better or worse PR than mine.

The Department of Homeland Security claimed the whole affair as a major victory against terrorism, thanks to the heightened awareness they had instilled throughout the populace and the increased security measures they had implemented across the nation.

The truth about Liz and Bomber's deaths got told in a number of news article sidebars, especially locally and in the Rockford area.

The RBR was dismantled, all of its holdings—including the Blowpipe missiles intended to deliver the main strike of Operation Stoneface—confiscated. Every member who could be accounted for was thoroughly grilled on activities they had participated in. A handful of those questioned were brought up on relatively minor charges.

I watched the Fourth of July fireworks one evening from the seat of a wheelchair rolled out onto the front lawn of the hospital. Margaret and Abby Bridger were there to watch with me. And Dusty. And Thunderbringer and Beatrice Sterling. B.U. and Mamie Gorcey showed up, too, packing a picnic feast of pan-fried chicken and homemade potato salad, and an ice chest full of pop and beer. We all stayed out there on the lawn for a long time after the fireworks display had ended. Talking and laughing. Genuinely and thoroughly enjoying one another's company.

Until one of the nurses came out and insisted it was time for me to go back in. As she wheeled me away from the others and they called their goodnights after me, I was keenly aware of how much I hated for the evening to end. And I also realized how close I felt to that gathering of good people who up until a few weeks ago had been total strangers yet as of that moment somehow felt like . . . family.

Jan arrived the next morning. She'd been following the news, naturally; picked up on the sketchy mention of my involvement. She said she waited for me to call her. When I hadn't, she said she couldn't wait any longer.

We made stiff, awkward small talk. Talked around the things

that were really on our minds, the things we *should* have been talking about.

Finally, she asked when I thought I might be getting out.

I was hoping for Thursday, I told her.

Next she asked when I thought I would be coming home.

Before answering, I glanced out the room's open doorway and saw Abby and Dusty coming down the hall. Then I heard myself say, "I'm not so sure I'm not already there."

ABOUT THE AUTHOR

Wayne D. Dundee is the author of nearly twenty short stories, three novellas, and five previous novels in the detective/mystery genre, most of them featuring his blue-collar private eye Joe Hannibal. His work has been translated into several languages and has been nominated for an Edgar, an Anthony, and six Shamus Awards. He is the founder and original editor of *Hardboiled Magazine.* You can learn more about Wayne Dundee by visiting his Web site at www.waynedundee.com.